Advance Praise for
The Still Point

"A gifted storyteller, Tammy Greenwood instantly transports you to the cutthroat, brutally competitive, and beautiful world of ballet in this richly detailed, expertly plotted, absorbing tale of friendship, motherhood, passion, and dreams, found, lost, and found again." —Heather Gudenkauf, *New York Times* bestselling author of *The Overnight Guest*

"With her meticulous writing and true-to-life characters, Tammy Greenwood takes readers on an intimate journey into the exclusive world of competitive ballet and the many lives affected by it. *The Still Point* is a must-read full of love, hope, desire and jealousy—a vivid, compelling and deeply nuanced look at a place where lives are forever shaped and changed." —Mary Kubica, *New York Times* bestselling author of *Just the Nicest Couple*

"A sensitive and deeply felt love letter to the joys—and struggles— of raising a dancer. Authentic and propulsive." —Meg Howrey, author of *They're Going to Love You* and *The Cranes Dance*

"Fans of 'Dance Moms' and Megan Abbott will love this literary take on the competitive world of elite ballet training. With Tammy Greenwood's firsthand knowledge of the subject, precise writing and well-drawn characters, *The Still Point* is an authentic and eloquent rumination on the ways that love—in all its forms—shapes our lives. Parental hopes, marital bonds, youthful passions: What does commitment mean in a life filled with inevitable changes?" —Zoje Stage, *USA Today* bestselling author of *Baby Teeth* and *Wonderland*

Praise for *Such a Pretty Girl*

"A gorgeously written, emotionally resonant novel about mothers and daughters." —Jillian Cantor, *USA Today* bestselling author of *Beautiful Little Fools* and *The Lost Letter*

"Magnetic. . . . This knotty story leaves readers reflecting on the limits of family obligations." —*Publishers Weekly*

Praise for *Keeping Lucy*

"A baby born less than perfect in the world's eyes, a mother persuaded that giving up her child is for the best, a lingering bond that pulls and tugs yet will not break. *Keeping Lucy* follows a mother willing to give up everything to save the child she's been told she must forget. This story will have readers not only rooting for Ginny and Lucy, but thinking about them long after the last page is turned." —Lisa Wingate, *New York Times* bestselling author of *Before We Were Yours*

"In T. Greenwood's latest page-turner, a betrayed mother discovers just how much she is willing to sacrifice for the safety of her child, deemed unwanted by even those most trusted. *Keeping Lucy* is a wholly absorbing tale in which the bonds of marriage, friendship, and family are pushed to the ultimate limit. A heartrending yet inspiring novel that kept me reading late into the night."
—Kristina McMorris, *New York Times* bestselling author of *Sold on a Monday* and *The Edge of Lost*

"A heartfelt tale of true friendship, a mother's unstoppable love, and the immeasurable fortitude of women." —*Booklist*

"An unabashed heart-tugger . . . a moving depiction of the primal power of a mother's love." —*Publishers Weekly*

Praise for *Two Rivers*

"*Two Rivers* is a dark and lovely elegy, filled with heartbreak that turns itself into hope and forgiveness. I felt so moved by this luminous novel."
—Luanne Rice, *New York Times* bestselling author

"A sensitive and suspenseful portrayal of family and the ties that bind."
—Lee Martin, author of *The Bright Forever* and *River of Heaven*

"T. Greenwood's novel is full of love, betrayal, lost hopes, and a burning question: is it ever too late to find redemption?"
—Miranda Beverly-Whittemore, author of *The Effects of Light* and the Janet Heidinger Kafka Prize-winning book *Set Me Free*

"A haunting story in which the sins of the past threaten to destroy the fragile equilibrium of the present. Ripe with surprising twists and heartbreakingly real characters, *Two Rivers* is a remarkable and complex look at race and forgiveness in small-town America." —Michelle Richmond, *New York Times* bestselling author of *The Year of Fog* and *No One You Know*

"*Two Rivers* is a stark, haunting story of redemption and salvation. T. Greenwood portrays a world of beauty and peace that, once disturbed, reverberates with searing pain and inescapable consequences; this is a story of a man who struggles with the deepest, darkest parts of his soul, and is able to fight his way to the surface to breathe again. But also— maybe more so—it is the story of a man who learns the true meaning of family: When I am with you, I am home. A memorable, powerful work."
—Garth Stein, *New York Times* bestselling author of *The Art of Racing in the Rain*

Praise for *Grace*

"A poetic, compelling story that glows in its subtle, yet searing examination of how we attempt to fill the potentially devastating fissures in our lives. Each character is masterfully drawn; each struggles in their own way to find peace amid tumultuous circumstance. With her always crisp imagery and fearless language, Greenwood doesn't back down from the hard issues or the darker sides of human psyche, managing to create astounding empathy and a balanced view of each player along the way. The story expertly builds to a breathtaking climax, leaving the reader with a clear understanding of how sometimes, only a moment of grace can save us." —Amy Hatvany, author of *Best Kept Secret*

"At once heartbreaking, thrilling and painfully beautiful. From the opening page to the breathless conclusion. . . . Greenwood again shows why she is one of our most gifted and lyrical storytellers." —Jim Kokoris, author of *The Pursuit of Other Interests*

"Greenwood has given us a family we are all fearful of becoming—creeping toward scandal, flirting with financial disaster, and hovering on the verge of dissolution. Grace is a masterpiece of small-town realism that is as harrowing as it is heartfelt." —Jim Ruland, author of *Big Lonesome*

"*Grace* amazes. Harrowing, heartfelt, and ultimately so realistically human in its terror and beauty that it may haunt you for days after you finish it. T. Greenwood has another gem here. Greenwood's mastery of character and her deep empathy for the human condition make you care what happens, especially in the book's furious final one hundred pages." —*The San Diego Union-Tribune*

"Exceptionally well-observed. Readers who enjoy insightful and sensitive family drama (Lionel Shriver's *We Need to Talk About Kevin;* Rosellen Brown's *Before and After*) will appreciate discovering Greenwood." —*Library Journal*

Praise for *Bodies of Water*

"A complex and compelling portrait of the painful intricacies of love and loyalty. Book clubs will find much to discuss in T. Greenwood's insightful story of two women caught between their hearts and their families." —Eleanor Brown, *New York Times* bestselling author of *The Weird Sisters*

"*Bodies of Water* is no ordinary love story, but a book of astonishing precision, lyrically told, raw in its honesty and gentle in its unfolding. What I find myself reveling in, pondering, savoring, really, is more than this book's uncommon beauty, though there is much beauty to be found within these pages. . . . A luminous, fearless, heart-wrenching story about the power of true love." —Ilie Ruby, author of *The Salt God's Daughter*

"T. Greenwood's *Bodies of Water* is a lyrical novel about the inexplicable nature of love, and the power a forbidden affair has to transform one woman's entire life. By turns beautiful and tragic, haunting and healing, I was captivated from the very first line. And Greenwood's moving story of love and loss, hope and redemption has stayed with me, long after I turned the last page." —Jillian Cantor, author of *Margot*

Praise for *Undressing the Moon*

"This beautiful story, eloquently told, demands attention."
—*Library Journal* (starred review)

"Greenwood has skillfully managed to create a novel with unforgettable characters, finely honed descriptions, and beautiful imagery."
—*Book Street USA*

"A lyrical, delicately affecting tale."
—*Publishers Weekly*

"Rarely has a writer rendered such highly charged topics . . . to so wrenching, yet so beautifully understated, an effect." —*The Los Angeles Times*

Praise for *Breathing Water*

"A poignant, clear-eyed first novel . . . filled with careful poetic description . . . the story is woven skillfully." —*The New York Times Book Review*

"A poignant debut . . . Greenwood sensitively and painstakingly unravels her protagonist's self-loathing and replaces it with a graceful dignity."
—*Publishers Weekly*

"A vivid, somberly engaging first book."
—Larry McMurtry

"With its strong characters, dramatic storytelling, and heartfelt narration, *Breathing Water* should establish T. Greenwood as an important young novelist who has the great gift of telling a serious and sometimes tragic story in an entertaining and pleasing way."
—Howard Frank Mosher, author of *Walking to Gatlinburg*

"An impressive first novel."
—*Booklist*

"*Breathing Water* is startling and fresh . . . Greenwood's novel is ripe with originality." —*The San Diego Union-Tribune*

THE
STILL
POINT

Other Books by the Author

Breathing Water
Nearer Than the Sky
Undressing the Moon
Two Rivers
The Hungry Season
This Glittering World
Grace
Bodies of Water
The Forever Bridge
Where I Lost Her
The Golden Hour
Rust & Stardust
Keeping Lucy
Such a Pretty Girl

THE
STILL
POINT

TAMMY GREENWOOD

KENSINGTON
PUBLISHING CORP.

www.kensingtonbooks.com

KENSINGTON BOOKS are published by
Kensington Publishing Corp.
119 West 40th Street
New York, NY 10018

All Kensington titles, imprints, and distributed lines are available at special quantity discounts for bulk purchases for sales promotion, premiums, fund-raising, educational, or institutional use.

This book is a work of fiction. Names, characters, businesses, organizations, places, events, and incidents either are the product of the author's imagination or are used fictitiously. Any resemblance to actual persons, living or dead, events, or locales is entirely coincidental.

To the extent that the image or images on the cover of this book depict a person or persons, such person or persons are merely models, and are not intended to portray any character or characters featured in the book.

Special book excerpts or customized printings can also be created to fit specific needs. For details, write or phone the office of the Kensington Sales Manager: Kensington Publishing Corp., 119 West 40th Street, New York, NY 10018. Attn. Sales Department. Phone: 1-800-221-2647.

The K with book logo Reg US Pat. & TM Off.

ISBN: 978-1-4967-3935-3 (ebook)

ISBN: 978-1-4967-3933-9

First Kensington Trade Paperback Printing: March 2024

10 9 8 7 6 5 4 3 2 1

Printed in the United States of America

For my ballet moms

Author's Note

There is a photo of my daughter at three years old, pudgy toddler body stuffed into a pair of pink tights and a black leotard, wild head of blond curls tipped forward as she studies her feet, which are carefully placed in first position. I captured the shot with my flip-phone after her first ballet class eighteen years ago. Looking at it now, it feels prescient, though of course, at the time I was busy documenting all of my two children's milestones: first steps, first words, first days of pre-school. I didn't know then that this was just the beginning of something that would determine the trajectory of her life.

When you watch a ballet performance, you are watching the culmination of not just a month's worth of rehearsals but years of hard work and sacrifice. The dancers onstage have spent their entire lives training for this moment. They are young women (and men) who have spent more hours in their ballet studios than in their homes. More time with their teachers than with their siblings. No proms, no homecomings, and often not even normal school.

But the sacrifices made by these dancers are only part of the story Because behind every dancer is a parent, usually (though not always) a mother. A mother who snaps a photo of her baby ballerina and then spends the next fifteen years driving to and from the dance studio. Who spends hours waiting in greenrooms and lounges, sewing pointe shoe ribbons, or hunched over a sewing machine, or stealing sleep in the car while her daughter practices. Who dreams alongside her.

There is a delicious sort of anticipation to being a ballet mom: each small moment accumulating, building, like individual notes rising to an uncertain crescendo. Of course, you know that at any moment, the needle might lift from the record. The music can end. There's a restlessness that accompanies this life, as well: you fear the worst and can only wish for the best. But for this, for her, you show up: day after day. All in pursuit of your child's elusive dreams.

Still, in the end, only a few will persist. Only a few will take that last final leap of faith and try to transform a childhood passion into a viable career. I would never have imagined that my own daughter would be one of those fearless few, the dream persisting into adulthood—and finally realized, with a ballet company contract this year.

I have wanted to write about the experience of raising a ballet dancer, about this strange and insular world, for a very long time, but I was never sure how to shape it. Like Ever, I wanted to write a love letter to my daughter. A love letter to ballet. A love letter to the other mothers who I know, would do anything to help their children realize their dreams.

The Still Point is this first and foremost: a love letter. But, because I am a fiction writer, not a memoirist, it is also a story of what happens when ambition becomes a dark thing. What happens when mothers go too far. Thankfully, my daughter never had a Savvy in her life, and these mothers are not the mothers of my own experience; no one has set anything on fire or kept a French ballet master stashed away in their guesthouse (as far as I know!).

Ballet moms, in the end, are just like every other mother—wanting their children to find happiness. Onstage, or off. So, my first *thank-you*s are to my many, many fellow ballet moms, but especially to Nina Garin, Agne Isidro, and Marsha Spitzer. How lucky we are to have found each other in the greenroom at SDSB all those years ago. Also, to the CPBP mamas and your amazing girls. Katrina Goldsmith, I miss you! And with so much love to Danielle Shapiro-Rudolph—for the years and years and years spent peering into studio windows and sitting in the audience. For the hours spent on the road to master classes and performances, auditions and competitions. Thank you for always having proper snacks in your bag and for your steadfast friendship. I adore you. Lastly, I am also so grateful to Dana Woolard Hughlett and Lisa Pasquale—because ballet moms never stop being ballet moms, even when their dancers grow up.

I started writing this novel before the pandemic, and there were many, many false starts. I am indebted to so many people who insisted the story was a worthwhile one to tell, even when I was ready to scrap it. Thank you to Amy Hatvany and Jillian Cantor for being my first readers as well as dear, dear friends. Thank you to my agent, David Forrer, whose intelligence and insight is matched only by his kindness and patience.

A special thanks to my editor, Wendy McCurdy, who insisted that I could fix what was broken in these pages and who held my hand for an entire year of revisions. I appreciate you. Thanks as well to the rest of my beloved Kensington team: Steve and Adam Zacharius, Lynn Cully, Elizabeth Trout, Carly Sommerstein, Alexandra Nicolajsen, Kristin McLaughlin, Matt Johnson, Lauren Jernigan, and Vida Engstrand, publicist extraordinaire. To Scott Heim, for the careful copyediting, and to Kris Noble for the cover, which is so beautiful I could cry.

Thank you as well to Neal Griffin, who is my go-to guy for all things law-enforcement, and to Marianne Reiner, who lovingly corrected my sometimes clumsy stabs at French.

As always, my heart is filled (and my writing fed) daily by my family. By Patrick, whose love is certain and sustaining. And Esmée, my other bright and beautiful kid, who—as a ballet sibling—endured all those afternoons in the greenroom, too.

Lastly, this novel would not exist without you, Mikaela, who took me along on this long, uncertain journey. I am so very proud of you—of the artist, and woman, you have become. *Merde* to you, in all that you do.

At the still point of the turning world. Neither flesh nor fleshless;
Neither from nor towards; at the still point, there the dance is . . .

—T. S. Eliot

Now I will dance you the war. . . . The war
which you did not prevent.

—Vaslav Nijinsky

Première

The world is on fire. This is what it looks like as she drives south along the winding coastal highway toward the theater. The sun has set, but the hills to the east, usually swallowed by the black of evening, are aglow now. Flickering. The air smells of smoke, and ash falls like snow around her.

She thinks about the spark that started this. That flick of the match against striker, the tiny flame trembling. The way it flared tentatively, then grew in confidence, glowing with heat. A flame feeds on the air around it, hungry for breath, but once it catches, there's little anyone can do to stop it.

A fire will not be ignored.

She grips the steering wheel and presses her foot on the gas, determined, but with each flicker and flash, she recalls everything she's left behind.

If this were a ballet, of course, the story would end with a dead girl. It is disturbing, really, how many ballets end this way: Juliet poisoned after the potion. Odette, the White Swan, drowning in the lake. Fragile Giselle, dying in her lover's embrace.

But she's never much cared for *The Dying Swan*, for *La Sylphide*. All those sad tragedies. She prefers the Firebird, dancing her infernal dance to cast her spell, to free the captive princesses from the wicked sorcerer.

The Firebird does not succumb. Even as flames leap from her wings' tips, the Firebird ascends from the smoldering embers and ash.

As the world burns around her, she takes flight.

Act I

Three months earlier

Ever

Ever Henderson felt twitchy as she drove Beatrice to the studio that afternoon for the first day of classes. Bea seemed jumpy, too, an odd mixture of excitement and irritation. It must have been the Santa Anas, those dry, wicked winds that roll down from the mountains in Southern California this time of year. When the winds come, the air temperature rises and humidity drops; the air electrified. The winds frazzle nerves, make people restless. Ornery and suspicious. Happily married couples suddenly find themselves squabbling, lifelong friends bickering. Old grievances get whipped up in the winds. Bad behavior abounds. They call them the *devil winds*, for the trouble they stir up.

Ever tried not to think about all the trouble swirling in her head since she got the message from her lawyer, Carl, that morning: *Ever, call me. I have news.* She hadn't returned the call yet. So long as she didn't call him back, his *news* would remain suspended, floating about in the ethers. It could be good or bad. Indefinitely indefinite. *Later,* she'd thought. After she'd dropped Bea off at ballet. But then he'd texted, **URGENT Can you swing by the office today? 4:30?**, and she'd agreed.

"Are you excited?" she asked Bea, forcing a smile. "To get back to the studio?"

Bea looked in the visor's mirror, touched the tip of her finger to an invisible blemish. "Yeah. I miss Miss V."

"And Olive?"

Bea shrugged, and her dismissiveness worried Ever. Olive hadn't been over since Bea got back from New York. Bea hadn't asked to go to Olive's, either. The girls had been best friends since they were ten, since the day Bea walked into Miss V.'s studio and Olive marched up to her like Pippi Longstocking, with her bright red hair and freckles, and took her hand. *Come stand next to me.* From that moment on, they had been thick as thieves, like sisters. For years, Olive had practically lived at their house; she knew where to find the honey in the cupboard, the trick of their fussy doorknob (a gentle twist and nudge of the hip), and Cobain never barked when she came to the door. Something was up with the girls.

Olive had stayed home this summer, opting for Vivienne's program rather than going to New York or Houston or Boston for a big company summer intensive as Bea had. Ever hadn't wanted Bea to go away, either; with Ethan gone and all of them still reeling in the aftermath, Ever had hoped she would stay home, *heal*, but Bea had insisted this was what she wanted. These summers away were all part of the grand plan: to train with the best teachers in the country, to build her resume, but mostly to be seen early on by the company directors so that later, when she was auditioning in a room full of dancers, they would remember her. Besides, even after all these months, Ever knew the house was so dense with sorrow, it was hard to breathe.

And so Ever had flown with her to New York to drop her off, and like the last three years, Bea had spent the summer training at NYRB. Ethan had been the worrier in the family, and Bea's first summer away at fourteen, he'd been reluctant. Some parents got apartments in the city where they stayed as chaperones, but Ethan taught private music lessons all summer when school was out, and Ever had Danny to take care of and classes of her own to teach, never mind the cost of subletting an apartment in Manhattan for six weeks. The only people Ever knew in the city were her editor and her agent, but they had both insisted that New York was one of the safest places on earth now—children growing up there were expected to take the subways alone by the time they were twelve. Still, Ethan had made Bea put both Leona and Edward's numbers in her phone, and each day that first summer he'd studied the tracker app they'd all installed, watching her icon traverse the map of the city. Ever had thought he was being overprotective; neither one of *them* had ever been tracked by their parents as teens. She'd been such a fool, she thought, to trust the world to be a benevolent place.

Bea had only been back for a week, and they were all trying to regain their equilibrium, whatever that meant now. With Bea gone, Ever had been on her own. Danny was busy at his job busing tables, at the beach, or at the skate park with his best friend, Dylan. She had bided her time puttering around the house, trying to write. She spent entire days staring at the blank screen, or traveling down one internet rabbit hole or another—"research," she might have justified if there was anyone to justify it to. But she didn't have a contract, which also meant she didn't have a deadline. "Take some time," Leona had said. "You'll write again when you're ready." Ever had no idea what *ready* looked like, though. The empty house had felt like a mausoleum, a monument to so many lost things. She was glad Bea was back, though her heart hurt when she thought about her graduating in June, about the girl-size hole she would leave in her world. Danny would follow in just a year, off to college, and she'd be completely alone.

"I can't believe this is your last year," Ever said. "It makes me sad."

Bea nodded but stared out the window.

"Is everybody coming back to the studio this fall?" she asked as they pulled into the lot.

"Mary quit," Bea said.

"*Mary* quit?" Mary O'Leary was a dark-haired, coltish girl, one of the strongest dancers at Costa de la Luna Conservatory of Ballet; Ever had been certain she'd be one of the few to make a career of it.

"She's doing water polo," Bea said.

"Wow," Ever said. "She's been at CLCB forever. Longer than you, even."

Ever was mystified by the girls, the ones whose lives, like Bea's, revolved around classes and rehearsals, who suddenly opted out.

They'd stop by the studio sometimes, their complexions now golden from days at the beach, their bodies filled out as if they'd been released from some sort of binding: their clothes showing new cleavage and bare legs, the sinewy muscles just memories now. They all seemed happy, though, released from this strange captivity.

"I really need to get my license," Bea said as they pulled into a parking space next to Savannah Jacobs, who was doing her hair in the BMW convertible her father had bought for her that spring. Ever had a few thoughts about that, and about Savannah as well, but kept them—mostly—to herself.

"I know, Bumble," Ever said. "We'll practice this fall."

Bea was seventeen, turning eighteen next June. She had her permit, but there simply hadn't been time for lessons; there was hardly time for *any* of those normal teenage milestones. She did online schooling and danced six days a week. While her friends from junior high went off to high school, their moms posting homecoming photos and prom photos and pictures of them behind the wheel (*Lookout, new driver on the road!* or *God help us!*), Bea was at the barre.

Ethan had always promised to teach the kids to drive. When Ever had been overwhelmed with the demands of two toddlers, she'd made him pinkie swear there would be a changing of the guard when they hit the teen years. "You get puberty, SATs, and driving," she'd joked. But by the time Bea got her permit, Ethan was sick, and in less than a year, he was gone.

Ever turned off the engine. The Volvo wagon had been Ethan's car—this beast with its COEXIST and BERNIE 2016 bumper stickers and its rusted muffler. He'd liked it because it accommodated his longboard. He'd also argued that its size made it safe, six feet of protection ahead of them and six feet behind. It felt like she was driving a tank, but now that her Jetta's clutch had gone, she was grateful to have it, despite the stained upholstery and the mystery scent (*wet dog? olives?*) coming from the floor mats.

"You don't need to come in," Bea said, her voice soft and her hazel eyes downcast.

"But it's the first day. I was going in to say hi to everybody." Ever had longed for the normalcy of this routine all summer.

"The moms aren't in there. Everybody else drove themselves." Bea gestured with her chin to Savannah Jacobs, who was still sitting in her car, looking at her reflection in the rearview mirror as she did her bun.

"Well, Olive doesn't even have her permit yet, so Lindsay will be here. I also need to fill out the registration papers and give Vivienne your tuition," Ever said, and felt the distinct plummeting feeling she experienced whenever she thought about money lately. And thinking about money made her think about the call from Carl again. Their meeting was in an hour.

Bea sighed and shut the car door, and—without acknowledging Savannah in the next space over, Ever noted—disappeared into the building.

Then, as if Ever had conjured her, Lindsay pulled into the lot. Ever waved, and behind glass, Lindsay's face bloomed into a beaming smile. She parked and threw open her door. Olive got out and went to Savannah's car, sliding into the passenger seat.

"*Hi!*" Lindsay said, embracing Ever tightly. Lindsay's hugs were always warm and long. Ever noticed she had lost weight; Lindsay was always dieting, inflating and deflating like a balloon. With her dark auburn hair and big brown eyes, Ever thought Lindsay was beautiful no matter her dress size, but Lindsay wouldn't hear it.

Lindsay Chase wasn't anyone Ever would have known if not for the studio. Despite living in the same town, they could be from totally different planets. The only thing they had in common was ballet, their daughters engaged in this daily ritual like congregants at the same church. But Lindsay had become one of Ever's best friends, a friendship forged over the last seven years as they sat for hours on end in the greenroom, embellishing tutus or sewing ribbons onto pointe shoes. Sometimes they just set up camp with their laptops: Ever writing and Lindsay, who was a realtor, working. They lived on opposite sides of town, however, and so their friendship played out mostly in the studio. With Bea away, they'd texted over the summer, gotten together for coffee a couple times, but Ever missed these daily interactions. They grounded her. She needed this.

Lindsay linked arms with her as they walked across the lot. "So, do you think he's in there?" she whispered.

"Who's that?" Ever asked.

"The new ballet master," Lindsay said.

"Vivienne hired somebody new?" Vivienne ran the studio alone, with only the help of Eloise, who taught the Littles. There had never been anyone else.

"Oh my god. Ever, don't you ever check your email?"

No. She almost *never* checked her email. She'd glance at it, of course, every few days, but unless there was a bill or something from Leona, she largely ignored the messages.

"It's Etienne Bernay," Lindsay said, eyes dancing.

"Etienne Bernay?"

In the last decade, Ever had gone from knowing nothing about ballet to knowing nearly everything. Thanks to Bea, she could list not only all the major ballet companies, but the names of their principal dancers, as well. There had been an article about Etienne Bernay in Bea's *Pointe Magazine* last spring; she'd read it while she was waiting for Bea to get out of a private lesson. He was a twenty-seven-year-old principal at Ballet de Paris. A wunderkind in the ballet world, his story a sort of miracle. Raised in one of Paris's dangerous and poverty-stricken *banlieues*, he was discovered in an after-school ballet program as a child and taken under the wing of the company's director. According to the article, he joined the corps at sixteen and quickly climbed the ranks. He was gifted, but undisciplined. He failed to show up for practices, purportedly got high prior to a performance before the Queen (though Bea had shown her the video on YouTube, and it was stunning—with him executing a series of flawless triple *sauts de Basque*), and had unapologetically had his torso tattooed with a bull's-eye, claiming he was always being unfairly targeted. (*C'est une métaphore*, he'd told the interviewer, winking devilishly.)

"So, you don't know about the documentary, either?" Lindsay said. "The scholarship?"

Ever shook her head. Documentary? *Scholarship?*

"Here," Lindsay said, handing Ever her phone, and she read the email announcing that there would be a visiting faculty member at CLCB this fall, a principal dancer from the Ballet de Paris, on "hiatus." He would not only be joining the faculty for the fall semester and assisting Vivienne with the Conservatory's production of *The Nutcracker*, but he would also be selecting one dancer to send back to the Ballet de Paris Académie for the spring term, on a scholarship he would sponsor. An award-winning filmmaker would be documenting the process.

"Crazy, right?" Lindsay said. "You seriously didn't know? Bea didn't say anything?"

If Bea had had any idea that Etienne Bernay was coming to CLCB, she would have been abuzz. Ballet de Paris was one of her dream companies. Ever felt a flicker ignite inside her. It had been so long since she'd felt anything like this, it took her several moments to recognize it.

Hope. That's what it was. Until Ethan's life insurance claim came through, she'd been trying to figure out how they would navigate the exorbitant cost of ballet. There was tuition, but soon they would also have to finance audition season; Bea insisted that video auditions were not the same as getting in front of a school or company's director. But this meant cross-country flights, a trip to Europe even. If Bea could skip all this, if she could simply be *chosen*, the burden would be lifted.

"Why here?" Ever asked. None of this made any sense. Their tiny coastal town, more than fifty miles south of Los Angeles, was hardly a celebrity hotspot, and Etienne Bernay was just that—a *celebrity*, in the world of ballet, at least.

"Apparently, Vivienne's known him since he was a kid," Lindsay said.

Vivienne never spoke of her past, but everyone knew she had danced all over the world: at Ballet de Paris herself, with a stint in

New York for Balanchine. And later with *Baryshnikov*. One rumor had it that he had followed her around like a lovesick puppy for months.

"He's taking over Level Six," Lindsay said, grabbing Ever's hand.

"Our girls?" Ever said.

"Our girls."

Lindsay

A scholarship. To the *Ballet de Paris Académie*. This could change everything for one of the girls. For *Olive*. For years, she had been overlooked by Vivienne. She was a strong, dynamic dancer, but she was not Vivienne's favorite, almost always relegated to the corps roles. She was reliable and consistent but—in Vivienne's eyes—just another competent dancer. A workhorse. Vivienne was a wonderful teacher, possibly the best in Southern California, but she had a narrow focus, and for years now it had been trained on Savannah Jacobs. Vivienne simply didn't *see* Olive. But now—a new teacher! A new set of eyes. Maybe he would see what made Olive special: that fire she had. A fire that, if Lindsay was being honest, was starting to dwindle lately.

She blamed Steve. This whole summer, it had felt like he was sabotaging Olive: letting her go off with Savvy to parties, bringing home junk food, allowing her to ditch classes when she was sunburned or tired or just feeling lazy. "It's the summer before senior year. Let her be a kid." But Lindsay knew what he was really saying, and likely so did Olive. He wanted her to act like a regular kid because he thought she *was* just a regular kid. He had never seen what was extraordinary in her, and with every day that passed, and every one of his dismissive comments, Lindsay had watched Olive's light dim.

Olive just needed something to renew that flame, and the scholarship might be it. Not only would it give her a goal to strive for, but if she somehow managed to actually get the scholarship, then it would prove Steve wrong. Prove them all wrong.

"It's hush-hush, of course," Nancy, the office manager at CLCB, had whispered to Lindsay earlier that summer, leaning across the reception desk, breath smelling like the butterscotch Lifesavers she sucked on whenever she quit smoking. "Don't want to get everybody worked up. Vivienne's worried about what will happen when word gets out." The moment people heard that Etienne Bernay was coming, ballet moms from all up and down the coast would descend on CLCB in desperate droves. The conservatory was intentionally small and selective. A family. Vivienne insisted that the visiting faculty would not change that.

Nancy was the guardian and distributor of most information at the studio. She was tough and a little bit mean, but, for some reason, she liked Lindsay. Back in June, Nancy had told her about Etienne Bernay, then lowered her voice to a husky hush. "Don't say *anything.*" Not being allowed to share the news had been torture, but Lindsay had kept her word. Though clearly, someone had looser lips than hers, because around the Fourth of July, the girls all seemed to know. It was only then that she'd figured it was okay to tell Steve, but he'd looked at her like she'd said they were having spaghetti for dinner. "Never heard of him," he'd said. She'd considered texting Ever, but she'd worried it might create some weirdness between them.

Of course, their daughters were such different dancers. Bea was ethereal, delicate: *Giselle, La Sylphide, White Swan.* Olive was fiery, fierce: *Kitri, Esmeralda, Black Swan.* But there was one scholarship. *One.* She didn't want to think about how this was going to change the dynamics at the studio, least of all between Olive and her best friend. Between Lindsay and Ever. But now it felt good to spill.

"So Bernay and the film crew got here a week ago," she told Ever as they made their way across the parking lot. "Josie said they're staying at that extended-stay motel by the freeway. Seacoast Suites?"

Josie Jacobs, Savannah's mother, had told Lindsay all of this over a glass of wine by her pool last week. With Bea in New York, Savvy and Olive had started hanging out more, and Lindsay had been forced into Josie's world. Being around Josie was something like a Tilt-a-Whirl ride: fun but also kind of nauseating. Also, every conversation she'd had with Josie that summer felt like a betrayal of Ever. It was silly, she knew; they were all grown-ups, but Ever (like the other mothers) had some strong opinions about Josie, and most were not good. Lindsay was glad that Bea was home now, that Ever was back at the studio, and that she could get off the ride.

"Oh my god, I have to pee," Lindsay said as they walked toward the front doors. "I've had like a gallon of cucumber juice today."

"You look skinny," Ever said. "Please tell me you're not on that awful liquid diet again."

Lindsay *was* on that awful liquid diet again, and she had lost twenty pounds so far, though while Ever had noticed, Steve had not. She wondered if she lost fifty pounds and her pants fell around her ankles, whether he might bat an eye. If she lost a hundred pounds and was nothing more than a sack of bones, maybe then he'd notice?

"I guess this means we can't go grab Ralberto's during class?" Ever asked.

"Not unless they've started making enchilada smoothies." Lindsay laughed.

"Hey, ladies!" a voice called from across the parking lot. Victor, one of the guys from Freezey's HVAC company across the parking lot, waved at them.

"Hey, Victor!" she said.

CLCB's studios were in an industrial park at the edge of town. One foggy day a few years ago, Lindsay had been waiting in the car for Olive; she'd gotten lost in one of Ever's novels for two hours before she realized she'd left her lights on. Victor saw her in a panic and offered to give her a jump. "Leave it running for a bit," he'd said, and motioned to the book on the seat, told her that his wife was a huge fan of Ever's novels. They'd been friendly ever since.

"Welcome back!" Victor said now, his smile wide. "You been working out, Lindsay?"

God, even Victor had noticed she'd lost weight, from *fifty feet* away. Goddamned Steve.

"Every day!" She curled her bare arm like Popeye and, for once, didn't worry about a sagging bicep.

"I can't believe this is our last year here," Ever said as they reached the door.

Before Ethan died, Ever had been like a living, breathing ray of sunshine: golden skin; sun-kissed, sandy hair; bright hazel eyes. But now, she looked like a shadow of herself.

Ever held onto Lindsay's wrist as if she were a flotation device; without Ethan, Ever was adrift. Lindsay knew the only way to save her was to *buoy* her. So, she linked her arm with Ever's and whispered, "Let's go check out *Monsieur Bernay*."

Bea

Bea had never kept a secret from her mother before. When she was little, her parents had called her "Howard Cosell" because after school, she'd replay every detail of her day: everything she ate, every game she played, even how many times she used the toilet. She couldn't help herself. Holding things in made her feel heavy, and all she wanted was lightness. To be filled with nothing but breath. But now here she was.

"Bea!" squealed Jazmin. Jaz was only thirteen, the youngest girl in Level 6. She'd been a rhythmic gymnast and competition dancer before she came to CLCB. Her mom, Melissa, was one of those crazy dance moms you always hear about; Jazmin already had fifty thousand followers on her mom-managed Instagram account. Jaz was sweet, though, and when she came running to Bea for a hug, Bea smiled.

Jaz's dark hair was slicked back into a high bun, a holdover from her competition days. Vivienne hated high buns; she insisted the girls wear chignons that skimmed their necks, but Melissa never seemed to get the memo.

"How was New York?" Jaz asked.

"It was great," Bea said, her words somehow making their way past the lump in her throat. "Oh! I brought you something!" She pulled a tiny snow globe out of her backpack. She had brought back souvenirs for all the girls in Level 6.

"I love it!" Jazmin said, and shook the plastic trinket, snow falling over the miniature Empire State Building. "So, are you excited?"

"Excited?" Bea asked.

"I wonder who'll get it." She lowered her voice. "Probably Savvy, but *I* hope it's you."

Sugar Plum. The poster on the bulletin board, the one with the photo of Savvy as Sugar Plum in last year's production, announced that *Nutcracker* auditions were in three weeks.

"We'll see," Bea said and shrugged.

Piano music was coming from Studio B. The new batch of Littles, the five- and six-year-olds, had class with Eloise; their mothers were lined up in the row of folding chairs in front of the window like people observing monkeys at the zoo.

The lobby was already full of the Level 6 kids, even though their class didn't start for another half hour. They were stretching, eating, looking at their phones. Bea's eyes did a quick scan, searching for Olive and Savvy. Neither had come inside yet. The Level 6 boys were all there, though, *Le Trio*: Luke, Nick, and Owen. Thankfully, only Owen looked up at her, smiled, and waved. Luke was on his phone, and Nick simply ignored her, and *she* ignored the throbbing in her chest. *Nick.*

She took a deep breath and went to the far corner of the lobby, where she set down her dance bag. She fiddled with her foam roller, rolling out her hip, then reached for her phone. When the bells on the door chimed, her body tensed, like a guitar string wound too tight.

"So, where is he?" Savvy asked in her silky voice.

"Nobody's seen him yet," someone said.

Bea looked up. Who were they talking about? A new student? Another boy? It was so rare to get a new boy, especially in Level 6. Most boys didn't make it past Level 3 before kids at school started taunting them or their fathers insisted they play soccer or football instead.

"Hey Bea, you're back," Savvy said coolly. Bea felt breathless. She thought about the Empire State Building key chain in her backpack, but knew she wouldn't give it to her.

Olive had come in with Savvy, but Bea couldn't look Olive in the eye, either. Instead, she returned to her phone, scrolling through some random Instagram feed, her hands trembling. She waited until she heard Savvy and the boys talking before she stole another glance. Savvy and Olive were now sitting on the floor with Nick and Luke in a loose circle. So, this was it. This was how it was going to be from now on. She couldn't wait to graduate and get out of here, though the thought of leaving also made her heart hurt.

The trouble—with Savvy, anyway—had started that spring when Miss V. had Bea understudy Savannah as Giselle. Mary, who usually understudied Savvy, was out with a "hamstring injury," though by then, everyone knew she was planning to quit. Bea had felt Savvy's disdain like something living and breathing, even seething between them. Every time Bea got a correction in class or Miss V. asked her to demonstrate a combination, Savvy looked irritated. It wasn't jealousy (Savvy had no reason to be jealous, after all—she was the best dancer at the studio, never mind the one with the boyfriend, the car, the pool, the *everything*), but derision. Like she didn't think Bea was worthy of being her understudy. Bea had felt Savvy's icy blue eyes on her, willing her to mess up. And it worked. *Fouettés* were the bane of her existence, and whenever she fell out of a turn, she could hear Savvy's knowing sigh.

It started with *Giselle*, but then came the bonfire. She and her mom had left for New York the morning after, but Bea didn't say a word to her about what happened. So much for "Howard Cosell." Her memory of the night was patchy, but the sickening feeling of regret was like an extra bag she'd carried onto the plane with them, one she'd quietly shoved into the overhead compartment, though it rattled around up there the whole way.

For the first few weeks in New York, she waited for the angry text from Savvy. But as time went by, she started to think maybe Savvy wouldn't find out. It had only been Bea and Olive, Luke, and Nick at the beach that night. Olive would certainly never say anything. Neither would the boys, definitely not Nick. Bea had still been too afraid to ask Olive, too embarrassed by what she *could* recall. She'd texted Olive a couple of times (*OMG! so hot here, miss you*), and sent her some Snaps of New York: her Creamsicle Float at Shake Shack, a guy dressed up like Big Bird sitting on a bench in Central Park, a photo of herself doing an arabesque in front of the fountain at Lincoln Center. Olive responded to the texts (*hot here too*), but she didn't open the Snaps. Her mom must have taken Snapchat away again. Last summer, Lindsay had banned Olive from all social media for a month when Olive cussed in a post.

Bea had searched Savvy's Instagram, and gleaned that Savvy and Nick were still together: photos taken of them in his Jeep, at the movie theater wearing 3D glasses, wrapped in a blanket on the jetty, staring out at the ocean. Savvy seemed happy, white-blond hair rippled with beach waves, tips dyed the same crystal blue as her eyes, and Bea had felt awash with relief. Maybe nothing would come of this after all, she'd thought.

But then one night, she was scrolling through Savvy's posts when she saw a bunch of pictures of Savvy with Olive's family, beach camping, their faces aglow in the flames of a campfire. Lindsay was in the background wearing a bright purple sarong. Olive's dad, Steve, was cooking burgers on a hibachi. Last was a photo of the two girls doing dual *saut de chat*s across the sand—their leaps in perfect synchronicity, the sunset burning behind them.

Olive hadn't said or posted anything about the trip coming early this year—the trip that *Bea* was usually invited to in August when she got back from New York. She and Olive looked forward to it every summer. Lindsay always made sure to get vegan marshmallows and veggie burgers for her. But this year . . . Olive had invited *Savvy*?

Bea scoured Olive's frustratingly sparse posts. Nothing. Lindsay must have taken away Instagram, too. She'd hesitated before searching Nick's account, heart racing, searching for something to explain how it was that Savvy had stolen her best friend. It was on Nick's account that she'd seen the photos of Olive and Savvy at a party, red Solo cups in hand. Olive almost never drank, but her eyes were glassy, and their short skirts were riding up, revealing a glimpse of Savvy's left muscled butt cheek. Olive had commented: *bottoms up*

LOL. The tap was accidental, the red heart icon blooming, and her own heart nearly stopped. That simple, clumsy tap would send an alert three thousand miles to both Nick's and Olive's phones, interrupting whatever they were doing with a message that Bea had liked the comment. Bea had quickly tapped the heart again, restoring it to its "unliked" state, but it was too late. It was literally like trying to unring a bell, and the reply from Olive almost immediately appeared, two words all in caps: *LOL STALKER.* Bea sighed, relieved, thinking Olive was joking, but when she returned to Olive's account, she'd been blocked. Just like that.

But why was *Olive* mad at her? She tried to remember their last conversation, but her memory of that night was scattered, fractured. Bits of glass in a kaleidoscope. Hands trembling, she had texted Olive: *you blocked me?* For five excruciating minutes, she'd watched the three dots hovering as Olive drafted her response; then, they disappeared.

It was humid and sticky that night in the dorm room that she and her roommate, Cassie, shared, a lazy fan spinning the air around. They left the windows open, and the noises from the street below kept her awake. A sob escaped Bea's lips, and Cassie said, "Hey, Bea, you okay?"

Bea had said *yes*, but tears ran hot down her cheeks.

She'd tried to put it out of her mind. Luckily, she was in classes all day (technique, pointe, variations or character, and rep), and so exhausted, she fell asleep early most nights. She kept hoping that Olive would unblock her, but each time she checked, she was still shut out.

"Don't worry," Cassie said when Bea explained. "You have *me*." Cassie was a good friend; they'd been roommates every summer since Bea was fourteen, but Bea had suddenly wanted nothing more than to just go home. She wanted to bicker with her brother and sit out on their rickety deck and watch the surfers bobbing on the waves. She wanted her mom to fill her favorite mug with chai tea, and she wanted Cobain, their old corgi, to curl up at her feet. She wanted her *dad.* He used to wax his surfboard while she read or did homework, and then give her head a kiss before he trotted down the steps to the beach below. Memories like this were like blisters on her toes, always popping up, fully formed. Stinging.

She'd been so homesick, worse than any other summer in New York, which was crazy, because now there was nothing to go home to. Her dad was gone. Danny spent most of his time with Dylan or at work. And apparently, her best friend in the world had ditched her. The fact that it seemed to be her fault only made it worse.

Across the room, Nick and Luke laughed loudly, startling her, and Bea put in her earbuds and turned up the volume on her phone. Her playlist was filled with her dad's favorite bands: De La Soul, Fugazi, Nirvana. All that '90s music she had grown up listening to, the music that made her feel, somehow, both closer to him and the sharp sting of his absence. It was like the exquisite pain of being *en pointe*, the agony of muscles stretched to their limits. Pain with a purpose. Because, if only for a few minutes, each song brought him back to her.

The bass boomed in her ears; she didn't notice that someone was standing there until he nudged her foot with his. Men's dance sneakers, black Adidas track pants, one pant leg rolled up, revealing a masculine calf, a tattooed spiral of barbed wire encircling it. She looked up, and the guy was bent over, hands on his knees. He tapped at his ear and was saying something to her. She yanked the earbuds out and blinked. Dark hair flopped over one brown eye, crooked nose, and sharp jaw. This guy looked just like *Etienne Bernay* from Ballet de Paris. What the hell?

"I said, what are you listening to?" The accent was definitely French.

"Oh. Um," she said. "A Tribe Called Quest?"

He held out his hand, palm up, and wiggled his fingers, motioning for her to hand him her phone, but she paused. She was hardly ready to hand her phone over to a total stranger. But was he a stranger, or was he Etienne Bernay? If so, what was he doing *here*?

She slowly handed him the phone. He put one earbud in and studied the screen.

"'Can I Kick It?'" he asked, smirking.

She nodded, stunned into silence.

"*Très bien,*" he said, and handed her back the phone and earbuds. Then he was gone—slipping into Studio A.

The room buzzed. When she glanced over at Olive, Savvy, and *Le Trio,* their jaws were slack.

"What's going on?" she whispered to Lizzy, who was stretching next to her.

"It's Etienne *Bernay,*" she said. "You didn't know? He's making a documentary, and he's picking one of us to bring back to the Ballet de Paris Académie. On scholarship."

Bea shook her head, which was pounding now. She reached with her right hand and pinched her left arm sharply. Not dreaming. This was real.

Suddenly, he, *Etienne Bernay,* leaned out of the doorway to the studio and beckoned them in. "*Allons-y,*" he said. "Come in. We have work to do."

Ever

"I'm going to the restroom," Lindsay said, squeezing Ever's arm. "I'll be right back."

The lobby was crowded with girls, a sea of pink. The Littles' moms sat perched on chairs near the smaller studio's window, bags filled with healthy snacks. Ever had been one of them once, brushing Bea's tawny hair into a bun as Bea sat on the floor between her legs, eating grapes. She missed those days, when she and the other mothers would sit and chat and watch while their daughters took class. Now, the girls either drove themselves or got dropped off. Mothers of Level 6 were unofficially banished from the main lobby, relegated to the stuffy greenroom down the hall if they opted to stay and wait. And peeking through the studio windows was tacitly forbidden. She pictured them, their girls, incubating inside that glass egg, Vivienne enclosing them inside her feathered embrace until they were all ready to fly away.

Vivienne. Ever pulled the postdated check from her purse and held her breath. She approached the reception area. Nancy was squinting at the computer screen in front of her, muttering. Ever gathered herself and lifted her chin. "Hi, Nancy!"

"Sign these releases," Nancy said, smacking two pieces of paper in front of her.

"For?"

"This goddamned *movie*." She lifted her chin toward the far end of the lobby, where a petite young woman with long, inky hair and laden with video equipment was talking on her phone, and a squat, balding guy was setting up a microphone. *"Ces sons ambients sont bons, oui?"* the woman asked the man. *"Les filles et les mamans?"*

The girls and the mothers. Ever picked out a few remembered French words from the year she and her family had lived at the naturist community in Belgium. She'd been little then and had absorbed the language like a cut flower in water.

Nancy motioned to the pen cup on the counter; each pen with a bright pink pompom attached to the top. Ever studied the form, which basically gave the filmmakers permission to both film the dancers and edit any footage taken, which could then be used *for any and all broadcasting, non-broadcasting, audio/visual, and/or exhibition purposes in any manner or media, in perpetuity, throughout the world.* It seemed sort of broad?

"Fill that one out for Beatrice." Nancy tapped the second sheet. "And this one for you."

"For *me?*"

"They want to interview the mothers, too. And *Bob,*" Nancy snipped.

Bob Ivers was the sole ballet dad at the studio. Clueless, bumbling Bob, a single father raising three daughters; his eldest, Phoebe, was one of the youngest girls in Level 6. Bob was sitting in a chair near the restroom door, with a clipboard and a pompom pen.

Ever quickly signed the papers and pushed them back across the counter.

"Is Vivienne in her office?" Ever asked.

"Outside," Nancy said. "Having a smoke."

Ever thought about going outside, but the idea of groveling while Vivienne smoked her Gauloise was unbearable. She set the post-dated check and the registration forms on the counter.

"Can you just let her know—"

Suddenly, the floor trembled, and the pounding bass of drums echoed through the lobby. Ever reflexively glanced toward the front doors; someone must have been driving past the studio with their windows down and their music up.

"What is *that?*" Nancy asked, standing, palms pressed against the counter's surface, neck craning toward the sound, which, Ever quickly realized, was not coming from outside but inside.

Recognition set in, like a punch to the gut. It was the kind of grief that squeezed her bowels, almost primitive, such a basic, human urge for release, though after a year, there really was nothing left to expel. That initial clenching was quickly followed by dizziness as she was transported: it was 1994, and she was in Ethan's ramshackle rental house near the beach in Santa Cruz: sand in the sheets, hip-hop and jazz. She shook her head, pulling herself from the riptide of nostalgia and grief, back to the moment. As though tumbled by the waves, she longed for her feet to find the ground again. She was at the *studio*, and the music was not coming from Ethan's old console stereo, but from Studio A.

"What the heck?" Lindsay asked as she emerged from the restroom.

Together they moved toward the studio window and, breaking those unspoken rules, peeked through the glass at the girls as their new teacher demonstrated the *tendu* combination, and the retro jazz hip-hop blasted from the speakers.

"What is he doing?" Lindsay said. "Vivienne is going to pitch a fit."

Etienne Bernay stood at the front by the mirrors. When he noticed the mothers watching—and they were all watching—his reflection winked at them. She felt her face flush with heat as she and all the other mothers backed away from the window. He turned to his audience of giggling girls. *"Vous êtes prêtes, n'est-ce pas?"* You're ready, no?

Just then, Vivienne swept into the lobby from outside, bringing the scent of cigarettes with her. She was scowling, seeming to search for the origin of the music.

Vivienne was in her early sixties; though she'd aged the way French women, the way French *ballet dancers,* anyway, do. Silver hair swept into a tidy bun at the nape of her neck. Most days she wore sheer skirts with a camisole leotard underneath, her shoulders like pale knobs, her clavicle a rigid hanger, her chest a row of bones. On chilly days, she'd wrap herself in a black ballet sweater, her thin legs enclosed in perfectly threadbare leg warmers. Elegance. She was the epitome of *aloof. Distant.* Even after all these years, Vivienne still intimidated Ever.

All the mothers watched Vivienne march toward Studio A, where the bass was beating like a wild heartbeat. She entered, and the music cut out. When she returned to the lobby, she was followed by a trail of giggles.

Ever checked the time. 4:15. She only had fifteen minutes until her meeting with Carl. She grabbed the check from the counter and took a deep breath.

"Vivienne?" she called out as Vivienne headed into her office.

"Oh, *bonjour*," she said, still scowling.

"I have the tuition check. I hope it's okay I postdated it—just a couple of days. We're still waiting . . . um . . . for Ethan's claim." Ever felt light headed, but Vivienne simply nodded and accepted the check.

"It is okay. *Merci.*"

She felt flushed with relief. It would be fine. She'd just have to pull a bit more from the line of credit this month. And maybe the news from Carl would be *good*? She hadn't allowed herself to hope that URGENT didn't mean calamity.

"Can Bea get a ride home with you later?" she asked Lindsay, who was filling out Nancy's forms. "I'm sorry; I know it's out of the way. But I have a meeting downtown with Carl, and I'm not sure how long it will be."

"Of course," Lindsay said. "Oh, shoot, is it about the claim?"

"Yeah. Finally. I also need to get the house ready for Sunday."

"Oh, the party!" Lindsay said, clearly flustered. "I'm sorry, I mean the memorial."

Every year for more than a decade, Ever and Ethan had hosted an end-of-summer party over Labor Day weekend. Lindsay was one of the few still there last year when the accident happened.

This year, Ethan's buddies had planned to paddle out on their surfboards at sunset to honor Ethan's life. But while it had felt like a lovely gesture back when they first brought it up, now—after a year—it felt like re-breaking someone's nose to set it right.

"You should do potluck," Lindsay said. "We'll all bring food. Actually, you know what? Forget that. I'm going to Costco Sunday after my open house. Give me a list. I'll get whatever you need." She paused and took Ever's hand. "Don't worry. I'm here for you."

Bea

Usually in class, Bea felt unburdened. At the barre, all those heavy things lifted. She imagined her sadness like vapor, like the marine layer lifting off the ocean. But when Etienne Bernay had decided to blast her dad's music through the speakers, she'd felt leaden.

For years, the Level 6s had dutifully stood at the barre and listened to the same piano music as they went through the same combinations. They were part of her body's memory, the movements so ingrained in her muscles and bones, they felt almost like a prayer. This new teacher, playing A Tribe Called Quest and making combinations up on the fly, felt blasphemous.

After Vivienne cut the music and stormed out, he'd dragged his feet like a scolded little boy (the girls stifling giggles), returning to his laptop where he cued Vivienne's music, rolling his eyes. And as the first few bars played, she was light again. Made of nothing but breath. But after the *rond de jambe* combination, as she automatically prepared for *fondus*, she heard a slithery whispering, snaking through the room. Jazmin poked her in the ribs, and she turned around. Jazmin's eyes were wide. Etienne Bernay was walking toward them. Did he think she'd been talking? Great, just what she needed was to be called out by the new teacher on the first day. Her limbs grew heavy again.

"You," he said, and pointed at Bea. *"Comment t'appelles-toi?"*

"Je m'appelle Beatrice," she said automatically, using the French pronunciation of her own name—*Beya-treece*. She'd been taking French since eighth grade, dreaming of Paris since she was thirteen. But she

never used it in class, not even with Vivienne. She could feel Savvy's gaze burning holes in her back.

He cocked his head, and a grin spread across his face. "Ah, *elle parle français*," he said to the class. "*Hip-hop girl*."

The heat had spread all the way to her ears now, and she was certain they were red because they were *burning*. Absently, her hand went to one of them, as if to squash out a fire.

"*Montre-leur!*" he said, and beckoned her with a curl of his index finger before he strutted to the front of the studio, where he turned on the music again. "Show them how to do."

All eyes on her, she took a deep breath and began. She focused on the feeling of the floor beneath her as she pushed her pinkie toe to the earth and her heel to the sky, articulating her feet, rolling through each joint, each muscle and little bone. It didn't matter that Savvy was shooting her death stares or that Olive wouldn't look at her, or that she could smell the heady scent of Nick's shampoo all the way across the room. She rode the music like a wave, gave in to its pull.

Bea felt breathless by the time she finished the first combination of jumps across the room, her body burning with the effort of flight. Male teachers always loved jumps, pushing them to go higher, higher. The boys stood in the back corner, hands on their knees, trying to catch their breath. She averted her eyes when Nick caught her watching them.

They'd done it on one side; now it was time to reverse it. Bea waited for her turn, running the combination over in her head, marking it with her arms. She tried to ignore Savvy and Olive, who were in the first group; Savvy always made sure she was in the first group. Usually Olive hung back. But not today. She had a feeling a lot of girls would be fighting for the front spots now. *Ballet de Paris. My god.*

"*Allez!*" Etienne barked at her group, clapping his hands and motioning them forward.

She moved across the floor in the *grand allegro* combination, aware of his eyes boring into her as she battled gravity.

Then they were done, and he was calling them to the center for *révérence*. *Révérence* was the time for them to catch their breath, to slow down, to linger. It is movement filled with gratitude and respect. Every time Bea went through the movements of *révérence*, her eyes inexplicably filled with tears, overwhelmed by a surge of emotion. Today was no different, though, maybe even worse. Because the end of class meant dealing with Olive. If she had her license, then she could just gather her stuff and go home, but without it, she was stuck here until her mom came.

They applauded the new teacher, who bowed his head, pressed his hand to his chest in humble gratitude, then slipped out the back door to smoke with the lady who had been videoing them and the guy with the mic.

Savvy, as always, kept her pointe shoes on and practiced pirouettes while one of the younger girls recorded her. Bea knew the video would show up on Savannah's public Instagram with a self-deprecating caption like, "work in progress" or "*en dedans* FAIL."

As Etienne came back into the studio, Savvy executed five perfect pirouettes, grinning smugly as Nick whistled. Bea sighed. Of course, Savvy would wind up with the scholarship. Bea should just give up right now.

Etienne walked past Bea and muttered, "*Quelle frimeuse.*"

What a show-off? Did he really say that? About Savvy? To her? She felt a small smile on her lips, despite herself.

Like Bea, Olive was sitting alone, taking off her pointe shoes. Bea peeled off her nasty toe pads and plucked the gel toe spacers from between her numb toes. Her bunions were throbbing, and she had corns between every single toe from her summer intensive. Her feet never hurt until the shoes came off. Then her toes felt like they were on fire.

She caught Olive's eye, but quickly looked back down. When she snuck a peek again, Olive was on her phone, but then Olive stood up, slipped on her trash bag pants, and strode noisily over to Bea. Bea held her breath, and for a moment, thought maybe things would just go back to normal.

"Hey, Liv," she said and smiled. "I got you something in New York." She reached into her bag, feeling around until she found the NY license plate magnet with Olive's name. She couldn't believe she'd found it. She and Olive could never find any tchotchkes with their names. She handed it to her, a peace offering. But Olive didn't even look at it.

"That's okay," Olive said, shaking her head. "You can give it to someone else."

"It has *your* name on it," Bea said, flummoxed.

Olive hoisted her bag onto her shoulder. "Your mom asked my mom to drive you home."

Bea felt tears springing to her eyes. "Liv, I'm sorry. For whatever it is that made you mad. What did I do? Did I say something? I don't really remember . . ."

The beginning of that night was clear, but after the first hour or so, the rest was just a blur of fire: the bonfire, the blazing heat of the vodka, the burn of her skin, of the sand. Fractals, branching out from the white-hot center of memory. There was some sort of argument, maybe? What had she done? Why did *Olive* hate her?

Olive eyed her with incredulity. "People feel bad for you. Because of what happened to your dad," she said. She shook her head. "But you're not a good person, Bea. You're just not."

"I—" Bea started.

"Anyway, my mom's waiting," she said, and turned away.

Lindsay

After they dropped Bea off at her house, Lindsay said, "You guys okay? You and Bea?"

Olive shrugged.

The girls hadn't spoken at all in the car. Olive had been on her phone, and when Lindsay glanced in the rearview mirror, she'd seen Bea leaning her head against the window, eyes closed.

"You two haven't seen each other in a couple months. Bumpy re entry?"

"Do I have to go to the memorial this weekend?" Olive asked.

Lindsay was taken aback.

"Greg Bardo's having a party, and Savvy invited me. I hardly ever get to go to parties, and it's the last one before school starts."

Lindsay felt a prick of anger. How could Olive even think of skipping a memorial for her best friend's father? Ethan had been like a second dad to Olive. He taught her to surf and to play bass guitar. He even built her a barre for her to use in the garage to practice at home.

"You went to a *bunch* of parties this summer. So that's totally not true. Seriously, what is going on with you guys?"

Olive's eyebrow twitched. "*Fine*, Mom. I'll go."

There were times lately when Lindsay felt like she'd failed as a mother. When she'd see a nasty flicker in her daughter, a bit of cruelty, a flash of ugliness, and she'd wonder what she'd done wrong. If it was too late to get back that sweet bubbly girl who was kind to everyone. She blamed Savvy, who seemed to bring out the worst in Olive.

"I'm sorry," Olive said. "It's just, Bea's, like, different lately."

"You mean since New York?" she asked. Some girls went away and came back full of themselves, but Bea was always humble. The opposite of Savvy.

Olive shrugged again.

"You'll work it out. You always do," she said, though honestly, Bea and Olive had never even bickered.

"Maybe," Olive said.

Lindsay opened the garage door and saw that Steve wasn't home yet. She pulled into her spot, leaving just enough room for Olive to get out, making sure to give Steve a wide berth for when he finally got home. He was always worried about their doors dinging each other.

Where was he? She checked her messages, but there was nothing from him, though that was not unusual. Lately she felt like a ghost in her own life. At some point in the last few years, he'd stopped kissing her goodbye when he went to work and at night before they rolled to their respective sides of their bed. Some days she thought that if she didn't initiate a conversation with him, he wouldn't say a single word to her. She had sneezed twelve times in a row the day before, the Santa Anas causing her allergies to flare up, and he didn't even bother with a single *bless you*, never mind twelve. They still had sex now and then, always in silence. Always in the middle of the night, their bodies going through the motions memorized so long ago. But in the morning, there was never any acknowledgment of what had felt, if only briefly, like intimacy.

She was ashamed to admit it, but sometimes she envied Ever. It was horrible, and she would never ever tell anyone this. Especially not Ever. But maybe, she thought, it would be easier if Steve were dead. Of course, she'd never *do* anything. This wasn't some *Dateline* episode; it was just her twisted fantasies (ones she couldn't even manage to bring up when she made her monthly visit to the confessional). But when he did this—disappeared at night with zero explanation—she entertained wicked thoughts: his midlife crisis sports car careening off the cliffs, the police coming to her home with the news. The outpouring of love from her friends and family.

When she allowed this grim fantasy to play out, it was never grief she felt at the prospect of Steve's demise, but *freedom*.

Why not just leave him, then? That, of course, was the thought that always butted in. The logical interloper in her murderous fantasies. But oddly, the idea of leaving Steve—of simply packing up her bags and walking out the door—seemed unfathomable. At least, if Steve were dead, no one would blame *her*. No one would speculate about what he'd been doing to cause her to break up their family. (*Well, she gained so much weight. I heard she was frigid. She was so consumed with Olive—her whole life wrapped up in her kid. She should have seen it coming.*) Well, she did see it coming. It was coming at her like a locomotive off the rails. It was easier to just pretend that all was well. Someone once told her *fake it until you make it*; well, she had the first part down.

"I'm going to take a bath," she said to Olive, who was sitting at the island in the kitchen eating leftover lo mein Steve had brought home. "Also, you shouldn't eat that."

Olive slurped the greasy noodles, ignoring her and looking at her phone, which was buzzing loudly on the concrete counter with a call from Savvy.

Ever

Ever was startled when Bea walked through the door. Was it nine already? She could barely account for the hours since she got home from Carl's. She was having difficulty grasping time lately; some days, it slowed, each minute insufferably long. Other days—like a sleepwalker waking—she'd return from wherever her mind had wandered, having lost hours.

"Hi," she said, motioning for Bea to come to her. "How was class? The new teacher?"

"Different."

"Different *good* or different *bad*?"

"Just different," she said. "Where's Danny?"

"Still at work," she said. It was the last week of summer before he went back to school, and he'd been taking on extra shifts. He knew things were tight; he never asked for money anymore and even offered to do the grocery shopping last week, but Ever had insisted that he keep his money in his pocket.

"I need a shower," Bea said, and slipped down the hall.

The old pipes in the house groaned, and Ever studied the bills spread out before her, like pieces of an unsolvable puzzle. Carl's voice echoed in her head, "I'm so sorry, Ever."

Carl was a good friend of Ethan's, a surfing buddy. He was also a lawyer, his office above Namaste Café on Main Street. The air had smelled cloyingly sweet as Ever climbed the stairs that afternoon. He'd greeted her at the door and ushered her into his office. After a quick hug, he motioned for her to sit.

His office was cramped and messy, more like a teenaged boy's room than the office of a respected attorney. His surfboard leaned up against one wall, and there were movie posters on the two larger walls: *Endless Summer* and *Point Break*. Matchbox woodies and VWs lined up along the windowsill.

"Well?" she'd asked, but she already knew from his apologetic eyes why she'd been summoned.

"I'm sorry." He frowned. "I finally got the letter today." He reached into the file with Ethan's name handwritten on the tab and pushed the letter across the desk to her. She scanned the opening and then the confirmation of what she'd been worrying about for almost a year.

"They denied," she said.

Carl took a deep breath. "Surfing's what they call a *high-risk hobby*."

"He started surfing before he could *walk*, Carl. He was more comfortable in the water than on the land. You *know* that," she pleaded, as if he had written the denial letter.

"I do know that, but the insurance company doesn't care. The only thing they care about is that he didn't disclose that he surfed on his application."

Ever's chest felt crushed. "He was *dying*. The doctor said he had weeks left. A month if he was lucky. He just wasn't strong enough to go out that night. It was an *accident*. Can we appeal? I can show them pictures. He has surfing trophies, medals."

"I spoke to the adjuster about filing an appeal, but it doesn't look good. They consider this a failure to disclose at best, material misrepresentation at worst. And in either case, it nullifies your policy. Showing his history as a surfer would make the omission even more egregious, I'm afraid."

She remembered the insurance people coming to their house all those years ago. She'd been pregnant with Bea. She'd felt so grown-up: having a baby, owning a house, getting life insurance. She couldn't even remember filling out the application; they'd probably just signed it quickly without bothering to read the fine print. It was almost twenty years ago. They were only *kids;* they thought they'd live to be a hundred.

She wanted to be angry at Ethan, to rage at his foolishness. But she was the one who had let him go out that night. She had *let him go.*

"But, how am I supposed to—" she started. ". . . *live?*"

"Well, you have Ethan's pension. Your job. And some royalties, right?"

She had almost laughed, but none of it was funny. There *was* Ethan's pension, of course. He'd taught music at the public middle school for nearly twenty years; still, this yielded hardly enough to cover their basic expenses. Never mind the hospital bills. Thankfully, they'd taken out a hefty home equity line of credit when he got sick. Though now, she was using this money to make the line of credit minimum payments. All of it felt like a snake eating its own tail. She couldn't help but wonder how long before it all closed in on itself. What then?

And none of this took ballet into consideration. Even when Ethan was healthy and working, it had been a challenge. Her income teaching writing classes barely covered the cost of Bea's pointe shoes each month. Luckily, Bea had gotten a partial tuition scholarship this summer, but CLCB's tuition was as much as some people's rent each month. She wasn't sure how much longer she could keep this up now. Never mind audition season.

"Could you pick up some extra work?" Carl asked.

She'd be happy to get a job, but who would hire her? And to do what? She'd been a writer for twenty years. When Ethan was alive, it hadn't mattered that her books weren't bestsellers. He'd made it possible for her to be an artist; his income, while modest, had kept them afloat. But now, the money from her last book was long gone, and her royalties were laughable.

"Are you writing?" he asked.

She grimaced. "If you call staring at a blank document *writing,* then yes."

He was right. She needed a new contract. This would get her

head above water. She needed to write again. But here was where it all fell apart. With Ethan gone, she needed to write, but without Ethan, she *couldn't*. Every time she sat down to work, she felt lost. As if her words had disappeared into the water with him that night.

"You should write about all those ballet moms," he said and chuckled. "I bet there's no lack of drama there."

"This is true."

"Listen. I know you don't want to think about this. But you have the house still," Carl said. "It's worth a lot more than you owe on it."

She'd swallowed hard, tears filling her eyes. "I am not selling our home, Carl."

He had sighed and nodded. "I hear you. I do. But just know the option is there."

She'd been waiting for almost a year for the claim to come through, worried, of course, but hopeful. In that time, the available line of credit had dwindled. The house was the only thing of value she had left. Maybe he was right. Maybe, once Bea left home, she should sell the house, move with Danny into a small apartment. *No.* This house had been in Ethan's family for decades. It was where they'd raised their children. It was where they had planned to grow old together. How could she surrender their home?

The shower turned off, and Bea came out of the bathroom in leggings and her dad's old fisherman sweater, which hung to her knees and nearly swallowed her whole.

"I'm so tired," Bea said, and came to her for a hug. "I'm going to bed."

"Okay. Love you, Bumble," she said. Ever could feel her ribs, even through the heavy wool, such a fragile cage around her own broken heart.

Lindsay

Their housekeeper, Sonia, had been at the house today. Sonia was the real ghost in this house—making sure everything was tidy and bright, and then slipping away before anyone could thank her. The linen closet was full of freshly laundered towels, still warm from their tumble in the dryer and smelling of the French lavender detergent Lindsay splurged on. She grabbed a couple and went to the master bathroom, which was sparkling clean.

As she undressed, she studied her reflection. Before she started the diet, she would undress in the dark, slipping into the shower or bathtub blind. But now that she had shed twenty pounds, she kept the lights on and gazed at her reflection in wonder. Lindsay felt *good* about herself. For the first time in years, she could bare her arms, sit at her desk without feeling her thighs spilling over the edges of her seat. She didn't huff and puff as she took the stairs to use the restroom (and now she *always* took the stairs to the restroom). She'd not only dropped two whole dress sizes, but—miracle of miracles—a shoe size, too. You know you're in dangerous territory when even your feet can stand to lose a few pounds.

She was turning fifty this year, and while her other friends who had reached the half-century mark had confirmed that women at fifty suddenly got that dubious superpower of invisibility (and really, what was the point of dieting if no one could see you anyway?), she wasn't ready to completely give up.

What had really gotten to her, though, was a photo on Facebook she'd been tagged in by a high school girlfriend. It was a picture of three girls in bikinis at the beach. It was clearly taken in the late

'80s, and the girl at the center was recognizable immediately as Sissy Carmichael, who had posted it. She looked exactly the same in her current profile picture (without the towering bangs, anyway). The girl to the right was Lisa Nguyen: a bright white, French-cut bathing suit and silky black feathered hair. But the third girl was the one who took Lindsay's breath away.

It was *Olive*. At least that was what she thought before realizing that there was no way in this space-time continuum that seventeen-year-old Sissy and Lisa could be on a beach with *her* own seventeen-year-old daughter. It wasn't Olive, it was *her*: Lindsay. Before. In a body exactly like Olive's: perky breasts, flat tummy, a cute little round butt. She remembered this body the way she recalled other lost things, with a deep yearning. Hot sand between her toes, the taste of a cherry popsicle, long hair tickling her bare back. She remembered the way it felt to walk across the beach, high school guys pressing their hands against their chests, falling onto the sand and sputtering like flopping fish at the sight of her. It was stupid, but she longed for this. Why hadn't she appreciated it then? She could hardly remember what it felt like to be *seen*.

She stepped onto the scales and felt an excited anticipation. When the digital numbers appeared, she squeezed her fists together. *Yes.* Twenty-one pounds down.

Smiling, she sat down on the toilet to pee, noting her shrinking thighs, but gasped as the pee began to trickle out. What the hell? It stung. Badly. She wiped gently, but still felt a sharp stab of pain.

Her heart raced as she leaned over to inspect. She rarely, if ever, looked down there. She felt like she was thirteen again, poking around trying to figure out what mysteries were hidden there, blushing with the same adolescent shame. She parted the flesh and caught her breath. A bump. A red, angry bump. She touched it gingerly, and the pain shot up into her shoulder.

She stood up, legs shaking, and lowered herself into the tub. She should look again; maybe it was nothing. An ingrown hair? Some kind of *pimple*? Her heart pounded as she flipped back through her memory; how long had it been since she and Steve last had sex?

Was there any way, this was? God no. It had to be some other joy-
ful byproduct of menopause, like the wiry hair she'd plucked from
her chin—mortified—last month. A middle-aged body is filled with
so many delightful surprises, like some horrifying second puberty
but without the antiquated pamphlets and corny videos shown by
the school nurse this time. There was Google, of course, though
she knew better than to start seeking info there. She'd made that
mistake once when Olive came home from class with deep purple
bruises on her hips. She'd diagnosed her with leukemia before they
realized it was from a new roll in contemporary class.

Maybe it would just go away. If not, she'd stop by the pharmacy
and get something to put on it. Hydrocortisone? Or antifungal
cream? It was *nothing*.

Steve came home at ten o'clock. She lay on her side of the bed,
eyes shut, and tried to glean from the scent he carried where he
might have been. Just like when she was pregnant with Olive, her
nose was working overtime lately, picking up smells like a blood-
hound's. She inhaled deeply, feigning sleep, and caught three distinct
odors, braided together: a boozy scent, and soap, and something else.
Familiar but foreign all at once, almost *buttery*?

She felt the sting down there, and rolled over, burying her face in
the freshly laundered pillowcase.

Josie

Josie Jacobs had pulled into the parking lot of CLCB as class was getting out. Savvy had driven herself to ballet, but Josie wasn't about to let her drive Etienne Bernay back to the house. Nancy had asked her to be discreet about the living arrangements they'd made for him. The rest of the "crew"—just a filmmaker and the sound guy—would stay at the Seacoast Suites over by the freeway, but that would not do for Etienne Bernay.

Nancy had called at the beginning of July and asked if Josie might be willing to put him up in her guesthouse. Vivienne lived in a tiny bungalow and didn't have the space. Nancy knew that Josie not only had an empty guesthouse now, but also a pool and Jacuzzi—good for sore muscles—as well as workout equipment, all that crap that Mark had bought when he turned forty but never used. She kept waiting for him to come get it, but then again, there was probably not much room at his new girlfriend's one-bedroom condo.

Now that Mark was gone, now that she was a single mom, *again*, Josie had already been planning to rent the guesthouse out to bring in some extra cash. The divorce wasn't final yet, but she'd gotten the house—well, sort of—Mark technically owned it, but he'd agreed to let her stay there. Until Savvy graduated, anyway, at which point the divorce would be final, the house would be sold, and he'd give her half the proceeds. He'd paid her a nice lump sum, too, but only because she'd agreed that there would be no alimony. Thankfully, Savvy's dad, Johnny, was generous with child support, spoiling Savvy rotten and sending a check to cover all her ballet expenses every month.

Nancy had told her there was no extra money to pay for Etienne's room, but that Vivienne would be happy to waive Savannah's tuition for the semester (a little detail Josie didn't plan to divulge to Johnny).

"Of course, this arrangement is hush-hush," Nancy had said.

Vivienne did not give out scholarships, and this wasn't a scholarship per se, but she and Nancy both knew the other mothers would see it this way, glomming onto this as evidence that Vivienne was playing favorites. Vivienne didn't *play* favorites; Savvy simply *was* her favorite. It only took about five minutes of watching class to realize that Savvy was in a whole different league than the rest of the girls. And with Mary gone now—*water polo, seriously?*—there was nothing, or rather *no one*, in her way. But optics were everything, and this might not look right to the other mothers. God, those horrid women would be practically apoplectic if they had any idea. *When* Savvy got the scholarship, Josie hardly needed those vicious women thinking she'd somehow cheated. Savannah did not need to cheat.

So, as Nancy had instructed, like some sort of criminal, she parked in the shadows, over by Freezey's. The plan was that he would come out after the girls, including Savannah, had left; they'd head to the rental car place to get his car, and then he'd follow her back to the house.

From her parking spot, Josie had watched the girls and the mothers spilling out of the studio doors. Olive had come out first, followed by her mom, Lindsay. Trailing behind them was Beatrice Henderson. Bea had been at New York Repertory Ballet all summer; Josie had secretly hoped she would be asked to stay at the company's year-round school so she wouldn't be back at the studio this fall. Of all the other girls, Bea was the one who had the most potential. Savvy was far beyond her in terms of actual polish, but Bea was naturally gifted with a few things that Savvy was not. In ballet, this was called *facility*—but what it really meant was that her body was *built* for ballet. She was petite, almost birdlike, with nonexistent breasts, short torso, long legs, and an elegant neck. She was the kind of dancer who simply walked into an audition and commanded attention even before she started to dance. She was the only thing close to competition for this scholarship. But while Bea might be a natural gem, Savannah was already cut and polished to a high shine.

"'Bye, Sav!" Olive waved to Savvy, who got into the Beamer Johnny had given her for her seventeenth birthday.

"See you guys tomorrow!"

"See you at school!"

A dozen car doors thunked shut. Then they had all pulled out of their spots and taken off. Nancy exited shortly after, marching across the lot to her own car. She was followed by a pretty brunette and a short bald guy, both carrying a bunch of equipment. Must be the film crew. They disappeared into a white van.

There were lights on inside the studio still, and she waited. And waited. Josie quickly checked her reflection in the visor. Her olive complexion was her Greek father's gift to her, but her blue eyes and flaxen hair came from her Danish mother. She was closer to forty than thirty now, but people still mistook her and Savvy for sisters.

Finally, Vivienne and a lanky, dark-haired guy came out. He lit a cigarette, took a deep drag, and exhaled a plume of smoke. He and Vivienne lingered for a moment before they kissed each other's cheeks. Vivienne gestured toward Josie's car, and he nodded, walking toward her with the same swashbuckling swagger Johnny had when they met back when they were still kids. *Sexy.* She'd seen videos of Bernay and photos, of course (Savvy had a poster of him on her wall, for Christ's sake), but in the flesh? *Damn.*

She rolled down the passenger window to the warm night and leaned across the seat. "Hey!" she said. "Etienne?" As if he could be anybody else.

"*Oui,* hello," he said, and tentatively opened the passenger door.

"I'm Josie." She reached out to shake his hand. Jesus, even his hands were sexy.

"*Enchanté*," he said, smiling. He tossed his cigarette to the ground and his backpack into the back, and then he stretched, cracking his neck, and climbed into the passenger seat.

"Are you hungry?" she asked. "Should we grab something before we get your things?"

He grinned. "How about a beer?"

Ever

Grief had fingers. The ghostly touch gentle as a wish, caressing with its sad strokes or, sometimes, poking at her, the way the kids used to in the wee hours of the morning. Dappled light, *Mommy and Daddy, wake up!* But other times, those fingers curled into fists, striking. Or suffocating. Nearly every morning since Ethan died, Ever had awoken breathless.

On Sunday morning, she gasped as she woke, and wondered if she should call the whole thing off. Really, no one would think any less of her if she were to cancel the memorial and just curl up in bed. The guys could still paddle out at sunset. She'd wave to them from the deck, her very own widow's walk. She had no idea what to do on the anniversary of her husband's death. Was she supposed to languish or push through her grief?

Lately, she felt like she was standing on the precipice of a cliff, staring down at her own life from a dizzying height. She should probably see someone, but the idea of sharing her troubles with a stranger made her throat close, so she'd used the tools at her disposal: yoga videos, CBD, and, occasionally, the special gummies stashed in her underwear drawer.

After the accident, Bea had sought solace at the barre, exorcising Ethan's ghost, *exercising* it. Released her grief in sweat. Danny had found distraction in his friends, in work. But what had she done? What progress had she made? A whole year later, the world kept moving while her sorrow stood still.

She heard a door shut down the hall, the sound of feet padding across the wood floors. "Morning," Bea said, and came to her for a hug. Ever buried her nose in Bea's hair, the tangled mess she so rarely saw with it always pulled back into a bun. Rather than releasing her after her usual quick squeeze, Bea held on, and Ever's throat hitched.

All Bea had been talking about all week was the scholarship. *Paris. Oh my god, Paris.* But when Ever tried to imagine her nearly six thousand miles away, sadness filled her, like liquid in a glass. She missed her already, and she wasn't even gone yet. She and Ethan had lamented the day that their little birds would fly from the nest; but she'd never thought that when it finally happened, she would be left alone in that hollow space.

"Mmm, smells good," Danny said as he loped into the kitchen before plopping down at the table and reaching for the pitcher of juice.

She'd woken early, tried (and failed) to write again, then made pancakes for Danny and a tofu scramble with bell peppers for Bea. She squeezed oranges from the tree in their yard, and put out a tub of Greek yogurt and a wooden bowl full of fresh raspberries from the farmers' market. She made coffee in the French press and tea for Bea in her favorite mug. Something about being seated around this table with her children made her feel grounded. So long as she had this—*oak, sunlight, the sea outside*—they might be able to survive. Even with Ethan gone, this was still their home.

The house on the cliffs had been Ethan's family's second home, their retreat. When he and his brothers were young, they spent their summers here with their mom while his dad stayed down in San Diego for work. After Ethan's father died, his brothers had all scattered to the wind—none of them in California anymore. None of them interested in the run-down bungalow. Ethan and she had inherited the house without a mortgage, but now they owed more than a hundred thousand dollars on it. Carl was right: this was nothing compared to what it was worth, but the monthly payments still had to be made. There were many times when the well ran dangerously dry that they could have sold it, but Ethan loved this house. He joked that he would die here, and then he did.

It had been a year. An entire year without him, but it still felt like any minute, he might just walk in through the French doors from the deck, dripping water on the scuffed hardwood floors.

Ever looked at the dusty floors. She really needed to clean. Ethan had been the one to scour the house each weekend: vacuuming the dog hair from under the furniture, scrubbing the grout and the sticky bins in the refrigerator. Having grown up in rustic cabins, most without indoor plumbing, Ever had watched his efforts both mystified and amused. It would have driven him mad to see the grubby floorboards and the dust.

"Can you guys help me clean today?" she asked the kids. "Danny, your room is really bad." Bea was tidy, but Danny was a slob. The room was not only messy but filthy, a collection of dirty plates teetering on every horizontal surface. Empty chip bags and energy drink cans tipped on their sides.

"Can I just close my door?" he said.

"*Can* you? Because right now the basket of laundry I put there last week is blocking it."

"I'm kidding, Mom. I'll clean," Danny said, and helped himself to a second stack of pancakes. "Can Dylan come tonight?"

"Of course. Anybody you want to invite. Are all the girls coming?" she asked Bea.

Bea had filled a bowl with yogurt and fruit. She squeezed the plastic bear, drizzling honey in concentric circles over her breakfast. She shrugged.

"I sent a text to the moms. I asked Nancy to invite Vivienne, the new teacher, too."

Bea's eyes widened, and she set down the honey. "Why would you do that?"

They had always invited not only friends and neighbors, but families from the studio as well. Vivienne, Nancy, and Eloise. Vivienne never came, of course; the boundaries between teacher and student were sacred to her. It had surprised Ever when she'd shown up to Ethan's funeral, touched her deeply.

"Bardo's having a party tonight. Some people might be there," Danny said, and chugged down his juice in a few gulps. Greg Bardo's mom was single; rumor was that she not only hosted but partied with the kids. It used to irritate Ever, but now she felt an odd commiseration. She was probably just lonely, and maybe having teenagers around filled a void.

"What about Olive? She'll be here, right?" she asked, but was met with silence, Bea's eyes downcast.

"She'll probably be at Bardo's, too," Bea said.

Ever's heart ached. She couldn't imagine that Olive would skip the memorial. Olive had loved Ethan, playfully called him *Dad*. When he passed, Lindsay said she'd been inconsolable. She'd try to talk to Bea about Olive later when Danny wasn't around.

"Well, Lindsay's offered to do the shopping. What would you guys like to eat tonight? We can do veggie kabobs on the grill if you want, Bea? You want fajitas, D?"

Ever flashed on a party she'd planned for the kids' seventh and eighth birthdays. (They were born exactly a year apart on the same day in June.) There'd been an outbreak of strep at school, and not a single kid could come. Ethan had run to the store and come back with a giant chocolate sheet cake anyway. They played games and whacked at a piñata until its candy guts spilled all over the deck. They ate almost the whole cake. By midnight, they all had sore throats and were trembling with fevers, but Danny said it was his favorite birthday ever. She'd had the profound and satisfying belief that all they needed was each other. But if that were true, what were they supposed to do now?

Lindsay

Lindsay had an open house from ten to one on Sunday, so she'd gone to eight o'clock Mass that morning. Alone as usual. Olive was exhausted from ballet, sleeping in on her only day off, and Steve had stopped going to church years ago. But she found comfort in the services. She loved the ritual of it. The predictability. At St. Mary's, things never changed. She always left Mass feeling a little bit better about the world. No small feat these days.

St. Mary's was also one of the few places outside the studio where she saw Vivienne, who sat in a pew near the back each week, also alone. Lindsay always smiled, and Vivienne nodded in acknowledgment, though they never chatted. But today, she couldn't help herself. As she passed her on her way to her own seat, she stopped and said softly, "Vivienne, I just wanted to say how amazing it is that the kids are getting to work with Mr. Bernay. Olive is *thrilled*." Of course, she had no idea if this were true or not. She'd barely spoken to Olive all week. Then she wondered if lying inside a church qualified as a mortal sin.

"He certainly is *challenging*," Vivienne had said vaguely, and returned to her missal.

What on earth did that mean?

After Communion, she returned to her kneeler and squeezed her eyes shut. *Please, God, let Olive get the scholarship. Also, make the bump go away?*

In the parking lot, she saw Vivienne again, but this time, Lindsay simply waved a goodbye before popping her trunk to make sure she'd loaded up her signs for the open house.

The property was one of those old bungalows along the cliffs, a little bit down the road from Ever and Ethan's. A thousand-square-foot Craftsman that had been uninhabited for several years: an inheritance. Someone's nest egg in the form of moldy drywall and asbestos tiles. Outdated appliances and popcorn ceilings. But Lindsay knew exactly how to make a home like this appeal to prospective buyers; it was simply a matter of suggestion. She had learned early on that no matter the condition of the home, she was never really selling the house but what the house could be. *Here? This is where the crib would go, of course,* she would offer a young couple. The same spot might become a place for an aspiring writer's desk or *place to paint?* She knew how to read people, intuiting exactly what they wanted and then showing them how a house might fulfill those desires. *This kitchen is perfect for entertaining,* she might tell a childless couple. Or, *When the kids come home, they can all gather here,* she'd offer the empty nesters. *It's just a block to the elementary school,* she'd say to the harried mother of three or to the old woman who, Lindsay suspected, fancied herself the neighborhood grandmother. She'd open the windows to the sounds of children playing, and the woman's eyes would sparkle with delight. She wasn't selling houses so much as dreams.

By the time the first couple showed up today (pregnant woman, broad-chested husband), she'd baked the tray of chocolate chip cookies she'd assembled at home in the outdated oven.

"Boy or girl?" Lindsay asked.

"Boy!" the dad said, beaming.

"There's a rope swing," she said. "In the backyard. It's amazing. Let me show you."

It didn't matter if no one else showed up. She was certain she'd have an offer by the time she pulled up the OPEN HOUSE signs.

She was good at this; she really was. But lately, after everyone was gone, all those hopeful glowing couples, after she'd shut the lights off and put the key back in the lockbox, she'd sit in her car and cry. She couldn't help but think that fifty percent of those newlyweds would eventually be divorced. That the economy might crash, and someone would miss a payment and then another and eventually lose the house. That some houses would be flooded or consumed by fire, some would tumble off these eroding cliffs. And even those couples who lasted, who managed to hold on, wouldn't be able to stop time. Their babies would grow up inside these walls, the children would become teenagers and then adults, the couples would grow old, and then there would one day be nothing but a FOR SALE sign out front. Open house days used to be exciting, but now they were *challenging*.

Josie

Melissa had come over to Josie's on Sunday afternoon, to try to catch a glimpse of the new ballet master. She'd been rattling on for hours about the scholarship, the documentary, speculating, hoping. She was Josie's best friend, but she was exhausting.

"So we *are* going tonight?" Melissa asked.

Josie knew she should go to Ethan's memorial. All the Level 6 families were invited; even Melissa thought they should make an appearance, and Melissa couldn't stand Ever Henderson or her elfin fairy daughter. It was still sad. Ethan had been a great guy, the kind of guy that made her feel hopeful that not all men were assholes. They used to say all the good ones were gay or taken, but as they all got older, it seemed she'd have to add *dead* to the list.

"BYOB is bring your own bong, right?" Melissa asked, snorting. Whenever Ever Henderson was around, Melissa's nose would twitch at the faint stink of sandalwood or patchouli or whatever it was she wore that made her smell like a walking headshop. "I swear though, if there's a drum circle, I am out of there."

They'd been sitting by the pool since noon, waiting for Etienne to emerge from the guesthouse. Until rehearsals started, the ballet studio was closed on Sundays. Josie had seen his light on and heard some godawful techno music coming from inside last night, but he hadn't come out today. Granted, the guesthouse was equipped with a mini fridge, a microwave, and a Keurig. She'd shown him where the Whole Foods was so he could pick up a few staples, told him he was welcome to use the kitchen. But he appeared to be living off delivery so far; pizza boxes, Panda Express cartons, and Chipotle bags filled the dumpster on the side of the house. He spent a good deal of time this first week elsewhere, probably with that minxy French camera girl at the Seacoast Suites. Just a hunch, but her hunches were usually pretty on the money.

That first night, she'd declined his offer to go get a beer, *so* not appropriate, and instead told him she had a fridge *full* of beers and he was welcome to help himself. She didn't add that her ex had left them behind. She'd given him a tour of the downstairs, then the backyard amenities, during which he drank the beer she'd offered. When he yawned and stretched, his shirt rose to reveal the perfectly taut and tattooed abs of a man almost ten years her junior. Trouble with a capital T. So, rather than offering him another beer, she'd shown him to the guesthouse, and since then, she'd hardly seen him. He slept in every morning that week and was at the studio teaching every night.

Melissa had only caught a quick glimpse of him at CLCB earlier in the week and had insisted on coming over so she might be "properly introduced." But, it appeared, he was using the whole day to sleep off whatever it was he'd been doing the night before.

"Well, let's go together at least. That way, we only need one excuse to leave early," Melissa said, standing up and walking to the edge of the pool, which was surrounded by a lush lawn that met the water's edge. The property backed up to a canyon, and the illusion was that the water dropped off into an abyss. It was Josie's favorite thing about the house. She'd miss this.

Melissa dipped her French-manicured toes into the water and glanced toward the guesthouse. She was wearing a bikini so small it looked like she'd borrowed it from Jaz. While the boobs were bought and paid for, the rest was earned by the hours Melissa spent at the gym. Josie liked to get her exercise more passively: hiking or biking. Swimming. She was also genetically blessed, which was basically just a humble way of saying she didn't *have* to work out.

Josie hadn't always been beautiful. As a child, she was on the chubby side. She also had a lazy eye and had to wear a patch all through third grade. But in middle school, while the rest of the girls

got braces or acne or fat, she got a body, and her face went from being pudgy to pretty. Like *really* pretty, though she honestly had no
idea until other people started noticing.

People like Alan Goldberg. Back then, they called it *scouting*.
She'd been scouted while she was with her mother at a restaurant
in LA. Her mother was shopping for a wedding dress, getting married to a guy she'd met at a bar three months before. Listless, long
legs stretched out, Josie had been sucking on a sweetened iced tea,
dreaming herself somewhere else, when a guy came up and politely
shook Josie's hand. Her mother had looked bewildered as he explained he was with a modeling agency, one that had repped both
Linda Evangelista and Cindy Crawford at the beginning of their
careers. He gave her his business card and made her promise she'd
reach out. Josie was fourteen.

Her mother thought modeling was stupid, or at least that's what
she said. She thought Josie should finish high school and go to cos-
metology school. Learn how to do hair, makeup. They lived in
Orange County; they were practically in Hollywood's backyard.
"What will you do when all of this . . ." she'd said, waving her hand
up and down at Josie's body, ". . . goes away?" Josie felt like she'd
cursed her with a wave of her hand. Like the reverse of Cinderella's
fairy godmother's *bibbidi-bobbidi-boo*.

Josie started high school, and Alan got her some local work, but
she was too young to get herself to LA where the real jobs were, so
she had to wait until she was sixteen before she could begin to work
in earnest. By the time she turned sixteen, her mom had already divorced the guy from the bar and was on husband number three, and
Josie was an emancipated minor with a GED and a little stash of cash
she'd saved from modeling and working at Baskin-Robbins. She got
an apartment in Venice Beach with a girl who had just moved from
some podunk town in Florida, "discovered" by one of Alan's guys at
Disney World when she was on a class field trip. Alan had co-signed
their lease, paid their first month's rent. At seventeen, she felt like
she was at the edge of the rest of her life. Though, within a year, it

was all over. She got pregnant, she got married to Johnny, and Alan Goldberg made sure she never got work again.

"I should go home and get ready," Melissa said, and gathered her beach towel and tote.

"Yeah, me too. I'll grab you at six."

"Is *he* going tonight?" Melissa asked, gesturing to the guesthouse with her chin.

Josie shrugged.

"What is he, a *vampire*?" Melissa laughed.

"Aren't they all?" she said.

Lindsay

An hour before sunset, Ever and Lindsay were in the kitchen assembling the fixings for the fajitas, which were sizzling on the grill outside under Steve's watchful eye.

Lindsay loved Ever's house. It was small but right on the cliffs, with a broad deck that faced the ocean. She and Steve lived in a sprawling, modern house across town in the foothills; Steve preferred new construction. Open floor plans and no clutter. But Ever's old house was cozy, with art and music and comfortable furniture. The periwinkle velvet couch Ever had found at a flea market was like something in a painting. Each room was a different jewel tone, like the inside of a traveler's caravan. It was always a bit messy, but in an artful way: books on the floor and every surface. Ethan's instruments strewn about as if an orchestra had just fled the scene. The forgotten pottery coffee cups were made by Ever's dad, who lived off the grid in Oregon. Whenever she stepped into this house, she felt a longing for a different kind of life.

"So, how are *you*, Linds?" Ever asked her. "I've been so distracted, I haven't even checked in to see how things are going with you. I'm such a terrible friend."

Lindsay shook her head. "Oh God, no. You have so much going on. I am so, so sorry about the claim. Is there really no way to appeal?"

"No, it's done," she said. "It's okay. But I mean it. I really want to hear about how you're doing. How are things with Steve?"

Lindsay didn't bring up her marital troubles with Ever anymore after Ethan died. It felt wrong to complain about her husband, who was still very much alive. But the bump had her in a tizzy.

"Actually, I found something . . . um . . . weird," she blurted.

Ever scowled and cocked her head.

"Like a *bump*," Lindsay clarified.

"Did you get your mammogram this year?" Ever asked, and Lindsay quickly realized her blunder. Ethan's illness had begun like this, too. A suspicious growth under his arm. One he ignored until it was too late.

"Oh, no, no . . . god, I'm sorry; I am such an idiot. Not that kind of bump. More like . . . just a weird thing, um," she said, and motioned to her nether regions. "Down *there.*"

"Oh," Ever said, her eyebrow raised.

Lindsay peeled an onion and felt her eyes burn.

"Is it itchy?" Ever whispered.

"Not really itchy? It hurts like a mother, though."

"Oh, no," Ever said, her face filled with concern.

"Hand me that knife," Lindsay said, wishing she hadn't opened her mouth about whatever was growing down there. But lately, it was all she could think about.

"I'm sure it's nothing," Ever said as she handed her the knife. "But promise me you'll make an appointment with your OB, okay? Just to make sure?"

"I will."

It took Ethan six months before he saw someone. By then, the cancer had spread into his lymph nodes. Within two months, it was in his lungs. She should be afraid of cancer, of course, but oddly, her bigger fear was that it wasn't her own body's betrayal, but *Steve's.*

She hoped that Ever hadn't noticed the catch in her throat. Ever was the one suffering through the anniversary of her own husband's death. Never mind the stupid insurance people screwing her over. Whatever was going on (or not going on, for that matter) between Lindsay's legs was likely a nuisance but manageable. She should never have brought it up.

"Oh, listen!" Lindsay said. "I totally forgot to mention this, and I hope it's okay . . . I asked Sonia to come by later. She'll do all the cleanup, so you can just be with your family tonight."

"You didn't need to do that," Ever said, but looked grateful.

"She's always looking for extra work. And she's amazing. It'll be like nobody was here."

"Thank you," Ever said. "For the food, for everything. You are a *great* friend."

The house was packed, filled with Ethan's surfer buddies and bandmates and fellow teachers, their neighbors, and even some of Ever's writing students. A few parents from the studio had come, but several had declined in a flurry of last-minute texts sent to the moms' group chat: *So sorry!* Amazing how many people had migraines or food poisoning or surprise visits from in-laws that day. Vivienne had declined, as expected, but sent a beautiful spray of dahlias, which Lindsay had put in one of Ever's dad's vases on the table with the appetizers.

Lindsay had been shocked when Josie and Melissa arrived, especially since Savvy was a no-show. Olive said she was at Greg Bardo's party, the one Olive kept angling to go to as well.

"Didn't they already do a memorial?" Olive had asked in the car.

"That was the *funeral*. Listen, I don't know what's going on with you girls, but Bea needs you tonight," she'd said, and Olive's sharp edges softened, if only a little.

The idea that Olive might be pushing Bea out, replacing her with Savvy, made Lindsay feel terrible. Worse, she felt complicit. The camping trip this summer had felt wrong from the get-go. Steve had reserved the dates without consulting her, but when she'd reminded him that Bea wouldn't be back until August, he'd shrugged and said, "Well, all the August spots are gone now." When Olive had asked if Savvy could take Bea's place, Lindsay had agreed, but that whole weekend, she'd felt queasy with guilt. Maybe that was why the girls weren't getting along?

Lindsay didn't like Savvy, a teenaged version of her mother: beautiful and self-satisfied. But worse, when Olive was around Savvy, she just wasn't herself. Olive had always been friendly and thoughtful. Kind to everyone. But when she was with Savvy, she acted sort of *mean*. On the camping trip, Lindsay had had to put the kibosh on several catty conversations about the other girls at the studio. Now this? It made her angry that Olive was turning her back on Bea, especially when she was going through such a hard time.

The doorbell rang, and Cobain made a half-hearted effort at barking.

"I'll get it," Lindsay said. She quickly ran water over her sticky hands and wiped them on the cherry-patterned apron she'd borrowed from Ever. Then she made her way through the crowd to the front door. "Excuse me," she said. "Pardon."

Outside, Etienne Bernay and the camera girl were standing on the threshold.

"Oh, hi there," Lindsay said, surprised. "Etienne, right? I'm Olive's mom. The redhead?" She wondered how many times she had said this. *Olive's mom? The redhead?* But not a bit of recognition crossed his face. Something about this made her feel anxious. Did Olive not stand out in class? "Lindsay Chase," she said.

He was dressed in dark jeans and dress shoes, with a white button-down shirt, open at the neck, where the forked tongue of a tattooed snake peeked out.

"This is Lotte," he said, gesturing to the girl, who was fiddling around in her bag.

Lotte wore a simple black linen shift, dark against pale skin. She looked up at Lindsay and smiled. She had a gap between her front teeth and full lips and that same French elegance that Vivienne had. Lotte pulled a fancy camera out of her bag.

"Oh! No, I'm sorry . . ." Lindsay started, shaking her head. "This is actually a celebration of life? I mean, it's probably not the best time to be—filming."

Lotte frowned. "*Tu as dit que ç'était une* fête," she said to Etienne, and then to Lindsay, "A *party?*"

"Oh, no. Well, I mean. It is. Kind of? But it's actually a *memorial*. For Beatrice's father."

"*Beatrice*," Etienne said, turning to Lotte.

"*La fille avec les bons pieds?*" Lotte asked, bright-eyed, and Etienne nodded.

Lindsay didn't speak French, but it was clear he knew exactly who Bea was.

"*Je suis désolé*. It is my fault," he said to Lindsay, and put his hand apologetically to his chest. "Vivienne said *celebration*. My English is not very good. We will go."

"Oh, no," Lindsay said, shaking her head. "Please come in. You can meet some of the other CLCB families." So *this* was why Josie had come. Josie could hardly ditch an opportunity like this; Lindsay was surprised she hadn't forced Savannah to come along to get some valuable face time with the new ballet master.

As they came inside, she got a whiff of his cologne. Normally, she hated scents on men, but this reminded her of a high school boyfriend. Alex had been just a kid with floppy hair and Converse high tops, but the smell of him—god, the smell of him made her body *respond*. Now her body was responding to a guy with a tattoo of a cobra on his neck like it had responded to absolutely nothing in months. Years, even. What was wrong with her?

She led them down the hallway to the kitchen, where a small group of girls from Level 6 were congregating. Their heads popped up, probably at that swoon-worthy smell.

"Ah, *mes filles*," he said, clasping his hands together in delight, and they all looked up, mouths opened like baby birds in a nest.

She didn't need to speak French to understand this. *My girls.*

Bea

"I miss him," Bea said.

"Me, too."

Bea and Danny had escaped the party and were down at the beach. Danny had eaten a couple of their mom's gummies earlier and was half asleep. They were lying on a faded turquoise Indian tapestry they had spread out on the sand. It was the same one they'd had since they were little: Bea used to lie on her stomach and trace the paisley pattern with her finger. The fabric smelled of coconut oil and surf wax. Of other summers.

How was it that a whole year had passed since her dad had disappeared into the water? Three hundred sixty-five days since she'd talked to him, hugged him. Fifty-two weeks since he'd filled a bucket with ice to help ease the pain of her inflamed toes, since he'd baked his special power bars (*Secret ingredient? Kumquats!*) for her to eat before ballet, since he'd played his guitar, improvising silly lyrics. What a beautiful life they'd had.

Of course, nothing truly beautiful lasts. Her dad had taught her that himself. *Beauty*, by nature, is fleeting. A monarch butterfly's life span is about nine months. A rose on the vine blooms for just one to two weeks. The first movement of Beethoven's Fifth Symphony is only seven minutes long, and Coltrane's version of "'Round Midnight" is under six. Fireflies only live for a few *hours* before they die. But what happens in those months, or weeks, or minutes, or moments, he said, are what count. What you do with that small amount of time you get is where beauty lies. This was the only way she could make sense of losing him.

She scooped a handful of sand and felt her eyes sting.

Why do you build them so close to the water? her mom would ask, shaking her head as her dad built one of his elaborate castles. *If you backed them up a few feet, they'd last longer.* But her mom never saw the world the way her father did. Didn't understand that some things aren't meant to stay.

Hamlet's "To Be or Not to Be" soliloquy only lasts about two minutes; so does the Black Swan variation from *Swan Lake.* There are usually about six hours between low and high tide. Just time enough to build something beautiful, before the sea sweeps it away.

"What do you think Dad would think of all this?" Danny asked, his eyes closed.

"The memorial?" Bea asked. It was chilly out, and she'd grabbed her dad's fisherman sweater, which still carried his sweet, grassy scent.

He shrugged, but Bea knew what he meant. He meant the *after.*

When he was alive, their dad had been the center of their family. The core. Exerting a centripetal force on them all, keeping them in a pleasant happy orbit around him. Now that he was gone, they were still spinning, but each on their own reckless trajectory.

"It feels like gravity is gone," Danny said. This was exactly what she'd been feeling: untethered. All the laws of the universe broken.

Danny opened his eyes and looked up at the dimming sky.

"Speaking of which, what's up with you and Olive?"

"What do you mean?"

"Luke told Dylan some shit," he said. "Something about a bonfire? Before you went to New York? You didn't mention anything about that."

Bea felt her chest heave, her heart cleave. She flashed on a memory of Luke handing her a cup. *You're a virgin, right?* he'd said. When she'd blushed (the fire, it was so hot), he'd said, *I mean, you don't drink.*

"What *kind* of shit?" she said.

"I don't know. He's just being a dick," he said.

She winced. She had thought about telling Danny what happened, or what she could recall of what happened. But the idea of recounting any of it to her brother made her feel hot with shame. They had always been almost as close as twins, but he was still her *brother*.

"Olive's just hanging out with Savvy more now," Bea said, feeling like she might cry.

"Is Olive here?" he asked, and they both looked back up at the house. The deck was strung with fairy lights, and there was music—though it sounded tinny and abstract from down here, the roar of the waves crashing against the shore, drowning it out.

"Yeah, but only because Lindsay made her come. Are you going to Bardo's house later?"

"Nah," he said, and she was overwhelmed with gratitude. Danny was a great brother.

"We should go back up there," Bea said. "Mom shouldn't be alone."

She knew the moment she said it, that it was nonsensical. The whole house was full of people who loved her, who loved their dad. Even so, when she thought of her mom's trajectory—her path since the accident—she was the one who'd gone farthest off course. She was like a planet that had somehow spun out of the sun's orbit and was alone in the universe. Aimless.

Ever

Just before sunset, when the world was tinged in gold, Ever stood on the beach, assembling the lanterns. She thought she'd ordered the ones that floated on the water, but when she'd gotten around to opening the package, she realized they were the kind you set off into the sky. "We can't use them," she'd said to Lindsay. "It's fire season."

"We're sending them out over the water," Lindsay said. "It's going to be fine. Besides, what are they going to do? Arrest you at your husband's memorial?"

Luckily, it quickly became clear that the lanterns would present no real danger of starting a fire; she could hardly get the practice one to stay lit.

"Help me with this?" she asked Danny, who had come back down from the house with Ethan's longboard under his arm. She felt a knot in her throat as he gingerly set it on the sand, fin-side up, the way Ethan had taught him.

Danny held the lantern for her while she tried to strike a match, but the breeze coming off the ocean kept blowing it out.

"I have a lighter," he said, and reached into the pocket of his board shorts, then looked at her with the blank face of someone who's been caught doing something wrong.

"I am not going to ask why you have that," she said.

He nodded gratefully, and flicked the spark wheel. The wick ignited, and the paper expanded. It was so beautiful, she felt like crying.

"Okay. Now put it out. I just wanted to make sure they worked," she said, and held her palm out. "And give me that lighter, please."

"It's just for incense," he said weakly.

As the sun set, people made their way from the house down to the beach. The surfers among them were all suiting up and prepping their surfboards. She and Danny lined the lanterns up along the beach; those who didn't paddle out could release them at the shore. Ethan's friend, Roger, had brought his guitar. Chet and Ashley had their instruments, too, and a friend of Danny's had some bongos. Roger began to pluck out "Ripple," a song that transported Ever back to the days when her parents and she were living in their van, following The Dead up and down the coast. She was only a toddler then, but she could still remember little things: cutting her bare foot on a piece of glass; her father showing her the Big Dipper through the van's skylight; the scent of weed and the tangy taste of apricot fruit leather they bought by the yard at the co-op. When she and Ethan met, he'd play her parents' music for her on his battered guitar, and it had made her feel both less homesick and more homesick all at once. She'd never had a real house; her family was transient most of her childhood: living on communal farms and in group houses and, for a stretch, in that van. The *music* had been her home.

She turned back to see the bungalow lit up like a jack-o'-lantern, windows filled with an autumnal glow. At first, she couldn't understand Ethan's attachment to this old house. To her, growing up, four walls had never provided anything other than shelter. When they first started dating, she'd assumed that they—like her own family— would live an itinerant life. She was a nomad, a wanderer. But after only a year of living here, the year she'd been pregnant with Bea, she began to appreciate the certainty of a slant of light, the familiarity of a house's breaths, its sighs. She came to realize that a house was more than drywall and plaster. It was like a body, the family inside its beating heart. The house. She could not lose this house.

Danny gave her a quick squeeze before jogging toward the water with the other surfers. Her friend, Koa, had made dozens of orchid leis, which she strung around everyone's necks before they went to the water. As Ever lit the first lantern, Ashley started to play the first plaintive notes of Van Morrison's "Song of Home" on her violin.

All down the beach, the lanterns lit up, and the music played. Their wedding song. That spring day a lifetime ago in Bonny Doon, they had danced barefoot to bluegrass music. Children ran through the fields of wildflowers, the air redolent with the scent of lavender. This song had been Chet and Ashley's gift to them that day. It was their gift to her now, though it felt like an empty box wrapped in pretty paper. She tried to delight in the moment, in the way the sky lit up with the flames, illuminating the circle of Ethan's friends bobbing on the water. But it only made her yearn for what was gone. For everything she'd lost a year ago, when Ethan kissed her on the head and then resolutely walked toward the water.

She felt someone touch her shoulder. "*Excusez-moi?* Is it okay?" Lotte asked, gesturing to her camera. "*Le feu?* It is so beautiful." The lanterns hovered over the ocean, as though the sky itself were on fire. Red and gold, flickering, reflected in the water below.

"Oh, yes," she said. "Please. Feel free."

"*Merci*," Lotte said, and trained her camera on the sky. But then they both noticed something in the distance, about a hundred yards down the beach.

Bea had slipped away from the crowd and was dancing quietly to the music, a shadow moving across the sand. Ever's heart swelled at the sight.

"Beatrice?" Lotte asked. "She is your daughter?"

Ever nodded. "Yes."

"*Oh, la vache!* She is so lovely."

Josie

When the bongos came out, Melissa nudged Josie. "Oh, for the love of ganja, let's go." Now was probably as good a time as any to ditch the party, *memorial*, whatever.

There were a few people Josie didn't know on the back deck, plus Olive's dad, Steve, at the grill. Melissa thought Steve Chase was hot. Josie didn't see it, but Melissa weirdly liked bald guys who were just a bit soft around the middle. He did have those big sleepy, brown eyes, but still.

"He's nice, too," Melissa had argued. "Sweet. Like a teddy bear."

Melissa had never been married to Jaz's dad, never married at all. For years, she ran an online business selling fitness wear, a line that eventually got picked up by Macy's. She'd sold the company and invested in real estate. She had two apartment complexes that paid all her bills, with property managers who handled the day-to-day while she spent her days at the gym or at the ballet studio. Josie envied her independence, the fact that she liked men, but didn't need them.

"He's married," Josie had reminded her on several occasions.

"*So?*" Melissa had said.

Seriously, had she forgotten that Josie's husband had just left her for a dental hygienist six months ago? *Read your fucking audience*, she wanted to say.

"'Bye, Steve!" Melissa said now, wiggling her fingers at him as they made their way across the deck toward the open patio doors to the house.

Steve looked up from the grill and smiled. "'Bye, ladies."

Inside, a housekeeper was filling a trash bag with paper cups and napkins and dirty paper plates. Josie dropped her empty cup into the bag.

Olive was sitting on a gaudy velvet couch in the living room, texting.

"Hey, Liv!" Josie said, and Olive looked up. "Savvy said to tell you to swing by Greg Bardo's later. You can sleep over at our house after if you want."

"My mom's making me stay here," Olive said.

"Oh, man," Josie said, pouting. "Sorry, girly."

Josie wasn't a mom who micromanaged her kid's life. She believed the harder you pushed, the harder a kid would resist. That had been the case between her and her own mom. Besides, Savvy would be eighteen next month, an adult. Because they were only eighteen years apart, Savvy was more like a friend than her daughter. They were close. Josie knew so many moms, ballet moms especially, whose kids turned on them when they'd finally had enough. She could see it happening with Olive and Lindsay. That would never happen with Savvy.

At the bottom of the driveway, the camera girl was standing in the middle of the quiet street, her camera out and focused on Etienne. He was leaning against a light post, smoking a cigarette. Like an old-fashioned movie star. Like James Dean.

"Hi guys!" Melissa said brightly. Loudly. Waving.

Etienne turned to them. *"Bonjour!"* The camera girl lowered her camera and looked at him questioningly. *"Les mamans,"* he explained.

The moms. Something about this made Josie wince. She wondered if the camera girl knew that Etienne was staying at *her* guesthouse.

"I'm Melissa," Melissa said, stepping forward, hand extended. "Jazmin's mom?"

Suddenly, the air cracked and resounded with a deep and violent *boom.*

An explosion. Coming from the Hendersons' house.

Lindsay

At the thunderous sound, everyone on the beach turned to look up at the house, the people in the water searching for an explanation as well, paddling back to shore. "What happened?" someone said. "Oh shit, I see fire."

Olive was in the house. Lindsay ran across the sand and darted up the steep wooden steps to the back deck. The air was smoky, charred. She stopped (not even winded, she noted) at the sight of Steve standing there, motionless and stunned, as flames leapt from the grill. She reached for the fire extinguisher Ever kept by the door and released the lever, quickly squashing the flames with foam.

"What happened?" she demanded when the immediate danger seemed to have passed, looking at stupid, stupefied Steve. Sonia had come outside, too, and was standing with her hand pressed against her mouth.

"I'll get ice," Sonia said, and slipped back inside.

Everyone who had been down on the beach had scrambled up the steps.

"*Steve*," Ever said, reaching the top of the stairs. "Are you okay?" She searched around frantically for the source of this disaster. "Oh my god, was it one of the *lanterns*?"

Steve shook his head, startled. "No, no. I was about to make the last of the *carne asada*, but the pilot in the grill was out. So, I went to re-light it, and I think the gas—the propane—was built up inside? As soon as I struck the match, it just *exploded*."

"I'll go get the first aid kit," Bea said, and ran into the house past Olive, who was standing with Josie and Melissa, whom Lindsay thought had left already.

Ever was trembling in her sundress, ghostly pale in the bright light on the deck. Lindsay slipped off her cardigan and put it around Ever's shoulders, recalling last year's party, the same terrified expression on her friend's face.

"Oh, honey. He's fine," Lindsay said. "Everything's fine."

Lindsay should have gone inside, too, helped Sonia and Bea find the first aid supplies. She definitely should have suggested they go to the hospital. But as she studied her husband, she was oddly frozen in place. Her legs felt like the cement pylons beneath the pier, holding her up. Why didn't she *feel* anything?

"Is he okay?" Melissa pushed through the crowd and moved him gently toward the porch light, which shone brightly in Steve's soot-covered face. "Are you hurt?"

"Just singed my eyebrows and eyelashes a little," he said, laughing awkwardly. "Luckily nothing up top to burn," he said, patting his head.

"Poor thing," Melissa cooed.

Sonia came out with a Ziploc bag of ice, which Melissa grabbed from her hand before pressing it gently to Steve's cheek.

"I was a candy striper in high school," Melissa said.

Steve looked at Lindsay as Melissa doted on him, wrapping his left hand with a bandage from the first aid kit Bea brought out. He seemed to want something from Lindsay. Comfort? Assurance? No. He was fine. *Fine.* It was just a scare. But his eyes were pleading.

"Should I get more ice?" Sonia asked.

He nodded, and Lindsay now recognized that look. He wasn't scared; he was *guilty.*

Ever

Ever felt herself splitting again, the fissure between past and present like a fault line. Now, she felt the tremble and quiver, the aftershock of this terrible quake. After it was over, the smell of burnt hair and the propane stink hanging in the air, everyone had quietly slipped out, one after another, giving those obligatory hugs that felt like bones. Only Lindsay lingered.

"Go with Steve," Ever said. "Sonia already cleaned up. I'll be fine."

A rumble. Last year, she'd been the one picking up the dirty plates and balled-up napkins, wineglasses and paper cups. Last year, she hadn't wanted to throw the party at all. Ethan was so sick. But he'd insisted. He was of the firm belief that his life should go on, even as it was winding down. She thought him a spinning top, in the wobbly final revolutions, a sort of staggering insistence. Carried only by momentum and habit and hope.

It had been a small gathering, and those who came didn't stay long. It was mostly their inner circle who lingered: the diehards who had been present through the treatments, close enough to Ethan to have witnessed his rapid decline. They were not shocked by his emaciated body, by the dark circles under his eyes or the glassy red sheen of his prednisone-bloated face, like a funhouse mirror distortion.

"The moon," he'd said, his voice crackling like a dying fire. "It's full tonight."

She was trying to pull the overstuffed trash bag from the trash can when he touched her back, causing her to shiver. Involuntary tremors often rocked her now, her body's seismic reactions. It took nothing but his fingertips grazing her cheek. The first few notes of a song. The scent of his soap.

"I'm going out," he said.

"Cool! I'll finish up here and come meet you outside," she'd said, releasing the bag's handles, then gripping them for another futile tug. "Bring a sweater, though. It's getting chilly."

"No, I mean out on the water."

"Surfing?" she asked, shaking her head. *No.*

"Just paddling out. It's still tonight."

She'd bent over the bag again, focused her energies, her strength, on pulling the bag from the canister. So goddamn stubborn.

"I just want to go out one more time. Just once more." He'd reminded her of Danny, a boy pleading.

"Okay. *Go*," she said, even as every bit of her resisted.

The bag finally relented, and it came out in a swoosh. Startled, she laughed. Incongruous and inappropriate. Nothing was as it should be, though. He'd reached for her, forcing her to set the bag down. She'd buried her face in his sunken chest. In the smell of grass. His bristly chin scraped her forehead when she pulled away.

She gasped as the memory, at the tremor it incited.

"You okay?" Lindsay asked now. *Here. Now.* "Hey."

Lindsay was holding her. Enclosing her. Keeping her up. She shook her head, because that is what a widow is supposed to do after a year, right? Shake it off. Move on. What was wrong with her that this pain was still so fresh? So raw?

"The explosion. God, Linds. Steve . . ."

"He's *fine*," Lindsay said, a hint of testiness in her voice (though it was the same irritation Ever had noted every time Lindsay mentioned Steve lately). "Everything is fine."

Lindsay took her hand and led her out of the kitchen to the couch, where she gave her a hot cup of tea.

"Sonia offered to drop Steve off at home so I can have the car. I'll stay here with you tonight; I'll be right here."

These were the same words that Lindsay had said a year ago, when the ambulance was gone, when the police were gone. When Ethan was gone, and there was nothing left but the record on the stereo, turning endlessly, the needle stuck in the last groove.

"Also, off topic?" Lindsay said, plopping down on the couch and resting her head on Ever's shoulder. "I think Steve's sleeping with Melissa."

Act II, Scene I

Josie

The night before *Nutcracker* auditions, Josie knocked on the guesthouse door to invite Etienne to join them for dinner. She'd made sure he was alone first, that that little twat, Lotte, wasn't around, checking the driveway and the street for the film crew's van. She had removed her apron and put on a pair of black jeans and a silk blouse. Casual but elegant, she thought.

It was a cliché, but her mother had taught her that the way to a man's heart was through his stomach. (A way to a man's heart was also through his zipper, but she'd learned that one all on her own.) Her mother had not taught her a lot, but she had shown her how to cook, passing on the recipes her own mother had given her— *from the old country.* Tonight, she'd made her mother's *braendende kearlighed*; it was simple but delicious, essentially just mashed potatoes with bacon and onions. Savvy, of course, wouldn't touch it (neither would she), but every man she'd ever made it for devoured it. God, she hoped he wasn't vegan. She'd dated a guy right after Mark left who was vegan, and it wound up being such a pain in the ass. He couldn't even eat popcorn at the movie theater, for Christ's sake.

Etienne seemed surprised by the invite, but said, *yes, yes,* of course he'd join them for dinner. Now, the three sat at the kitchen island, a bottle of wine from Mark's stash breathing on the counter. One perk from Mark's shacking up with the hygienist was that he'd left his wine collection behind. There was a lifetime's worth of cabernet in the wine cellar.

"Can *I* have some?" Savvy asked, holding out her tumbler.

"Sure. In three years," she said, pouring wine into Etienne's glass and then her own.

"In France, we drink wine in our baby bottles," Etienne said, and laughed.

"See? In France I would be legal," Savannah said, and pouted.

"Well, when you get to *France*, you can drink all the wine you'd like," she said, then realized that might be a bit presumptuous, though there was hardly any doubt in her mind that Savvy would be the one heading off to the Ballet de Paris come January.

Savvy was in her pajamas already: a pair of worn sweatpants, a camisole tank, her hair hanging down in beachy waves, the ends a faded blue from a summer dalliance. Josie had warned her that Vivienne would lose it if she saw even a strand of sapphire sticking out of her bun, but Savvy had brushed her off.

"You really need to get that trimmed," Josie said, and gestured to the blue tips of her hair.

Savannah ignored her and scooped some salad onto her plate, plucked out the sliced black olives, and tossed them back into the salad bowl.

"So, Etienne," Josie said, smiling and serving him potatoes from the Le Creuset her mother had given her when she and Johnny got married. "Will you be using Vivienne's choreography for *The Nutcracker*?"

Etienne took a swig of wine, and wiped his mouth with the back of his hand. "I will do my own version."

"Your own version?" Josie said.

"Yes. I will . . . *borrow*? From Nureyev. From Baryshnikov."

Savvy's mouth dropped open, and her eyes widened. "There's no Sugar Plum in those versions," she said.

"No Sugar Plum," he said, smiling sympathetically, as if he'd just revealed that he'd run over her dog. Josie's heart dropped. Without a Sugar Plum, what role would Savvy . . .

"But then, who . . . I mean . . . ." Savvy said.

Etienne regarded her intently across the steaming vat of potatoes, eyebrow raised.

"It's just, I've been Sugar Plum for the last three years, I kind of assumed . . ."

"In my version, the lead role, the prima, is *Marie*. No Clara. No Sugar Plum."

Josie and Savannah had gone to ABT's production in Orange County several times. Ratmansky's version did not have a Sugar Plum Fairy either, only an adult Clara. But there was a child Clara in that version, as well. Melissa was going to flip. Jaz was finally tall enough, old enough to be Clara, but definitely not old enough to play an adult role.

Etienne reached for another helping of potatoes and meat.

Savannah gawked. "But . . ."

Josie wanted to kick her, but they were at the island, not the table, and so she couldn't get her in the shins without Etienne seeing.

"It sounds amazing," Josie said, *corrected*, with an undertone of scolding in her voice that she hoped Savvy could read. "I can't wait to see what you do with it. Honestly, I'm happy to see things shaken up a bit." Though this was not at all what she wanted to see. She liked things as they were. As they were supposed to be.

"Well, you see, that is what I do best," he said, and held out his empty glass, shaking it. "Shake things up."

Bea

"You'll do great," Bea's mom said. "Just remember *S.M.O.G.*" Her mom had agreed to let her drive to auditions today. It was Saturday, early, so not much traffic. She'd offered to move the car onto the street so Bea wouldn't have to back down their steep driveway, but Bea had insisted she needed to learn how to do this. Seriously; how hard could it be? She could execute complicated ballet combinations effortlessly; the coordination of head and neck and feet and knees. Multitasking was her specialty. Still, when her mother buckled herself in, Bea could practically smell her fear.

"Okay. Good. Signal, Mirror, Over the shoulder . . . now Go!"

She did as she was instructed, and soon they were at the foot of the drive and then cruising down the street. Her mom seemed to relax a little, too, and she even pulled out her phone when it dinged with a text, which she scanned, frowning.

"Everything okay?" Bea asked.

"Yeah, just a bank notification," she said.

Bea tilted her head.

"Low balance. I need to transfer some money. It's nothing."

Bea knew things were tight right now. She didn't even dare ask her mom for new pointe shoes. She'd been rotating the pairs she had left over from the summer, Jet-gluing them to keep them alive. She'd dug through the small pile of dead shoes she had, searching for ones that might be salvageable. The pair she'd brought for today was workable; she just prayed they'd get her through auditions before they completely died. Lizzy had an extra pair of Grishkos in her size she offered to sell her for thirty dollars. Bea normally wore

Russians, but at this point, she just needed a pair she could dance in. She hadn't resorted to digging through Vivienne's Lost and Found yet, but she would if she needed to. Once, she'd found a brand-new pair of flats there. Nobody claimed them, and so she'd slipped them quietly onto her feet. Later, a knee-length character skirt she just had to take in a little at the waist. She'd even found a Yumiko, but those were custom leotards, and whoever had left it there would recognize it if she wore it to class.

Savvy and Olive ordered their pointe shoes in bulk directly from Russia, their moms dishing out hundreds of dollars at once. Bea bought hers one pair at a time, except for this summer before her intensive, when she made a GoFundMe. Everyone had felt so bad about her dad, she'd raised twice as much as she needed for shoes and used the extra for her MetroCard.

She had to remind herself she was lucky to train at a conservatory like CLCB. Ballet was expensive. Even before her dad passed, she'd been planning to audition for trainee positions for next year. Trainees usually weren't paid, but at least they didn't have tuition expenses. Worst case, she'd thought she might be able to get into a company's school on scholarship. But then Etienne Bernay had shown up. She didn't believe in angels or Heaven or God, but still, it felt like somebody somewhere might be keeping an eye out for her. She didn't just want this scholarship, like every other girl at the studio; she needed it. Her family needed it.

"I saw you were writing this morning. Are you working on a new book?" she ventured.

"Maybe," her mom said.

Her mom had stopped writing when her dad got sick, but this morning, while Bea warmed up at her portable barre in the living room, her mom sat at the kitchen table, clacking away at her laptop, the patio doors open. Before her dad died, he would go out surfing early, and her mom would work. Though it made her happy to see her mom writing again, the open doors had made her eyes sting, as if her mom was still waiting for her dad to return to the deck, shaking his wet head, before walking into the house.

"You need to start signaling now, and slow down, so you can make the turn," her mom said as they approached the studio. "Just pull up here, put it in park, and leave the car running." Bea was grateful she wouldn't have to try to fit the Volvo in between Josie and Lindsay's expensive cars; it would be like trying to dock a cruise ship in a slip made for a rowboat.

She undid her seat belt and slid out of the driver's seat. Her mom got behind the wheel while Bea retrieved her water bottle and dance bag from the back. "Oh, shoot," her mom said through the window. "Is there a performance fee? What was it last year? A hundred?"

"I don't think so," Bea lied, knowing her mom had likely not read the email Vivienne sent out. Her mom looked relieved.

This morning, when Bea had pulled the cork stopper from her piggy bank's belly, she'd found exactly a hundred dollars. She'd had to dip into it several times this past year, every time her mother got that pained expression that said, *Please, please don't ask me for money.*

"Wait. Should I stay? Looks like the other moms are here?" She motioned to Josie and Lindsay's cars. Bea thought about all the other auditions. All the years her mom came along with snacks and spare tights. She remembered her mom pinning the crinkly audition numbers on her leotards, her purse always filled with spare safety pins.

"It's okay," Bea said. "We all know Savvy's going to be Sugar Plum. I'm just hoping for anything other than Mirliton. I *cannot* do Mirliton again."

What she was really hoping was that she'd get Dewdrop, the soloist role in the "Waltz of the Flowers." Getting Dewdrop would enable her to do other roles, as well: Snow and maybe even Arabian, though Vivienne always chose the darker-skinned, darker-haired girls for Arabian, the bendy ones with flexible backs and bigger boobs. Zoraiya would probably be Arabian lead again. God, ballet could be so awful, and it killed her that Vivienne kept playing into those racist stereotypes. She dreamed of dancing at a company that was more progressive; she wondered if Ballet de Paris was making any strides toward inclusivity. *Stop*, she thought.

"Okay," her mom said. "You did a really good job today. You can drive home, too, if you want. What time are you out again?"

"Three, I think," Bea said.

"Come here," her mom said, and Bea leaned down and hugged her through the open window. "*Merde*, Bumble."

"Thanks, Mama," she said, feeling like a little girl again and wishing, for a moment, she was.

As soon as she got inside the lobby, she remembered why the moms were here. The interviews. The lobby was packed. The greenroom door was closed, with a sign that said, DO NOT ENTER: FILMING IN PROGRESS. While Etienne and Vivienne ran the auditions, Lotte would be interviewing and filming the moms. There had been a link to a sign-up sheet in that email her mom had missed. That's why Josie and Lindsay were here, sitting together, chatting near the bathroom door. Crap, her mom should be here for this.

She quickly dug her phone out of her dance bag and texted her. But as she was typing, the app shut down. Damn it. Her phone was her mom's old one, too old for updates even, glitching all the time lately; she needed a new one, but a new phone was definitely not in her mom's budget. Hopefully, the film people could do the interview when her mom came back to pick her up.

Vivienne was in Studio B, auditioning the Littles, and on the Studio A window, a sign said Etienne would be doing a warm-up class for the Level 6s at noon before their auditions. It was only eleven-thirty, but there were already a bunch of kids in the studio stretching. It was loud with excited chatter and the deep laughter of the boys.

The boys. Bea was usually grateful for how their energy balanced things out. All those female hormones synching up could be overwhelming. There were days when every girl in the class (except for some of the youngers who hadn't started yet) were on their period. The air felt charged on those days; each of them tightly wound, like un-sprung springs. Other times, a lovely peacefulness descended on the class, and it was almost harmonious.

Over the last several years, the girls had all cycled through crushes on *Le Trio*. People assumed that all male dancers were gay, a tired ballet cliché. But, as far as Bea knew, all three boys in the class liked girls. Though when they danced together, they were just bodies. Hands and sweat and legs. Touching was not sexual or even romantic. They were a machine made of parts; flesh and muscle functioning like cogs and wheels. At least they had been before. They hadn't had a partnering class since she got home; she was nervous even thinking about it now.

Savvy and Olive weren't in the lobby; they were probably in the dressing room. She and Olive used to change together, too, as easy and unselfconscious around each other as sisters.

She kept replaying the conversation she'd had with Olive the first day back at class: her attempt to apologize, and Olive's cruel words. *You're not a good person*, she'd said. Bea *was* a good person. She'd just made a mistake; she'd been mad at Savvy. She'd been drinking. But why was *Olive* so angry about it? What she and Nick had done was painfully clear in her memory, but every time she tried to remember what had happened between her and Olive that night, it felt like fog rolling across the stage of her memory, obscuring everything.

She walked into the studio now, head down, and made her way to her spot at the barre along the back wall. She had to walk past Nick and Luke to get there, and she caught Nick staring at her. He'd never do that if Savvy were in the room. Luke punched him in the arm and leaned in to whisper something. Her skin prickled. Owen was alone in the corner, stretching and reading; he hadn't been hanging out with the guys as much lately, using every spare minute to study for his SATs.

"Hey, Bea," he said. Owen was half Japanese, with light brown skin and intense green eyes. He was kind of nerdy but super nice. And cute.

"Hi," she said, and smiled.

A few other heads popped up as she walked across the studio, and a couple girls said "Hi." She wasn't a *total* pariah, anyway.

Olive and Savvy finally came in at 11:45, bumping shoulders as they looked at something together on Savvy's phone.

Focus, she thought. She was glad Etienne was doing a warm-up class. Going into an audition cold was the worst. Plus, Etienne's classes were so different from Miss V's. Exhausting, but fun. She could do Vivienne's combinations in her sleep—and sometimes did. (She woke herself up one night doing *frappés*, her feet tangled in the sheets.) But Etienne was unpredictable. Some days, he would do a three-hour barre, focusing on technique. Other days, he seemed restless and would hurry them through barre so they could get to center, where they never knew what he would throw at them. Some students who were amazing in Vivienne's classes were like fish flopping around out of water in his. You had to be quick to keep up, and he had no patience for those who were slow on the uptake. She and Savvy had no problem adjusting. But Jaz floundered. So did Olive.

"You!" he'd called out one afternoon last week, when Olive kept bungling a *petite allegro* combination. "You look like—" He pantomimed someone moving slowly across the floor, dragging his feet clumsily. "How do you say, *une limace*? *En Anglais?*" He was staring right at Bea, waiting for her to act as translator, a role into which she had unwillingly fallen.

"Une limace?" she asked, dredging her memory for the word.

"It is, an insect?" he said, making antennae with his fingers. *"C'est orange?"*

"A *slug*?" she said, stunned, as Olive's face flushed.

Etienne clapped his hands and pointed. "Yes. You are like a slug."

Olive marched to the edge of the room, where she fiddled, frustrated, with her pointe shoe ribbons, as if it were her shoes rather than her feet that had failed her. Bea wanted to go to her, to hug her. Why was he so mean to her? But when Olive stood up again, she crossed her arms angrily and glared at Bea, as though *she* were the one who had insulted her.

"Come back, my little slug," he had said, beseeching Olive, palms pressed together. "Come, come. It is okay. I still love you."

At this, all the girls in the class, except for Bea and Olive, tittered, and Olive's face reached an even deeper shade of crimson. After that, Olive had gone from cold to downright icy toward Bea.

Today, as he warmed them up at the barre, Olive seemed to have checked out completely. If she danced like this during auditions, she'd be lucky to get even a corps role. When Olive tried, she was amazing. But lately, she *was* sluggish. Even lazy. It was like she didn't care anymore. Normally, Bea would talk to her about it. Find out what was going on. But this wasn't her business. Not anymore. Olive had made that clear.

Bea needed to focus on herself. On Dewdrop, on the scholarship.

This was just a warm-up class, and so it was short, ending with a couple quick combinations across the floor. That was when her left shoe died.

Lindsay

"You're up!" Nancy boomed from her post at the front desk, and Lindsay practically jumped out of her skin. After Josie was called into the greenroom for her interview, Lindsay had pulled up the listing for that run-down cottage on the cliffs on her laptop. The first offer had fallen through when the young couple freaked out about the disclosures. The pregnant woman was terrified of mold. Never mind that it had been remediated six months ago. Never mind that every house that close to the beach was crawling with it.

"Right now?" she asked. Nancy now stood arms akimbo in the doorway, extra bedraggled today: platinum hair in a sloppy bun, yoga pants, and an oversized CLCB sweatshirt like a strung-out, middle-aged cheerleader. Though this was simply her *Nutcracker* uniform; she'd look like this until she cleaned up for opening night.

"Yes, now!" Nancy said, full volume, before turning on her heel.

Lindsay closed her laptop. The owners were eager to sell, so she'd urged them to drop their price a bit. Mold or no, she'd get this thing sold soon. God, that stupid disclosure. Some things were better left hidden, though secrets have a way of rearing their ugly little heads.

She hadn't told Steve about the bump. What exactly would she say? "I think you gave me a VD? Maybe you should let *Melissa* know?" She held out hope that it was nothing—both the bump and whatever that strange moment at Ethan's memorial was. Despite her instincts, which told her to steer clear of WebMD, she'd gone on to the symptom checker and typed in "red bump," at which point she was prompted, "Could you be pregnant?" which gave her pause for exactly three and a half seconds of pure terror before she remembered she hadn't had a period in two months. But wait. That was a symptom of pregnancy itself. *No, no.* She was almost fifty and sweating like a pig most nights as hot flashes came in waves. *No,* she'd clicked. At this point, she was given several possible diagnoses: *Shingles, Hives, Bed Bugs,* and there, at the bottom of the list, *Genital Warts.* Of the dozen or so possible explanations, only this one was sexually transmitted, and with only a "Fair" match to her symptoms, no less. She felt relief wash over her. But maybe "red bump" was too vague. It lacked geographical specificity, anyway. She trembled as she typed *vulv . . .* and the option of *vulvular lesion* popped up. And *click, click, click,* a brand-new list: *Herpes, Genital Warts, Scabies.* Scabies?!

But what if it *wasn't* a VD? If Steve hadn't done anything wrong, and she accused him, that would be a disaster. But that look she'd seen cross his face when Melissa was all over him at Ethan's memorial? What was that?

After the initial shock of what it seemed to imply, she'd attempted to debunk the theory. First off, Melissa Knolls was a full-time stage mom. She homeschooled Jazmin and spent the rest of her time at the studio. She and Jaz were almost always together; an affair would be hard to pull off. Secondly, Lindsay had always thought Steve was nice-looking, but Melissa, with her various *enhancements,* was definitely in a different league, if not an entirely different game, than her husband.

So, despite what her gut was telling her, she'd figured (hoped) she'd simply read too much into whatever that was at the memorial. And whatever was going on down *there* was probably just another perk of menopause. No need to confront Steve yet. First, she'd try to get rid of it on her own. If it persisted, she'd call her OB-GYN and make an appointment.

Josie was talking to Nancy as Lindsay made her way to the greenroom door.

"I just hate the *secrecy,*" Josie said quietly. "It feels so devious. You know?" With that, she lifted her chin toward the greenroom door, catching Lindsay's eye.

What was she talking about?

Josie and Melissa were best friends; was she talking about Steve? If not, what on earth did she mean? What other secrets could she possibly be keeping, and why would she be talking about them with Nancy? No, it couldn't be Steve. She was being paranoid. It had to be something to do with ballet. With Etienne? Maybe he'd already decided to give the scholarship to Savannah? This possibility stoked a hot little flame of anger.

Lindsay tentatively knocked on the closed greenroom door.

Lotte opened it and gestured for her to come in, as though Lindsay had shown up uninvited. "Sit here," she said, and her breath smelled like cigarettes.

Lindsay sat down on the stool in front of the backdrop, the lights brighter than the sun on her face.

Josie

"What are your dreams for your daughter?" Lotte had asked as she aimed the camera at her face, like this was an interrogation instead of an interview.

"*My* dreams?"

"Yes. A mother always has a dream for her child, no?"

For some reason, Josie had felt like she was being led into a trap.

"Happiness," she said. "Of course."

"Of course," Lotte said. "But for her career. Where would you like to see her one day?"

"Well, I'd love to see her onstage at the Ballet de Paris," Josie offered with a grin. That's what Lotte was looking for, right? That's what this whole documentary was about. The scholarship. The bright future of one dancer. But *Josie's* dreams for Savvy? It was more than this, more than they could capture in a sound bite. What she wanted, what she *really* wanted, was for Savvy to *be* something. Like Josie, Savvy wasn't good at school. She did high school online, getting mostly Cs. If Savvy were to apply to college, Josie knew there would be little but disappointment for her. She'd likely have to do two years at community college with hopes of transferring to a four-year university, and Josie feared she might not even make it through community college. Then what? Pray she would meet someone who could support her? Rely on some stupid *guy* to give her the life she deserved? Of course, Josie had managed in this way, but a mom always wants more for her daughter.

On paper, Savvy was perfectly average. But on the stage? She was perfection. A one-in-a-thousand kind of dancer. It didn't matter that math had been bringing her to tears since the fourth grade, or that her English papers came back graffitied in red. None of that mattered when the curtain rose. Under the lights, Savvy was flawless.

Josie suddenly recalled the afternoon not long after she'd moved to LA when Alan Goldberg, the agent who had scouted her, called her into his office to review the photos that had come back from her portfolio shoot. He'd pushed the stack of 8 x 10s across his desk, a sly grin on his face. She could have been one of the models in any of her mother's magazines: *Vogue. Elle. Mademoiselle.* She remembered the way her hands had trembled as she studied them. Her first thought had been how proud her mother would be. Perhaps a girl's dreams and her mother's *are* intertwined.

"Baudelaire. The poet?" Lotte said. "He says, 'The more delicate and ambitious the soul, the further do dreams estrange it from possible things.'"

Josie smiled and then struck back. "Well, Savvy might be ambitious. But she's definitely *not* delicate." It was true. Savvy, like Josie, was tough. A fighter. She might crumble in front of a history exam, but tasked with thirty-two *fouettés* in *Swan Lake*, she didn't flinch. And she didn't fall. And she didn't *fail.* There was no one at the studio besides Savvy who could do this.

But after the camera was off, Josie stood up and made her way to the door, feeling uneasy. For whatever reason, it felt like this girl, Lotte, had it out for her. For Savvy. And who knew how much influence she had over Etienne, over the decision about the scholarship. Best to tread lightly. She was starting to think that having him in the guesthouse was not a good idea. Not if it was pissing this chick off.

"How was it?" Nancy had asked as Josie emerged from the greenroom.

Josie leaned over the reception desk, glancing around first to make sure nobody was listening, though she knew someone was *always* listening at the studio.

"That girl," she said, gesturing with a nod to the greenroom door. "I don't think she's thrilled about her boyfriend staying at our house."

Nancy chuckled, shaking her head. "Don't worry about *her.* She's only bent out of shape that she's stuck at that shitty motel."

"I guess," Josie had said. "But I just hate the secrecy. It feels so devious. You know?"

The Level 6 kids were all still in the studio with Etienne, and she had a bunch of stuff to get done at home, so she'd patted the counter and said, "Have Savvy text me when they get out?"

When Josie had turned around, Lindsay was staring at her, listening, her face pale, and she'd given Josie a look that was unreadable. *Shit.*

Lindsay

After the interview, Lindsay rushed out of CLCB and raced downtown. Her co-worker, Deanne, had the flu and had asked if she could show a prospective buyer a condo at noon; she said Lindsay could have the client, the sale too, if she covered for her.

It was already eleven-thirty, and Saturdays were busy downtown; she was hoping she'd be able to find a place to park. Downtown Costa de la Luna was a four-block stretch of shops and restaurants. When Lindsay was growing up, there had been headshops and co-ops, used bookstores and coffee shops. Now there was a Whole Foods, a mini Target, and Starbucks. There were a few businesses that had managed to survive the corporatization, but everything that had given Costa de la Luna its character and charm was slowly being replaced either with chains or craft breweries. Seriously, how many craft breweries does one town need?

The condo was in an older building at the top of the street, next to St. Mary's. When she was a kid, the building had been a bank. Now, the main floor was a fancy wine and cheese shop (the wine kept in the old bank vault), and upstairs were eight one-bedroom units. She'd never shown a unit in this building, but assumed the residents were either retired folks wanting to remain independent or younger couples who saw this as a starter home that could yield them a hefty bit of equity when they were ready to truly domesticate. Most of her clients were couples like this, with their entire lives awaiting them.

It was an odd nostalgia she felt as she opened the door to the condo: though for a past she'd never had. For a future that Olive *might* have. If Olive wound up dancing in New York or San Francisco (or Paris!), she'd have to live crammed into a five hundred square foot apartment with at least a couple other girls. Lindsay imagined the pink tights hanging from the exposed pipes, and she could almost hear the city sounds from the street below filtering through the windows. She could nearly smell the sweet sharp scent of *girls*. Of youth. She felt a little glint of joy whenever she thought of Olive's bright and exciting future. Because Lindsay didn't go to college, she'd never lived in a dorm and had roommates; she'd gone straight from her childhood bedroom into Steve's house, which had felt so grown-up and sophisticated at the time. Now, it just felt like she'd missed out.

This unit was small and nondescript, with none of the charm that a New York City walk-up or Parisian flat would have. The "expansive view" described in the listing was of a brick wall. The kitchen was dated, the floors pitched like a steeply raked stage. If she set her pen down in the living room, it would probably roll all the way to the bedroom. She quickly assessed its selling points *(Wine downstairs! Free alley parking! High ceilings!)* and opened the windows, allowing in the ocean breeze and the faint smell of weed coming from the alley behind the high-end dispensary next door. A boomer client might be transported by the scent to their younger years. *Nostalgic living!* A wink and a nod would do for a millennial prospect.

At 11:55, she opened the door and waited for Deanne's client. But as she looked down the dark hallway, she saw nothing. Finally, she heard someone coming up the steps. She straightened her skirt, ran her hand over her hair, and smiled.

"Oh," he said, surprised. "Hi!"

It took her a moment to place him without his gray Freezey's uniform. Today he was dressed in gently worn blue jeans and a chambray button-down shirt. Without his Freezey's baseball cap on, she could see he had silky black hair. A whole head of it.

"Victor!" Lindsay said. "Hi!"

It was like the time she'd seen her math teacher slumped over at a bar in the local steakhouse in high school. Completely out of context. Like seeing a polar bear at the beach. They stood awkwardly in the doorway for a second.

"This is the condo for sale, right? Are you the agent? Deanne said she was sick, so someone else would be here to meet me."

"Oh, oh, yes! Sorry. You're here to see the condo! Deanne didn't give me a name. Come in." She turned and entered the condo, and her brain went through its usual calculations, trying to figure out the best tack to take with this prospective buyer. But wait. Why was he here?

"Are you looking for an investment property?" she asked, as Victor opened the door to the economy-sized fridge and leaned in to inspect. "I heard that people who Vrbo these condos are making hand over fist."

He poked his head out of the fridge and smiled. "No, it's for me."

"Oh," she said.

"My wife and I, we're, um, separating."

"Oh, no," she said. "I'm sorry."

He shook his head. "Don't be sorry. It's been a long time coming. Now that our son is off at college, my wife thought it was time."

Lindsay knew a lot of couples who had lived through miserable marriages, then filed for divorce the second they dropped their kids off at the dorms. Whenever she heard these stories, she fantasized about doing the same. The delicious liberation they must feel. Imagine that car ride home! But then she'd think of those poor college freshmen, probably wondering how long their parents had been silently enduring one another for their sake. Or worse, what about that first Christmas break? Would Victor's kid come home to *this*? The condo suddenly looked even sadder and shabbier than it had before. She couldn't imagine putting Olive through that.

"Well," she said. "I'm sorry anyway. Divorce is never easy."

"Actually, she hasn't filed yet. I am kind of hoping she changes her mind. I'm just giving her the space she needs. Absence makes the heart grow fonder, right?"

"Right," Lindsay said. "Well, you could always convert it into a rental later. I mean, if you make up."

Victor walked over to the living room window and twisted the stick that controlled the vertical blinds, revealing the brick wall.

"Nice view," he said, grinning. He had dimples, she noted. Two of them.

"You can *kind* of see the ocean from the bedroom," she offered. She motioned for him to join her in the ten-by-ten-foot bedroom where, as advertised, a westward-facing window provided a glimpse of the ocean. A fragment of blue.

"Does the furniture convey?" he asked.

"I think so?" she said. "I'll double check with the sellers. Sorry. I don't have all the info, since this is Deanne's listing. I'll find out."

"I used to go to that church growing up," he said, motioning to St. Mary's. The church bell tower was right outside the bedroom window.

"St. Mary's is *my* church, too!" she said.

As if on cue, the church bells began to ring out. It was deafening, but Victor was unfazed. If he was any other client, she would have said, "Isn't it lovely?" or "No need to set an alarm!"

"Let me show you the bathroom," she said instead, and motioned for him to follow her.

Later, as they stood in the living room, he took one last look around. "It's perfect. But I'm not sure it's in my budget. My wife offered to let me live in the garage—it's converted and everything— but that feels kind of pathetic," he said.

She shook her head, though it did sound sad. She thought of her own garage with its sterile gray walls, empty save for their cars and Olive's barre. Steve was not a guy who owned tools.

"Deanne said the seller is very motivated," she said. "If you make a reasonable offer, I'm sure they'll work with you. I can put in a good word, too. Since we're friends." That was weird. *Were* they friends?

He took a deep breath and smiled. She noted his front tooth had the tiniest chip. Something about that was endearing. "Hey," he said. "Do you want to go get a coffee?"

"Are you making an offer?" she asked, and felt her face flush red with the double entendre. Oh my god, what was wrong with her?

"I think so," he said, pretending as though she hadn't practically thrown her panties at him.

"I'll text the owner."

Bea

Vivienne's auditions were nothing like this. First off, Etienne dismissed half the Level 6 girls before they even put on their pointe shoes. "I have seen enough," he said.

"But I didn't even *audition*!" Jaz said; she had been waiting to be Clara for years, but there would be no Clara in Etienne's version. Only *Marie*, who would be played by one of the older girls. No Cavalier. Not even a Snow King. The Snow Queen would have a *solo* instead of a *pas de deux*. Bea had stayed up half the night studying the video of last year's performance, memorizing the roles of both Dewdrop and Sugar Plum. For what? There was no Sugar Plum.

The dismissed girls walked out of the studio in bitter silence. She could practically hear the buzz of their disbelief after the door had closed. If Vivienne was smart, she'd deadbolt herself inside her office. The moms were going to go ballistic as soon as they found out.

Le Trio stood in the corner, looking confused. If there was no Cavalier, only a Prince, what would the other two be? Party scene dads? The Rat King? There was always the Russian dance, of course. Chinese? But that was what, a whopping minute and a half onstage?

"I'd better not be freaking Mother Ginger," Luke said, loud enough for everyone to hear.

"No Mother Ginger," Etienne said. "No comedy in my version."

God, no Mother Ginger meant no Polichinelles, no little ones to come tumbling out from under her enormous skirt. Every girl at the studio started out as a Polichinelle. The Littles' mothers were going to lose it.

"I will be Prince, of course," Etienne said as he marched up to

Olive and studied her from head to toe before turning and walking up to Savvy, who took an audibly deep breath and squeezed her shoulder blades together. "And so, I must choose my partner first."

Whoever was cast as Marie would partner with Etienne Bernay? *My god.*

Vivienne always auditioned from the bottom up: dismissing people until only the biggest roles were left to fill. It had the effect of building anticipation and excitement. Even if it was always the same people cast in the same roles, there was still that electric time when anything was possible. This was crazy.

"You are too . . . *slow*," he said to Olive. "Go."

"What?" Olive's eyes widened, and her face was red. Bea felt her throat thicken with compassion. "This is such a joke," Olive whispered.

"Livvie," she said, but Olive stormed past her.

"Faster, *ma petite* slug," he said, then pressed his finger to his lips as he paced up and down the line of remaining girls. He tapped four girls on their sharp shoulders who held their breaths expectantly until he jerked his thumb toward the door.

The only four left were Savvy, Zoraiya, Phoebe. And Bea.

He taught them the new *pas*, but it seemed as if he were making it up as he went along. At one point, Savvy made eye contact with Bea, as if to say, *What is going on?* but the moment of connection was lost when he called Savvy up to demonstrate. As she flawlessly performed the new choreography, Bea's heart sank. She was gorgeous. Perfect. It wasn't going to be any different this time around, even with a different teacher.

"That was great," Bea said to Savvy. Like she needed Bea to tell her how good she was.

He repeated the process with the other girls, with Bea last. She prayed that the Jet-glue she'd managed to sneak onto the shank of her dead shoe after warm-ups would do the trick. But as she moved into an arabesque, her foot sank into the box: nothing but weakened cardboard, satin, and her own sheer will to keep her up. Still, she managed. Maybe he wouldn't notice. Maybe he'd be mesmerized by her extensions, by her impeccable turnout, by how much she wanted this. God, she wanted this more than anything she'd ever wanted in her life.

"Stop," he said, as she was mid-pirouette. "Your shoes are bad."

She thought about the hundred dollars she'd given Nancy for the performance fee. She should have made up an excuse, bought herself some time, and bought the extra pair of shoes from Lizzy. He would cast Savvy as Marie. Savvy would dance the role beautifully, and then she'd receive the scholarship. It was over.

"Okay, okay," he said, and stepped back, examining them as if they were flowers in a flower shop. Or cuts of meat in a freezer. Of course, this was just the way the world of ballet worked. She'd been to enough auditions to know what it felt like to be assessed and scrutinized. She knew how interest can turn to disinterest with a single misstep. One bad day could mean the difference between having a future and having nothing.

"You," he said, tipping his chin at Bea. "You will be Marie."

What?

Savvy's hand went to her mouth, and Bea felt dizzy. She curtsied and quickly moved to the barre, which she clung to, feeling like she might collapse.

"Will there be a second cast?" Savvy asked, her voice trembling, as Etienne walked to the front of the studio, where he sat down and tapped at the laptop, which controlled the music.

"No, *ma chère*," Etienne said. "There is only one performance. No need for a second cast. This is not Ballet Season at Lincoln Center."

Only one performance?

"What about an understudy?" Savvy asked, and her eyes widened. Bea knew this was how Savvy kept from crying. She'd seen the same expression when Savvy was working through a groin injury but refused to stop dancing.

Etienne cocked his head and shook his finger at her. "*You* are stubborn. Like a fox."

"You mean like an *ox*," Nick said from over in the corner, and Savvy shot him a glare.

"I thought it was stubborn like a *mule*," Phoebe said softly.

"Vivienne always casts an understudy for the lead," Savvy persisted. "In case someone gets sick. Or *injured*." She looked back at Bea, her expression mildly threatening.

"*Pah. Understudies*," he said abruptly, as if the word were something rotten in his mouth. "I danced *Don Quixote* with a temperature of forty." He winked at Bea.

"You will be the Raindrop," he said to Savvy.

"*What?*"

"Among the pretty flowers?" he said and flapped his arms around condescendingly, which got a few snickers from the boys.

"*Dewdrop*," she corrected.

"That is all for today," he said, and clapped his hands. "Rehearsals begin next week."

Savvy forced a smile, curtsied, and walked toward the barre where Bea was standing. The air practically sizzled with her rage.

"I'm sorry," Bea blurted, and Savvy looked at her, confused. "I mean . . ."

"Don't be *sorry*," Savvy said. "Jesus. You got the part. Fair and square. What's the *matter* with you?"

Ever

Ever pulled into CLCB's parking lot at two-thirty, early for a change. Parents were strictly forbidden from observing auditions. An email went out, signs were posted, and Nancy made a speech. Nothing could deter some mothers, though, and when a dogged few were caught trying to peek through the slats of the drawn vertical blinds in the studio windows, Vivienne had gone so far as taping butcher paper over the glass. Ever figured if Bea wasn't finished yet, she'd sit in her car and wait. Try to get some work done.

This morning, while Bea warmed up in the living room, she'd opened the document she hadn't looked at in almost two years. Surprisingly, as she reread the draft she'd abandoned when Ethan was first diagnosed, she felt a sliver of excitement. She'd reread the fifty pages she'd written and then quickly written ten more, which weren't terrible. She tried not to think about the uphill battle she had in front of her with this one; she couldn't allow the business end of things to paralyze her. She would focus on the writing. On the words. On the story. On the magical feeling of spinning a glistening web with only her fingers and the keys of her laptop or the fine thread of ink in her notebook. If she started thinking beyond that—to all those things she could not control—she would never write another word.

It had been four years since her last novel, *Black Evenings*, came out, since the debacle from which she was still recovering. *Black Evenings* was a historical novel about Audrey Hepburn, focusing on her early life as a ballet dancer and the secret concerts she performed in to raise money for the Dutch Resistance. It had taken Ever two solid years of researching and another two to complete the novel. When it was done, she knew she'd written something special. It was not only about a beloved icon, but a book with big themes: resistance, resilience, the power of art. It was the novel, she had thought, that was, *finally*, going to make her career. It would be what people in publishing call a "break out."

Her agent, Leona, loved the book and managed to pique enough interest for it to go to auction. After more than a decade of only moderate interest in her work and modest advances to pay for that work, she had hardly known what to do when editors had attempted to court her with promised book tours and major marketing campaigns. In the end, Leona had managed to negotiate a low six-figure deal with Edward. All the stars had seemed aligned, and *her* star— Leona assured her—was finally rising. "Tenth time's a charm," Leona had joked. *Black Evenings* was slated to come out in June; her publicist assured her it would be on every summer list. Maybe even the *book of the summer*. She and Ethan went out to celebrate, and he'd said, "I am so glad people are finally seeing how wonderful your work is. You deserve this."

But then, that spring without warning, the other novel about Audrey Hepburn came out: *Black Dresses*. This one not about Hepburn's heroism, but her scandalous romances. Worst of all, it was written by an author who regularly perched at the top of the *New York Times* bestseller list. Though Ever's book was a hundred times better written (she knew this because she managed to get an ARC of *Black Dresses* from her editor—it really was just fluff), it didn't matter. There was one branch to sit upon on this tree, and that woman's talons were sharp. The other author had been sent to BookExpo, where a billboard with her novel's cover loomed above the crowds. She was the darling of the librarians, the book bloggers, Bookstagram. Her launch party was at the restaurant inside Tiffany: Ever had watched the livestream on Facebook with an agonizing curiosity. Even when *Black Dresses* got skewered by *The New Yorker*, it had been such a colorful review, it had gone viral, and as if in defiance, *Black Dresses* had flown to the tippy top of the *New York Times* bestseller list and hovered there. For *a year*. Meanwhile, *Black Evenings* received nary a mainstream review, none of the hype. And it just wouldn't end. When the paperback of *Black Dresses* was released, *The Today Show* picked it as a book club selection. Then came the Netflix series, the Golden Globe. It was like watching her own dream unfold slowly for someone else. Ever had never seen writing as a competitive sport before now, but Lindsay had joked there must be a way to take this author out at the knees. "I'll Tonya Harding her for you," Lindsay said. "I will." It was as if the stars were not aligned at all, but conspiring against her in a cosmic joke.

Of course, Ethan had been with her through it all. When he caught her obsessing, he'd pull her away from the internet: from Amazon, where her own poor book flopped like a dying fish, from *Entertainment Weekly* (Really? A full-page ad?), from the podcast interviews (Wait, she has a British accent? I read she was born in Hoboken!), from the author's Facebook posts of her events, to which her adoring fans wore their black dresses and pearls.

"You're better than this," Ethan had said solemnly during one of her pity parties. And while he'd meant to be supportive, it had stung. Was she better than this? Or had she become bitter and jealous? Her ambition was making her ugly, angry. This woman's success had ignited an awful spark in her, one she worried might engulf her in flames. Thankfully, Ethan had been there to extinguish it. "You need to get back to work," he'd said. "Make your art. Forget the rest."

He was right. He always was. When she became unmoored, he knew how to steer her back to what mattered. Dutifully, she'd started researching her next book, this time finding an obscure historical figure's story to tell (settling on a female inventor nicknamed *Lady Edison*), hoping nobody would swipe *this* idea out from under her. Luckily, as far as she knew, Beulah Louise Henry hadn't had any scandalous Hollywood affairs.

Ever had been working on it for months when Ethan was diagnosed. She'd set it aside to care for him, assuming he would get better, and she would get back to work. Just a brief sabbatical. But the hiatus stretched on and on, until she hardly remembered what it felt like for an idea to consume her. After he passed away, it all felt so pointless, every word a struggle. But this morning, somehow, she'd found the determination to open the document and pick up where she left off. She'd been lost in her work when Bea told her it was time to leave for auditions. She was eager to get back to it after she dropped Bea off. The hours had passed so quickly, she'd hardly even thought about the auditions, or anything else, for that matter.

She lowered the car window, figured she could keep writing in the car, but the sun was beating through the glass, causing sweat to trickle down her neck, her reading glasses to slip down her nose. Hopefully, she could work inside.

But the lobby was, as expected, a madhouse.

"Where have you been?" Nancy asked, coming out from behind the reception desk and taking Ever by the elbow.

She held her breath. Oh god, what had happened? Was Bea hurt? She thought about all the possible disasters. A broken ankle, a snapped Achilles, a dislocated knee. If she knew anything, it was that there were a million ways the world can fall apart.

"Where is she?"

"Who?" Nancy asked.

"*Bea*," she said, feeling the muscles in her neck tensing.

"I don't know where Bea is. But they're wrapping up the interviews, and you're the only one they haven't talked to yet. Get in there!"

Damn it. The documentary.

"Right now?" Ever asked, looking down at her wrinkled skirt. Had she even looked in a mirror today? "I'm a mess."

Nancy scowled and peered at her over the top of her glasses.

"Well, they can't just skip the mother of the *lead*," she said.

"The *lead*?"

Nancy squeezed her elbow and guided her toward the green-room.

"Yes," Nancy said, her butterscotch breath sweet as she leaned in. "Your girly has gone and dethroned the queen."

Bea

Bea just wanted to go home. She'd gotten exactly what she wanted—more than she wanted!—then why did she feel so horrible? She waited for her mom to come out of the greenroom, pretending to be absorbed in reinforcing the ribbons on her pointe shoes. But the shoes were dead. She'd have to ask her mom if she had a credit card. Dancing the lead, she'd be going through pairs faster than usual. There were a couple of girls at the studio who were ambassadors for pointe shoe companies, posting photos of themselves wearing their gear and gushing about how much they loved their shoes in exchange for free pairs. But that whole process would likely take far too long. She needed them *now.* Mary once sold pictures of her feet to some creepy guy on the internet, and he'd Venmoed her a hundred dollars. She couldn't quite stomach that option. Maybe she could set up another GoFundMe? No. Doing that again so soon felt like begging.

Behind her, she heard someone crying, though girls were always crying in the studio. Injuries—both physical and emotional—were a daily occurrence. But the hiccup-y sobs weren't like the muffled whimpering of someone with a twisted ankle or a bruised ego.

"Jaz?" Jazmin was sitting in the corner, knees drawn to her chest. "You okay?"

Bea sat down next to her and put her arm tentatively over her shoulder in a side hug. You had to be careful. Some girls might cry but didn't want to be touched—to be pitied. She'd made that mistake with Savvy once. Her groin injury had brought her to tears, but when Bea offered to get her some ice from the greenroom fridge, she'd practically bitten Bea's head off, though Savvy's words often had teeth. She hoped today's sharpness—*What is* wrong *with you?*—was just that: a snap of the jaw.

"My mom is going to be so mad," Jaz said.

Bea shook her head. "It's not your fault. You're just too young to be Marie."

Jaz swallowed another sob.

"I'm sure you'll get another good part. Maybe a doll in the party scene?"

"But I won't get the scholarship now," Jaz said.

Bea felt a pinch in her stomach. Had Jazmin really thought she might be in the running for the scholarship to Ballet de Paris? She was *thirteen*.

"Nancy told my mom that Ballet de Paris wants girls starting in the school when they're young like me," Jaz said, wiping at her eyes. "That way, they can shape them into what they want. I'm the youngest one in Level Six."

Bea had always thought of Jaz as a sort of mascot in Level 6. A little sister. She'd never felt competitive with her, but now, she felt a distinct sense of unease. What if this were true? What if Etienne *was* looking for a younger dancer, someone more malleable? Someone who hadn't fully hit puberty yet? That put a whole bunch of other girls in the running: Phoebe, Lizzy. God, maybe even some of the Level 4 and 5 girls? At the Bolshoi in Russia, children as young as nine were uprooted from their homes and ferreted away to train. She'd watched the documentaries. Overseas, ballet was not seen as a recreational activity but a calling, one that began as soon as a dancer could put their feet into first position. Was Bea too *old*? She was only seventeen, but maybe it was too late for her. Maybe Nancy knew something the others didn't?

Savvy and Olive came out of the dressing room wearing high-waisted shorts and tight tanks over bikini tops, strings tied at the neck and hanging down between their shoulder blades. Olive's skin was milky white with freckles like a speckled sparrow egg, while Savvy's skin was a golden shell.

She felt a sharp pang. Last year, when she'd gotten back from New York, she and Olive had practically lived at the beach when they weren't at the studio. Sunburnt, salt-crusted skin, and happy. Her dad had been so sick then, and being with Olive was the only time she felt normal. If only for a few sun-soaked hours.

Savvy had stolen Olive. Though maybe Bea deserved it. Tit for tat. All that. Still, as far as she could tell, Savvy didn't know about what happened with Nick at the bonfire, so this wasn't revenge. She was just being her awful self. Bea really needed to talk to Olive when Savvy wasn't around, if that were even possible anymore. Find out what she'd done to make her so mad. When she and Danny were little, and one of them had done something to upset the other, her dad would always insist the perpetrator ask the victim what he or she could do to make it better. Her dad said that apologies were hollow, that actions spoke louder than words. But what could she do when she didn't really remember exactly what she had done to upset Olive? She did recall a conversation with her, an argument maybe? But every time it started to crystalize in her memory, it just as quickly dissolved again.

Outside, Nick honked, and Savvy and Olive both jumped and giggled, grabbing each other's hands as they walked briskly toward her. Bea braced herself, but they only breezed past, close enough that Bea could smell the scent of Olive's deodorant (Secret, Powder Fresh), and acted as though Bea wasn't there.

Her mom came out of the greenroom a minute later, like she was stumbling out of a dream. Bea scrambled to her feet and met her. She reached for Bea's hands and gripped them, whispering. "Nancy said you got *the lead*?"

Bea nodded, the happiness she'd been forced to tamp down now about to bubble over.

"I am so proud of you, Bumble," Ever whispered. "Daddy would be so proud of you, too."

Bea winced.

Outside, Nick was idling. He drove one of those open Jeeps, no windows or doors. Olive and Savvy were in the jump seats, singing along to whatever he had on the radio. There were surfboards strapped to the roll bars.

"Do you still want to drive home?" her mom asked.

Bea shook her head. There was no way she was going to try to back that beast of a Volvo out of the parking space with all of them sitting here watching her.

Owen came out behind them and touched Bea's arm. "Hey Bea, congrats on Marie."

"Thanks," she said.

"Dude, you want to come to the beach with us?" Luke said to Owen.

"Nah, thanks," Owen said. "I have to work."

"Let's go," Savvy said.

"How about some ice cream? To celebrate?" her mom said, and Bea felt her skin flush with shame. What was she, a little girl? "Your brother's working today. I'll text him we're coming." Bea nodded but didn't speak. If she did, she knew she'd cry. She'd just gotten everything she'd ever wanted. The *lead*. But she felt like someone had punched her in the gut.

Josie

"Last chance," Josie said into the dead air at the other end of the line when Mark, again, did not pick up her call.

Sunday. She imagined Mark and the hygienist, *Erica*, cozied up together in bed or having a late brunch at some cute café. She could practically see him, with his sharp nose and sun-weathered face, as he leaned over, brushed a lock of hair behind Erica's ear, and gazed into her eyes. Tender and attentive. Making her feel special. Seen. He was *good*, the kind of guy who made up for his lack of looks with tons of charm. She'd fallen for it herself. She could hardly blame the girl.

"If you change your mind and want your stuff, you can find it at the homeless shelter."

After the interview with Lotte, she'd felt edgy, and so she'd gone home. She'd planned to spend the rest of the day packing up Mark's shit. He'd left behind almost everything, as if he'd died instead of ditched her. Had he really been so eager to get away that he didn't need his clothes, his good watch, his shoes? She had half a mind to have a bonfire at the beach, but she was worried that it might not be good for the environment. She cared about that sort of thing, after all. So instead she'd opted to fill up a half dozen garbage bags with his dress shirts and ties, with his workout clothes and his shoes. She figured she'd drop it all off at the shelter; some lucky homeless dude might find himself in a Brooks Brothers button-down and Burberry wing tips. She imagined Mark driving past a guy in the median wearing his Tom Ford suit and felt almost giddy.

Of course, she'd offered to give him his crap back. Told him she'd make herself scarce for an afternoon. But he said he didn't need any-thing. Erica's place was small; he had everything he needed. That "things" didn't matter to him anymore.

Who even *was* he now? For years, he'd been working fifty-, sixty-hour weeks, so focused on building his company, building a future for them. And he'd ditched it all. For what? *Erica?* Erica, who had scraped the plaque off his teeth, off *her* teeth, for the last three years. Erica with her big baby-doll eyes and lashes and her four-leaf clover wrist tattoo. Josie wondered how it had started. Was it with the loose crown he'd had replaced? Or was it later, when his wisdom tooth was acting up? How does one even flirt when you've got somebody's hands in your freaking mouth?

Whatever. Onward. She yanked his dress shirts from their hang-ers, noting that Mark and Etienne were roughly the same size. She wondered if he might be interested in some of this stuff. She thought she could just leave the clothes with a note to take what he'd like, but as she was stuffing a pair of Ferragamos into the bag, her phone dinged with a text from Savvy.

DEW EFFING DROP

Josie felt her heart plummet. What the hell?

MOM

Who's the lead? she wrote back.

Who do you think?! Going to the beach back later ILY

Acid crept up the back of her throat. Dewdrop? It was a solo role, yes, but after years as Sugar Plum, it was a demotion. She wondered if Lotte had somehow orchestrated this, whispered in Etienne's ear. She clearly was not a fan of Savvy's; that had been abundantly clear in the interview. Jesus Christ. Well, this was a disaster. It had to be Beatrice. There wasn't anyone else who could possibly carry the lead role. Though who even knew what the lead was anymore, now that he'd done away with Sugar Plum. Shake things up? This was like a goddamn earthquake.

What happened? she texted back, then immediately realized that Savvy would read this as blame. But *something* must have happened for him to cast Bea instead of her. She racked her brain. What time had Savvy gone to bed last night? What did she have for breakfast? Maybe she'd been too relaxed with her lately. Savvy had been staying out later all summer, sleeping in. She didn't always eat well. Josie had caught her at least a couple of times cooking up a big bowl of mac and cheese for lunch rather than eating a salad like she was sure Bea was doing. She imagined the Hendersons' cupboards full of healthy options: granola and hemp seeds and dried seaweed. Rabbit food.

Could this be her fault? She'd been distracted with Mark's sudden departure. She hadn't been paying as much attention as she should to Savvy over the summer. She was only seventeen, still a kid. Just because Josie had been on her own for almost a year at her age, didn't mean that Savvy was equipped to take care of herself.

The Whole Foods was just down the road from the homeless shelter. She figured she'd drop off Mark's stuff, load up on some healthy food, and then empty out the cupboards. Get rid of the junk. The meat. They'd go vegetarian. She was going to have a fresh start. She and Savvy both. Kale smoothies for breakfast and salads for lunch. Steamed veggies, *quinoa*. Maybe she could talk her into doing a few laps in the pool in the morning. It would be good for them both.

Also, she reassured herself, the casting still might change. Etienne didn't know the girls—he probably just saw in Bea what everybody saw at first glance. *Her lines, her lines.* God, if she had to hear another word about Bea's *lines.* As if a girl were little more than a collection of angles: legs and arms and neck, nothing but a series of pencil strokes. When rehearsals started, Etienne would realize that Savannah was clearly more fleshed out than Beatrice Henderson. Savvy's *lines* might not be as elegant, but who cared about elegance when you had a powerhouse? Once he saw her really dance, he would change his mind. And even if nothing changed, just because Bea got Marie did *not* mean she'd get the scholarship.

After she'd dumped Mark's clothes at the homeless shelter, she felt good about herself. The workers were all so appreciative, thanking her as she handed them bag after bag. Of course, they had no idea how many thousands of dollars' worth of stuff she was relinquishing.

They probably would have treated her the same if she'd been dumping off a broken toaster. But she still felt like she'd done a good deed, and doing good deeds was good for the soul. And for the skin, apparently. When she caught her reflection on the way into the Whole Foods, she was practically glowing. Fuck Mark. And fuck Erica. She was starting fresh.

She filled up her cart with all the healthy things, remembering reading once that you should only shop the perimeter of the store: produce, dairy, perishables. Avoid anything in cans or boxes. She even bought a few glass jars and stood at the bulk dispensers, filling them with nuts and grains and coffee beans. By the time she left the store, she felt like a brand-new Josie. She loaded up her car, then decided she'd swing by Namaste Café to grab a chai latte to go. Or, better yet, one of their cleansing teas. She was on a roll.

As she studied the chalkboard over the counter at Namaste, she heard a familiar laugh. It took her a moment to place it. Lindsay Chase? She turned around, and sure enough, there Lindsay was at a table with a guy who looked familiar, though she had no idea why. It certainly wasn't *Steve*.

Lindsay was a realtor; of course, she probably met clients at coffee shops all the time, but the way Lindsay was playing with her hair and smiling didn't seem like she was talking about mold remediation or termite tents. Lindsay Chase. What do you know? Miss *Holier-than-Thou* with her fourteen-carat-gold cross and her "Olive and I will be feeding the homeless on Thanksgiving if anyone wants to join us" texts to the CLCB parents' group chat. Damn, why did this guy look so familiar? He was good-looking. Dark skin, dimples. Then it hit her. He was one of those guys from the HVAC place near the studio. Seriously? A *repair guy*? Granted, he cleaned up well, but still.

She couldn't decide if she should say anything to Lindsay or not; they were friends, after all. But when the barista hollered out "Josie?" Lindsay caught Josie's eye. It took only the surprise on Lindsay's face to confirm Josie's suspicions.

"Hi, Linds," she said, clutching her detoxifying tea, which smelled like grass and looked like puke.

"Oh, hi!" Lindsay said as Josie approached their table. "Josie, this is Victor. He works at Freezey's by the studio. He's shopping for a condo. You know the ones next to the St. Mary's?" Smiling too big and talking too much. Something was definitely going on.

"Hi," Josie said to Victor, and wondered if *he* was married, too. Probably. She thought of Mark and Erica, and felt some of that earlier rage creeping back.

"You want to join us?" Lindsay asked, and motioned to an empty seat.

Was Victor blushing? Poor Steve! She really hated cheaters.

"Can't. I've got groceries in the car. But you know, after the girls get back from the beach, Olive is welcome to join us for dinner. Stay over if she wants. It'll be nice for you and Steve to have a night alone?"

Lindsay nodded, her eyes downcast now. "Thanks."

Oh my god. Melissa was going to die.

Ever

"I am so proud of you, Bumble. Tell me everything that happened," Ever said once they were in the car, and Bea caught her up on what sounded like a chaotic audition process.

"Was Savannah disappointed?" Ever asked.

"I think she was in shock," Bea said.

For years now, every CLCB performance had centered on Savannah Jacobs. Vivienne's "auditions" were simply a formality that ended with the same result every time. Savvy was a beautiful dancer, of course, but it always felt inherently unfair. Ever would love to have seen one of the less accomplished girls dance the lead; she would much have preferred to see Olive or Zoraiya or even little Phoebe be given the chance to shine for just a moment. And obviously, Bea had been waiting for this day for years.

Why don't you tell us when you knew? Lotte had asked Ever in the greenroom, the camera's eye winking at her.

Knew? she'd asked.

Yes, that this was serious. Your daughter's dancing.

Ever and Ethan joked that Bea began dancing in her crib. As a baby, the only way they could get her to sleep was to put on a classical CD, and lying on her back, she would kick and kick until she passed out. There were videos, taken with Ever's old flip phone: Bea twirling in a tutu, walking on tippy-toes across the room, arms made into an "O" over her head, taking a series of dramatic bows for her imaginary audience.

Of course, wanting to be a ballerina is no extraordinary thing at three years old. There had to have been forty little girls, chubby legs stuffed like sausages into pale pink tights and leotards, at Miss Joy's School of Dance, stumbling about like tiny drunken sailors. But as Ever sat watching class with the other mothers, she could see an intensity in Bea's expression. She didn't giggle or twirl aimlessly about the room. She didn't pick her nose or zone out. She was only three, but she was *focused.*

When you dream of your child's future, the image is usually hazy. And as hard as you search for clues into the woman your daughter might one day become, it's mostly wishful thinking. *Look at the way she holds a crayon already—could she be a painter? See how she loves to pitch a tent in the playroom? Maybe one day she'll climb Mount Everest.* Or *Look at that! She loves animals so much; maybe she'll be a veterinarian when she grows up.* But this was different. This glimpse. Like a stolen glance at a crystal ball, the future played out in those spindly limbs, that piercing gaze, that gentle turn of slender wrist. It felt *prescient.*

And so, Bea danced. Lessons once a week at first, and then twice. When Bea was ten, Miss Joy told Ever that she had no more to offer her, and if there was even the smallest chance that Bea wanted to pursue ballet professionally one day, it was Ever and Ethan's *duty* to seek someone who could properly prepare her for a career. The idea that Bea might have even an inkling, at ten years old, of what to do with the rest of her life felt ludicrous. But what if this *was* her calling? Ever had started writing stories when she was Bea's age; she had known that she wanted to be a writer forever. And so, the next day, Ever called the number Miss Joy had given her and spoke to Nancy at CLCB, who said to bring Bea in for an assessment, though it quickly became obvious that Vivienne was assessing not only Bea, but Ever and Ethan, as well.

After the placement class, Vivienne had beckoned them into her office, leaving Bea to stretch in the lobby.

"The good news is Beatrice has tremendous *facility. Potential.* Long legs, loose hips, natural turnout. Her head, it's a little large, but she is still growing. It's impossible, of course, until they are older to know certain things . . ." She looked at Ever, and Ever quickly realized

Vivienne was gauging any genetic land mines that might be waiting for her.

"Small breasts. Narrow hips," Vivienne said in a hushed tone, though Ever didn't know whether she was referring to Bea or herself, though either way, Ever felt an odd sense of relief. "But she is behind. For her age. That *recreational* ballet school . . ." she said, with a clear tone of disdain. "There is much catching up to do. I will need to undo some bad habits. I must work with her privately. Have you considered homeschooling?"

Ethan snorted. Ethan was a public-school music teacher. His world revolved around the middle school in their neighborhood, where Bea would enter the sixth grade that fall.

"Homeschooling?" Ever *worked* at home. The idea of having even one kid home with her all day again was daunting.

"It is not necessary yet, of course. But eventually, it will be too much to train intensively and attend regular school. Many upper-level students study online."

Ethan was shaking his head, his knee jumping up and down. Ever gently squeezed his thigh to make him stop.

"What most impresses me, though," Vivienne said. "It is not her body, but her *ear*. Her musicality. I must assume one of you is musical?"

Ethan tried but failed to hide his pride. "I teach music!"

"Brilliant," Vivienne said, clapping her hands together. "What a gift. She is *gifted*."

Bea had been exuberant, and when they told her she would be going *en pointe*, her eyes had filled with tears. When Ever brought her to CLCB for her first class that fall, her pink mesh bag with a brand-new pair of tiny pointe shoes nestled inside like two delicate birds, Ever felt an odd sense that she was delivering her to her destiny.

Over the next seven years, there were so many things that happened that Ever could not predict, but this one thing had been certain. And she had watched that opaque vision in the crystal ball sharpen. With each class, each private lesson, each performance, the prophecy becoming clearer.

Now this. The lead. Finally. It felt foretold.

★   ★   ★

The café where Danny worked was just a little shack on the pier, but they served the best fish tacos in town. They also had a huge selection of ice cream, a ten-foot-long freezer with colorful buckets of any flavor you could imagine. For years, almost every Friday night, they would take a family walk down the beach to the pier, where they'd get cones and watch the sun set. The kids and she tried all the flavors, but Ethan stuck to Rocky Road.

Today, they sat in the corner by the window. Danny came out of the kitchen, spotted them, and smiled. His hair had gotten so long over the summer, a floppy golden mess of curls. He wiped his hands on his apron and came over to the table, resting his palms on its edge. These were Ethan's hands. Long fingers. *Piano fingers*, Ethan had marveled when he was a baby. But the piano lessons had come and gone in favor of guitar. Then those fingers had been used to grip a volleyball, a baseball, and—for about five minutes—a pen (he was a *great* writer but gave that up in sixth grade). Bea's future felt clear, but Danny's was fuzzy.

"Congrats!" he said, and ruffled Bea's hair like Ethan might have if he were here. "So did Savvy implode?"

"Stop," Ever scolded. She and Ethan had tried to teach the kids to be humble and gracious, though Ever herself was bursting with pride. It was the same way she'd felt the day when she got the contract for *Black Evenings*. Like every bit of her hard work was finally paying off. But then again, look how well that had turned out. Best not to get ahead of herself, like that mouse who gets the cookie but then needs milk, then a straw, then a napkin, too. Best to simply enjoy the cookie. Or, in this case, the ice cream.

"You guys want some tacos?" Danny asked.

"Just a scoop of raspberry gelato," Bea said.

"I'll have a Rocky Road," Ever said, her eyes stinging. "Two scoops."

That night, Ever dreamed of Ethan. When he was alive, he was never in her dreams, but after he passed away, suddenly there he was. It was like the opposite of grief: those moments in which she could see him and smell him and hear his voice again, when his hand brushed her shoulder or grazed her hip. Though the simple bliss of having him back, if only for a moment recalled in the half-light of morning as she wiped a warm streak of drool from her cheek, turned quickly into the worst sort of sorrow.

In this dream, they were in bed. When she rubbed her foot against Ethan's calf, it was gritty with sand. Warm.

"She *did* it," she whispered to him, her heart so full of pride it was practically spilling over with it. He was the only person in the world with whom she could share this. Who would understand. "Our little Bumblebee got the lead."

When she rolled over and found his shoulder, she licked it, like a cat, tasting the salt on her tongue. But her tongue did not meet flesh, and when she woke, she realized it was only salty tears running into her mouth.

Lindsay

Olive had texted that Bea got the lead, Savvy was Dewdrop, and the rest of the casting hadn't been announced yet. **Maybe you'll get Spanish?** Lindsay asked, but Olive only replied: **Spending the night at Savvy's.**

Lindsay and Steve sat alone at the kitchen island, eating Chinese takeout, though she'd told him a hundred times she couldn't eat it on her diet. As he loaded up his plate, she scooped a cup of steamed white rice from one carton and a few pieces of broccoli from the beef and broccoli vat. She stopped short of rinsing off the greasy oyster sauce.

When Olive was little, she and Steve used to look forward to nights alone when she had sleepovers or went to her grandparents'. Olive was often gone now, but instead of being exciting, like playing hooky from parenting, these nights felt bleak: like a preview of their lives once Olive was out of the house. Tonight, they ate quietly, making small talk about the various things that demanded their attention: the guest room that needed cleaning out, the clogged drain in Olive's bathroom, a charge on the credit card for a custom leotard Lindsay had ordered from Japan.

Steve was the one who handled their finances: he took care of the bills, invested, put money into a savings account, into Olive's college fund. She worried about that money, wondered if they'd be allowed to access it for a pre-professional ballet program instead of a university. Steve didn't like the idea of Olive forgoing college; he thought it was ridiculous to even consider. This was one of many things he and Lindsay disagreed on, the starting point of most arguments lately. Tonight, apparently, would be no exception.

"The next SAT date is October fifth," he said. "I signed her up today."

"She has rehearsals on Saturdays," Lindsay said.

"She can miss one rehearsal."

"I thought we'd decided she wasn't taking the SATs," Lindsay said.

"Well, *I* decided that it's smart not to close any doors." He dumped another mound of greasy lo mein noodles on his plate.

"She doesn't want to go to college, Steve. She wants to dance."

"She can dance in college. Probably even get a scholarship," he argued, though she'd told him again and again that this was not the typical path for a classical ballet dancer. Contemporary dancers, modern dancers, those were the girls who could go to a traditional college. If you were a classical ballet dancer, companies wanted you young. She often thought of the whole process like the fattening of calves for veal. No matter what you did, you couldn't make veal from a cow.

Olive would be eighteen soon. Lindsay feared she might even be too old already. Some companies started snatching girls up at sixteen, seventeen. She had studied the rosters of second-company dancers on the websites of every major company in the U.S. Some looked like babies still in their headshots: so many elongated necks and bare shoulders. Translucent skin hardly touched by the sun.

"And what will she do when her dance career ends at twenty-five? Wait tables?"

She winced. Steve had met her when she, herself, was waiting tables. Living with her parents to save money while she studied for her real estate license. God, he could be such an ass.

"I suppose she could find some rich guy to marry," she snapped. "Pop out a kid or two. Maybe get her real estate license. Build a career and reputation from the ground up."

Steve scowled. "You know that's not what I meant."

"She knows you don't believe in her," she said, shaking her head and loading her plate with the salad she'd put together when he called from the Chinese restaurant. "You pushing for her to go to college gives her the message that you don't believe she can make it as a dancer."

"Well, can she?" he snapped. "I mean, *really*? She's not even the best dancer at her own studio. There are at least two or three girls that are better than she is."

Lindsay felt like he'd taken his chopstick and stabbed her.

"It's not about being 'the best,'" she said. "It's about being an artist. Having a special quality. Every company wants something different. She just needs to find the right match." But maybe he was right. Just because you wanted something badly didn't make it possible. You can't will things into being; their floundering marriage was case in point.

"How many of Vivienne's students have gone on to be professional dancers?" he asked.

"What?"

"How many of her students have gotten actual *jobs*?"

"Well, there's Amber," she said. Amber Markopoulos was Vivienne's star student five years ago. She left home at sixteen for a school aligned with a company in Germany. She'd gone on to dance in the corps for a year before snapping her Achilles. "She would still be there if she hadn't been injured. Hugh is at Boston." Hugh had left Vivienne's for Boston's school and had slowly risen to the second company and then to the corps. "Sarah Nelson is a trainee at Joffrey."

"So nobody is getting a paycheck right now? Not one of her dancers?"

"I just *told you*, Hugh is in the corps at Boston."

"*Girls,*" he said. "You told me yourself it's easier for boys."

Though it was true—boys did have an easier time—she felt like he was challenging her. He always needed to be right, to have the last word. And for years, decades, she'd let him. Until recently, she knew exactly what her role was: to give in. For twenty years, she'd been rolling over. But now she couldn't stop pushing back. Stupid menopause. It was making her crazy. It was making her fed up. With everything. She'd gone from being a doormat to being a doorstop.

"What do you want me to say, Steve?" she asked, setting down her fork.

"What do you mean?"

"I mean, what is it you want from me? Do you want me to tell you you're right? That she doesn't have a chance at this? That the last fifteen years were some sort of huge mistake?"

"You're being ridiculous," he said, and stood up, leaving his plate at the table. "I don't need to be yelled at. I worked my ass off all week. I'm exhausted. I'm going to go relax on the couch. If you calm down and would like to join me, to have a nice night in, that's up to you."

Calm down? She hated him. God, how she hated him.

As she stood up, she felt that dreadful tingle again. The *bump.* She'd thought tonight she could do some reconnaissance. They were long overdue for their monthly roll in the hay. While they were at it, she could do some snooping. If it was what she worried it might be, there would have to be some evidence of it on him, too, right? But there was no way in hell now. (Though she wished a pox upon him. All *over* him.) Instead, she studied the table littered with the remains of dinner and started to take the plates to the sink. But then she stopped, set them down.

Normally, she'd put the salad in Tupperware, wrap the leftover Chinese for him to bring to work for lunch on Monday.

I worked my ass off all week, he'd said.

Well, I worked too, you shithead, she mumbled, and she left everything there. Let him deal with it. She was going to bed. But first she was going to put some more cream on that bump and try to make it all just disappear.

Josie

Josie heard Savvy and Olive pull up, the mechanical whir of the garage door, the bell-like tinkle of their laughter. She'd insisted at first that Savvy keep the fact that Etienne was living in the guesthouse a secret, but realized this would effectively mean that Savvy wouldn't be able to have friends over until the holidays, and frankly, she loved it when the girls came over. Especially with Mark gone now, she liked having them around.

When Savvy had asked if Olive could stay over Saturday after *Nutcracker* auditions, Josie had agreed but made her promise they'd leave Etienne alone, though most nights, he didn't come back home until almost three a.m. anyway, and the girls would likely already be fast asleep by then. And so what if they did run into him? He was just a tenant, and she was his landlady. Though it did sound a bit porny when you put it like that. She still swore Olive to secrecy. The other girls could not know; the *moms* could not know.

"Remember. Not a word," she reminded Olive now, pulling out a couple of fizzy waters from the fridge. "The moms might get the wrong idea. That his being here gives Sav an unfair advantage."

"I promise." Olive made to zip her lips.

"Like it matters anyway," Savvy said, sounding defeated. "He's probably already decided who he's giving the scholarship to."

"What makes you say that?" Josie said, feeling anger bubbling up in her throat along with the sip of chardonnay she'd just taken.

"Well, he's *all over* Bea."

"What do you mean?" Josie asked.

"Oh, nothing. Whatever. Can we get Domino's?"

Josie thought about the three hundred dollars she'd dropped on healthy crap at Whole Foods quietly spoiling (no preservatives!) in her cupboard.

"Sure," she said.

By ten o'clock, she was starting to get a headache. Wine always gave her a headache; but she didn't like beer and, other than the occasional poolside margarita, drinking cocktails at home made her feel like an alcoholic. Tonight, she'd had at least three full glasses, enjoying gossiping with the girls as they talked about the studio, about the documentary, about the scholarship. About the fact that Etienne had cast Bea in the lead, and what that meant for the rest of them.

"So, Bea must have improved a lot over the summer?" Josie asked. Savvy's comment about Etienne being *all over her* kept niggling at her.

"I guess." Savvy shrugged and turned to Olive. "Oh my god, did you hear Jaz in the bathroom after auditions? She told me it's the stomach flu, but I'm kind of worried about her. She's super bummed about Clara."

"I've heard her before," Olive said, and Josie put her hands over her ears and made a point of *la-la-la*-ing. She did not want to have to decide whether to share this with Melissa, though it was probably nothing serious. Half the time, girls Jaz's age just wanted people to *think* they had eating disorders.

Olive was reaching for another slice, and Josie had to resist the urge to tell her maybe she should take it easy on the pizza. That was Lindsay's job. Josie was Olive's friend, not her mom.

Eventually, she left the girls alone downstairs to watch *Center Stage* for the millionth time. They needed their space, after all; she wasn't one of *those* moms, always up in their business. There was a balance, she thought, between being fun and being *annoying*.

Lying in bed, she opened Instagram, but she was a little too buzzed to focus. She woke up when her phone dropped onto her lap, and she reached over to click off her light. Of course, now she was wide awake, her head pounding. Then she heard splashing sounds.

She'd taken out her contacts and couldn't find her glasses, and when she stood up to look out the window, she felt seriously woozy. Outside she could see the eerie aqua glow of the pool and make out a blurry Savvy, sitting on the steps in the shallow end, her golden hair, tipped in blue, like a mermaid's in the iridescent blue light. Josie scanned the backyard, searching for Olive, but didn't see her anywhere. Oh, there she was, on the chaise lounge behind the palm tree, wrapped in a fluffy pink towel. Between the wine and her shitty eyes, it was a bit of a blur.

She should have opened the windows and called the girls in. They were right outside the guesthouse. What if Etienne came out? No, she was being ridiculous. He probably wasn't even home. And if he was, it was harmless. Just a little night swimming, and it had been so very, very hot.

Act II, Scene II

Ever

"Good morning!" Ever said brightly as she walked into her classroom at The Center on Monday morning. It was only nine o'clock, but the room was already sticky with heat. She wondered if the heat wave would ever break.

While anyone was welcome to join The Center's writing groups, the demographic leaned toward the retirement set. Eighty-year-old Henry was always the first one there. Today, he was perched in his favorite spot at the table by the window, sunlight falling on his black-and-white-marbled composition book. In his former life, he'd been an entertainment attorney. Betty, a retired psychiatric nurse, arrived as Ever was struggling to get the heavy window open to let some air in. The building was old, and the windows were impossible. Betty was followed by Sid and Clementine. The oldest in the group, they had been married a stunning sixty years; they wore matching royal blue tracksuits their kids had made. *#CoupleGoals*, Bea joked when Ever talked about them. Doris was out today, and so Martha was last, pushing her walker slowly through the doorway, scowling. Poor Martha was rage on a plate some days, and it looked like today might be one of those days.

"Good morning, Martha," Ever said sweetly, gently touching the old woman's stooped shoulder before making her way back to the conference table to set up her laptop and pull out her Sticky Note-marked books. Ever liked to begin each class with a prompt before having them freewrite for twenty minutes or so.

"Okay, guys, let's go ahead and get started . . ."

Someone knocked gently on the open door before peering in.

Bob?

Phoebe's dad, from the studio, stood at the entrance to the class-room, looking lost.

"Bob!" she said, "Are you here for . . . ?"

Bob was a widower raising three girls on his own. The youngest had just started kindergarten. He, like Ever, had lost his spouse to a freak accident (something involving a city garbage truck?). It was a strange thing to have in common with someone. Maybe he was here for the bereavement group? There was a group of grieving widows and widowers that met down the hall on Mondays, as well. Some-times they had to shut the door when the crying got too loud. But no, he had a notebook tucked under his arm and seemed hesitant.

"Hi. Um, Lindsay mentioned a while back that you led a writing group, and I've been meaning to start writing again, so I thought I'd give it a try. Can I—I mean, is it okay to just walk in?"

The other members of the group were studying him warily, pro-prietary about their group. Ever waited for Martha to make some snide comment and send him packing.

"Guys!" Ever said to break the tension. "This is my friend, Bob. His daughter dances with Bea." This would melt the ice. They all loved Bea and Danny. Some of them had known the kids since they were in elementary school. There had been many sick days when Danny or Bea had to come with her to class: coloring books at the ready.

Bob had buzz-cut blond hair and was short and muscular, like a wrestler or a gymnast. Phoebe, who was willowy and tall, must have taken after her mother. Bob was a friendly guy, a sort of mas-cot among the moms. She and Lindsay had even tried to show him how to sew pointe shoes, but his fingers were too thick and clumsy. They had all taken Bob under their respective wings at some point. Phoebe, too. Dads weren't allowed in the dressing rooms, of course, and so they'd made sure she always had help backstage.

It was odd to have her worlds colliding this way, but stranger things had happened.

Bob waved awkwardly to the group and took a seat near the far end of the table.

"That's Doris's seat," Martha snapped.

Bob jumped up, his face reddening. "Oh, sorry! Is there a better spot?"

Clementine motioned to the seat next to Doris's empty one. Doris wouldn't be there today because she'd just had oral surgery. TEN TEETH REMOVED, she'd emailed earlier.

After everyone had gotten settled in, Ever said, "Bob, why don't you introduce yourself. Tell us a bit about who you are and what you're working on. Why you'd like to join the group?"

Bob explained that now that his youngest daughter was in school, he was hoping he could get back to a novel he'd been writing off and on since he graduated from college. He said he'd set it aside when his wife passed, but now, he figured, was as good a time as any to pull it out again. Who knew! *Bob*, an aspiring writer. She wondered for a moment how it was he could be in a writing class on a Monday morning instead of busy at work and then recalled something Nancy had said about his wife's accident. He'd won a huge settlement with the city. She felt a stitch of envy at the thought of her own disastrous insurance situation.

"Well, welcome," she said. She pulled out her folder and read from her list of ideas. She quickly selected a poem by Philip Larkin, "Home Is So Sad," to read as a prompt. It had always spoken to her, this sad elegy to a home, but even more so now.

She knew the poem by heart, but she held the book up to give her eyes a place to rest as she read aloud. It was a short poem, just two stanzas, but by the time she got to the end, she felt a swell of emotion. She hoped nobody noticed the hitch in her voice.

"Today, we're going to write about *home*. It can be a place or just a feeling. Twenty minutes." She sat down with her laptop open and began to write, trying to capture that feeling the poem evoked, her mind wandering to their kitchen table, that oak centerpiece where her family's life had played out over the last nearly twenty years.

The first night she and Ethan had spent in the house, the only furniture they had was what had been left behind: a lumpy double bed, a stained fold-out couch, and this table. It, like the house, had been in Ethan's family for as long as he could remember. He told her that he and his brothers used to put a blanket over it to make a fort when they were little. He'd shown her all the quirks of the house: the loose floorboard in a closet that lifted to reveal a hiding place. The attic where they used to stash bottles of beer pilfered from their dad. The view of the pier from the smallest bedroom, and the fireworks released off the end most summer nights.

She was in the throes of morning sickness the day they moved in, able to do little but lie on the uncomfortable bed and stare at the ceiling. (*See, doesn't that water stain look like boobs?!* he'd said and laughed, and she'd imagined him and his brothers staring at their X-rated ceiling.) He'd spent the day running trips back and forth to the hardware store, to thrift stores, to friends', gathering the things they needed. When her nausea subsided, she went to the kitchen and made spaghetti. Then she'd gone through her own boxes holding her meager collection of things and found an Indian-print tapestry, which she laid over the table. She realized with delight that it hung almost all the way to the floor. She gathered some candles and ducked underneath. He found her there when he returned, their dinner picnic-style in the fort she'd made. He'd brought her ginger ale and clinked his beer bottle against her glass, before leaning forward and kissing her. *Welcome home*, he'd said.

Later, as everyone was leaving the classroom, Bob lingered, writing her a check. "I'm so glad you're joining us," she said to him as she gathered her things.

"Thanks. And congrats to Beatrice," Bob said. "Phoebe told me about her getting cast as Marie. She must be so excited to have the lead. Whatever anybody else says, I think Etienne being here is good for the studio. Giving some of the *other* girls a chance for once."

Was that a bit of snark? She thought of Bob as being sort of oblivious to the rumblings at the studio, the grievances of the mothers.

But here he was, quietly acknowledging exactly what they all had been thinking but never, ever saying—except in whispers. It *was* time for someone else to get a chance. Someone other than Savannah Jacobs.

"Thanks," Ever said, ignoring his innuendo. She didn't want to be one of those nasty parents talking behind the kids' backs. "Bea's really excited. Nervous, too, of course."

Bob hoisted his messenger bag up and over his shoulder. "I'm going to be helping Etienne build the sets," Bob said. "I'm not very good with a needle and thread, but I'm pretty good with power tools."

"The sets?"

For years and years, Vivienne had used the same backdrops and props for *The Nutcracker*: the Christmas tree that grew during Clara's dream scene, the sleigh that took her and the Nutcracker Prince off to the Land of the Sweets. The thrones, where they sat during the second act, the giant lollipops and oversized foil-covered candies.

"Etienne wants all new backdrops and props. He asked me if I could help him out."

"Oh," she said. Etienne had been talking to Bob? So far as Ever knew, Etienne didn't speak to the parents at all. He certainly hadn't spoken to Ever. He didn't even acknowledge the parents unless he had to, avoiding the lobby and greenroom where they congregated. He, like Vivienne, was *aloof*. She figured it was a French thing. She tried to picture Etienne approaching Bob, asking for his help. He wouldn't speak to the mothers, but he'd talk to Bob?

"That's great," she said. "The old sets are pretty tired."

"He's got some terrific ideas. We went down to Tijuana together yesterday and checked out a backdrop rental company."

"Mexico?" she asked. Etienne and Bob had driven all the way to Tijuana together?

"They have a really vibrant arts community down there. I had no idea. The backdrops are hand-painted, beautiful. Cheaper to buy down there than to rent here. And I've got a truck."

"Wow, that's great," she repeated dumbly. "It will be a beautiful production, I'm sure."

Ever felt dizzy, trying to process what she was hearing. Etienne and Bob were best friends now?

"Well, thanks for letting me join the group," he said, and awkwardly made his way to the door. "I'll see you at the studio for rehearsals on Saturday?"

"Sure thing," she said, but she was distracted, a strange pit in her stomach.

Bea

Saturday was the first day of rehearsals, and Vivienne had finally posted the official cast list. A crowd was hovering and buzzing at the bulletin board. Little girls on tiptoes, older kids standing back and squinting to see over them. Of course, Bea already knew her part, and so she waited until the group had scattered to quickly snap a photo of the list, pretending she was just taking a picture of the rehearsal schedule hanging next to it.

As she stretched, she studied the cast list, her eyes widening. Her being cast as Marie was only the first upset. Second, *Phoebe* had been cast as Snow Queen. Everyone wanted a chance at Snow Queen with the gorgeous towering crystal tiara; the older girls in Level 6 were going to be pissed. Phoebe was a beautiful dancer, and once the older girls were gone, she would definitely start getting more attention. Even so, Miss V. would never have given this role to her. She was only fourteen. Bea scanned the lobby and saw Phoebe standing with her dad, Bob; he was beaming at her, squeezing both of her hands.

Bea looked back at the list, zoomed in and searched for Savvy's name. Savvy had been cast as both Dewdrop and Spanish lead, as well as in Snow corps. Of course, Savvy was upset about not getting Marie, but to Bea, this seemed like a pretty good alternative. Lots of challenges, lots of time onstage. Maybe even more than Marie.

Another shocker: Jaz had not only not been cast as Clara (since there was no Clara), but she wasn't cast as one of the dolls, either. Instead, she'd been relegated to Party Girl and a Rat. Just like every other twelve- and thirteen-year-old at the studio. Bea quickly looked around the lobby again; she didn't see Jaz anywhere. Melissa was going to be livid.

Zoraiya would be Arabian lead, just as Bea had expected. She searched the list for Mirliton, assuming this is where Olive would be, but her name wasn't there, either. She kept searching and finally found Olive under "Waltz of the Flowers." A corps role. She studied the Snow list, too, but Olive's name wasn't there, either. Her heart sank. For the past eight years, she and Olive had always read the cast list together, excited when they got to be in the same scenes. Disappointed when they were separated. But this was horrible.

She watched as Olive made her way to the bulletin board and expectantly scanned the list with her finger; then, understanding followed by disappointment setting in. It didn't matter that Olive and she were going through a rough patch. This wasn't fair. She wanted nothing more than to go talk to her, to give her a hug. But there was Savvy, putting her arm around Olive's shoulder, leading her away from the list.

Bea swallowed hard and looked back down at her phone, zooming in on the rehearsal schedule. The morning would be dedicated to the Party Scene, then Snow, with Miss V. and Etienne both directing. In the afternoon, Miss V. and Eloise would take the younger kids to rehearse the Fight scene, while Etienne worked with all the Act II roles. Tomorrow, Sunday, were the soloists: *Marie, Snow Queen, and Dewdrop.* Her, Phoebe, and Savvy. *Great.*

The Party Scene in *The Nutcracker* was mostly pantomime and acting, very little dancing. Bea had never been Clara. The year she was the right height was in seventh grade, but that year, Mary was cast, with Savvy—who was new that year—as understudy. Bea had danced nearly every role *but* the lead. She could do the Party scene in her sleep. Even though she'd never been Clara, she'd learned the choreography (always quietly memorizing, marking on the side).

In Etienne's version, the key story elements were the same, but as the morning progressed, and he taught them the choreography, the whole thing felt a bit darker somehow. Drosselmeyer had always creeped her out, but in Etienne's version, his role was even darker. His "toys"—the Harlequin and Columbine dolls—were more lifeless and puppet-like than in Miss V.'s version. It felt sort of sinister.

Etienne had little patience for the younger kids. After only an hour, he dismissed them all. "Isn't it, *comment dit-on? Nap time?*" Jaz gave Bea a look somewhere between shock and accusation as she picked up her things and left when Etienne shooed them out.

Etienne paced back and forth across the floor, as if trying to decide what to do next. This was hardly the methodical process that Miss V. employed for rehearsals. He completely ditched the posted schedule after only an hour.

"I am tired of Act I," he said. "Where are the Arabs?"

"The *Arabs?*" Phoebe whispered to Bea.

"You know." He pressed his palms together over his head, wriggled his hips.

"The *Arabians?*" Bea said to him, mortified.

"*Oui!*" he said, and clapped.

"Um, I think the schedule says Act II parts don't need to be back until two," Phoebe said.

"They are not here?" he said, frowning.

"They might be? People come early to warm up sometimes."

Savvy and Olive had shown up together. But the boys weren't there yet. Nick and Luke had been cast in Russian; Owen would be Chinese. No Snow King; Phoebe would be doing a solo for Snow. Someone must have clued the boys in to the cast list.

She'd heard mumblings that Nick and Luke were planning to try out for another studio's *Nutcracker*. They were both good enough to get the role of Cavalier in any of the other local studios' productions, all of which were desperate for boys. Owen, however, said he'd be happy with whatever part he got. Only Nick seemed seriously put out. Nick, like Savvy, was the default lead in every production. Bea hated his audacity, the way he assumed that the role belonged to him. Ever since the auditions, he'd been acting like a kid who got his sand bucket stolen at the beach.

The beach. The bonfire. She'd put that fractured night inside a special box in her mind, closed it, locked it up, but she could still taste the metallic key on her tongue.

"Tell them to come in," Etienne said to Phoebe, who poked her head out into the lobby and beckoned the Arabian girls in.

Bea stretched off to the side by the door, observing.

"You must be like a *snake*," he said to Zoraiya. Bea had always thought she was an amazing dancer, though Zoraiya only took ballet to improve her technique for modern and contemporary. Bea followed her dance account on Instagram and could never reconcile the powerful, confident dancer she saw there with the daintier version of Zoraiya in this studio. Zoraiya was a senior, too, and would be auditioning for companies and schools in January, as well; she wanted to dance with Alvin Ailey one day, and Bea had no doubt she would.

Etienne demonstrated the choreography, the serpentine moves of his choreography.

"Pretend there is a man who is playing this music. The . . . ?" he looked to Bea, pantomiming someone playing a flute.

"Snake charmer?" she offered.

"Yes!" he said, and clapped his hands. "There is a *charmer*, who is using his music to make you dance."

Zoraiya was accustomed to moving her body in this way. The other three Arabian girls tittered and stiffly tried to follow along.

"Good, good," he said as Zoraiya danced, his eyes focused on her.

"But you girls," he said, waving his arms dismissively at the other three. "You dance like a rubber chicken."

They giggled again. But he wasn't laughing.

"Go."

"What?" Lizzy said.

"I need snakes, not chickens," he said. "Fly away." With that, he waved his arms dismissively. When the girls stood there, stunned, dumb, he flapped his arms and clucked.

The three girls walked briskly past her, leaving just Bea and Zoraiya in the studio, and Etienne clasped his hands together as if in prayer, then bowed to Zoraiya, who smiled. *"Merci, merci.* That is all for today. Now, you, come," Etienne said, motioning to Bea.

She scrambled to her feet, tucking the loose end of her ribbon in near her ankle.

Lotte sat perched on a stool in the corner, quietly filming. She'd been at every class so far. She couldn't figure out how old Lotte was exactly; she could be as young as twenty, but maybe as old as thirty. She was as thin as a dancer herself, and very *French.* Black hair swept into a sleek ponytail that ran down her back like an actual pony's tail. She wore tight camisoles without a bra and loose-fitting jeans, rolled up. Bea wondered if she was a dancer, too. A few girls thought she might be Etienne's girlfriend, but Bea wasn't sure. They smoked together during breaks. Lotte brought him coffee and Mexican food from Ralberto's, which seemed more like something an assistant would do than a girlfriend, though maybe in France, this is what girlfriends did. Or maybe this is what Etienne Bernay's girlfriend did.

Lotte was in the far corner of the studio, fiddling with the camera she kept on a tripod, and Bea stood awkwardly in the center as he went to his laptop to search for the music. But it wasn't the "Dance of the Sugar Plum Fairy" that began to play; rather, the music for Snow.

"In Nureyev's version," he said, sitting down on the bench, "Drosselmeyer and the Prince are played by the same dancer. They are both Marie's . . ." he said, twirling his finger by his head. *"Son rêve.* Her *dream*? She is dreaming of her lover."

Bea felt her skin prickle, as the haunting music filled the studio. Snow had always been her favorite, but now it embarrassed her.

"Close your eyes and *écoute,*" he said, and tapped his ear. *"Listen."*

She dutifully closed her eyes. She sensed him walking to the floor and moving behind her. Still, when she felt his fingers on her ribs, light as snowflakes, she caught her breath. Her eyes shot open, but she squeezed them shut again when his reflection *tsk-tsk*ed her in the mirror.

"In this version," he said, "Marie is a little girl in Act One; then in Act Two, the dark magician is transformed into her prince, and she is transformed from a girl into a young woman. The snow queen casts the spell."

The music felt different now, a haunting lament. Her heart felt heavy as the wordless chorus began.

"Okay. Now watch," he said. She opened her eyes, and he quickly demonstrated the choreography. She imprinted it in her memory the way she had trained herself to do.

"Tu comprends?"

Bea felt like she was floating, as if she had become completely disembodied. She was always so acutely aware of her body: every sinew, every muscle, every joint and bone and breath. Sometimes she felt like she was *only* a body. As if her skin were the only real thing. But here, now, she felt transcendent. Bea's dad used to meditate on the deck as the sun rose. *What's it like?* she'd asked. *Peaceful*, he said. *Try it.* She had never had any luck with meditating, but dancing occupied her body and quieted her mind.

Now, as the choreography became one with her body, as her muscles memorized the movements, her thoughts stilled. When she stopped, she realized she hadn't been breathing except in shallow sips and felt like she was gulping for breath.

Etienne had moved to the front of the studio with his back to the mirrors. His muscled arms were crossed and his head tilted.

"You have seventeen years, no?" he asked.

She nodded.

"When is your birthday?"

"June twentieth," she said.

"Aha. So, on June nineteen, you are a little girl. But when you wake up in the morning on June twenty, and you are not a little girl anymore. While you sleep, you *transform*."

He moved behind her again, studying them both in the mirror.

"Relevé," he said, his fingers nudging her ribs. She rose *en pointe*, lifted her leg into *passé*, and he began to turn her. "It is magic, yes?"

She was both here and not here. Both awake and asleep. Both girl and woman. In the mirror, she could see the tattoo on his arm. It was a snake, curling around and around his bicep, to his collarbone, forked tongue licking his neck. *Charmed.* She blinked hard, as if waking from a dream, and looked to the corner—embarrassed, realizing that Lotte had been filming this whole time. But when Bea looked to the camera, the red eye blinking at them, Lotte just smiled and winked at her.

Lindsay

Well??? Lindsay texted Olive.

Olive had spent the night at Savvy's, so the girls had gone straight to the studio this morning. Nancy told Lindsay earlier in the week that the cast list would be posted today. But Olive didn't respond, and as the morning progressed and no answer came, Lindsay worried this could only mean bad news. She'd thought about texting Ever or Josie to ask if they'd seen the list yet, but both of their girls already knew their parts. Besides, she was starting to have a bad feeling about all of this.

What time should I get you? she tried at noon. No response.

Then at three o'clock, just as Lindsay pulled into the CLCB lot, her phone dinged: **Going to S's again tonight Don't come**

She huffed and parked the car next to Ever's Volvo. Ever was sitting in the driver's seat, working on her laptop. She thought about texting Olive again about the casting, but knew she'd probably not get an answer. She was here now, anyway; she could check the cast list herself.

Maybe you guys should invite Bea? she wrote, but Olive ignored this, too.

She and Ever hadn't spoken at all about the apparent dissolution of the girls' friendship, but she could feel it between them, a trembling current.

She got out of the car and tapped on the Volvo's passenger window. Ever looked up, startled, and rolled the window down.

"Hi!" Ever said brightly.

"Are you working?" she asked, motioning to the laptop.

"No! I mean yes, but I'm glad you're here. Oh! I brought you some CBD. Come sit."

Lindsay climbed into the passenger seat. Ever had suggested she try CBD for her little issue. If it could prevent an epileptic seizure, maybe it could make her bump disappear, too.

Lindsay leaned over and gave Ever a hug. Ever closed her laptop and reached into her bag, pulling out a little brown bottle.

"This was Ethan's. Different brand than the one I use. It's all yours. But you really should talk to somebody at the dispensary about dosage. Are you taking it orally? Or, are you, like, just putting it directly on it?"

Lindsay hadn't really thought about it. She hadn't read beyond the Google search results confirming she wasn't the only one to try to make a potential STD go away with cannabis. She'd been, frankly, too worried to start clicking through. She'd assumed the application was topical, but now she didn't know. Maybe she'd try that first? Put it in her tea if that didn't do any good?

"Will I get—um—high?"

Ever laughed. "No, CBD doesn't have the THC. This is pure medicine. But if you want, I have some of that too?"

Lindsay blushed and shook her head. "No, that's okay. But thank you for this," she said, and put the vial in her purse. "How much do I owe you?" she asked, but Ever waved her hand dismissively. The last time she refused money for something, Lindsay quietly Venmoed her some cash. Yes. She'd do that again. She'd already researched the cost; a bottle like this was about sixty-five dollars. Almost enough for a new pair of pointe shoes. Olive told her Bea had auditioned on a dead pair. She should also look through Olive's stash and see what she had. She and Bea wore the same brand, model, and size even, though Bea's feet were one width size narrower. She recalled she had at least a few pairs she'd ordered last summer, ones she'd sewn ribbons onto before realizing she'd gotten the wrong width. There was no returning them at that point, and she hadn't gotten around to trying to sell them to anybody at the studio.

"A new book?" Lindsay asked, gesturing to her laptop. She knew how paralyzed Ever had been ever since her last book came out. Lindsay had loved *Black Evenings*; it was beautiful and powerful. She didn't understand publishing at all. It seemed like a cruel business. Not so different from ballet, she thought.

"I think so!" Ever brightened. "I'm putting together a proposal for my agent. Hoping to get it sent off next week."

"That's awesome," Lindsay said. "I really need a new book to read."

"Well, we'll see if this one goes anywhere."

"Listen, I'll let you get back to work. I need to go see the cast list. Olive is totally ignoring my texts."

At the mention of Olive, she saw Ever stiffen.

Lindsay sighed. "So, listen, I'm not sure what's going on between the girls, but I'm sorry. I hate this."

Ever's eyes grew glossy, but she seemed grateful that someone had finally acknowledged the elephant stomping through the room. "Me, too."

"Do you want me to talk to Olive about it?" Lindsay asked.

Ever shook her head. "They don't need us interfering. It might make it worse."

"Okay," Lindsay said. "I'm sure it's just a little squabble between sisters."

"I hope so," Ever said, but she seemed unconvinced.

Lindsay heard the yelling before she even opened the studio door. Melissa stood at the counter, one hand clutching Jaz's dance bag and the other gesturing wildly.

"This is *ridiculous*," she said to Nancy, and a few heads swiveled around. "We've been at this studio for *five years*. Between tuition and privates, we literally pay the rent here. Then this *narcissist* comes in and starts messing with our daughters' futures? And for what? Some stupid documentary? Why is Vivienne allowing this to happen? She is going to lose students, *good* students. I am so freaking close to pulling Jaz."

"Well, if you pull her now, there's no refund on the performance fee," Nancy said coldly. She did not suffer being yelled at *at all*.

"I'm not talking about the production," Melissa said. "I'm talking about pulling her from CLCB." With that, she turned on her very high heels and reached for Jaz, who was standing back, head hung low.

When Melissa realized her tantrum was on full display, and that Lindsay had been watching, Melissa stopped. Her face was red, her free fist clenched.

"You and Steve should consider pulling Olive, too," she said. "She didn't get jack shit, either."

Hearing Melissa say Steve's name made her hot, but then the rest of what she'd said registered. She walked swiftly to the cast list and ran her finger down the list. No Olive, not anywhere, except for Flowers.

Josie

Melissa called on Sunday morning as Josie was pulling home-made muffins out of the oven. The sweet steam wafted into her face and made her eyes sting.

"I don't know what to do," Melissa said. "All the other studios have already cast their *Nutcracker*s. Where would we even go?"

This wouldn't be the first time Melissa left CLCB. She'd always been a studio-hopper, jumping from one place to the next when she didn't get her way. She'd moved all the way to Vegas for six months for Jaz to train at a school that was cranking out competition winners. She'd only come back to CLCB because of some rift with the studio owner. She could find another studio if she was willing to relocate again, but she, like Josie, knew that Vivienne was the best there was. She'd be stupid to pull her now. There was a bunch of girls graduating this year, and once they were gone, Vivienne's attention and focus would shift to Jaz and Phoebe.

Josie plucked the hot muffins from the tins and arranged them on a plate.

"None of this stuff with Etienne is appropriate," Melissa said.

Josie tensed. "What do you mean, appropriate?"

"Letting him hijack *Nutcracker*, Vivienne having you hide him in your guesthouse. Can you imagine what will happen when that comes out?"

"How would it come out?"

"Well, you said Olive knows, right? All she has to do is slip up and say something to Lindsay or Steve . . . Steve says she talks to him more than she talks to Lindsay lately."

"Where did you see Steve?" she asked. Olive's dad never came to the studio.

"I talked to him at the memorial. Why?"

"Is something going on with you and Steve Chase?" Josie blurted, and then lowered her voice, remembering Olive was upstairs with Savvy after sleeping over again.

"What the hell does that mean?" Melissa asked.

"Just a vibe," Josie said.

"I *like* Steve. He's a good guy. What's wrong with that?"

"He's *married*," Josie said. Again.

"I know that," Melissa said. "Jesus. I thought we were talking about Etienne."

"Sorry," Josie said, but she'd had a bad feeling about this since the memorial. She didn't feel particularly loyal to any of the moms at the studio, but Melissa being so casual about another woman's husband pissed her off. Though she *had* caught Lindsay flirting with that HVAC guy, so maybe Steve was fair game?

"So, what are you going to do?" Josie said. "About Jaz."

Melissa sighed. "I don't know. I feel like we should probably stick it out until the scholarship is announced, but we already know who's getting that."

Normally, she'd assume she meant Savvy, but for some reason, Josie felt her spine go rigid. "Really? Who?"

"Seriously?" Melissa scoffed. "*Beatrice*. Jaz says he's totally obsessed with her."

"What does that mean?" Josie asked, though Savvy had said basically the same thing.

"Jaz said he uses her to demonstrate everything, and she's the only one he offers corrections to. It seems like he's already made up his mind."

Josie needed to take all of this with a grain of salt. Melissa was pissed that Jaz had been passed over for the lead. This was just her jealousy and anger coming out. Josie was sure Etienne wasn't *obsessed* with Beatrice. Seriously. Sure, she'd gotten the lead, but Savvy had been entrusted with *two* major roles. Maybe if she talked to Etienne, she could get a sense of what it was he was looking for. It was his scholarship, after all, one he was sponsoring himself. She just needed to find out what he wanted in a dancer and make sure Savvy gave it to him.

It was Sunday, and Savvy had rehearsals with the other soloists for the first time today. Nancy said the film crew would be conducting interviews with the girls today, too. Savvy could really turn it on when there were lights and cameras on her. She had this going for her, anyway. Not like that meek little waif, Beatrice, who practically withered if you spoke to her.

"Give yourself a couple days to cool off. You'll figure it out," she said to Melissa. Then she remembered what the girls had said about Jaz throwing up. "Hey, is Jaz doing okay?"

"She's fine." Melissa frowned. "Just heartbroken."

Upstairs, Savvy and Olive were still sleeping. Josie had gotten up early to make these healthy muffins, using the almond flour and flaxseeds she'd gotten on her Whole Foods spree. Now she placed a few of them, hot to the touch, into a cloth napkin and made her way out through the patio doors to the guesthouse.

The heat had finally broken; the morning air even had a bit of a bite to it. It was fall, after all, almost October now. Steam rose off the heated pool. She'd go for a swim later.

She knocked tentatively on Etienne's door, and then a bit louder when there was no response. Eventually, she heard some rustling inside. When he opened the door, he was wearing only a pair of boxer briefs, and a slow grin. *Jesus*, Josie thought. He stretched one arm over his head, the other stifling a yawn. Stupidly, she held the muffins out to him.

"*Dancer fuel*," she said. "I made them for Savvy and Olive. Almond butter, banana, and date. With flaxseeds. Gluten-free, too."

He took a muffin, tore off the top, and popped it in his mouth, chewing a couple of times before swallowing. His Adam's apple bobbed; and she remembered the time when she was eight and a neighbor boy made her watch while he fed a live mouse to his snake.

"And I really just wanted to say thank you. Savvy's so grateful for the roles. She's done Sugar Plum so many times, she's super excited to learn Dewdrop and Spanish. To expand her repertoire."

He cocked his head and seemed to be trying to quash a second yawn.

"Anyway," she said, feeling like an awkward teenager. "I should get the girls up. Long day ahead for all of you." She turned to go.

"She's very good," he said.

"What's that?" she asked, turning back to him.

"*Ta fille.* Savannah," he said. "That is why you are here, with your . . . *muffins?*"

She focused on the center of the target tattoo on his chest, because she couldn't look him in the eye.

He peeled the accordioned paper wrapper off the muffin bottom and ate it, and Josie felt her body radiating the heat of her embarrassment. Seriously, what was she, thirteen?

"She works very hard," she said. This was the response she had crafted over many years of Savvy being the standout student: humble while still acknowledging the truth of the compliment. But it also asserted that Savvy had earned every bit of praise being offered.

"They all work hard," he said. "But some want it more. They are hungry."

Yes, that was exactly it. This was what truly differentiated the girls at this point. Thanks to Vivienne, they all had nearly flawless technique. Some were gifted with artistry, as well. But the desire? You couldn't teach passion. Olive seemed to have lost it. Jazmin didn't have it, not really (though Melissa had it in spades). Even Mary, for all her natural facility and ability, was just as content playing a game of water polo as she was performing a solo variation. But Savvy? She *wanted* it. Badly. And he could see that. He had to know Savvy wasn't like any of the others. That she was special. But he hadn't said "She is hungry." He'd said, "They." He was talking about not just Savvy but Bea as well, with her raw ambition. Josie had seen it, too. Bea was like every lovesick girl she'd ever known, though it was not a boy, but ballet, that she loved.

"Well," Josie said, snapping back to the moment, one where a nearly naked Etienne was brushing the crumbs from her healthy muffins off his muscled abs. "If *you* are hungry; there are more of those in the kitchen. Just come in and help yourself."

Bea

"Good morning," Nancy said on Tuesday morning as she unlocked the door to the studio to let Bea in. She seemed to be in a good mood today. Maybe it was the change in weather. The air outside was suddenly almost chilly. The Santa Anas had retreated, the heat wave over. Bea wore her favorite gray sweater tights and a long-sleeve leotard with her CLCB puffer vest over it. It would be cold in the studio; at least Miss V. allowed her to wear warm-ups during her privates.

She trailed behind Nancy into the dark lobby, and Nancy turned on the fluorescent lights, which flickered and hummed, and then unlocked Studio B so she could go warm up.

"Vivienne will be here in about ten minutes. Traffic's backed up. She said to turn the heater on in the studio if you want."

"Will Lotte be here today?" Bea asked.

"Not until later," Nancy said.

Lotte had conducted the interviews with the soloists during rehearsals on Sunday afternoon. Bea had been so anxious, and grateful when Lotte wound up being very friendly.

"Je t'en prie, assieds toi," Lotte had said, motioning for Bea to sit in a chair positioned on a bright pink backdrop in the makeshift studio they'd made in the greenroom. There were lights and umbrellas stationed all around her. Lotte sat facing her, next to the camera, which was on a tripod. The sound guy was not around.

"I'm kind of nervous," Bea had blurted. Her leotard was already sweat-stained from rehearsals, and the heat from the lights wasn't helping.

"No, no," Lotte said, and smiled. "Pretend we are just girlfriends having a chat."

She nodded, but the bright lights made her feel as if she were onstage.

"I will ask questions, and you answer," Lotte said. "Do not be scared. I don't bite."

She had started with simple things: when did Bea start dancing, how long had she known she wanted to be a professional dancer, what was her dream role? And with each question, Bea felt more relaxed.

"Tell me about your family," Lotte asked. "You have a little brother?"

"Yes. Danny. He's sixteen."

"He is a dancer, too?"

Bea laughed. "Oh my god. No."

Lotte looked at her, out from behind the camera, her eyes dark and warm. "You lost your father. Recently."

She nodded, unable to speak. She wasn't expecting to talk about her dad.

"My papa, he passed when I was a girl, too," Lotte said. "When I was ten years old."

"Oh, no," Bea said. Ten years old? She tried to imagine what her life would look like if her father had died when she was ten. She was ten when she started dancing with Vivienne. "That's so young. I'm sorry."

Lotte smiled sadly. "*Oui*, I wasn't ready."

That was exactly what she felt like. She hadn't been ready for him to go. Even with him being sick, with months to prepare. Because in the end, he'd died suddenly. It did not feel fair.

"*La vie est un flambeau toujours prêt à s'éteindre*," Lotte said, leaning forward, hands clasped together, arms on her knees. "*Life is a torch, always ready to go out.* And that is why we must make art; to keep the flame burning."

Bea's eyes filled with tears. "He used to build sandcastles," she said. "But they always got swept away."

Why was she telling Lotte this?

"It drove my mom crazy. Why waste all that time on something that just disappears? But ballet is like that, too. We dance, and then it's all just a memory."

"Yes!" Lotte said, sitting up and clapping her hands together. "And that is why *I* make films! To capture those memories, to seize them. To hold on."

When they were finished, Lotte had squeezed Bea's shoulder. "That was lovely. See, no need to be nervous. You are a natural. *Tu es douée.*"

She had left feeling strangely peaceful. It had been nice to talk to someone who knew exactly how she felt.

Miss V. came into the studio as Bea was warming up, stretching out her left hamstring, which was always tight. Bea inhaled the distinct scent of her floral perfume and cigarettes.

"*Bonjour,* Beatrice," Miss V. said.

"Good morning." She quickly stood up, peeled off her vest, but left her sweater tights on.

During privates, Vivienne was not the same stern teacher she was during class. Bea had been working one-on-one with Miss V. since she came to CLCB. She'd been afraid of her back then; during her first private lesson, she'd been too frightened to say a word. But now, as she got older, Miss V. had become more like family than a teacher. Like an aunt, or even a second mom. Bea enjoyed Etienne's classes, but she missed Miss V. Tuesdays and Thursdays were the only days she got to work with her anymore. She tried not to think about what it would be like when she left CLCB, when she emerged from the soft cocoon of this studio. Some days, she wished she could stop time. Stay here. Never grow up.

Bea moved to the barre where Miss V. usually had her start, but Miss V. clucked her tongue and beckoned her over to where she sat at the front of the room, her back to the mirror. Bea stood awkwardly before her. This was how Miss V. began most lectures: a cool assessment of Bea's progress followed by gentle instructions or cau-

tions or vague metaphors Bea sometimes understood and sometimes
wondered at for days after.

"First, congratulations," she said. "On Marie."

Bea involuntarily curtsied. *"Merci,"* she said.

"Etienne is very impressed with you," she said.

Bea realized she was holding her breath and willed herself to
breathe.

"You have been waiting a long time for a principal role. Now, it
is your turn," she said.

Bea felt warmth spreading through her limbs.

"But please, and I do not mean to be—negative?"

Bea felt the heat drain from her, and she shivered.

"But, Etienne, since he was a child, he is *whimsical*. He changes
his mind often."

Bea felt like she might cry. Was Miss V. going to tell her that Etienne had changed his mind about the role?

"Oh, no, no," Miss V. said. "Please, I don't mean to frighten you.
It is just that I care for you. Men like Etienne, they can be careless. I
do not want his . . . *caprice*? To hurt you."

What was Miss V. saying? What sort of warning was this?

"It's okay," Bea said, more to herself than to anyone else. "I will
work hard." This was the only answer in ballet. The only thing she
had any control over whatsoever.

"Yes, my dear. You will. Let us get started."

It was a good private, a strong turning day, with lots of com-
pliments from Miss V., a lesson that ended with a hug and words
of encouragement, but Bea couldn't shake the feeling that Miss V.
knew something she didn't. Had Etienne already decided about the
scholarship, and Miss V. was preparing her? Or maybe her role in the
lead was not set in stone. Whatever it was, it had felt ominous. By
the time everyone began showing up for class at three o'clock, she'd
almost worked herself into an anxiety attack. She usually walked
from the studio over to the market that sold pre-packaged salads for
lunch, but she felt queasy. She had to force herself to eat a protein bar
so she wouldn't pass out in class.

She made small talk with some of the girls as they stretched and gossiped in the lobby while Zoraiya, then Jazmin, did their private lessons with Miss V. She was talking to Lizzy when Savvy and Nick came in holding hands, Savvy leaning into Nick. Her hair wasn't up yet, and she hadn't changed. She'd cut the blue out of her hair—but it still fell below her shoulders like a curtain of pale yellow silk. Olive was nowhere in sight.

"Where's Olive?" Jaz asked Savvy since, apparently, now they came as a pair.

"She's *sick*," Savvy said, making air quotes.

This was code word for ditching. Lots of them did it—when they had tests to study for or occasionally events at school they couldn't get out of.

"Do we have *pas* today?" Bea asked. Bea hadn't been around Savvy without Olive attached to her hip since classes started.

"No idea," Savvy said. "Etienne told me this morning that he's going to be taking over *pas* classes, too. But not sure if that starts today or not."

Savvy was *talking* to her. Being friendly, even. So friendly, the fact that Savvy seemed to have spoken to Etienne this morning almost got past her.

"This morning?" Bea asked, feeling unsettled.

Savvy looked down, rifling through her bag. "Oh yeah—my mom had me text him about the rehearsal schedule. To ask about *pas* class, too."

"Oh," Bea said.

"Shit, I left my water bottle in the car," Savvy said.

Bea stretched into a center split and leaned forward, resting her head on her arms. She closed her eyes, still feeling uneasy, looking up when she saw a pair of Converse.

"Hey," Owen said, and sat down next to her.

"Hi," she said, self-conscious about the funk coming from her toe pads, which she'd left out to dry after her private. She shoved them into the mesh bag where she kept her pointe shoes.

"I like your shirt," she said, nodding at his blue Grateful Dead T.

"My dad was at this show," he said. "With Santana at Angel's Camp. 1987."

"Oh my god, I bet my mom was there, too," she said. "Her family followed The Dead around for a while."

"Really? Wow. That's so cool."

"*Hippies*," she said. It embarrassed her a little, but Owen didn't seem to be judging her.

He took a deep breath. "So, I actually have a question. And no big deal if you don't want to, but I was wondering if you might want to come to HoCo with me? I wasn't planning on going, but then I figured it was the last one I'd have a chance to go to, since we're graduating. I have to get there late because of class, and since you'll be here too . . . I mean, that's not the only reason I'm asking, but anyway. Would you want to go? To Homecoming?"

Homecoming. A dance. She'd never gone to a dance. Not the late-afternoon ones in middle school. Not a single high school prom or formal. For Christmas one year, Danny gave her a T-shirt that said, SORRY, I'VE GOT BALLET. She and Olive had planned to go to Olive's Homecoming and Prom together this year. "To be like *normal* girls for once in our lives," Olive had said. Though even as she said this, there was a sort of pride beneath the self-deprecating surface. They weren't like normal girls. They were special.

Owen didn't go to the public high school with Luke, Nick, and Olive. He went to a small Catholic K-12 school where he'd been since kindergarten.

"No worries if you're not into it," he said, and reached for his bag as if to get up. "It'll probably be boring."

"Um, no. That would be cool! I'd like to go," she said.

"Really? I've wanted to ask you for a while now, but I was nervous."

She waited for him to say he was just kidding, but he was serious.

"Well, don't be," she said. "I'm totally not even scary."

"You're a little scary," he teased, and she smiled.

He stood up and shook his pant leg back down. "I figure we can go after class that Friday, catch the last two hours. It's the same night as CLHS's HoCo. We could meet everybody at Denny's after?"

Her heart sank. The last thing she wanted was to spend any time with "everybody."

"Or not," he said, smiling.

Owen hadn't been at the bonfire that night. He probably had no idea what had happened with Nick.

Ever

Don't forget tuition, Bea had texted. October first. A whole new slew of payments due. When Ever arrived at the studio on Tuesday night with another post-dated tuition check, she'd felt defeated, despite having had a relatively productive day writing.

Her plan was to get a hundred solid pages, along with a synopsis of the Lady Edison novel, to Leona within the next week. She hoped Leona would be so pleased with her work she'd suggest they submit it to Edward, her editor, try to secure a new contract on the proposal alone. If he offered a decent advance, then the whole insurance situation wouldn't be so dire. If it was a *really* good advance, it wouldn't matter at all. She was seasoned enough in this business to know the latter scenario was highly unlikely—the air still smoky after the crash and burn of *Black Evenings*. But what else was there to do but keep working and hope?

Ever hadn't spoken to Lindsay since Saturday when the cast list went up, unsure of how to broach the subject with her. Though maybe Lindsay wasn't upset. It seemed like Olive had been pulling away from ballet a bit in the last year or so; maybe Lindsay felt it, too. But when Ever walked into the studio that Tuesday afternoon, it quickly became clear that Lindsay *was* upset about the casting. Very upset. She was hunched over the reception desk, talking in hushed voices with Nancy. *Scholarship*, she heard Lindsay say, in a whisper.

A little, mean thought pricked at Ever, one she quickly squashed: Olive didn't *need* the scholarship. Lindsay and Steve could afford to send her to any pre-professional school or training program she got

into. They had no financial burdens, no financial concerns whatsoever, as far as Ever could tell. They were people who sent their kid to
public school because they chose to. They opted for the public high
school, their alma mater, over the expensive Catholic school because
of school pride, not because the forty-thousand-dollar tuition at St.
Mary's was cost-prohibitive.

Lindsay hadn't even looked up when Ever came into the lobby;
she was so engrossed in her conversation. "Well, with Bea in the
lead . . . it seems like he's already made up his mind . . ." Lindsay
said, and Ever felt like she had the first day of junior high after years
of homeschooling, when she'd been in the bathroom listening as
two girls talked about the *dirty hippie* in their math class, only to realize it was *her* they were talking about.

When she heard Bea's name, whispered in a sort of frustrated hiss
from her best friend's lips, she thought another wicked little thought,
sharp as a thumbtack: *Your daughter doesn't deserve this.* Olive could
be a powerful dancer, but was uninterested lately. Lazy. Bea had said
Etienne called her a *slug.* She had all the potential that any of these
girls had, the same opportunities, more even, and she'd squandered
them. Hanging out with Savvy. Going to the beach and parties, all
while Bea was working so hard.

Ever hated herself. How could she have such awful thoughts
about Olive?

"Hi, Linds," Ever said, gently touching Lindsay's back.

"Oh," Lindsay said, startled, red-faced. "Ever!"

Ever took a deep breath and blinked her eyes, trying not to cry.

"Hi," Lindsay said, and hugged her. "I'm sorry. I am just such a
wreck over this."

Of course, she was. How could she not be disappointed? Ever felt
ashamed for every thought that had scuttled across her brain. This
scholarship business was crazy-making.

"How *is* Olive?" Ever asked gently.

"She's actually at home sick today. She says it's some kind of stomach bug, but I think she might be avoiding coming in. This whole

thing is messing with her head. She'd kill me if she knew I was here."

"That's tough," Ever said, then worried that that sounded condescending. Easy for her to say; Bea had just gotten everything she'd wanted. "I'm sorry."

"Oh god, whatever for?" Lindsay said, but her dismissal felt forced.

Lindsay

The CBD didn't work. She'd given it almost two weeks, but if anything, whatever it was had gotten worse. It was itchy now, too. Itchy and bumpy and horrid. She'd finally called her OB-GYN, and on Friday afternoon, she sat in the waiting room, thumbing through an old *Good Housekeeping* magazine, mindlessly scanning recipes for cobbler and advice about how to communicate with your teen.

"Lindsay Chase?" The nurse stood in the doorway with her clipboard, looking at her sympathetically. Or was she just imagining that? All the nurse knew was that she was here for her annual exam.

Lindsay stood up and, forcing a smile, made her way across the waiting room to the doorway, where the nurse ushered her in and motioned to the scales. Out of habit, she slipped off her shoes and shrugged off her sweater before stepping on. As the nurse slid the weight across, she exhaled, as if the air inside her lungs could change the reading.

"Wow! You've lost some weight," the nurse said.

"Twenty-two pounds," Lindsay said.

"That is *amazing*. Good for you. I should get some tips from you."

Lindsay followed her down the hallway to the examination room, where she left her to change into a paper gown. The AC was cranked up, and her body was covered in goosebumps as she sat on the table. She was reaching for her sweater when there was a knock on the door.

"Come in!" she said. This was always the worst, the awkward exchange of pleasantries before the exam. At least Dr. Ramachandra was gentle and kind. Lindsay had never had to divulge something like this before, though; the most embarrassing thing she'd ever admitted to was painful intercourse, but the doctor had simply recommended a lubricant. She hadn't treated her like it was shameful. Even so, STDs were not something she'd ever thought she'd be worried about. Seriously, who got an STD at *forty-nine*?

"Okay, scooch back," the doctor said. "Open up your gown, and I'll do a quick breast exam."

She laid back and opened the gown. She felt so exposed, especially given the arctic temperatures in the room. At least the doctor's hands were warm.

"I see you've lost some weight," she said, though unlike the nurse, her face was serious.

"Twenty-two pounds."

"Was it intentional?" she asked, kneading her left boob.

"Yes. I've been dieting. I mean, eating healthier." Olive had told her *diet* was a taboo word now.

"And exercise?" Right boob.

"I work out every day," she said.

"That's good. Okay, you can close up," she said, and motioned to her gown. Lindsay pulled it across her breasts. "Feet up," she said. "Oh, cute socks."

The socks had been a Christmas gift from Olive. They looked like ballet slippers, with pink "ribbons" printed on the ankle part. As she put her feet into the stirrups and wiggled her butt down the table, the doctor moved to the stool and said, "Your daughter is a dancer, right?"

Lindsay felt the same swell of pride she always felt when people asked about Olive. She never broached the subject on her own; she hated when other moms somehow managed to work their daughters' dancing into every conversation, but when someone opened that door, she never hesitated to walk through.

"Yes! She trains at Costa de la Luna Conservatory," she said.

"That's right. She's a . . . junior?" the doctor asked, as she prepped the items on the tray. Lindsay focused on the conversation and avoided looking at the various instruments of torture.

"Senior."

"Does she know where she wants to go to college?"

The SATs had been last Saturday. Steve had not backed down, and oddly, Olive hadn't put up a fight, either. When Lindsay cautioned this would mean missing rehearsals, Olive had said, "I have one part. In the back. He literally won't know I'm missing."

The doctor's hands were cold now. Down there.

"No, no college. Maybe someday, but this year she'll audition for trainee positions, or pre-professional schools. There's a scholarship she's hoping for—for the school at Ballet de Paris?"

"Oh, wow! Paris! That is amazing. She must be very talented."

Lindsay flinched when the doctor's fingers touched the bump. Her knees stiffened, and her legs automatically squeezed together.

The doctor looked up at her. "Did that hurt you?"

She nodded, trying not to cry. Dr. Ramachandra returned to her task, and Lindsay could feel her fingers gently prodding. She closed her eyes and tried to imagine she was somewhere else. At the beach. In her own bed. Anywhere but here.

"How long has this been bothering you?" the doctor asked, and Lindsay shrugged. She kept poking around; each time she touched the spot, Lindsay caught her breath.

"What do you think . . ." she started. "Is it . . . ?" The words wouldn't come.

"I'm going to screen for everything," the doctor said, her tone suddenly all business. "Take a little sample here."

Ouch.

"Sorry. Okay, now this is going to be cold."

Lindsay squeezed her eyes shut tightly as the icy speculum entered and opened.

The doctor completed the more intrusive part of the exam in silence and then stood up and peeled off her gloves. She tilted her head and seemed to study Lindsay. Lindsay sat up, gathering herself together the best she could, though the tears had fallen down her cheeks.

Dr. Ramachandra reached for her arm and squeezed it gently, looked her in the eyes. "Well, this should be quite a year for your daughter," she said. "You must be so proud of her."

The doctor smiled, went to the computer, and tapped in her notes. "Did you have any other concerns today?" *Concerns.* God, it felt like *all* Lindsay had were concerns these days, but she shook her head.

"We're going to figure this out. It might be nothing at all," she said. "Or it might be something. Let's just take this one step at a time."

It would be a week, Dr. Ramachandra said. Until the tests came back. A week of freedom before her life went back to normal, or her worst fears were confirmed.

Ever

"Danny, can you get that?" Ever hollered from the garage when the doorbell rang, and Coby started barking, though Danny was probably asleep. It was Saturday, no school. He'd gone surfing early, then disappeared into his cluttered cave of a bedroom again.

After dropping Bea off at rehearsals that morning, she'd finished her book proposal. She'd re-read it at least a half dozen times before drafting an email to Leona and clicking *Send*. Now, it was out of her hands; she simply had to wait. She thought she'd distract herself by decorating the house for Halloween. She was in the garage, searching for the orange bins.

When the kids were small, Ever and Ethan used to host huge Halloween parties. Costumes, bobbing for apples, that game where you string donuts up and the kids eat them without using their hands. She used to make the kids' costumes; once, she spent a whole weekend making a pirate outfit for Bea and a feathered parrot costume for Danny. Danny had always been Bea's sidekick: the black cat to her witch, the Sebastian to her Ariel, the white rabbit to her Alice. Ethan loved Halloween: from the ghoulish decorations to the gutting of pumpkins. Last year, after Ethan passed, she had left the decorations in the garage. It had been too difficult to carry on with their beloved traditions, every fake tombstone a mocking reminder. But this year was likely Bea's last one at home. No party, but at least they could make the house festive. She would put pumpkins on the stoop. She would string cobwebs in the corners and fill the glass pumpkin jar with candy corns.

She was dragging the Halloween bin from the back corner of the garage when she heard Cobain barking again.

"Coby!" she said, exasperated as she emerged from the garage into the kitchen to find him scratching at the front door.

Outside, there was a package on the doorstep, but it didn't appear to have come from the post office. No mailing label or return address, just EVER & BEA written in Sharpie across one of the sealed flaps. Curious, she lifted the box and brought it into the house.

She used a kitchen knife to open the box. A sheet of paper lay on top, a poem bordered with Halloween images of witches and ghosts. *You've Been Boo'd!* She scanned the poem, remembering the years when the kids had lived for this Halloween tradition: anonymous treats showing up on the doorstep with the instruction to pass the kindness on. How many times had they snuck up to a friend's doorstep with a basket of goodies? But the kids were grown. What could this be?

Inside the box were stacks of pointe shoe boxes. Lindsay had mentioned that Olive had a couple pairs that were too narrow, but there had to be a dozen pairs in here. At least a thousand dollars' worth of shoes. She removed a box, lifted the flap, and unwrapped the tissue. The shoes were brand new, but with ribbons sewn on. She checked the other pairs and saw they all had ribbons, too. Shoes that have been sewn can't be returned; Lindsay knew this.

She looked around the kitchen for something she could offer her friend in return, but what could possibly match this kindness? She scanned the windowsill with the little pots of fresh herbs, the antique milk bottle with a bunch of wilting roses from the bush in the front yard. A chipped yellow mixing bowl her dad had made. Maybe she could bake her a cake? Probably not on her diet.

And she felt awful for begrudging Olive a chance at the scholarship. Lindsay was her best friend. Generous and thoughtful. Supportive and kind. This stupid scholarship was bringing out the worst in her.

Lindsay

Olive was sullen in the passenger seat as Lindsay backed out of the garage to take her to rehearsals on Saturday morning. Sonia had just pulled up in her van and was lugging her cleaning supplies up the walkway.

"Hi Sonia!" Lindsay said through the open car window.

"Good morning, Mrs. Chase."

Sonia had been working for them for seven or eight years, though Lindsay had no idea how old she was. Forty, maybe? Forty-five? She, like Lindsay, was a little overweight, but she had beautiful dark hair she wore in a ponytail. A plain face, but a warm and friendly smile. Lindsay didn't know much about Sonia's life except that she had been taking classes at the community college for several years and lived with her mother and her son on the other side of town. She'd brought him, a quiet boy named Oscar, with her once or twice. But that was ages ago; he had to be eleven or twelve now.

"I left some brownies on the counter! They're gluten- and sugar-free. Make sure to bring some home to Oscar," Lindsay said, and Sonia gave her a thumbs-up.

"Rehearsals start in twenty minutes," Olive said, the first time she'd spoken all morning.

Since the SATs, Olive had been quiet. Not angry necessarily—that was a different kind of quiet—but distant. Distracted. Today, she sat in silence all the way to the studio, despite Lindsay's best efforts to engage her in conversation.

"So how are rehearsals going?"

Nothing.

"Have they said when the documentary will be out?"

Shrug.

"I wonder when they'll announce the scholarship."

Silence.

Lindsay kept driving through the foggy morning, the marine layer a wall of white. They could be driving off a cliff and not realize it until they were mid-air.

One last effort: "Ever said that Bea really likes Etienne's choreography; that it's really challenging."

Olive exhaled loudly.

"What?"

"Of course, Bea likes the choreography," she said. "She's the *lead*."

Lindsay felt heartsick. First, she couldn't understand Olive's bitterness against Bea, who had been like a sister to her. Bea, who had sat at their dining room table a thousand times, who had played a million games of Sorry and Scrabble sprawled out on the floor of Olive's bedroom. Bea who had lost her dad and had, apparently now, lost her best friend. But it wasn't just this that made her sad; it was the resignation in Olive's voice, the tone of defeat.

"Well, Nancy told me that Etienne likes fiery dancers," she said. "It's not over just because you didn't get a big part. The scholarship is still up for grabs."

"This is a waste of time, Mom," Olive said.

"What's a waste of time?" Lindsay turned to her, and Olive gestured wildly to her dance bag on the floor.

"This. *Ballet*. I practically live at the studio. And for what?"

"Oh, jeez Louise," Lindsay said. "Is this about homecoming?"

Homecoming was tonight. Starting at seven o'clock. Rehearsals were from noon to eight. Olive had pleaded to skip. Her friends from school were spending the day at the salon, getting their hair and nails done. Getting together at a friend's house to get dressed before heading to the high school. Lindsay herself had felt a twinge of regret, recalling her own senior homecoming.

"You ditched last Saturday for the SATs. You can't miss any more classes or rehearsals," Lindsay had said.

Lindsay knew Olive was an underdog with regards to this scholarship, but skipping rehearsals for a school dance would send the wrong message. Lindsay had reminded her that it was often the reliable dancers who made the strongest impression. The ones who, regardless of casting, *showed up*. The ones who learned every part and could step in at a moment's notice to dance any role. Olive had told Lindsay that Etienne didn't "believe" in understudies. "Even better then," she'd offered. "Nobody else will be prepared. Learn everything. You never know. *Nutcracker* season is flu season, too." Olive knew this better than anyone; two years ago, when she was supposed to dance Arabian and Chinese, she'd been taken out by the flu.

Olive had asked to skip class before, of course. When she was sick. When her tendinitis was flaring up. Once, when there was a class field trip to Disneyland. But she, like all the other Level 6 girls, understood that sacrifices needed to be made.

Olive had only backed down from her HoCo campaign when Savannah texted that she didn't think they should skip. The compromise was that Olive would get a ride with Savvy and Nick to the dance as soon as rehearsals were over. The girls would bring their dresses and hang them up in the dressing room. There wouldn't be time to go home for showers, so they'd likely just leave their hair up, put on some makeup and heels, and go. They'd only miss about an hour.

"I'm going to swing by the studio at eight so I can get some photos," Lindsay said.

"Seriously?" Olive said. "Why?"

"Because it's your senior year! Homecoming?"

"You just spent the last three weeks convincing me how stupid it was, Mom. You can't have it both ways."

Lindsay sighed.

"Also, we're leaving the second rehearsals get out, so—"

"So, I'll be there early."

They pulled into the parking lot at the studio, and her phone rang through the Bluetooth. The screen said: Costa de la Luna Obstetrics and Gynecology.

Olive looked at the screen and then at Lindsay, her face a question mark.

"Just trying to schedule a mammogram," she said. "Next month is Breast Cancer Awareness Month. I always schedule an appointment for November."

"But it's Saturday," Olive said, and a momentary flash of something crossed her face. Fear? Was she thinking of Ethan? Olive was worried about her.

"I should get this," Lindsay said, her heart pounding now. Almost loud enough to hear.

"Okay," Olive said as she got out of the car. "I'll see you after rehearsals."

She started to touch the screen to accept the call, but then, trembling, sent it to voicemail. She waited, and the voice message alert dinged. She considered ignoring it. Really, she could just delete the message. She could switch doctors, never ever get the results. But none of that changed anything. Not really. It would be like ignoring cancer. Or a dying marriage.

Outside, Melissa was unloading Jazmin's dance bag from her trunk. She caught Lindsay's eye, waved a half-hearted, obligatory, wave. *Thunk.* So, she hadn't left the studio after all. *Terrific.*

She turned off the Bluetooth and held the phone to her ear.

"Hi, Lindsay. This is Dr. Ramachandra. I'm sorry to bother you on the weekend. I had to swing by the office this morning, and I saw that we got the test results from the lab. I thought you'd rather know now than wait until Monday. I'm here for another half hour or so."

This could not be good. Before she returned the call, she ran through the possible scenarios in her head, though she had been doing this every night, all night, for weeks. So, if the bump was some sort of VD, she'd have to confront Steve. But how? Send him a text? **Hey, Steve, doctor says I have herpes. Talk tonight?** Maybe an email: "Dear Steve, Not sure how to tell you this . . ." Or God, a phone call or, worse, a conversation over dinner? She tried to imagine his response and couldn't. Would he deny or confess? If so, to what? It made her nauseous thinking about where he could have picked it up. Then she recalled that look on his face when Melissa was fawning over him at the memorial. Now, she watched Melissa, who was wearing a very short flowy sort of romper, usher Jazmin through the front door and wondered if her suspicions about Melissa and Steve were just paranoia or something to truly worry about. Did *Melissa* have herpes? By the time her mind circled back around to this sort of speculation, her head was pounding.

She took a deep breath before picking up her phone.

"Hi, Dr. Ramachandra? This is Lindsay Chase." Lindsay felt a cold bead of sweat trickle down from her armpit. "I just got your message?"

"Oh, hi, Lindsay!"

She felt as if someone were sitting on her chest.

"So, we got the test results. Good news is, it's totally treatable. Bad news is, the medicine has to come from a compound lab, which means it's more expensive."

Her vision vignetted. "What *is* it?"

"Well, I'm going to prescribe a hormone cream as well as a steroid. The steroid you can get at your local CVS, but the estrogen has to come from a special pharmacy."

"No, what's the diagnosis?" Lindsay's voice was at least an octave higher than usual.

"Oh," Dr. Ramachandra said. "I'm so sorry. Not enough coffee. It's an inflammatory skin disorder, an autoimmune issue; it can be triggered by hormonal shifts."

"Wait," Lindsay said, chest tight. "It's from *menopause*? Not from . . ."

"Your STD screenings were all clear," she said.

She felt like she might hyperventilate. Every bit of worry and fear and rage was suddenly suspended around her like smoke after a fire. Tears ran down her cheeks. Sweat ran down her sides. She was a weeping, leaking mess. She wasn't being cheated on; she was just *old*.

"Thank you, thank you so much," she said.

"I would like to go ahead and do a little more blood work, though. Check your hormone levels. And with your recent weight loss, I want to make sure there isn't something else going on."

Something else going on? Like what? She thought of Ethan again. *Cancer?* No, the weight loss was from the cucumber soup. From working out.

The boot on her chest pressed downward. Her lungs emptied of air, and her mouth opened involuntarily, allowing a shuddering sigh to escape.

"Can you swing by the lab early next week?"

"Of course," she said.

It should have felt like relief. Like a release. That pesky little bump was not the punctuation mark at the end of her marriage, but the end of her fertility. She should have felt the weight of this burden lifting, but instead, she felt a sinking feeling. The prognosis was good; the steroid cream would make it all go away. Except the sad truth was, it didn't really make her problems with Steve go away at all.

The tap on her glass startled her. She looked up and saw Victor standing there. She quickly lowered the window, wiping at her eyes.

"Hey," he said brightly, and then, noticing her tears, cocked his head. "Wait. You okay?"

Lindsay nodded. "Yes, actually. I'm totally fine."

"You sure? It looks like you've been crying."

"I have been," she said, and smiled.

"Oh. Happy tears. The best kind."

She smiled. "Oh, I meant to call you this afternoon. We've got a closing date on the condo. How does November first sound?"

"That's *great*," he said. "My wife will be very happy to get her couch back."

"Well, I guess I'll see you soon," she said.

"I'm clocking off early today; do you want to go grab a coffee? Or happy hour? I definitely owe you a drink."

"Oh, no. I mean, I'm on my way home."

"Okay," he said, and smiled, backing away from the car as she turned on the engine.

She was plagued by a horrific sense of guilt as she backed out, and Victor kept standing there looking at her a bit quizzically. Had she led him to believe there was something going on between them? They'd had coffee. But she had coffee with lots of clients. They'd chatted on the phone. So what? So they'd talked about their lives. About their kids. He couldn't possibly have thought she was flirting? *Was* she flirting?

She shook her head as she backed out of the parking space, then pulled out of the lot. She waved at him and then gripped the wheel.

It wasn't every day you got such life-changing information. Such a reprieve. But then why did she feel like this? Sort of *unwell*. Whatever was going on didn't seem like the appropriate response. As she pulled onto the highway, the realization snapped like a rubber band against the tender underside of her wrist. Was it possible she was—*disappointed*?

Act II, Scene III

Josie

Josie sat at home alone on Saturday night, with a fire in the fire-place and a glass of wine in her hand. Her phone dinged with a text from Savvy, a photo from HoCo. Nick and Savvy looked like they could be in a magazine; you'd never guess Savvy had come straight from the studio. Must be all those years of quick changes backstage had prepared her. The dress was navy blue, a deep V-cut in the front and backless. Floor-length. So many girls insisted on unflattering spandex and sequins, like sparkly sausage casings. But Savvy's gown was elegant. Classy. Nick's tux was also simple and stylish. Together, they looked perfect.

Savvy and Nick had been dating for about a year; but honestly, Josie had never been sure it was a good idea. First off, she worried about them being at the same studio. What would happen when they broke up? Second, she didn't want anything holding Savvy back from any opportunities that might come her way, least of all a stupid boy. But beyond all that, there was something *familiar* about Nick. Josie had dated a dozen egotistical assholes, a few bona fide narcissists, and one full-blown sociopath. From the beginning, she'd gotten a weird vibe from Nick. Like he was playing a part. Like he was always onstage. The guy never turned it off. And worse, he talked and talked, but when Savvy offered her own thoughts or opinions, he interrupted or corrected or, worse, ignored her. Savvy's face would fall when he did this, but for some reason, she just took it. Savvy was normally in the spotlight, but with Nick, she fell into the shadows. She didn't stand up for herself, and that made Josie livid.

Of course, Josie kept this to herself. Sometimes, you need to let things run their course. She knew from experience that when a narcissist makes a choice between his own selfish desires and his girlfriend's needs, the girlfriend *never* wins. As soon as Nick got into college or got an offer to go dance somewhere, he'd leave Savvy in his dust. Savvy just needed to get the scholarship and go. Start her life with no baggage. She was turning eighteen in a week; it was time to leave those childish things behind. Including her first love.

The log crumbled into a pile of ash, and she picked up her phone when it buzzed, expecting another photo from Savvy.

WTF You've got a guy staying in MY guesthouse?? CALL ME

Oh Jesus, Mark. Don't get your panties in a twist. She was furious. Also, how the hell did he know about Etienne? She started to text him back but stopped. Wait, *his* guesthouse? Since they split up, Mark never passed up an opportunity to remind her that everything she had was his.

She didn't owe him anything. Not even an explanation.

Bea

"In 1985, this was a luxury ride," Owen said as he opened the car door for her. He drove an old Buick; the ceiling upholstery was sagging, and Bea could feel the springs in the passenger seat. She had assumed she was the only middle-class kid at the studio; she'd never paid attention to Owen's car before. She wondered how his parents afforded private school.

"My dad teaches English at St. Mary's," he said, as if reading her mind. "Free tuition."

"Oh! My dad was a teacher too," she said. "Middle school, though. Music."

How was it they hadn't talked about any of this stuff before? It was amazing that she knew his body practically as well as her own, and she didn't even know where he lived.

"I have an older brother," he said when she asked if he had siblings. "He's pretty messed up, though. In and out of rehab. Which sucks, because he's like the smartest person I know. He got a perfect score on the SAT. He had a full ride to UCLA."

"Wow," she said. "I had no idea."

"I don't exactly broadcast it," he said. "It's been really hard on my parents."

She thought of her own mom, the despair that hung around her like fog.

Homecoming was a mistake. She knew it the second she and Owen walked toward the yacht club. He'd said that everyone at his school was nice, and his friends were looking forward to meeting her. But she still felt uneasy. The parking lot was full of BMWs and

Lexuses. The few kids who weren't already inside looked like they were on the red carpet: dresses like whispery wishes and tailored tuxes. Bea's dress, the yellow taffeta gown she'd gotten on clearance at Macy's for the Youth American Grand Prix awards last year, had been rolled up in her dance bag and was wrinkled now. Her bunions were throbbing inside the heels she'd picked up at Goodwill.

The music coming from inside was loud, the bass heavy. She tried to imagine walking into a room full of strangers in her wrinkled dress and secondhand shoes. She tried to picture herself walking out onto the dance floor with Owen; she didn't even know how to dance. Not like that, anyway. For the last couple of weeks, she'd watched so many YouTube videos and TikToks. She'd studied the moves and did her best to replicate them in the mirror. It was funny how complex ballet choreography presented no challenge to her, but tackling a thirty-second TikTok dance felt like putting an octopus in a straitjacket.

"You okay?" Owen squeezed her hand as they stood at the entrance to the club.

"I'm not really good at this," she said, and he looked puzzled. "Like, being a normal teenager," she explained.

"I have an idea," he said, and took her hand, leading her to the exit. "Come on."

She took her shoes off the second they climbed over the sea wall onto the sand. Her feet had never been happier. They walked across the beach toward the water, which twinkled in the lights of the city, and the moon, which was full and bright.

"They call that a Hunter's Moon," Owen said, pointing up.

"Why?"

"I think it's because it happens in October. Hunters would use the full moon to track and kill their prey—to, like, stock up for the winter."

"That's delightful," she said, and laughed.

"It's called a *blood moon,* too," he said.

"Even better."

The air was chilly, and she pulled her mom's borrowed shawl

over her bare shoulders. When they reached the shore, the cold water washed over her feet. The saltwater bit at her blisters, but it felt
good. Sharp.

"When I was little," she said, "my dad told me that at night, the
ocean swallows the sun like a peach, and then spits out the pit. And
that's the moon," she said.

"You must miss him a lot," Owen said.

She nodded but kept her words inside so she wouldn't cry.

A wave crashed against the sand, and the water rushed toward
them, drenching the bottom of her dress. The chiffon, which had
felt like feathers or clouds, now felt like an anchor.

She remembered something. About the bonfire. But it was tangled up with something someone said about her dad? Olive? Then
Nick's hand, pulling her away from the fire. How heavy her legs had
felt as she stumbled after him. How powerless and graceless and ill.

"You okay?" Owen asked.

But her breath abruptly left her, like the wave receding back into
the sea. The sand, the earth beneath her pulled away. An undertow,
sucking her under. A rip tide she couldn't fight.

Lindsay

Two weeks after homecoming, Lindsay still hadn't found the time to get the follow-up lab work done. She'd been busy prepping for Victor's closing on November first: too busy to argue with Olive about ballet, too busy to argue with Steve about ballet. Or anything else, for that matter. Too busy to wonder what was supposed to happen now. Before the doctor called, she'd been gearing up for a confrontation, preparing herself for the worst-case scenario. Now, it was *over*. It felt like she'd been wandering around in a maze for the last two months only to get to the center, walls all around her, and no idea how to get out.

Olive was going to Savvy's birthday party tonight. Savvy would be the first of the girls to celebrate her eighteenth, with Olive just over a month behind. She had no idea how it had crept up on her. And it *had* crept up on her. Olive's childhood felt like it had lasted forever, the days of infancy endless, the years of elementary school a string of a million similar days, the thousands of hours at the studio, the slow progression from child to adolescent to young adulthood, and then, now, without warning, it was almost here. She'd had eighteen years to prepare for this; why did she feel so blindsided?

"I need to get Savvy a present," Olive said, licking Cheeto dust from her fingers.

"Oh my god, why are you eating Cheetos? This is why you keep getting sick."

It was nine o'clock, and Olive was still in her pajamas. She'd been "sick" a lot lately. No fever, but all sorts of ailments: stomachache, headache, nausea, sinus pain.

"I can grab a present for her while you're at rehearsals this after-noon. What time do you have to be there. Two?"

"I'm not going to rehearsals," she said. "I'm sick."

"Then you're not going to a birthday party," Lindsay said, reach-ing into her bag for the inspection report for the condo. She hadn't had time to review it yet and had promised she'd go over it this weekend and meet with Victor on Monday.

"I'm too sick to *dance*, but I'll be okay to sit in a restaurant for a couple of hours," Olive said. "Savvy's my best friend."

"*Bea* is your best friend," Lindsay snapped.

"*Was*," Olive muttered, and tossed the empty Cheeto bag on the counter.

Lindsay didn't have time for this. She didn't want to get into it—any of it—with Olive right now. She checked the time. She was showing clients a house close by at eleven o'clock, then taking Olive to class, then hosting an open house from two until four.

"So *anyway*," Olive said, "Daddy says that during Christmas break, he's taking me up the coast to tour some schools."

"What do you mean?"

"The UCs. Santa Barbara, Santa Cruz. The common app is due November thirtieth."

"That's right after the show," Lindsay said dumbly.

"It's due before I'll have a chance to visit, but I figure I'll just ap-ply to all of them and visit after. Daddy said we can also go check out UCLA. My stats probably aren't good enough, but I'm a legacy, so that might help?"

UCLA was Steve's alma mater. She should have known he'd be pushing for this, this *Plan B* that had rarely been spoken of until now. She knew that for some girls—girls like Bea and Savvy—there simply was no Plan B; that a backup plan was only for people who were willing to settle.

"I might even apply to NYU, too," she said. "Dad says to apply anywhere I want."

College was what most seniors aspired to, but this felt like an admission of defeat. Why was she feeling so let down? Any other parent would be thrilled with these prospects.

"Well, USC has an amazing dance program," Lindsay said, biting her tongue and holding back tears. It was true. Their program was incredible, highly selective. There was still a chance, she supposed, that she could go on to a professional career if she went somewhere like USC. "I heard Owen is applying there; you should talk to him about it."

"Oh, I wouldn't major in dance," Olive said, and it felt like the wind had been knocked out of her.

"What?"

Olive took a deep breath, and her mouth twitched. "This is it, Mom," she said softly. Her dark eyes looked sad and a little scared. "I don't want to dance after this year."

Josie

Josie didn't respond to Mark's text about Etienne and the guest-house. If he was doing it to get her riled up, he could go bark up some other tree. He couldn't intimidate her. Seriously. He was the one who left *her*. Who she had at the house was her business, and hers alone, though it niggled at her, like a sliver under tender skin, working its way to the surface every now and then. It had felt like a threat. And she still had no idea how he found out about her "tenant."

She had tried to put Mark out of her mind, focusing instead on the plans for Savvy's birthday party. She'd thought about having it at the house, but the illicit houseguest made that impossible. So instead, she'd booked their favorite Italian restaurant and told Savvy she could bring ten of her closest friends. But because Johnny was footing the bill for it, the one stipulation was that he'd be there, as well.

It pissed her off that every bit of "generosity" had strings attached. What she wouldn't give to have something that truly belonged to her. She thought of how big her dreams had been when she was Savvy's age. How close she'd come. And how quickly she'd lost it all. Now, here they all were eighteen years later, and the only thing she had to show for any of it was Savvy.

Eighteen. She had no idea how it was that Savvy was eighteen, when she'd been a baby just yesterday. The baby Josie hadn't planned for, but the one whom she had loved more than she ever thought possible. She remembered bringing her home to her and Johnny's little apartment when she was only a day old, and thinking, even as

Johnny nuzzled her against his chest, "She's mine. She belongs to me."

Late Saturday afternoon, as she was putting together the goodie bags for the party, the doorbell rang, but rather than wait for her to answer the door, she heard his fingers punching in the code (the one she'd changed, of course) and then the firm bang of a fist.

She took a deep breath and went to the door, peered through the beveled glass at Mark's face. She could tell that he was pissed. She opened the door and stared at him, this stupid asshole who had once looked at her like she was the only woman in the world. Those same eyes now gazed at her like she was nothing more than a piece of shit he'd just stepped in.

"Come on in," she said, but he'd already barged into the kitchen. He opened the fridge, looked inside like he still lived there, and pulled out a beer. He dragged a barstool out from the island and sat down. He seemed a little messy? Probably stopped by some bar for happy hour on his way over. Trouble in dental paradise?

"Let me guess, Erica left you for somebody in her grade at school?"

Mark took a long swallow of the beer, then reached for a goodie bag—a pink cinch sack she'd filled with star-shaped, foil-covered chocolates. She snatched it back.

"You think this is wise?" he said, apropos of nothing. "Having this guy around Savvy?"

"I really don't need parenting tips from someone who's shacking up with a child."

"Well, in case you've forgotten, this is still my house. And I don't recall giving you permission to sublease the guesthouse."

She fumed. This wasn't about Savvy. This was about *her*. He owned the house, and everything in it, it seemed, including *her*.

"What do you *want*?" she asked.

"I want him out of my house," he said.

"He'll be out by December."

Mark scowled at her. It was the same game of chicken they'd played too many times to count in the last year. He liked to play tough, but in the end, he wasn't.

He surveyed the kitchen. "You know, I'm actually considering putting the house on the market."

"What?" she said. "I have the house until Savvy graduates."

"Actually, no. I said you could have the house until Savvy is an adult. As of tomorrow, that's the case."

Wait. *What?*

"That's bullshit, Mark."

"It's not bullshit. It's *contractual.* Just because you didn't read it . . ."

She felt her face flushing with heat. With anger. He'd been so civil as they divvied things up. He'd promised she could continue living in the house, rent-free; he'd drawn up an agreement. Once Savvy graduated, she'd use her half of the proceeds to buy a two-bedroom condo by the beach. This was the plan; what they'd agreed to. The arrangement had seemed fair; she had no idea he'd pull this shit.

"You *promised* me. Why are you doing this?" she asked. She could have sworn he said that he wouldn't sell until next summer. She hadn't bothered to read the fine print, because she'd trusted him. What was she supposed to do now? Uproot their lives during *Nutcracker*? Savvy needed to be focused right now, on ballet, on the scholarship.

"I'll reconsider if you get rid of him," he said.

After he left, she paced. She was still wringing her hands at the kitchen island when Savvy came home. Savvy tossed her dance bag by the door and collapsed on a barstool, where she kicked off her warm-up booties, and pulled the bobby pins out of her bun.

Josie forced a smile and reached out to stroke her hair. "Happy birthday, girly. So, you're all grown up now," she said, trying not to cry. "Right?"

Bea

Savvy made no effort to hide the fact that she was having a birth-day party that night and that Bea wasn't invited. Nick and Luke were going, Olive and Zoraiya. Owen had bowed out on his invite, told Savvy that he had an essay to write for AP American Lit. But after they'd all left, Owen lingered at the studio.

Bea was practicing the Italian *fouettés* she had to do in the coda at the end of the *grand pas* with Etienne. They required both strength and stamina, two things she was still working on. Lotte was filming, which only made it worse; knowing that she was capturing every flaw and imperfection was paralyzing.

"Hey, do you need a ride home tonight?" Owen asked when she sat down on the floor next to him, exhausted and frustrated.

"Sure," she said. Her mom had said to call when she was ready, but Bea figured she'd probably be happy to not have to drive. Her mom was in her pajamas by six p.m. most nights lately—that was if she bothered to get dressed at all.

Bea gathered her things and threw on her clothes, and they headed into the lobby. "*À demain,*" she said, waving to Lotte and then to Etienne and Vivienne, who were in the lobby discussing something with Nancy.

"*Bonne nuit,*" Etienne said, waving.

She followed Owen out to the parking lot.

"Still no license yet?" he asked.

"Not yet." She'd gone as far as scheduling her driver's test for the week before the show, but she still wasn't sure she could pass. She could do the route between the studio and their house without any problems, but she hadn't been on the freeway yet.

"So do you want to go straight home, or would you like to go get a coffee or something? French fries?" he asked. "S'mores?"

"S'mores would be awesome," she said.

"Okay, I might have oversold myself. I can definitely get you French fries though."

They got two large fries at the McDonald's drive-through, but she didn't want to go home yet. She'd texted her mom that she was getting a ride, picking up food; she still had some time.

"Hey," she said. "You wanna see something cool?"

"Sure," he said. "I'm up for anything."

Owen was so cute, with earnest eyes and a wide smile.

"It's one of my best qualities," he said. "My enthusiasm. I'm basically a golden retriever in human form."

She directed him to the foothills near Olive's house, and her heart tripped a bit as they coasted down Olive's wide street. She remembered riding bikes here with Olive, pedaling furiously up the hill and then flying down, hands releasing the handlebars, the wind blowing through their hair, the ribbons at their handlebars flapping colorfully in the breeze. When was the last time they did that?

"Park here," she said when they reached the end of the cul-de-sac. The entrance to the urban trail was barely visible in the feeble glow of a streetlight.

They got out, and he said, "You should grab your bag. Car locks don't work."

She used her phone as a flashlight as they walked along the narrow path that wound up the canyon's hillside. By the time they got to the clearing near the top, they were both breathless.

The fig tree was just as she remembered it, though she and Olive hadn't been here in over a year now. They'd first discovered it when they were eleven, the year they both went *en pointe*.

"Whoa! It looks like something from Middle Earth," he said, gazing at the enormous tree and its tangled limbs.

"I know, right?" she said. She reached for his hand and led him across the exposed roots, like ropy snakes twisting and turning above ground. She located the familiar crook in the trunk and hoisted herself up onto one of the main limbs. Owen followed behind, her flashlight brightening their way as they navigated the branches.

From the edge of the limb, the view was of the sparkling city beyond.

"Wow," he said. "This is amazing. That's Costa de la Luna over there?"

"Yeah. But that's not what I wanted you to see," she said, pointing the light up at the canopy of leaves. "Look up."

There, hanging from the branches, were her and Olive's collection of old pointe shoes. Tattered silken ornaments. Hundreds of them.

"Wow!" he said.

"Olive and I called this our *Toi Toi Toi* Tree. You know, like a Good Luck tree? It's stupid. But we totally used to think it was magical. Whenever we retired a pair of pointe shoes, we'd string them up here and make a wish."

She thought of all those wishes: for luck in competitions, in auditions. For a good grade on a test or a paper, and—later—for her dad to be well again. The last time she'd come here, she'd strung up her shoes, then couldn't stop crying. Olive had just held her. She missed Olive. She missed being eleven and making wishes on shoes and believing in magic.

"Can *I* make one?" he asked. "Do you have a pair of dead shoes in your backpack?"

She still had the pair she'd worn to the audition with Etienne in her bag.

"Sure. Here." She gave him one and kept the other one.

"Like this?" he asked, standing up and reaching into the foliage to tie the ribbons.

"Yep—and it's like a birthday wish. It has to be the first one that comes to your mind, and you can't say it out loud. Otherwise it won't come true."

"Wow, so many rules."

She stood up and tied the other shoe to a branch, closing her eyes and wishing for the first thing that came to mind. *Please let me win the scholarship.* She sucked in her breath; she should have used the wish for her mom—for her to sell her new book, for her to stop being so sad. She should have wished for Olive to forgive her. For Savvy to never find out about the bonfire. How could she have wasted it on something that was probably never going to happen?

Silently, they climbed out of the tree. Owen took her hand, and they made their way back down the path to the car, walking quickly and then running, succumbing to gravity. The steep decline was hard on her knees, but it felt so good to run, so nice to leave that wish in the tree. At least now it was out of her hands, a weight lifted off her. Fate would decide now.

When they got back to the car, they were laughing. Big belly laughs. The kind of laughter she hadn't had in so long. Then it petered out, like a chattering audience growing quiet when the house-lights go out and the curtains open.

She knew it was coming, but the kiss still surprised her. It was soft and warm and sweet. It wasn't her first kiss. But it was the first kiss that felt like this. Nice.

"Wow, I didn't expect it to happen so quickly," he said, as he stepped back.

"What's that?"

"My wish to come true," he said, and wiggled his eyebrows.

"That's cheesy," she said.

"*You're* cheesy."

They got into the car, but her heart wouldn't stop racing. Any of the hurt she'd felt about being excluded from Savvy's party was gone now. Owen turned the key; warm air blasted from the vents, and Nirvana blasted from the stereo. "Heart-Shaped Box."

"Oh! I love Nirvana!" she said. "Our dog's name is Cobain. We also had a cat named Love. But she was kind of mean, and then she got eaten by a coyote."

"That's amazing."

"It happens all the time. They live in the canyons."

"Not the coyote part. The Kurt and Courtney part."

"*Cobain* and *Love*. But Love died," she said.

"Love never dies."

"Oh my god. Somebody should put you on a cracker, you're so cheesy."

At this, he kissed her again, quickly, before turning his gaze back to the road as they drove slowly past Olive's house.

Then there was someone driving behind them, the high beams blinding.

"What the hell?" she said.

Owen gazed into the rearview and then the side-view mirror. "It's a van."

She turned around and looked out the rear window. "I think it's *Lotte*," she said. "What is she doing here?"

Ever

Ever had selected "Strawberries," a poem by Edwin Morgan, to inspire their writing exercise on Monday morning. It was one of her favorites, a simple poem about a couple eating strawberries together on a porch as a storm rolls in.

"I want you to try to recall a quiet moment with another person. Try to remember all the sensory details. Think about the smells, the tastes. The textures of the moment. Give your reader the vicarious experience of *being* in that place," she said, and dutifully, they all began. She opened her laptop, thought for a moment, and put her fingers on the keys.

In college, when she and Ethan had just started dating, they'd decided to take a road trip to Big Sur to visit the Henry Miller Library. They'd packed a tent, a hibachi, sleeping bags. The library ended up being closed, and it began pouring rain as they were pitching their tent; cooking outside was impossible. Soaked and shivering, they'd found a restaurant overlooking the water. Ethan told her that Henry Miller and Anaïs Nin would come here. He'd bought her a copy of *The Four-Chambered Heart* at a used bookstore, and they'd rented *Henry and June* that winter. Sitting at the bar, she'd felt as if *she* were in a film. This is what falling in love felt like, she thought: *cinematic*, each moment imbued with import. Even simply walking down the street—or riding on the back of his beach cruiser, holding on to his soft T-shirt—felt dramatic.

They had hardly any money left after paying for their campsite, so they asked for a basket of bread and the cheapest bottle of wine on the menu. She caught a glimpse of their reflections in the mirror behind the bar, through the glass and amber liquid in the bottles lined up there. She was drenched, but she felt pretty and just so happy.

She pointed to the restaurant's name on the menu. "What does *Nepenthe* mean?"

"Remember? It was in *The Odyssey*," he said. They'd met in a Humanities seminar. "It's a drug. Egyptian, I think? It can make you forget your grief."

"Would you take a drug like that?" she asked, turning to him. "To forget your sorrow?"

She remembered the way his long, beautiful fingers dragged a crusty piece of bread through a swirl of olive oil and red wine vinegar on the plate before them. The drip of it on the wooden bar. The way he stopped and looked at her, shaking his head.

"No," he said. "Grief is good."

"How so?"

"It means you had something worth grieving."

"But what if *I* died," she said boldly, a little tipsy. "You wouldn't want to forget your *excruciating pain and heartache*? Not even if some Egyptian guy gave you a magic potion?"

"Nope," he said firmly, setting that soaked piece of bread on the rim of his plate. "Heartache is proof that you loved someone." At the word *loved*, she felt the heat of the cheap wine spreading down her shoulders, flooding her.

"You love me?" she asked. No boy had ever told her that before.

His eyes were sparkly. "I do."

She wondered now, if she had this elixir, if she could simply forget the pain that had settled in her chest, would she? Would the absence of her grief somehow negate that she had loved him, and he had loved her?

Sid, sweating in his velour tracksuit, suddenly stood up from the table. His wife, Clementine, gripped his hand.

"I'm not feeling very well," he said.

"Oh, no," she said, pulled out of her reverie. "Should I call someone?"

"No, no. Just indigestion." He patted Clementine's hand.

"Let's go home," Clementine said, and stood up as well. Together, they hobbled out of the classroom.

Ever returned to her writing, but the spell was broken. She used to be so good at handling interruptions, like diving back into a dream after being woken, but she struggled now to capture what it felt like to be in that bar with Ethan. When she tried to conjure his face, the details were shadowy, and the lack of clarity filled her with dread.

She tried to write, but oddly, her thoughts turned to Bea. She could tell something was going on between Bea and Owen. Some tight bud of something about to bloom. But instead of feeling happy for her, she wanted to warn her. To keep her safe from what seemed like inevitable heartache.

Lindsay

Olive had gone back to school that Monday morning after being out "sick" again all last week. She said Savvy would drive her to and from ballet; she didn't need Lindsay at all. Olive had hardly said a word to Lindsay after she'd made her big announcement about wanting to quit ballet, and Lindsay had felt too stunned to do much beyond hope she'd only been lashing out, flirting with quitting the way all the girls did at some point. Well, most girls. Savvy and Bea probably never even entertained the idea.

When Mary O'Leary quit, Lindsay had felt awful for her mother, Cathy. She'd bumped into her over the summer at the CVS, where Cathy was buying eardrops. "Mary's got swimmer's ear," she had said by way of explanation, the heft of what this meant hanging between them for a moment, and her expression almost grief-stricken.

For the last fifteen years, Lindsay's life, like all the moms', had revolved around ballet: driving Olive to class, waiting for her to get out of class. Keeping her body healthy: visits to physical therapists, massage therapists, acupuncturists, and chiropractors. Hundreds of hours sitting in the greenroom, miles on the road to competitions and auditions. She knew better than to try to calculate how many tens of thousands of dollars spent.

They were all aware that it might end one day, of course. Mary was evidence of this. A few girls fell away as each year passed. It was like the longest game of musical chairs ever. Now there were only a few seats and just as many girls, plus one, circling, circling. Would it really be Olive who stood still when the music stopped, all the seats taken?

She could never explain to Steve what this felt like; his investment in all of this had been purely financial, like a stock he'd watched suddenly plummet, the only option to sell it off as quickly as he could to recoup what remained. Ever would understand, of course, but it felt unfair to burden her with this: to drag her down with her sad lament just as Bea's star was rising. And, she was beginning to suspect, everyone had seen this coming except for her.

No. Olive had said she would finish out the year, and Lindsay had felt a little glimmer of hope at this. If she didn't get the scholarship, there was still YAGP semifinals in January. Vivienne had talked about doing *Swan Lake* as the spring show. If Savvy was sent off to Paris, she'd need a Black Swan.

Still, as she drove along the coast that afternoon to meet Victor to go over the inspector's report, Lindsay's heart sank with the sun. She parked and stood staring out at the view, feeling despondent. But when she turned back to the café, she saw Victor sitting at a table by the window. He smiled at her and waved, so happy to see her—to *see* her!—and her heart lightened.

Upstairs in the condo, they read the inspector's report together—examined a missing tile in the bathroom, the ancient pipes under the sink, the crack in the bedroom window.

"It feels so strange," Victor said, looking out the window at that sliver of blazing sky.

"What's that?" Lindsay asked. She was having difficulty focusing.

He sat down at the foot of the bed and set his coffee cup on the end table. He sighed. "I guess this is really happening. Twenty years of marriage, and now this."

A surge of sympathy flooded her.

"I know," she said, nodding. "Actually, my husband and I . . ." she trailed off. What was she going to say? To this guy she hardly knew? This casual acquaintance? Her *buyer*. Tell him that her marriage was falling apart, too? That her daughter was talking about abandoning her dreams? That she felt like a colossal failure as both wife and mother?

"Mind if I sit down?" she asked, suddenly feeling light-headed. Dieting always made her feel a bit faint.

She sat next to Victor, and together they looked out the window at the fiery sky.

"Are you okay?" he asked. His hand was warm when he put it over hers. Soft and tender and kind.

"I am," she said. "I'm sorry. I don't know what's wrong with me."

The church bells began to ring, six o'clock. They both laughed at the deafening noise. But he didn't let go of her hand. And she didn't pull it away.

She smiled at Victor when the bells stopped ringing. "I really should go," she said.

"Me, too," Victor said, and lifted his hand.

But she could still feel his rough palm the whole way home. She wondered if Steve would be able to see its imprint there. If Olive would somehow know.

Ever

Vivienne had always allowed the kids to wear their costumes to class on Halloween, one of her few concessions to childhood. Of course, the costumes needed to allow freedom of movement, so they usually incorporated tutus. Over the years, Bea had been a "ballerina cat," a "ballerina vampire," and last year, she and Olive had been Ketchup and Mustard—wearing red and yellow tutus. But this year, Bea didn't dress up. Of course, Ever had known she'd grow out of it someday, though she suspected this decision not to partici pate had more to do with Olive.

She'd asked Bea several times what was going on, but each time she just shrugged, said she and Olive had grown apart. But even as she tried to act nonchalant, Ever saw a deep hurt in her eyes. Why couldn't Bea just talk to her? She worried that not only were Bea and Olive growing apart, but that *she* and Bea were becoming distant, too. If this was what her children growing up meant, she wasn't sure she could take it.

When they walked into the building, she could see that Olive and Savvy had, unlike Bea, dressed up, in white and black tutus with jaunty silver caps on their heads: *Salt* and *Pepper*. The Littles were all in costume, of course: kitties and witches, a half dozen Elsas, a sad-looking taco, and a tiny antlered Bambi. One mom, wearing yoga clothes, was trying to coerce her howling six-year-old into doing some stretches. The girl, dressed in a red leotard and tights, devil's horns affixed to her head, was not having it.

Bob was also in the lobby, tapping away at his laptop. So far, he had declined to share his writing in class. She was curious what he was working on now. Sci-fi, she figured. Guys like Bob were always writing sci-fi.

Nancy was yelling at the Level 6s to quiet down. The noise level in the lobby was much higher than usual. If she were Vivienne, she'd probably give the kids Halloween off.

"What time are you done tonight?" she asked Bea.

"Eight, but Owen and I are going to go to the early show of *Rocky Horror*. It starts at nine; I'll be home by midnight. If that's okay?"

"Sure," she said, smiling. "I'll hand out candy." On her way home, she'd swing by the drugstore and buy some chocolate. She'd already decorated the front stoop so that kids in the neighborhood would know she was giving out candy. Danny had helped her string orange twinkle lights in the windows.

"Save me some Kit Kats?" Bea said.

"Of course." Next year, Bea would be somewhere else for Halloween. And back here, would she even be in the house, or would she and Danny be in an apartment somewhere? So many things were coming to an end. Too many things.

She gave Nancy the November tuition, a small miracle of more financial finagling, and watched Lotte focus her camera on one chubby Little in a bee costume who was buzzing about the lobby, zigzagging through the crowd, and Ever felt the sting of nostalgia again.

"Hi, Bob!" she said. "Working on your book?"

"I am!" He smiled.

Her phone buzzed in her purse, and she quickly pulled it out: an email notification. From Leona. *Call me!*

She quickly calculated how long it had been since she sent off the proposal: just over two weeks. Too fast to respond to a manuscript, but maybe not too fast for a proposal? She hadn't heard anything after the initial acknowledgment from Leona's assistant that it had come through, along with a promise to circle back around after she'd had a chance to read it. She must have read it.

She felt both excited and anxious as she looked around the room. Nobody here had any idea what was at stake with this call. A *yes* from Leona was the first step toward a new contract, a new advance, a new chance to revive her career. To keep the house.

She'd sent the proposal along with an email she hoped might gently impart how much she needed to get a new contract. "Hope you love it," she'd said, which was authorspeak for *God, please tell me you can sell this thing.*

She stepped outside and dialed Leona's cell.

"Hey," Leona said, her tone apologetic.

No, no, no. Ever felt like she might collapse. She leaned against the building. Waiting.

"Listen, Ever, I know how hard you've been working on this . . ."

Ever's heart pitched.

"But it just, ugh, how do I say this. It just doesn't feel like *you.*"

Leona kept talking, but the words all swam together, and Ever felt like she was drowning.

Josie

"We're such *snacks*," Melissa said, smacking her lipsticked lips together in the bar's restroom mirror. Melissa was always trying out the new words Jaz brought home from the older kids at ballet. She was like a walking urban dictionary. It was embarrassing.

Jaz was staying at her cousin's house after trick-or-treating, a rare sleepover, and so Melissa had suggested they go to Maisie's. Melissa was dressed up like a genie, flat belly bare and gravity-defying boobs on full display. Josie adjusted her cat ears and studied her reflection. False eyelashes, black smudge on her nose, and eyeliner whiskers on her cheeks. She wore a black silky blouse unbuttoned just enough and a pair of tight black leather pants tucked into teetering boots. Standard sexy kitten costume; she could anticipate the *pussy* jokes that would come by the night's end. God, men were so predictable.

Melissa had insisted it was time Josie put herself back on the market. She was teasing—this was how they talked about being single— but for some reason, it bothered her now. The idea that she was a commodity, that she could be purchased like a pound of ground beef or a pork tenderloin, made her feel a little nauseous.

Maisie's was one of five bars in downtown Costa de la Luna, but the only one with live music. The dance floor was packed with people, and with every drink, Melissa became more insistent on getting Josie out onto the dance floor. Normally, Josie loved to dance. But tonight, she felt listless. Restless. At least the music was good; the bass was booming inside her, and with the noise, she didn't have to make conversation.

This friendship, she thought, was—like most of her relationships—

one based on an exchange. For Melissa, Josie was more mentor than friend. Josie provided her guidance and hope; Melissa clung to Savvy's successes as if they were somehow a guarantee of her own child's—if only she followed the steps that Josie had taken to get her there. And for Josie? She got to feel like a teacher, as if she had some valuable wisdom to impart. It felt good when Melissa wanted to know: *What's the best summer program? Who's the best photographer? The best pointe shoe fitter? What are the best shoes?* Being with Melissa made her feel like an expert.

"That guy's been checking you out all night," Melissa said, after knocking back her fourth sugar-rimmed Lemon Drop. "You should go ask him to dance."

The guy in question was sitting at the bar, good looking enough, Josie supposed. But her eye was trained to look for certain things. A receding hairline could be forgiven in the presence of a Rolex. A BMW key ring next to a hand with hairy knuckles? Okay. But a hot guy in a cheap suit? Hard pass. This one, she quickly assessed, was paying for at least one failed marriage (likely with a couple of kids). Sacrifices had been made: good (pre-divorce) shoes, but the shirt was Nordstrom Rack at best. The top-shelf bourbon cocktail was an expensive habit, but the ill-fitting pants meant he'd gained weight and didn't have the funds to get a new wardrobe. All of this gleaned in a single, though lingering, glance, but it was enough that he noticed her checking him out and lifted that overpriced cocktail he couldn't afford as if in cheers.

"You should go for it," Melissa said, and then, sensing her hesitation, added, "You don't have to marry him, you know."

Josie knew this, but she also knew when something would go nowhere, and she was too damned old to screw around. She'd come to the sad but vaguely comforting acceptance that most things in life were transactional. She pitied those who didn't get that.

She drank the Lemon Drops that Melissa kept ordering because they were sweet and went down easy, the liquid filling up that hollow place with a warm, lovely, sunshine-y feeling.

"Okay, fine. Let's go dance," Josie said.

Melissa, who was a couple of drinks ahead of her, stumbled onto the dance floor, giggling, and Josie followed. The floor was packed with people, most in costume: masks and capes and various Party City ensembles, and it all seemed ludicrous and it all seemed a little sad, and so she closed her eyes and let the music carry her away.

"I need another drink," Melissa said when the song ended, and disappeared from the dance floor, but Josie kept dancing.

The hands on her hips startled her, and her eyes shot open. She was ready to sock whoever had decided to grope her, but it took only a moment to realize that the man, wearing a purple and gold Mardi Gras mask, was *Etienne*. She recognized the woodsy cologne, and his body, which seemed as comfortable on a filthy barroom dance floor as the stage.

She scanned the room, searching for Melissa, and spotted her chatting up that sad sap at the bar. Etienne beckoned her deeper into the crowd, and she followed. This was not a good idea. If Melissa saw this, she'd go apeshit. But his body felt so good against hers, and his hands wouldn't let her go. So she leaned in, moved to the rhythm, giving him what he, like all men, wanted, and expected that it would be clear what it was she wanted in return.

She felt fingernails digging into her arm. Melissa hissed in her ear. "Let's *go*."

"Sorry," she mumbled to Etienne, and he pressed his hand to his heart before slipping back into the crowd.

As they gathered their things from their table, Melissa was silent.

"You okay?" Josie asked, heart thumping, but Melissa just fished around in her purse for her phone. She looked up at Josie, her eyes unfocused and angry.

"Do you want me to call us a Lyft?" Josie asked brightly.

"I see it now," Melissa hissed. "Mark's always said that you've got no limits when it comes to her."

"Mark said *what*?" she asked.

"*Sa-van-nah*," Melissa said, drawing out the word. She was really drunk, her words slippery, dangerous. "You're *prima*."

"What are you talking about?"

Melissa had found her phone and started tapping at the screen. "I really didn't think you'd go *this* far, but when opportunity knocks, you answer, right? Invite it in for a drink and a quick screw?"

"You're wasted," Josie said.

"And you . . . you're a . . ." Melissa slurred the word, but Josie heard it loud and clear. And then Melissa stormed out.

Bea

Bea had never been to *Rocky Horror* before. Owen had brought the props: rice, toilet paper, rubber gloves. He showed her what to do and introduced her to some friends of his from his school. She was swept up in the mayhem and tangled in toilet paper by the time they stumbled out of the theater. It was only eleven o'clock, and she didn't want to go home. She still had an hour until curfew (she had a curfew now!), and no ballet until the next afternoon.

"I'm starving," she said. "I totally forgot to eat after class."

"Let's go to Denny's for pancakes," Owen said.

"Oh my god, I would kill or die for a pancake."

"Hey, I can get you a pancake without you murdering anyone or sacrificing your own life," Owen said, chucking her in the arm.

They drove across town to the Denny's in the strip mall by the freeway. The mall was usually deserted: an aquarium supply shop, a sketchy-looking massage parlor, and furniture rental store. But tonight, there had to have been fifty teenagers in costumes in line to get in. Bea and Owen sat on a bench outside the aquarium shop after giving their names to the hostess, who said it could be a half hour wait. In the window, there was a large fish tank filled with orange clown fish. She remembered Danny, after watching *Finding Nemo*, would cling to their dad whenever they went out to wade in the water, afraid they'd get separated.

A group of boys were vaping over by the darkened Rent-a-Center. Others congregated on a grassy median in the parking lot. It felt like Owen had opened a door, one she'd been looking at for years, wondering what was on the other side. Like Alice and the door to Wonderland, she'd been too big to fit through. There was a whole other life out here, one she knew existed, but had only caught glimpses of before. But tonight felt different. Like she belonged here. After all this time, and just as she was preparing to leave for good.

Feeling bold, she took his hand and squeezed it. "I like hanging out with you," she said.

Owen said, "Awww," and rested his head against her shoulder. Her heart fluttered.

"Hey," someone said. When she looked up, Nick, Luke, Savvy, and Olive were standing there. Her fluttering heart rose to her throat and hovered there.

"Hey, Bea," Savvy said. "Cute *shirt*." It was Owen's Grateful Dead T-shirt she'd borrowed to change into after class. Was she making fun of her?

Savvy was a little glassy-eyed, leaning against Nick. She and Olive had also changed out of their costumes and were both wearing short, nearly identical dresses. She noticed Savvy had a burning cigarette in her hand; that was new. There were girls at NYRB who smoked; they said it helped stave off their appetites. She wondered if Olive had started smoking, too.

"Hi," Bea said to Savvy, and then, "hi, Liv."

Olive stared at the ground. The tips of Bea's ears burned.

"You guys on the list for a table?" Luke asked. "Can we crash? The line is crazy."

"We just asked for a two-top," Owen said.

"A *tube top*?" Savvy giggled.

"*Two-top*, a table for two people," Owen clarified. He, like Danny, bused tables at a restaurant. He even paid half his own tuition at the studio.

"How *cozy*," Luke said, and punched Nick in the shoulder. Nick scowled at Owen.

"Let's just get in line," Olive said impatiently. Then they were gone.

"Actually, I should probably go home," Bea said, standing up.

"Okay," he said. "We can grab some drive-through if you want. Taco Bell chalupa on me?"

"I'm okay. I really should just get home to my mom. She's alone tonight."

As they drove back toward the coast, Owen said, "I'm sorry about Olive. Luke said you and she had some sort of fight? At the beach?"

What had Luke told him? And Nick? Was *that* what all this was about? His being so nice, all these dates? Did he think she would do that . . . with him? She looked out the window, nauseated. She felt Owen's hand on her arm. Gentle. "Hey," he said. "I didn't mean to make you upset."

"I don't know what the guys told you. I heard Luke was saying some stuff . . . about me, but it's not . . . whatever he's saying."

He looked confused. "What happened with Luke?"

She shook her head. He didn't know. Why had she opened her mouth?

Lindsay

As Olive ate breakfast, Lindsay studied her calendar. Friday was one of those days that Lindsay hated: jam-packed, every minute swallowed up. At home, the cupboards were empty on Fridays, but the laundry hampers were full. Thank god for Sonia, who had arrived at seven o'clock and was already upstairs stripping the sheets, likely still warm with their sleep. At work, Fridays were the best days to post new listings, prompting buyers to schedule weekend visits. She also seemed to always have closings on Fridays, and today was no exception. Everything was set to go with Victor's condo. At three o'clock, they were meeting at the title attorney's office to close.

She was going to miss spending time with Victor. Of course, she knew she'd still run into him in the parking lot at the studio every now and then, but it had been so nice having coffee and chatting. They had a lot in common, and he was just so kind. It was innocent, of course, but it also felt a *little* bit illicit. A secret friendship she didn't talk about with anyone. Steve had a life that existed beyond the walls of their home: work, his co-workers, his golf buddies, and whomever he was spending time with when he wasn't at home. He was away so much, he could probably have a whole other family—a second life. Once she'd read about a woman who found out that her husband had another wife and two other kids. In an entirely different state. She'd felt baffled: how could she not know? Well, it appears, just like this.

She had to drop Olive off at school at eight o'clock, which left her the morning to get her new listings posted. She still needed to get the blood work done, though the bump—as promised—had almost completely disappeared with the steroid cream. The lab took walk-ins, so she figured she'd swing by the hospital on her way to the attorney's office at three o'clock. After the closing, she'd go back to work to get ready for the weekend open houses before going to the grocery store.

"What's your schedule look like this weekend?" she asked Olive. They were four weeks and counting until *Nutcracker* now, which meant rehearsals during the week, as well as on Saturdays and Sundays.

"Bardo might be having another party Saturday night."

"Well, they're broadcasting the Bolshoi's *Don Q* at the theater on Sunday night. I thought we could ask Ever and Bea if they'd like to go." The theater offered a whole series of ballets each season; last year, the four of them had gone to see them all.

Olive took a deep breath and set her spoon down. She looked at Lindsay, exasperated.

"Listen, Liv. Friendships aren't like piano lessons or softball or Girl Scouts," Lindsay said, realizing even as she said it that she was starting something she didn't have time to finish. But she couldn't stop herself. "You can't just *quit*."

"I didn't quit the friendship, Mom," she said.

"Well, that's what it feels like," Lindsay said. "It feels like you ditched Bea for Savvy. And honestly, it breaks my heart. You two have been best friends since you were ten years old. How can you act like all those years didn't happen?"

"Well, you and Daddy have been married for almost thirty years now, and you've ditched *him*."

Lindsay felt like she'd been slapped.

"What is that supposed to mean?"

Olive's eyes were glossy. "Josie *saw* you at Namaste with that guy from Freezey's."

Lindsay was trembling. The top of her hand, where he'd touched her, seemed to pulsate.

"He's my *client*. I meet clients for coffee all the time."

"Whatever," Olive said, wiping as a tear fell.

Olive hadn't cried in front of her for ages. Lindsay was overwhelmed with guilt.

"Livvie, you can't possibly think . . ." but her voice trailed off. She thought about hugging her, trying to explain, but then decided the best thing to do would be to pretend the conversation hadn't suddenly veered off-track like that. To acknowledge it, was to own up to it. But she hadn't done anything wrong. Goddamn Josie Jacobs.

"I was just *saying*," Lindsay said, her heart pounding, relentless, "that Bea is like your *sister*, Liv. I don't understand what she could have done to make you walk away from her."

"Why aren't you listening to me?" Olive said, her face so red now, her freckles almost disappeared. "She walked away from *me*. It was *her*."

"What are you talking about?" Lindsay said.

"Nothing, Mom. Bea is perfect. Perfect dancer, perfect family, perfect everything. *Whatever*." And with that, she grabbed her bag and stormed out of the kitchen.

Despite being slammed with work that morning, she couldn't stop thinking about Olive's accusations about Victor. The closing was this afternoon, and now she found that she was dreading seeing him.

At noon, she grabbed a salad at the Trader Joe's near work, planning to eat it while she waited at the lab. But the lab was remarkably empty, just her and an old man with an eyepatch and the volunteer who offered her a warm cookie. The old Lindsay would have taken two, but instead she shook her head and said, "No, thank you."

The phlebotomist was new; she could tell by her eagerness to please and her apologies as she poked and then poked again. Lindsay was starting to feel light-headed: no breakfast and no lunch. When the needle finally slipped into her vein, she felt her vision going dark at the edges and the sensation of falling, followed by a vacuum silence in her ears, then the startled yelp of the poor phlebotomist.

When she came to, a nurse was helping her back up onto the chair. The lady with the cookies was handing her a paper cup of orange juice, which she took and drank obediently.

"Did I pass out?" she asked.

"You certainly did," the nurse said. "So, we're going to keep you here for a bit, just to make sure you're okay. Is there someone who could give you a ride?"

She thought of Steve, though he rarely, if ever, answered her texts on Friday afternoons, leaving work early to golf.

"What time is it?" she asked.

"It's about quarter to three," the cookie and juice lady said.

"Oh, crap," she said. *Victor's closing.* She took a deep breath and reached into her bag for her phone. "Hey Victor, I hate to ask you this. But could you possibly pick me up on your way to the attorney's office? I'm at the hospital."

"What? Are you *okay*?"

"Yes," she said. "I guess I *swooned* a little getting my blood drawn."

"Handsome phlebotomist?" he asked.

"Ha! No such luck. Just no time for breakfast today." She felt woozy, the edges going fuzzy and then dark again. She leaned over and put her head between her knees. What a nightmare.

Victor showed up, and the nurses insisted on wheeling her out of the hospital to his car. She felt ridiculous. Luckily, Victor had pulled up into a space right out front, and so the nurse didn't have to wheel her very far. Victor took her arm and helped her up—and she got the oddest sensation—she imagined herself one day wheelchair-bound, her husband gently taking her arm to help her up. But try as she might, she could not imagine Steve doing this.

She felt like she might swoon again. Good lord. What was wrong with her?

"You okay?" he asked, and gripped her elbow.

She nodded.

"Mrs. Chase?" Startled, she looked up and saw Savannah Jacobs on the walkway. Savvy studied her, then Victor, her blue eyes wide and fluttery. *Oh, crap.*

"Savvy," she said, feeling heat rush to her limbs. "What are you doing here?"

"I have a PT appointment on Fridays in this building," Savvy said, motioning to the doors. "For my tendinitis."

"Oh," Lindsay said.

"What are *you* doing here?" she asked, though she wasn't looking at Lindsay, but squarely at Victor.

Bea

"Pick a boy, and line up," Etienne said. It was Tuesday, partnering class.

Bea had not been looking forward to partnering, where it would be nearly impossible to avoid Nick. Still, she'd walked into the studio, chin up, pretending everything was okay. She had done the same thing each time she went to visit her dad at the hospital last year. She was tough.

"'Tis just a flesh wound!" her dad would tease in his Monty Python voice, any time she got hurt and brushed it off. She'd gotten her appendix out when she was six—admitted on Friday night and back in her first-grade classroom on Monday, ballet class by the following Friday. She'd had four adult teeth removed when she was twelve with only a couple of shots of Novocaine. She regularly lost toenails and kept dancing. She could do this.

Vivienne assigned partners, pairing the girls with boys who were the right height and strength for the lifts. Being one of the smallest Level 6 girls, she tended to be paired with Owen; he was the shortest of *Le Trio*. He was also the weakest in terms of strength, but even he could lift her easily into a shoulder sit or an angel lift. They danced well together; she felt she could trust him. Trust was the most important thing in partnering.

Etienne, however, didn't bother assigning partners. Instead, he had three boys stand in the center and told the girls to line up behind them in even groups. Their choice. There were twelve girls, so each boy had a line of four. Normally, she, Jaz, Phoebe, and Lizzy—the shortest girls—danced with Owen. But now, as she moved to stand behind him, there were already four girls there. For whatever reason, a newer girl named Sophia had jumped from Nick's ship. It was probably because Owen wasn't cocky like Nick, never blamed his partner when something went wrong. Plus, he didn't dig his fingers into your ribs when lifting you up. Once Nick had left three thumb-shaped bruises on her hip like inky fingerprints for days after. She thought about asking Jaz if she'd mind going to Nick, who needed one more girl. But since the casting for *Nutcracker*, nobody was doing Bea any favors, and no one seemed willing to budge.

"*Vas-y, Beatrice,*" Etienne said impatiently, and so she quickly ran across the floor to Nick's line. She was last in line, at least, which gave her time to learn the new combination they were doing. She'd done *pas* classes all summer at NYRB, and her partnering skills had gotten better. But her summer partner had been an incredible dancer, a boy who trained in Russia during the school year, able to lift her as if she were a feather.

She watched Nick and Savvy first. She used to envy the ease and synchronicity of their movements. The way their bodies appeared to work together toward a common goal: to make the audience feel like they were witnessing something private. In the best *pas de deux*, in Bea's opinion, the audience wasn't a spectator, but a *voyeur*.

She remembered a night when her dad was sick, and she'd gotten up to get some water. The porchlight was illuminating the deck, and she'd moved to go turn it off, thinking someone had left it on. But when she heard the music, she stopped. Her mom and dad were standing together outside, leaning into each other, moving to the muffled sounds of Van Morrison. Her dad looked like a ghost in that faint light, and her mom looked *ravaged*. For a moment, her mind translated this moment into a ballet, into the adagio of two lovers, one dying, the other who would rather die than lose him. It was achingly beautiful, she thought, the way they danced, their bodies holding each other up. But just as quickly, the truth of what she was seeing became clear. This was no *Romeo and Juliet*, not Nureyev and Fonteyn clinging to each other, Romeo dancing with Juliet's lifeless body, refusing to accept her death. This was her mom. And her dad.

This was no performance, but rather a private dance never intended to have an audience.

She looked at Nick now and remembered dancing on the sand, the heat of the bonfire, the heat of her own skin. The heat of his hands on her bare waist. *No.*

"*Très bien,*" Etienne said, clapping as Savvy completed six pirouettes and then moved sharply into a flawless arabesque which she held, in Bea's opinion, a few moments too long. *Quelle frimeuse.* Savvy didn't need Nick; she was holding herself up. She was strong, and Nick was lazy. Even with her. *Especially* with her, because he could be.

Zoraiya was next, then Olive. She watched Olive with a sinking feeling. She'd put on a little weight over the summer, always struggling to keep it down, fighting her sweet tooth. When they were younger, Bea loved going to Olive's house, because of her ever-present stash of Sour Patch Kids and Junior Mints, Pringles and Flaming Hot Cheetos she kept in a plastic bin under her bed. "Where do you get *this*?" Bea had marveled at the stockpile. It was as if she had an entire 7-11 under her bed. "My dad," she'd said. "My mom would kill him if she knew." But worse than the change in Olive's body was that she just seemed checked out. Like she was only going through the motions. And Olive, unlike Savvy, was not strong enough to hold herself up, and so when Nick failed to support her when she did the *penché*, her leg extended over her as she reached to the floor, she almost fell on her face.

"Sloppy," Etienne said dismissively as Olive struggled to her feet. Nick smirked.

"I am talking about you," Etienne said to Nick. "Next!" Etienne said, and moved to where Owen was partnering with Jaz.

As Bea and Nick got into position, with her standing in front of him, she felt his fingers on her pelvis. His breath was hot on her neck, yet goosebumps rose to the surface of her skin. It had started like this that night. Was he remembering, too?

The music began, and she tried to focus. She *plié*d in fourth and began the pirouette, feeling his hands on her, his fingers turning her, touching her. She held her breath.

The sand had been cold under her bare feet, but the fire was warm, and so was the liquor that slipped down her throat. Everything melted.

"Beatrice, *inspire et expire*," Etienne said. "You must breathe. You are like a balloon, about to pop." Etienne clapped his hands together as she completed a turn. It startled them both, and Nick flinched, pinching her under her ribs. Bea bent forward into a *penché*, extending her leg up behind her with her foot slowly rising toward the ceiling, pressed her chest toward her standing leg, and prayed that Nick would do his job. But she felt his grip on her loosening. She engaged her muscles, using every ounce of her strength and control to hold the *penché*. But it was her weaker leg, and Nick was *not* doing his job. She was completely alone. She felt the energy extended through both her legs; she winged her foot as if in defiance. She would not only survive this alone, she would be beautiful. This jerk was not going to destroy her; she'd worked too hard.

But, she *wasn't* strong enough, and she could feel herself losing control. When her ankle gave, and she fell, her palms slapped the floor, and both knees knocked to the ground. She scrambled to her feet, and Etienne stormed toward Nick.

"You are *dangereux*," Etienne snapped. "*Je vais te montrer*. I will show you."

Etienne gripped Bea's waist, nudging her into the *penché* again. Her palms stung. Her ankle thudded with pain.

He scolded Nick as he demonstrated. "You must keep your back straight, your arms straight and strong. You must pull back to keep her from falling over."

Nick stood to the side, arms crossed, as he watched Etienne.

"No *promenade*, just *arabesque*," Etienne said to her, and his hands were guiding her. The pain in her ankle was intense.

Bea lowered her leg, and Etienne released her. Close to her ear, he muttered under his breath. "*Je suis désolé*. I am sorry. *Il est un imbécile*."

Nick suddenly seemed to comprehend *le français*. He marched toward the door and picked up his water bottle by its plastic loop, face red with fury.

Everyone was silent.

"Why are we even here?" Nick said to Owen and Luke. He shook his head, then turned to Lotte, perched in the corner, capturing his tantrum with her camera. "None of *us* are going to get the scholarship," he said, motioning to the other boys.

Owen looked down. He clearly didn't want any part of this.

"Luke?" Nick said, waiting for him to follow him out.

"*Dude*," Luke said, and threw his hands up in surrender. "I'm just here to dance." Then he said more softly, "You need to chill out."

"*Seriously?* You're cool with this?" he said. "You *really* think he's going to bring one of *us* back to Paris?"

Luke shrugged.

"Because I have news for you. *You're* not getting it," he said to Owen, who flushed red. "And neither are you," he said, turning to Luke. Then he stared pointedly at Bea and Etienne. "Not unless he decides he wants to sleep with one of you, too."

Bea felt her bowels twist. What was Nick implying? Was he saying Etienne was *attracted* to her? The idea of anyone thinking this made her want to cry. She looked at Savvy and Olive, but they both just stared at the floor.

"What the hell?" Luke said, stepping toward Nick.

"Seriously," he continued. "We all know what it's going to take to get this scholarship. But do what you need to do, *dude*."

"*Excusez-moi*," Etienne said to Bea, and walked calmly to the door. He opened it, and with a grand gesture, he motioned for Nick to leave. "*Foutez le camp*," he said to Nick. "In English, that means *Get the hell out of my class*."

"Thanks for having my back, *Luke*," Nick hissed.

After Nick charged out, the electrified air in the studio seemed to buzz, then still. Etienne clapped his hands together and took Nick's place. "Let us get back to work," he said and, to her horror, he winked at Bea.

After class, Etienne disappeared into the office with Vivienne, who called him in as soon as they had all applauded and curtsied and thanked him for class. Bea wondered if Nick's mother had somehow already caught wind of what had happened. Nobody kept their pointe shoes on to keep practicing, but rather quietly got ready to go home. Everyone was speaking in whispers.

Bea retreated to the far corner of the studio, where she sat down and took off her pointe shoes, her ankle swelling once released from the ribbons. Savvy and Olive were sitting with Luke, close enough for her to hear them.

"Nick's got a right to be upset," Savvy said.

"Sure, all three of us guys do, but what the hell?" Luke said. "Calling me out, making it sound like I'm . . . ?"

"*Gay?*" Olive said, giggling.

"Liv," Savvy scolded. "Who cares if Luke's gay or not?"

"I'm not *gay*," Luke said. "Jesus."

"I'm just teasing," Savvy said, and squeezed Luke's knee.

He pulled his leg back and jumped to his feet. "Well, whatever. One less person to compete with," he said. "Fuck Nick."

"Aw, you guys will kiss and make up soon," Savvy said. "You always do."

"You think he's so great," Luke said angrily. "You have no idea."

Bea looked up, heart thumping, as if she'd just done a series of *sauts de chat* across the floor.

"What's *that* supposed to mean?" Savvy said, her smile fading. She caught Bea's eye, and Bea quickly looked down again.

"Nothing," Luke said. "Whatever. See you guys tomorrow."

Josie

Josie had not spoken to Melissa and had carefully avoided Etienne all week after the *incident*, or whatever that was at Maisie's on Halloween. She'd had way too much to drink that night. Really, maybe she'd quit drinking for her New Year's resolution. Nothing good ever came of loneliness and liquor. There it was: the sad truth. She was *lonely*.

When Mark left, it had still been summer vacation. It was easy to forget about him without school and ballet taking up all of Savvy's time. She and Olive buzzing about had kept her occupied. But now, her days were long, filled with little besides hours online and tending to the house. She made elaborate dinners only to have Savvy come home after ballet and go straight to bed. She took hikes in the canyon and swam late in the afternoon after Etienne took off to teach. She watched a lot of TV and played a lot of Candy Crush.

She had no idea what she would do once Savvy was gone. As much as she wanted her to get the scholarship, to go to Paris to start her career, she also couldn't fathom what a day would look like without her. She'd been taking care of Savvy since she was eighteen years old. After she got pregnant, after Alan Goldberg ruined her career, she'd focused all her energy into raising Savvy. She was her world, but soon, Savvy would be gone, too.

No wonder she'd been susceptible. That's all it was. Just a bit of loneliness. She was vulnerable, and he was . . . *hot*. Never mind that he held her daughter's future in his hands. But Melissa's words stung. She wasn't a *whore*. That's not what this was about.

Her plan was to pretend she didn't remember dancing with him, act like it didn't happen. Hell, if Mark could carry on with the hygienist and act completely innocent for months, then she could certainly pretend as though she hadn't danced a little dirty with someone. Also, he'd been wearing a mask. How could she even be certain it *was* him?

On Sunday, the doorbell rang. Nobody ever just popped over, so her first thought was that Mark had come back to thump his chest again. Or maybe it was Melissa coming to apologize. But as she looked through the peephole, she saw it wasn't Mark or Melissa but a guy with a binder and a clipboard. Probably a Jehovah's Witness, or somebody from the mega-church over by Home Depot. With Thanksgiving only a few weeks away, they probably wanted her to either give cash or convert.

She opened the door and said, "Can I help you?"

"Hi, Mrs. Jacobs?"

"Yes," she said. She'd kept Johnny's last name, but the Mrs. was a leftover from Mark.

"I'm Sam Gorski. I'm here to do the appraisal?"

"Appraisal?"

Sam Gorski looked at her like she was an Alzheimer's patient.

"For the house. You're the tenant, correct?"

"What are you talking about?"

The man looked stricken. "My understanding is the owner has a potential buyer. I'm here to do the bank appraisal for the lender. They said that arrangements had been made with the tenant."

She had her phone out before Sam Gorski could even step foot into the foyer.

AN APPRAISAL? WTF MARK

Mark texted back.

Craziest thing! I've got a client who wants to buy the house. Sight unseen.

"Come in," she said. "But you should know that my ex did not discuss this with me."

"Oh," Sam Gorski said, confused. "Your ex-*husband* is the owner?"

"My ex-husband is a cheating, lying asshole."

Sam Gorski reddened. "I'm so sorry," he said.

"Well, it's not *your* fault," she said, and took a deep breath. She would not let Mark rattle her. "Would you like some coffee?"

"Sure," he said. "And I'm so sorry about this. I'll try to be quick."

She led him to the kitchen, where she had a full pot of coffee brewed. She poured him a cup, handed it to him, and as he sipped it, she texted Mark back. **Next time, a heads up would be appreciated. I have company, and so this is super awkward.** She'd just let him stew in whatever visual that gave him.

Then, as if he'd been conjured, Etienne Bernay stumbled in through the patio doors, in pajama bottoms and nothing else. Like some sleepy Adonis, barefoot and messy-haired.

"*Bonjour,*" he said, his voice gravelly with cigarettes. "Oh, *pardonez-moi.*"

"Oh, no," she said, and beckoned him in. "We were just having some coffee. Join us?"

Sam Gorski's face turned a shade of red she'd never seen on human flesh before. "Well, all righty then," he said. "If you don't mind, I'm going to start to take some measurements?"

Bea

"Did Nick *quit?*" Bea asked Owen on Sunday at rehearsals.

Nick had not come back to the studio after the blow-up with Etienne. Almost a whole week, and he hadn't shown up for class or rehearsals. But oddly, his absence made Bea more anxious rather than less. He'd been so angry: at her, at Luke, at Etienne. He'd even snapped at Savvy. At least with him at the studio, she could gauge how he and Savvy were doing. As long as they were still together, still happy, everything would be fine. But with him gone, it was like trying to solve a problem with only half of an equation. A missing variable. Savvy herself was unreadable. Some days she was polite, *nice* even, asking Bea if she could borrow some toe tape or offering her a PowerBar when Bea realized she'd forgotten to pack a snack. Civil.

"No idea," Owen said.

"Luke hasn't said anything?"

"He and Luke aren't speaking. Luke is pissed about him calling him out in front of Etienne. To be honest, I'm glad he's gone," he said.

She wasn't sure what that meant. How much Owen knew about the bonfire. He'd seemed oblivious when she brought it up on Halloween, though he also seemed to have distanced himself from Nick lately. She hoped it was simply a coincidence. Nick had always been a jerk. And Owen was a really great guy.

"Hey, how is your ankle?" he asked, reaching out and touching the swollen bump.

Owen had seen her rubbing the Arnica into her ankle after the fall during partnering class; otherwise, she would have kept it to herself.

"It's okay." The truth was, something was wrong. It wasn't broken, but it wasn't okay, either. Probably a sprain. She'd had one once before, when she was eleven. Back then, her mom had just pulled her out of class for three weeks until it was better. There was no way to take off three weeks now. She was simply going to have to work through it.

Luckily, it was not her standing leg for the *pas* with Etienne, or for *pirouettes* and *fouettés*. She could almost forget when she was dancing that anything was wrong. But at the barre, that was when she noticed it the most, when every muscle and joint and tendon was exercised. And when they did *grand allegro*. She endured the big jumps with her usual resignation and determination. *'Tis just a flesh wound*, she thought. She simply did not have time or room in her life for an injury right now, and to reveal that weakness to anyone, especially Etienne, would only hurt her when it came to the scholarship.

The scholarship. No one had said yet when it would be announced; not even Nancy seemed to know. She'd heard a rumor that it might be after *The Nutcracker*, though that could mean the night of the performance or in the days following before Etienne returned to France. Either way, it felt like an infinity away. She just wanted to know already, so she could either celebrate or start preparing for auditions.

Today, she tried to stay focused on her part, but between the twirling thoughts about the scholarship and Nick and the ever-present panging in her ankle, she was off her game.

"*Non*," Etienne said, shaking his head, exasperated when she fell out of yet another turn.

"Sorry," she mumbled, and quickly recovered, pushing herself to do it again and again. Eventually, he gave up on her and moved on to the next part of the piece. And there was Lotte, capturing everything from her perch in the corner. If nothing else, Bea was ready to have that camera gone: every single misstep, every imperfection preserved forever.

Miss V. and Eloise were also now observing rehearsals, focused mostly on the Littles. But during the older girls' variations and the *pas de deux,* Vivienne sat in her wooden rolling chair, watching and offering the occasional correction. *Use your plié!* her refrain with Bea. *Softer arms!* to Savvy. Today, after they had run the second act, and after everyone had curtsied to both her and Etienne, Miss V. said, "Beatrice? Come see me in my office when you are dressed."

Everyone looked at Bea, eyes wide.

Oh my god. Was this how it would happen? Was she pulling her aside to let her know she was getting the scholarship?

She hurriedly gathered her things, took off her pointe shoes, and pulled on her warm-ups.

"Good luck," Owen said, squeezing her hand.

Savvy, who had been friendly all day, turned cold as she walked past her and Olive.

She knocked on Miss V.'s door. In all these years, she had only been in her office a couple times: once when she was promoted to Level 6 midway through the year, and one time when Miss V. called her parents in to say it was time to start thinking about the online school.

Miss V. opened the door and beckoned her in. "Have a seat," she said. Bea's eyes quickly scanned the framed photos of Miss V. dancing when she was not much older than Bea was now. The dreamy black-and-white photos of her in *Romeo and Juliet* with Baryshnikov.

This is where your life begins, she thought. *Here. Now. Hold on to this moment.*

She smiled expectantly at Miss V., who did not return her smile, her expression serious.

"You are injured."

Bea felt her limbs go numb. She shook her head. "No," she said. "No, no, I'm fine."

"Etienne told me that Nicholas dropped you. That your ankle twisted. I was watching today, and I can see you are in pain."

"I'm totally fine," Bea said, shaking her head.

When she was eleven years old, Miss V. had told her she needed to see a chiropractor, because her shoulders were misaligned. The chiropractor had confirmed she needed an adjustment, that one shoulder was about a quarter inch higher than the other. Miss V. knew when she was coming down with something, not by a runny nose or a cough but by her breathing. She knew Bea's body better than anyone did, better than she herself did. After the bonfire, she had been so glad she was going to New York, where none of the teachers could see, in a single glance, what she had done. Miss V. would have known.

"Let me see," Miss V. said now, and Bea reluctantly removed her bootie and rolled up her convertible tights. Miss V. motioned for her to put her foot in her lap, and she studied it as though it were a wounded baby bird, gently turning it side to side, having Bea flex her foot, which sent a searing pain all the way to her shoulder. She could not stop her body from flinching, wincing.

"You need rest," she said. "This is a sprain."

Bea shook her head.

"I want you to take the week off. No class. No rehearsal."

Bea's heart heaved. *No, no, no.*

"What about Marie?" she said.

"I am not concerned with . . ." and she flicked her hand vaguely toward the door. "*This.* I am concerned with your future. You are almost grown now, and part of what you must learn is to listen to your body. Soon, I will not be with you to tell you when it is time to rest."

"I can't take time off," she pleaded. "The show, it's so soon."

"*Pah.* One week. The performance is almost three weeks away."

"Can I at least mark it?" she asked. "Do the work that doesn't use this ankle?" With this, she looked at her ankle and hated its weakness, the pale flesh with the slightly bluish hue beneath, betraying the injury.

"*Rest,*" Miss V. said. "We will have someone stand in for you. Just one week."

"Who?" she blurted.

"One week, sweetheart, and then you will be healed and ready to step back in. You may not listen to your body, but you must listen to me."

Ever

"How is Bea's ankle?" Bob asked after he'd settled at the table at The Center on Monday morning, his face filled with sympathy. But was it genuine, or was he calculating what this might mean for Phoebe? Bea had said there were no understudies, but if she couldn't perform, someone would need to step in.

"It's okay," Ever said firmly. "Just a minor sprain; she's resting it this week."

Bob nodded. "Good, good."

The truth was, when Bea had come limping out of the studio the day before, Ever had felt like everything was unraveling. When Bea got her first pair of pointe shoes, Vivienne had taught her how to sew the ribbons to the slippers, cautioning her they would quickly fray if she didn't hold a flame to the edges, cauterizing the fragile fibers. As Ever sat in the urgent care waiting room, it had taken every effort not to envision Bea's dreams slowly and certainly coming undone, this injury the beginning of the end. Fortunately, the doctor assured her it was minor.

"Well, please let her know Phoebe and I are thinking of her."

"I will," she said, but Bob's compassion felt disingenuous, his smile strained.

"Can we get started already?" Martha snapped from across the table. "I'm eighty-two; I haven't got a lot of time to waste here."

Ever had struggled this morning to find a passage that might inspire her students. She worried they would know she'd lost her writing mojo. The call with Leona last week had been a huge blow. But after reviewing the excerpt, *she* wasn't in love with it, either. She'd been trying to write a book that would sell. That never worked; it contradicted what she told her students about writing what you care most about. *Then your passion will seep into your sentences.* She really wasn't passionate about Lady Edison, and Leona could tell. The cumulative effect of all this was that she was starting to feel like a sham. She wondered if her writing career was over. Maybe she'd ask Koa whether she needed help at the front desk of the yoga studio. Was forty-five too old to just start over?

"Listen," Leona had said. "Why don't you try writing a short story? Or an essay?"

"About what?"

"Anything," she said. "Just a thousand words. Maybe a novel is too overwhelming right now. Baby steps. It's like an injury. You have to get back in shape, build your confidence. Your strength. Plus, if we can place it at a major outlet, you could actually make some money. I've got a good friend at the *Times*. Maybe something for the 'Modern Love' column?"

She'd agreed but had felt defeated.

"Write about love," Ever said to her class now. "Any kind you choose."

She wrote, but every sentence was a struggle. She was crossing out a whole paragraph when her phone rattled on the table. She flipped it over and saw a number she didn't recognize. Probably spam. When it buzzed, she whisked the phone into her lap and saw that there was a new voicemail.

"Five-minute warning," she said.

She usually didn't leave the classroom while her students were writing, but what if this was an emergency? She couldn't imagine it would be, though. Danny was at school, and Bea was at home, exiled from the studio.

She glanced around the conference table, noting that everyone appeared lost in their writing. She stood up and murmured, "I'll be right back. Keep writing."

In the hallway, the smell of whatever they were making for lunch at The Center filled the halls with a nauseating yet familiar scent. It reminded her of the hospital cafeteria. She quickly pressed *Play* on the voicemail, holding her breath. Whoever was on the other end cleared his throat. "Hello, this is Frank Gregory at Costa de la Luna High. I'm the new vice-principal. I need to speak to you about your son. Danny? There's been a bit of an *incident*. If you could please call me back as soon as possible, I'd appreciate it."

Trembling, she quickly returned the call and was patched through to Mr. Gregory's office.

"Is Danny okay?" She thought about the fact that he'd ditched the skateboarding helmet he'd worn through middle school the moment he started high school. She imagined a cracked skull, a bleeding brain. But then again, why would a vice-principal be the one to call if that were the case? Usually nurses broke the news of broken bones.

"I'd rather not go into the particulars over the phone," he said. "He's fine, but I do really need you or Danny's father to come by the school as soon as possible."

He *was* new. Everyone at the high school knew about what happened to Ethan. He'd taught nearly every student there when they were in middle school. There had been GoFundMe campaigns and even a 5K race to raise money for their hospital bills; he was *beloved*.

She could see through the window into her classroom that everyone was still diligently writing. The twenty minutes were up, but there were forty minutes of class left. Martha was sure to get snippy if Ever said she needed to leave. The class was free to The Center's members, but that didn't keep her from making sure she got her money's worth.

"I'm in the middle of teaching a class," she said into the phone. "Is this urgent?"

"If there's any way you can get here in the next half hour, that would be great. It's . . . well, he's been detained," he said.

"Detained?"

"By the school police."

Josie

On Monday morning, Josie had woken up still fuming after the visit from the appraiser. When Mark sent her to voicemail for the tenth time, she got in the car and drove to the dentist's office. At 11:45, she told the (thankfully) unfamiliar receptionist she was just waiting for a friend to come out, and sat down, grabbing a tattered *Cosmo* to read until noon, when the office would close for an hour, and the hygienists and dentists would head out to grab their lunches.

Erica didn't seem to recognize Josie at first. Normally, she saw Josie lying back with her mouth open and a bright light in her face; she likely wasn't expecting her boyfriend's ex to be sitting, reading about multiple orgasms, in the waiting room at her work.

"Erica!" Josie said as Erica whisked past her in her scrubs, hot pink scattered with a pattern of turquoise dinosaurs, a pair of white rubber Crocs on her feet. Mark left her for *this*?

Erica smiled at her broadly, assuming—of course—that Josie was a patient, but as the recognition set in, she looked like she was deciding whether to flee or to fight.

"Oh, hi, Josie. Actually, I'm sorry, but I have to run. I only have forty-five minutes for lunch," Erica said, and began to walk toward the doors. *Flight.*

Josie stood up and repeated, *"Erica,"* as though Erica were a toddler. Well, she practically was, Josie noted. "Please," she said this time. "Let me walk with you. I just want to talk for a minute."

The receptionist who had been so warm and friendly now looked a bit concerned, but Erica bravely nodded at her; was this a silent signal that it wasn't necessary to press the panic button under her desk?

Josie trailed behind Erica's fast clip all the way to the elevator, and then they stood, waiting silently until the doors opened. Inside the elevator, Erica finally spoke.

"I *told* him it's not fair," she said. "Just so you know."

Josie scowled.

"Selling the house," she said. "If that's what this is about. I'm actually on your side."

Josie felt her heart sink as the elevator descended.

Erica turned to her. "My parents got divorced when I was ten. Me and my mom had to move into a studio apartment, and my dad stayed in the house where I grew up. I hated him. I told Mark that Savannah is going to hate him, too, if he takes your house away. He's her stepdad. He still loves her."

Josie was struggling to find words to respond. All the fury she'd felt had nowhere to go, but it was still there, spinning inside her. Trapped in the elevator.

"Wow, you're amazing," Josie snapped. "You'll swoop in and steal my husband, but you draw the line at stealing my house?"

The elevator dinged, and they exited into the lobby. Erica turned to Josie again, her mouth twitching. "Listen," she said. "He told me your marriage was over. That all you care about is Savannah's ballet career. That he felt *alone* when he was with you." Erica was crying now; Josie was rendered speechless. It was her turn now to fight or take flight.

"Well," Josie said. "You can tell your *boyfriend* that I'm not leaving. It's my *home*. My daughter's home. I'll burn it to the ground before I let him force me out."

Lindsay

On Monday morning, Lindsay weighed herself in the locker room after forty minutes on the treadmill. She'd steered clear of the scales for the last three weeks when she realized she hadn't lost a single pound in over a month. She'd heard about this so-called plateau. The only way to combat it was to keep working out, eating well, and eventually, she'd get over the hump. Now she stepped on and grimaced. She had, somehow, *gained* five pounds. Seriously? She'd been eating like a rabbit for months. She ran three miles a day. Twice a week, a personal trainer had his way with her on his torture devices. *Damn it.* She stepped off and stepped back on. Maybe it was wrong. And it was. This time, it registered *seven* pounds more than her last reading.

Feeling defeated, she showered and got dressed. She had a quiet day ahead of her today, just some paperwork in the office, and then she had to go take some pictures for a new listing in Josie's neighborhood; Victor's sale was finished.

She had been rattled after running into Savvy at the lab. Of course, it seemed suspicious: her coming out of a medical building, Victor holding her up like an invalid. She'd waited for the fallout, for Olive to come at her with more of her vitriol, her accusations. Though Olive hadn't said anything. There was nothing going on with Victor; then why did she feel so guilty?

After the closing, he'd shaken her hand, all business. But if this were the case, why had her heart sunk as they said their goodbyes? And why had she not closed things out the way she did with all her other clients? He'd moved into the condo over the weekend, but she still hadn't given him a housewarming gift. She always got a closing gift for her clients: a welcome mat, a Home Depot gift card for the fixer-upper, a framed map of Costa de la Luna for those new to town. She'd once given a newly married couple an orange tree. But she'd found herself at a loss as to what might be an appropriate gift for Victor. And, honestly, maybe she knew that completing this last ritual would ensure they'd now both go their separate ways.

On Mondays, there was a Farmer's Market downtown. They blocked off the whole main street, and people came out to sell flowers and fruits and veggies, as well as fresh fish and art. She decided she'd stop by the market on her way to Josie's neighborhood. She wandered around for a while, ignored the pastries and cookies, and instead picked up a butternut squash and a bunch of kale. Next, she stopped at a booth filled with watercolor paintings of local landmarks: the pier, the beach, and *there*, a lovely little watercolor of St. Mary's. It was perfect. She could swing by Freezey's tomorrow to drop it off, maybe peek in at the studio and catch a glimpse of partnering class while she was at it. She hadn't given up hope that Olive would change her mind about leaving the studio. This stupid scholarship had simply thrown the girls off. *The Nutcracker* was in just a few weeks. Olive would remember everything she loved about performing. Things would get back to normal.

She put the produce and the painting in her car and buckled up. Her phone rang. The screen read: Costa de la Luna Obstetrics and Gynecology.

"Hi, is this Lindsay Chase? This is Bettina. I'm a nurse at CDL OB-GYN."

The blood work. She'd forgotten. It had been over a week now; they must have just gotten the results. Luckily, it was only the nurse. The doctor would have called if anything were wrong.

"I am so, so sorry. Dr. Ramachandra has been out with the flu for a week now. She would have gotten back to you if she'd been here."

Lindsay felt a rush of heat in her face. "Is everything okay?"

"Actually, um, *yes?*" she said.

THE STILL POINT 239

"Oh, phew. Terrific. Thanks so much for calling to let me know," she said, and put the car in reverse.

"Um, wait," the nurse stumbled. "I'm calling because all the blood work is *fine*, but the routine test we ran for pregnancy came back positive."

"What?"

"You're pregnant."

Ever

At the high school, Ever sat in the car, heart racing. She thought of her yoga practice, trying to pay attention to her breathing. But when her heart wouldn't slow, she reached into the glove box and pulled out the gummies she'd picked up at the dispensary over the weekend. *No.* She didn't want to have an anxiety attack, but she also didn't want to go into the school stoned. She kept running over the phone conversation. Danny had been detained by the school police? She ran through the list of possible transgressions: Cheating? Drugs? A weapon? Her heart nearly stopped at the thought of those troubled kids on the news, the ones who, out of nowhere, wreaked havoc and violence against their classmates. Nobody ever saw it coming. She shook her head; those terrible thoughts rattled loose like dry beans in a can. This was *Danny.* Sweet Danny, with his easy smile and inner calm. Just like his dad.

No. There had to be a mistake. Danny struggled with rules, but he would never do anything to hurt anyone. He might not always respect authority, but he had tremendous respect for other people. He was compassionate and kind. But then again, she hardly saw him anymore. Since Ethan died, he'd been at home less and less. She'd been distracted. Lost in her own grief. Would she have even noticed if he were spiraling, too? What if she had failed him somehow?

Inside, the receptionist was on the phone and did not look up. "If you swing by the store and grab some ground beef, I can make tacos tonight." Ever waited as the woman ran down her grocery list. The clock hanging behind the reception desk ticked loudly.

"Gotta go," she said into the receiver, and then to Ever, "Can I help you?"

"Hi, yes. I'm Danny Henderson's mother?" she said. This usually brought her pride, but now she felt shame burning her ears.

"Oh," the woman said, and for a moment, it felt like she was some sort of celebrity. "We've been waiting for you."

Ever thought about asking this woman, in her smart blue cardigan, to fill her in, prepare her so she was ready for whatever awaited her behind the door. But her throat seemed to have closed, the questions trapped inside, and so she simply followed her into the office.

It took a moment to orient herself. Sitting behind the desk was a man, the VP, presumably. A school resource officer stood beside the desk, arms crossed. And sitting in two chairs were Danny and another boy. The other boy was bent forward, elbows on his knees, long hair obscuring his face. He looked up, and when he saw Ever, his cheeks turned a deep red. It was Luke. From the studio. *Luke?* She barely recognized him out of his usual uniform of black tights and white dancer's T-shirt. His mother, Jenny, sat next to him, staring ahead, eyes glazed. Danny was sitting upright, hands clasped in his lap. As Ever walked in, he started to stand up.

"Sit down," the officer said.

"What happened?" she mouthed to Danny, and his eyes pleaded with her. "What's going on?" she managed, searching the grown-up faces in the room for an answer.

Mr. Gregory stood up and reached across his desk to shake her hand. Awkwardly, she returned the gesture. "Hi, Mrs. Henderson. Thanks for coming. Please, have a seat. Our principal is out sick today, so I'll be handling this matter."

Ever sat down in the chair next to Danny and tentatively put a hand on his back.

Mr. Gregory took a deep, somewhat exasperated breath, and said, "So, this morning during first period, the smoke alarms went off. We didn't have a scheduled drill, and so obviously, there was cause for concern. Fortunately, our students followed the protocol for a fire drill and all evacuated the building. We've had fires before, of course, though not so much now that kids are vaping instead of smoking cigarettes."

Ever thought, *Oh, shit, Danny was smoking in the bathroom.* Probably weed? As she thought about the pure calm of those gummies, she felt like the definition of hypocrisy.

"Smoking?" she asked, though she wasn't sure whom she was asking.

"Oh, sorry. No. The point is that everyone was outside because of the alarm, and this is when the—altercation—occurred."

She looked at Danny for an answer, but he simply lowered his head again.

"According to the other students, your son—unprovoked—attacked Mr. Lawson."

"I don't understand." She felt her world upending. She gripped the chair's arms. Danny? Danny was one of the gentlest kids she'd ever known. He'd never hit *anyone* before.

"I'm new here, but I've been told that these are both good boys. Boys who, as far as their school records show, have never been in trouble before. The school is willing to deal with this internally and administer a reasonable punishment. Likely suspension. For Danny."

"Suspension?" Ever said. Danny would be applying to colleges next year. Would this ruin his chances of getting into a university?

"Of course, the victim obviously has the option of pressing formal charges. In which case, we'll need to reach out to law enforcement."

Ever thought about what being formally charged with assault might do to his future and looked fearfully at Jenny, who took a deep breath.

Luke shook his head, sharply. "No, Mom. It's okay."

"I know Danny's had a rough time this year. With losing his dad and everything," Jenny said, but her voice was threaded with suppressed anger. "We won't press any charges, but we expect a replacement of Luke's iPhone. Immediately."

"His iPhone?" Ever asked.

"Mr. Lawson's phone was damaged during the fight," the counselor said. "Danny apparently stomped on it."

Ever felt breathless as she calculated what a new iPhone would cost them.

"Okay," the counselor said, clapping his hands as if he'd just negotiated peace in the Middle East. "Officer Cushman, is this okay with you?" The officer nodded.

"I'm going to recommend a week's suspension for you, Danny. Any tests you miss will need to be made up, and the grading repercussions of your absence will be up to your individual teachers. You're free to go, Luke. And, Mrs. Lawson, I am so sorry about all of this."

Ever and Danny left together twenty minutes later, after signing multiple forms and enduring the scrutiny of at least a half dozen administrators and faculty, who came in and out of the office. It wasn't until they returned to the Volvo that Ever exploded.

"What the hell, Danny?"

His lip trembled in a way it hadn't since the days after Ethan's death. He shook his head.

"Did Luke do something to you? I didn't know you guys even knew each other."

Danny gazed out the window, and she studied his boyish profile. He would never hurt anyone unless there was good reason. She pressed her hand against her chest to still her heart.

"You can tell me," she said, reaching out and touching his arm. "Whatever it was that started this. Did he do something to you?"

"Not me, Mom," he said, exasperated. "It was Bea."

Bea

Without class and rehearsals, this was going to be a long week. On Monday morning, she'd woken up late and did homework; still, by noon she'd already finished most of her assignments for the week. Without ballet, what was she supposed to do with herself? She'd sworn to Miss V. that she wouldn't touch the portable barre at home. Maybe she could do some yoga or something that didn't involve her ankle?

She had zero appetite, but she also knew that if she didn't eat, her blood sugar would be low, and she'd feel even more miserable than she already did. She threw together a small salad, and was sprinkling some feta crumbles on top when Danny and her mom came through the door.

"What are you doing home?" she asked.

Danny's head was hung low, and his hands were shoved deep in his pockets. He wouldn't look at her.

"Give me your phone," her mom said, and he pulled it out of his pocket. Her mom put it in the basket on top of the fridge. "You'll get this back at the end of the week. And you're going to need to pay to replace Luke's."

Luke's?

Danny sat down at the kitchen table and put his head in his hands, and her mom turned the burner on under the tea kettle.

"What happened?" Bea asked, and when Danny didn't answer, she turned to her mom. "What's going on?"

Her mom looked stricken, and Bea felt the same way she'd felt the

night of the accident, in the first few minutes before concern turned
to terror.

"Mom?" she said again, her voice cracking.

"I think you need to tell your sister what's going on," her mom
said, and reached for a mug in the cupboard.

Bea set her fork down, and Danny finally looked up. Her mom
poured the hot water over a tea bag in her mug and left them alone
in the kitchen. Danny grimaced and then explained.

There was a *video*. A video that Luke took at the bonfire. Luke
was pissed at Nick, and so he'd sent it to a small group chat of guys,
joking that he could totally blow up Nick and Savvy's relationship
whenever he wanted. One of the guys in the chat had forwarded it
to Danny.

"Who else has seen it?" she asked, mortified.

"I don't know," Danny said. "Just the guys in the chat, I think?"

"What about Savvy?" she asked, her mind reeling with what all
of this meant.

"I told Luke to delete it. At least now that his phone's broken, he
can't send it to anybody else," he said.

"But one of the other guys in the chat can," she said. "Danny, this
is bad. Now everybody's going to be wondering why you went after
Luke. They're going to find out. *Savvy* is going to find out."

"I'm really sorry," he said, his eyes pleading with her. "Those
guys are such assholes."

"I'm going to my room," she said, head pounding. "This is so
bad."

Even if Savvy hadn't seen it yet, Bea knew it was like a live grenade tossed into a room. It was bound to go off. Once something
was recorded, it was just a few clicks away from global dissemina-
tion. She'd been so careful never to allow anyone to take videos of
her that she wouldn't want her parents or teachers to see. But now,
there was video of her on the worst night of her life. Her head

throbbed as she tried to run through the possible scenarios of what might happen when that grenade went off. Once Savvy found out, she would be furious. And rightfully so. She'd be sure to make Bea's life at the studio a nightmare. She'd already turned Bea's best friend against her, and that was before she knew what had happened between Bea and Nick. She had no idea what Savvy was capable of if she actually had a valid reason to be pissed.

Someone knocked on her door.

"What?" she said, exasperated.

"Can I come in?" Her mom gently pushed the door open. She sat on the edge of the bed, where Bea lay curled up into herself. "Let's talk through this."

Bea closed her eyes.

"Danny said you were dancing with Nick, flirting? At the beach?"

Her eyes shot open. "Oh my god, you didn't watch the video, did you?"

"No," her mom said, shaking her head. "Danny just gave me the gist of it. He said you and Nick were . . . together?"

Bea threw her head back against the pillow. "Mom, I really don't want to talk about this."

"Did you and Nick . . ." Her mom's face was pained as her eyes searched Bea's for an answer. "Did he *hurt* you, Bea?"

Bea sat up, took a deep breath. "No, Mom," she said. "I wanted to be there. I didn't care about Savvy. I made a mistake. I'm not a good person. I'm just not."

Lindsay

*P*regnant. Now everything made sense. The weight loss plateau. The nausea. The light-headedness, that wild sense of smell she had. Not getting her period. She'd thought she was going through menopause, that her fertile days were over. But it was literally the exact opposite. Dr. Ramachandra's nurse had suggested she come in as soon as possible, given this was a "geriatric" pregnancy due to her advanced maternal age. There would be tests: a lot of them. She could have some decisions to make. Difficult ones.

She and Steve had tried to get pregnant for years. She'd miscarried four times, each pregnancy lasting excruciatingly longer than the previous one, the fourth one ending at almost five months. Steve had suggested they resign themselves to being a family of two, when she got pregnant again. Though it wasn't until she went to the hospital with contractions that she believed it was really happening. And when she held Olive, with her shock of penny-colored hair, in her arms, she knew this was what she had been made for. Her whole life had been leading to this single moment. Of course, everyone told her it was just baby bliss, that surge of hormones every new mother experiences. That as soon as the hormone levels dipped, after a few weeks of sleepless nights, after she'd been pooped on and everything she owned smelled like sour milk, she'd come down off that high. But she didn't. She loved every moment of being a mother.

Another baby. *My god.*

She drove out to Josie's neighborhood and let herself into the empty property she was listing to take photos. The house had been staged with nondescript furniture and boring art. Fake flowers in vases and unread books on the shelves. Staging was meant to help prospective buyers imagine their lives here, to envision a future. But it was all so phony. All of it so incredibly sad.

When she'd gotten all the photos she needed, using a wide angle to create the illusion of space, she sat at the kitchen island and created the listing on her laptop, spinning the house's boring details into a generic, one-size-fits-all dream: *vaulted ceilings, light and bright, newly painted and ready to make your own.* She sat outside by the *pristine pool, recently retiled* and called her clients, delivering good news to some, breaking bad news to others. She fired off a few emails and then figured she should probably just head home.

All the way back to the house, she tried to think of how she would tell Steve, but couldn't. At least he wouldn't be home until tonight. Maybe not even until late. This would give her time to think. To process. To plan.

But as she pulled into the cul-de-sac, she noticed that Steve's car was in the driveway. That was odd. For a moment, she worried that he had somehow found out about the baby. Would the doctor have called him, too? She was pretty sure this was not the case. HIPAA laws and all that? No, more likely, he'd simply forgotten something at the house. Or maybe he'd come home to grab some lunch? But it was almost three-thirty. It was also a twenty-minute drive to and from his office to their house. Was he sick? The flu was going around. But if he'd come home sick, why was he parked in the driveway rather than in the garage?

She parked behind his car and thought about how she would break this news to him. He'd think it was a joke. She imagined what would happen as the realization settled in. The way he rubbed his palm across his bald pate whenever he was upset. The silent calculating of what this meant for their retirement plans. She imagined the stupid questions he would ask: *How could this happen? I thought you were going through menopause. What are you going to do about it?* He had been practically counting down the days until Olive flew from the nest. He would not be thrilled that this old bird was about to lay another egg.

But wait. What did *she* want? What did this mean for *her*? There had been so much pressure raising an only child. Only one chance to get things right. The first pancake theory of parenting—people always screwed up the first one: burnt edges or uncooked middle. But now, like a gift, here was a second chance. A ladle full of fresh batter and a hot griddle. She could do it better this time.

Maybe she wasn't being fair to Steve. Maybe this could actually bring them closer together. She recalled those early days with Olive, when they were a new little family. Steve had been as much in love with their baby girl as Lindsay was. This love was something they shared. Maybe the real problem was that, with Olive leaving soon, the one thing that bound them together was disappearing. A baby could be the glue to fix those cracks. Maybe?

She clicked the garage door opener, but as the doors opened, she cocked her head, confused. Why was Sonia's van in the garage? It was Monday. She hadn't said anything about needing to come a day early. And besides, Sonia usually parked on the street. But now here was her van, backed into Lindsay's spot.

Oh my god. Was it possible? Steve and *Sonia*? Sonia, who had washed their sheets, had been slipping between them with *Steve*?

Lindsay sat in the car, engine idling, while she imagined storming through the house, catching them. She wondered if she would scream or cry or just silently stand there as the horror unfolded, like a movie, before her eyes. She pictured Steve in some embarrassing, compromising, position; Sonia and her beautiful hair spread out on Lindsay's own pillowcase. She tried to come up with whatever biting remarks someone in this situation should offer. But oddly, she drew a blank. Because it wasn't rage, but sad resignation she felt; she had been *right*. Wrong about the *who*, but not about the *what*. Not Melissa with her Instagram-ready body. *Sonia* with her kind smile and sensible shoes. Lindsay wondered how long this had been going on.

And then it hit her. Sonia had been bringing him ice from Ever's kitchen the night of the memorial. After the explosion. She'd looked right through Sonia that night. It served her right for not seeing what was right under her nose.

Tearfully, she searched the glove box for a scrap of paper. Should she slip a note under Sonia's windshield wiper? A little heads-up that the jig was up? That she didn't have to pretend anymore. That nobody did. A sob escaped her lips as she located her pen, and she startled when the garage door to the kitchen opened, and Steve stuck his head out.

He was shirtless, wearing only a pair of shorts and a scowl. He was paunchy and pale, the dark curls on his chest glistening with sweat. When he realized it was her, he glowered.

He motioned for her to roll down the window.

For a moment, she resisted. Because the second he spoke, she'd have a choice to make. To stay or to leave.

"Jesus, is your phone dead?" he asked.

"What?"

"Your phone. I've texted you like forty times."

Confused, she looked to the cup holder, where she usually kept her phone. After the call from the doctor's office, she must have tossed it in her purse. She fumbled around and pulled it out. Ten texts from Steve.

"George next door heard it and called me. Luckily, Sonia was able to come, and the plumber is on his way."

"Plumber?"

"Yes. The hot water heater upstairs exploded, and we've got water pouring down through the light fixtures. I've been moving furniture, and Sonia brought the wet vac." He gestured to the back of the van. She could see now the van's rear doors were open, Sonia's supplies at the ready. "It's a total disaster in there."

She shook her head. None of this made sense. Or, perhaps, all of it made perfect sense. Sonia and Steve weren't sleeping together. That was ludicrous. It was so ludicrous, she felt laughter starting to bubble inside her; then she was laughing like she hadn't in years.

"What the hell is wrong with you?" Steve said.

She shook her head again. Tears coming down her cheeks.

"Nothing is wrong with me. Nothing at all."

"Well, Jesus, can you at least get inside and help out?"

She looked at Steve and felt a tsunami of sorrow envelop her. She didn't love him anymore. Hadn't in a long time. The marriage was shattered, not cracked. There was nothing that could fix this. Not even a baby. Especially not a baby.

"I can't stay," Lindsay said. "I'm sorry."

She rolled the window up and slowly backed out of the garage, Steve following then, standing shirtless in the driveway, bewildered. There it was, the expression she'd seen after the grill blew up. It wasn't guilt. He was just clueless, as always, in the face of disaster.

In the street, she shifted into drive and turned on the radio. Thanksgiving was a couple weeks away, but the pop station had already switched over to its 24/7 Christmas programming. When the first few notes of "What Child Is This?" hummed through the speakers, she felt another startled sob escape her lips. At the stop sign, she idled, but only for a moment, then clicked her blinker and headed downtown to St. Mary's.

In the back of the quiet cathedral, she sat down in a pew and looked at the stained-glass windows, the last bits of daylight filtering through. Maybe after this, she would take a walk down on the beach for the sunset, see if the seals were out. She pulled the kneeler down and knelt, hands resting on the back of the pew in front of her. She closed her eyes.

So, she had been wrong. Her mother had told her that a woman's instincts were reliable. That if your intuition says that something is wrong or dangerous, it likely is. That you should follow your gut rather than your heart or even your head. But her instincts had misfired. And then misfired again. What else was she wrong about? How could she trust her own judgment about anything? As far as she could tell, Steve wasn't cheating. He didn't give her a venereal disease. And he wasn't pretending to be Arnold Schwarzenegger with the housekeeper.

Maybe everything that had been happening the last few months, all her wild suspicions about an affair, had not been jealousy at all. Maybe she'd simply been looking for an excuse to leave, for a way out. She'd been searching for a reason to go that would absolve her of any responsibility. She was a coward. This was her decision, and it was time that she found the courage she needed to make it.

She said a quick prayer and crossed herself. When she stood up, the late afternoon sun was pouring through the crimson glass, and when she held up her hands, they were bathed in orange and red light.

As the sun blazed on the horizon, she left the church and went to her car. But when she sat down in the driver's seat, she couldn't bring herself to turn the engine on. She didn't want to go home. Then she spied the package she'd left on the passenger seat after the doctor's call.

Gift in hand, she walked to the old bank building. Upstairs, she knocked on the door, and Victor answered, still wearing his uniform. He seemed surprised to see her, but quietly ushered her inside.

She thrust the package toward him. "I just came by to give you this. It's a housewarming gift. I meant to give it to you last week."

He took the tissue paper–wrapped package and opened it. He smiled broadly, dimples deep, as he studied the tiny painting of the church, but when he looked up at her again, he frowned.

"Let me get you some water," he said. "You're a little pale."

"I'm pregnant," she blurted.

He nodded slowly. No shock. No judgment. No *holy shit*.

"Also, my daughter hates me," she added.

He reached for her hand and squeezed it gently. "That's not true," he said.

She shook her head.

"Listen," he said. "I've been watching the way you are with your daughter, all these years. You're a really good mother, Lindsay. You are a *great* mom."

No one had said this to her. Not Steve. Not Olive. Not even Ever or any of her other friends. It was the simplest sentence. Five words. Bigger than *I love you*.

She moved toward him, tears streaming hot down her cheeks now, and he opened his arms to her. She fit inside his hug like it was made for her. Like a puzzle piece locking into place. But when her phone rang, she pulled away. *Olive.* She felt flush with shame, as if Olive had caught her in Victor's embrace.

"Mom?"

"Hi, Livvie," she said, moving out into the hallway. "What's up? Why aren't you in class?"

"Etienne put me in *Spanish,*" Olive whispered. "Bea's injured, so he had to move people around."

"*Spanish?*" Etienne had chosen Olive to take over Spanish? It was a solo role in his version. It had been *Savvy's* role. *Yes.* This was all Olive had needed—just a little acknowledgment. Lindsay's heart trilled. "Wait. *What?* Bea's injured?"

"I have to go back in in a minute. I don't know if this is like permanent or what, but I have to stay late tonight to learn his choreography. Can you get me at nine o'clock?" Buried in her request was something familiar, forgotten. Excitement?

"Of course," she said.

She hung up and returned to Victor, who was sitting on the bed now.

"I'm sorry," she said. "I've got to get going."

"Of course," he said, standing up and giving her another, though briefer, hug. "Thank you for the gift."

"Thank *you,*" she said.

Through the window, the setting sun was burning now, the whole sky ablaze.

Josie

When Savvy came home from ballet on Monday night, she went straight to the shower. Josie figured she'd had a long night at the studio. They were in the final weeks until *Nutcracker*, and Etienne had them working every day.

Josie hadn't spoken to Melissa since their blow-up on Halloween, but her anger kept simmering, though that was nothing compared to the rage she felt after her confrontation with Erica earlier today. She'd thought talking to her husband's mistress would make her feel better, but it had done the opposite. The things Mark had said about her? It felt like she'd been sucker punched. He felt *alone* in the marriage. Because of Savvy. But she was a mother first, long before she met him. The more she thought about it, the angrier she got. Just wait until Erica got knocked up. Then he'd take the back seat again. A man can never win if he makes a woman choose between him and her child. Never. Savvy came first. She would always come first.

Mark was right. Josie would do anything for Savvy. Everything she'd done from the moment she found out she was pregnant was for her daughter. Josie had been eighteen, a baby herself, but she'd made the adult choice to keep her. To raise her. She'd sacrificed everything, including her blossoming career, when Alan Goldberg had made her choose. She'd taken care of her day and night while Johnny went to law school and then grew his practice, only for them to slowly grow apart, for him to leave her. Johnny supported Savvy, of course, but she herself had gone without for years. She'd thought about getting her associate's degree, but that would mean time away from Savvy, and Savvy needed her. School for Savvy was a struggle from the beginning, and so Josie had read aloud to her, helped her with math as much as she was able. She picked her up from elementary school every day, right when the bell rang, so she wouldn't be stuck in aftercare like she had been when her mom had been off drinking or doing whatever it was she did instead of parenting. Josie was *there*, even if things were hard. Especially when things were hard.

When she and Johnny split up (just as her mother predicted, as Alan predicted), she'd struggled for five years as a single mom to give Savvy everything she needed before she met Mark. No one could ever make her feel guilty for that.

Really, if she were being honest, she'd only married Mark because she was tired of struggling, and he was rich and willing to be with a single mom. She'd never been attracted to him, not the way she had been with Johnny. And now, she was pretty sure, she'd never been in love with him, either. But she had done what needed to be done. And in return, Mark got Josie—a hot, younger wife. Good sex, regularly doled out. She had held up her end of the bargain. And yet, here they all were.

She *had* been consumed with Savvy's ballet career. Of course, she had been—ballet was going to keep Savvy from ever being in a situation like hers. And it was this, more than anything, that drove her to get the best teachers and training. Private lessons. Pilates. Chiropractors and acupuncturists and massage therapists. She had done whatever it took to keep Savvy focused. To keep her eyes on that prize. And now, that prize was here. And yet now, that prize was in the hands of another arrogant, egotistical man. Jesus. Why had she thought it would ever be any different for Savvy?

Stewing, she put together a plate of the stir fry she'd fixed earlier and popped it in the microwave. She also made a quick smoothie: Savvy's favorite, with clementines and frozen raspberries. She would miss these late dinners together when Savvy was gone.

They had a lot to catch up on tonight. Savvy had told her that Nick stormed out last week, that he was pissed at Etienne. Of course, he was; he was just bigheaded enough to believe there had been even

the slightest chance of Etienne giving one of the boys the scholarship. She was hoping, frankly, that Nick might move to a different
studio. With him no longer at ballet, maybe things between them
would peter out, and when Savvy got the scholarship, she would
have absolutely nothing holding her back.

Savvy also said that Bea would be out all week with a sprained
ankle. It was terrible, but her first thought had been *relief*. Certainly,
Bea would be a less desirable candidate for the scholarship with an
injury. And, if it was bad enough, he might have to put someone—
maybe Savvy—in as Marie permanently. It felt like things were finally happening as they were supposed to. This was Savvy's destiny.
God, she sounded like Ever. Next thing you knew, she'd be buying
crystals and meditating.

When the microwave beeped, she pulled out the plate, steam rising off the baby corns and water chestnuts. She gave the smoothie
one last spin in the NutriBullet and then heard Savvy padding down
the stairs.

"Hey Sav, come have some dinner."

Savvy was in her fluffy pink bathrobe, with her hair spun up in a
towel turban. She looked ghostly without her makeup.

"You okay?" she asked as Savvy plopped down at the counter.

Savvy reached for the fork and a napkin from the holder.

"So . . ." Josie said, as she gently pushed the steaming plate in
front of Savvy. "Is Etienne having you take over for Bea this week?
To play Marie?"

Savvy's eyes were red. Had she been crying?

"What's going on?" Josie asked, heat rushing to her face.

Savvy pulled her phone out of her robe pocket and set it on the
counter. She was always sharing videos with Josie. Videos of her
friends. Of girls doing fifteen pirouettes. But now Savvy looked mo-
rose. She pushed the phone toward her, and Josie picked it up.

"Luke took this," Savvy said. "He sent it out to a bunch of guys at
school this morning. He's pissed at Nick, and so I guess this was like,
his way of getting back at him?"

"Wait. Is that Bea?" Josie asked, squinting at the screen.

"Keep watching," she said.

"Oh my god," Josie said. "That's Nick?"

"Yeah. That's *Nick*."

All the anger that she had been feeling: at Mark, at Erica, at Melissa. None of it compared to what she felt right now.

That asshole Nick; she had never trusted him. And that bitch Beatrice? Josie was practically blind with rage as she studied the screen.

"Oh, also?" Savvy said. "*Everybody* knows that Etienne is staying in the guesthouse. That little brat Jaz decided to tell the whole studio. I thought you and Melissa were friends."

Ever

On Tuesday morning, Ever woke up feeling out of sorts. Everything was falling apart. Just two years ago, she would have risen early to a quiet house (Bea still sleeping, and Ethan and Danny out surfing together). Ethan would have made coffee before he left. She would have taken a moment to breathe in the smells of her home: that musky aroma of sandalwood, the pervasive scent of the ocean, and the biting citrus smell of fresh-squeezed juice. She would have silently expressed her gratitude. She always, always appreciated the simple pleasures of her life.

And yet—this tremendous gratitude she'd cultivated in the end made it all so much worse. Because when you are grateful for everything, there's even more to lose, even the milky beam of sunlight she passed through becoming precious. *Nepenthe.*

If Ethan were here, now, coming up the stairs from the beach, she would ask him to have a cup of coffee with her before getting ready for school. He would kiss her and say, *Sure thing. Get my zipper?* And he would present his back to her, that familiar back, her finger hooking into the loop and pulling the zipper down to reveal his cold skin, which she might press her cheek against. The constellation of freckles on his shoulders as familiar as the stars in the sky. She could navigate anything with that certainty to guide her. But now, she was drifting, farther and farther out to sea.

"What's going on?" he would ask her.

And she'd tell him about Danny, about Bea, and they would figure out what to do. Together. But now, as she slipped quietly into the kitchen, the quiet kitchen slipped from the one of her memory into the one of reality. There was no coffee brewed. No juice. The sandalwood scent was oppressive, and outside, the waves were crashing almost angrily against the sand.

Bea was still sleeping, but she'd heard Danny get up. Through the patio doors, she saw him bent over the surfboard, and for one illogical, desperate moment, she thought it was Ethan. That he had somehow found his way home again. Just a cruel trick of her mind. A ridiculous flirtation with the impossible. It was Danny, of course, waxing his surfboard. Hunched over, wetsuit peeled to the waist, *like a banana*, was what he'd said to Ethan the first time he saw him this way. How old was he? Four? Five?

"Good morning," she said, poking her head out.

"Morning. I'm still allowed to surf, right?"

He was suspended from school all week, but what sort of punishment should *she* dole out? Fighting was serious. She and Ethan had never tolerated violence. They didn't let Danny play violent video games or watch movies with guns. They were peaceful people.

She knew they were lucky that Luke's parents didn't press charges. They could have ruined his life right then and there. God, how many times had they escaped from possible disasters? How many near misses were they allowed? Had they gotten a reset after Ethan?

She'd told Danny that he was going to have to pay for the phone, hand over every dime he made at the café until he'd paid her back. She'd put the new phone on a credit card, one so close to the limit she wasn't sure it would process. She'd taken away his phone, the video trapped inside.

She needed to see the video. If she was going to help Bea, she needed to know exactly what had happened between her and Nick.

"Actually," she said as Danny reached for his board, "I need you to show me the video. Of Bea."

"I don't think it's a good idea, Mom. Bea doesn't want you to watch."

"Danny," she said. "I need to see it."

In the kitchen, Ever returned Danny's phone to him from where she'd stashed it on top of the fridge, and he plugged it in, powered it up. Alerts sounded, and his screen was a flurry of notifications. He looked at the screen, transfixed. She gave him a few moments before she said again, "Find the video, Danny."

He hung his head, searched through his texts, and reluctantly handed her the phone.

"You can go surfing now," she said. "Be safe."

He reluctantly left her in the kitchen, and she watched as he retrieved his surfboard from the deck and headed down the steps to the beach.

Ever glanced down the quiet hallway toward Bea's closed door again and then slipped out onto the back deck, sitting in the shade as she clicked to expand the video to full screen.

It was dark at first, voices a jumble. Cacophony. Laughter, tinny music. Then the camera focused, the clarity almost startling. Bea was standing in front of a bonfire, wearing a very short pair of cutoff denim shorts, her long legs bare, glowing in the light of the flames. Her eyes were closed, and she was swaying to the music. Ever had seen her do this when she was running variations over in her head, her arms marking the *port de bras*. Trancelike, alone inside the music, inside herself. Though this time, Bea was unsteady, swaying, a drink in her hand.

Ever felt a vague sense of betrayal. Bea and Danny had always told her everything. She knew which kids from school and at the studio drank, which kids smoked or stole pills from their parents' medicine cabinets, which ones were having sex. She knew Bea had done none of these things. This was like watching a stranger, like someone Ever didn't know at all.

When Nick came up behind her and rested his chin on her shoulder, Bea's eyes were closed. She was so far away. When Bea opened her eyes, they were glazed, unfocused, reflecting the fire, but revealing nothing.

Nick turned her around to face him and started dancing with her, pushing his body against hers, running his hands up and down her back, his forehead pressed against hers. His fingers lingered at the frayed cuffs of her cutoffs, at the place where the denim ended and her flesh began. Bea pulled away from him and began to dance on her own, but the movements were not the usual elegant, controlled choreography. Instead, she was moving clumsily, drunkenly, *sexually*: hands pressed against her knees as she gyrated. What was Bea thinking? Beyond the drinking, this was Nick, Savvy's boyfriend. But here she was, flirting, beckoning him to come closer with one curled finger. Though to Ever, she looked like a little girl playing grown-up.

Nick gave her a *Who, me?* look, and she nodded and reached both hands toward him. When he took them, she pulled him close again, and she started to grind against him. Then they were kissing. Sloppy, desperate. Whoever was holding the camera—Luke, she supposed—hooted and said, "Damn, Savvy is gonna be *pissed*."

At this, Bea turned to the camera, eyes unfocused, as she flipped the camera off and slurred, "Fuck Savvy."

Ever sucked in her breath. She had to force herself to look at the screen, though tears had filled her eyes, making it difficult to focus. She wiped her tears with the cuff of her shirt. Who was this girl? She didn't recognize her; she'd never seen her act like this. She realized with horror that she was *ashamed* of her.

Olive was there in the frame then, gently reaching out for Bea's arm. "Come on, Bea. Let's call an Uber."

Bea hung onto Nick. "You go. I'm staying."

Olive tried again, tugging her arm this time. "Bea. Come on. Let's go home."

Bea yanked her arm away from Olive's grip and whirled around, that spindly arm lashing out, the back of her hand making contact with Olive's face. Hard.

Luke hooted again, his voice a screech. "Holy shit! Cat fight!"

Olive looked straight at the camera. She was holding her right eye, astonished. Bea had *hit* her, but it didn't seem to register with Bea, who was bleary-eyed and swaying.

Ever felt stunned but forced herself to keep watching.

"Wow. Your dad would be super proud of you right now," Olive said angrily. "I really wish he were here to see this. His *sweet* Beatrice."

At this, Bea stopped and swayed again. She looked like she might say something, like she was trying to gather the words to defend herself, but they were lost. She was searching for something that was out of reach.

"My dad . . ." she said, and Ever felt dizzy. "Don't talk about my dad."

"I'm going home," Olive said, then disappeared out of the frame.

Now it appeared that Luke had gotten bored and moved the camera to other things: the fire, Olive gathering her stuff. But in the periphery, she could see the fire. Bea and Nick's silhouettes. Nick reached for Bea's hand. She was swaying again, and she shook her head.

Ever zoomed in. Nick was tugging at Bea's hand, and she tripped, dropping her cup and falling to her knees. He helped her up, then pulled her hand again, and she stumbled after him. The sound was garbled: laughter, music, the crackling fire.

"What are you doing?" Bea asked. She was standing by the patio doors in her pajamas, her face red, her eyes glossy.

"*Bea*," Ever said, her body aflame.

Bea

All week, Bea stayed in her room except to eat. Even then, she silently made her meals and took them back to her room. Her mom tried to get her to come out, pleaded with her to talk, but she refused. She wondered if she could simply hide out in here until graduation, when she could leave Costa de la Luna for good.

After finishing her schoolwork each morning, she did some sanctioned floor-barre exercises, then studied YouTube videos of Svetlana Zakharova and Polina Semionova. She tried to make herself eat and then slept. Hours and hours, she slipped into frenzied dreams, as if she were afflicted with a fever instead of crippling shame. By Thursday, she felt the same way you feel after being home sick for a week, and so she'd finally showered.

Of course, she knew she couldn't really stay here forever. She needed to go back to the studio. She had *The Nutcracker* performance still, though she felt the scholarship slipping away from her, like one of her dad's sand castles being consumed by the surf. And worst of all, she deserved it. She'd screwed up, and this was the price she had to pay.

With each passing day away from the studio, she also became more and more certain that Etienne had only been toying with her. And when she got the text from Zoraiya, **OMG. Etienne is LIVING IN SAVVY'S GUESTHOUSE WTF???,** she knew it was over. That was probably what Vivienne had been trying to warn her about. Why she'd even allowed herself to dream was beyond her.

With a new sense of purpose, she sat at her desk, creating a spreadsheet of ballet companies and their audition dates. She researched tuition scholarships and which trainee programs offered stipends and pointe shoe budgets. She went so far as to research airline tickets, mapping out her auditions on a printed U.S. map, color-coded: red for ones requiring a flight and pink for those places she could drive to. She'd get her license, drive wherever she needed to go.

When Sunday came around, and she was allowed to go back to ballet, she almost considered just staying home. She still had no idea if Savvy had seen the video yet and what to expect if she had.

"We really need to talk about this," her mom said to Bea as she drove to rehearsals.

Bea gripped the steering wheel tightly, shook her head, and felt the tips of her ears burning red. Ever since she caught her mom watching the video, which she still had not been able to bring herself to watch, she'd refused to speak to her. She was angry with her for breaking her promise, but mostly she was just ashamed.

"Why would Luke do that to you?" her mom said.

"Do what?"

"Record you instead of help you? I thought you were friends."

"Everyone videos everything, Mom," she said, exasperated. Seriously, this was her own fault. She'd been such an idiot to think that this would all just go away.

Her mom often talked wistfully about the years before the internet—before cell phones and Snapchat and Instagram. Bea had never understood it until now. Her parents had been allowed to make mistakes without worrying about them being revealed to the world. They'd grown up without having every movement tracked on an app, without every conversation recorded for infinity in someone's text stream. She'd always assumed her mom was just afraid of technology, but now Bea understood. How easy life must have been back then. How free.

"Can we please not, Mom? I need to focus on driving," she said, turning briefly toward her. "I'm sorry about what I did. I just want to move on."

"Okay. But you can always talk to me, Bumble. I know I haven't

been as—*available?*—as I used to be. But I'm still here. I really am."
When she looked at her again, her mom's eyes were wet. She hated
seeing her mother cry; she especially hated *making* her mother cry.

"I can deal with it, Mama. It'll be okay."

But she knew the moment she stepped into the lobby that it wasn't
okay. Everyone stared at her, for one thing, and then parted as if she
were Moses as she made her way past the reception desk to the studio
doors. Lotte was in the lobby, too, with her camera, capturing this
collective head turning, jaw dropping, whispering.

She kept her head down, and made her way into Studio A, which
was, thankfully, empty. She'd been stretching at home all week,
and had, in the last couple of days, done some modified work at the
portable barre, but it was not the same as being at the studio. Now,
she did some *pliés*. She was grateful for the pain: the stiffness of her
joints, the tightness of her tendons and muscles, gave her something
to concentrate on.

Etienne came in, followed by Lotte with her camera.

"Beatrice," he said. "*Bon retour.* How is your ankle?"

"All better," she lied. It was actually about eighty percent, but she
wasn't going to tell him that.

"Very good. Today, you may take class—but you will observe
rehearsals."

"What?"

"I have made some changes."

"Oh, no, I'm fine," she said. "My ankle, it's fine."

"I am sure. But for today, you may observe."

"The performance is in less than two weeks. I am *fine.*"

"I know," he said, smiling. "Do not worry, *ma choupette.*"

Lotte smiled and snapped the legs of her tripod open like she was
cracking bones.

Etienne said not to worry, but worry is exactly what she did.
After class, she obediently sat stretching in the corner, worrying as
everyone took their places for Snow.

But Phoebe, the Snow Queen, was standing in the wrong spot.
She was supposed to come on from downstage left, but instead,

she was positioned upstage right, with Savvy in Phoebe's spot, and when the music began, it was Savvy who walked onstage. *What?* He'd taken Snow Queen away from Phoebe and given it to Savvy? Phoebe must be crushed. Bea covered her mouth with her hand, but Phoebe didn't seem upset. She was smiling, *broadly,* as she and a Level 5 boy, the young Nutcracker Prince, walked arm in arm across the stage. This made no sense.

Phoebe had been stepping in for Bea as Marie? Her heart was racing.

The whirling, haunting snow music began to play, and she watched Savvy dance. She was hypnotic, wicked. Gorgeous and terrifying. When she caught Bea's eyes, she somehow smiled and glared at the same time, and with that single glance, she relayed exactly what Bea had been fearing.

Savvy *knew.*

Of course, she'd seen the video, and now the secret was out, the lie exposed, and Savvy would want revenge. Bea had taken something of hers, and now she would take the only thing in the world that Bea wanted. *The scholarship.*

Bea's legs felt numb, paralyzed. Even her throbbing ankle was stricken with a complete absence of sensation. She grabbed her water bottle, suddenly overwhelmed with thirst, but she realized she was having difficulty swallowing, as well. Her head and heart were pounding in time to the music. She somehow made it to her knees and then to her feet, and despite not being able to feel them at all, she ran quickly out of the studio into the bathroom.

She got out her phone to text her mom to come get her, and saw that there was a text from an unknown number, nobody in her contacts. Below the text was a link to a TikTok video. *Oh my god.* Someone had posted the video to TikTok?

Her phone glitched, the app closing down. Then the phone itself shut down. She felt a sob escape her lips. She clicked the On button again and again, until it finally powered up and she was able to get back to the text. Trembling, she clicked on the link.

Ever

On Sunday, when she went to pick Bea up from rehearsals, Ever saw Lindsay in her car in the parking lot. Lindsay rolled down the window, and said, "Hey! Do you have a minute?"

"Of course," she said, and Lindsay motioned for her to open the passenger door.

"Sorry about the mess," Lindsay said, moving a box from the passenger seat to the back, which was *filled* with boxes.

"Is this stuff for the shelter?" Every year Lindsay did a clothing drive right around Thanksgiving. Ever had been meaning to go through their old coats. Ethan's coats.

"I'm leaving Steve," Lindsay said.

"Oh, Linds," she said. Lindsay hadn't been happy in her marriage forever, but she was stunned that she'd actually, finally, done it.

"Was it . . . *Melissa*?" Ever whispered.

Lindsay laughed, even as fresh tears fell down her cheeks. "No. Actually I don't honestly know. But I'm just . . . done."

"Are you okay?" Ever asked, and squeezed Lindsay's hand.

"I am," she said, as if she were startled by this truth. "I'm checking into a motel room today. I can't be in the house with him, and he refuses to go anywhere."

"Stay with us," Ever said. She could bunk with Bea, give Lindsay her room. But then she thought about Bea and Olive. That would never work.

"Thank you," Lindsay said. "But right now, I think I just need to be alone for a bit."

"How is Olive?" she asked.

"Well, Etienne put her in Spanish," Lindsay said, her face brightening. "So that's amazing. She's wanted that role forever."

"But what does she think about all *this*?" Ever said, motioning to the boxes.

Lindsay shrugged. "She's furious. She thinks I'm cheating on Steve."

"*What?*"

"Oh, Ever. It's just so terrible. Josie saw me and Victor meeting at Namaste, and Savvy ran into him picking me up from the medical building. Long story, but I passed out getting blood drawn, and Victor came to get me on the way to his closing. It's all such a mess."

Ever felt exasperated. Seriously. Nearly every bit of drama playing out at the studio could be traced back to Josie and Savvy.

"Oh my god!" Lindsay said. "Did you hear about the guesthouse!"

"Guesthouse?"

"Apparently, Etienne has been living in Josie's guesthouse. This whole time. Olive never said a word; she said Josie swore her to secrecy. But Melissa got pissed at Josie and spilled."

"Wow," Ever said. She had no idea how to respond. What this meant. Josie had been hosting Etienne at her house this whole time; did this mean the competition for the scholarship had been rigged from the start? None of this felt fair.

"I told Olive she really needs to think hard about that friendship," Lindsay said. "Savvy and her mother are just . . ."

"*Wait*," Ever said, shaking her head, "Did you say you were getting *blood drawn*? I thought everything was okay." Ever felt the same creeping fear she'd felt after Ethan told her he had to have some tests done. He'd been so cavalier. So nonchalant.

Lindsay laughed, even as she kept crying. "So, I'm pregnant."

Ever's jaw fell open. "Oh my god."

"I know, right?" she said. "Olive doesn't know yet, so please don't say anything to Bea."

"What are you going to do?" she asked. She imagined what it would be like to be on the far end of middle age, with the prospect of starting over like this, becoming a mother again. A baby? Nothing could have surprised her more.

Ever's phone buzzed. **MOM I need u**

"Oh, shoot," she said. "I'm so sorry. That's Bea. I hope it's not her ankle. Call me tonight? We'll talk more then, okay?"

The lobby was filled with mothers. Racks of *Nutcracker* costumes, folding tables opened with sewing machines set up like a makeshift sweatshop. This had been her job for years. She knew each of those costumes as intimately as her own wardrobe. After Ethan died, she'd been absolved from these duties. Now, they'd been passed on to the next generation of mothers.

She walked over to see if Bea was in Studio A. They appeared to be rehearsing the second act. The music for Spanish was playing, and Olive was dancing; she looked positively radiant. Happy.

"Where's Bea?" she asked Nancy, feeling the same desperate fear she'd felt whenever the kids wandered away from her in the store when they were little.

"She's been in the bathroom for the last twenty minutes," Nancy said.

"Is she sick?" Ever asked as she glanced toward the closed restroom door, and Nancy shrugged.

Ever went to the door and knocked gently. "Bea?" She noted a few heads pop up from the sewing machines. "Bea?" she said again. "It's Mom."

She heard the door unlock, and Ever stepped inside to find Bea sitting on the floor, knees drawn to her chest, her body shaking.

"The video's on TikTok now," she said. "There are over twenty thousand views. What am I going to do? What if Vivienne sees?"

Twenty thousand people?

"Who posted this?" Ever asked, anger burning in her chest. "Luke?"

Bea shook her head, and she let out a shuddering breath. "It was *Olive*."

Bea

How could Olive do this to her? Bea played the TikTok video over and over. Watched herself as if she were watching any other stupid drunk girl on the app: #drunkgirl #drunkgirlanthem #girlfight. She clicked on the other TikToks that used the audio of Luke's hoot, "Holy shit! Cat fight!" She agonized over the duetted videos, where other girls reenacted the clumsy smack of her arm into Olive's eye.

Every inch of her body crawled with shame. And with each viewing, she remembered more and more. That night, which had been not much more than a blur, came into sharper focus with each viewing, the fog that had hung over the memory lifting as she watched everything play out before her on the screen.

It was the night before she left for New York. The boys invited them to meet them at the beach after class. Olive had pleaded with her, said it would be fun.

"It's the last time we'll see each other until August. Please?" Olive said. "Savvy won't be there. She's with her dad for the next two weeks."

Things had been terrible with Savvy ever since Miss V. had Bea understudy Giselle. She'd gone from vaguely annoyed with Bea to angry. Then, on the night of the performance, Savvy had approached her in the dressing room as Bea was getting dressed for her role as a Willi, and she thought that Savvy might be about to make peace with her. Savvy had remained injury- and illness-free, and she would dance the lead—like she had danced every lead—as planned. Order had been restored.

"Hey, I heard you got a scholarship to NYRB this summer," Savvy said.

Bea was so surprised. She was going to congratulate her?

"Just fifty percent," she said.

"Oh, that's too bad."

This didn't feel like a compliment. "It's my fourth summer. I like it there."

"Yeah. But if they really wanted you, they'd probably give you a full ride."

Bea's ears grew hot. Savvy had a way of ruining everything.

"All those big company intensives are just about making money, anyway. They jack up the tuition and then offer 'scholarships.' The best dancers don't pay a dime for their training at those schools, and they don't send you *home* at the end of the summer." With this, she laughed a little, as if Bea were an idiot. Bea couldn't believe Savvy had managed to stab her fifteen different ways in a single sentence.

"Anyway, *merde*," Savvy had chirped, and breezed out of the room.

Thank God, Savvy was gone now.

They'd gotten dressed for the bonfire at Olive's house; she'd borrowed a pair of Olive's shorts, and Olive had done her makeup: liquid eyeliner and false eyelashes making her eyes look dramatic, as if she were going onstage. And thick, arched eyebrows. She remembered feeling like someone else when Steve dropped them off at the beach parking lot and they made their way to meet the guys.

She expected *Le Trio* to be there, but it was just Luke and Nick.

"Where's Owen?" she asked, suddenly feeling kind of hesitant about the whole thing. Nick and Luke barely acknowledged her at the studio. But at least Owen was always nice.

"His cousin's got a birthday party," Luke said.

She hadn't planned on drinking, but when the boys pulled out the bottle of vodka they'd pilfered from Luke's parents' liquor cabinet, she and Olive accepted. She figured maybe she could just drink a little bit—that way, she wouldn't seem like a prude. And those couple of sips made Bea feel looser. Warm. Happy. Everything Savvy had said backstage became pliable, her cruel words like putty. Even the sharp sadness she'd been carrying with her since her dad passed started to soften, the razor-like edges dulled. A shard tumbled by the sea into a piece of sea glass.

"Well, look at *you*," Nick had said, and she'd felt *iridescent*.

It was nice to have someone admiring her. No one had ever looked at her the way Nick was looking at her. The fact that he was Savvy's boyfriend made it somehow even better. She knew it was wrong, but Savvy's meanness seemed to justify this.

Olive had seen what was happening. Now, Bea remembered Olive trying to steer her away from Nick. "Oh my god—sea sparkle!" Olive had said, pointing at the glowing blue bioluminescence on the receding waves. "*Bea*, come with me."

But she was too sleepy to go hiking around, her legs jelly beneath her. She kept tripping, the sand making an unsteady surface. When the music came on, that Billie Eilish song, "Bad Guy," she felt the music in her marrow. The beat thrumming inside her.

"No, I want to stay here and *dance*," she said. She'd had too much to drink; her vision was kaleidoscoping, but Nick's hands held her steady. His hands on her hips, his lips on her lips. The warm fire, his warm tongue. It felt *good*.

She didn't remember the argument with Olive until she saw the video. She did remember Olive trying to pull her from the dream, to make her go home, but she didn't want to go home. Home was where her dad's absence felt like a bottomless pit. She wanted to be *here*. In the firelight. In a boy's arms. The luminous blue of the ocean. The gleaming stars in the sky. A normal girl for the first time in her life.

But watching herself now, on the video, lashing out at Olive, saying "Fuck Savvy," was mortifying. This was her body, her face, her voice, but it wasn't her.

She vaguely recalled the way the sour-tasting liquor had climbed up her throat, Olive's anger, and Nick pulling her arm as she stumbled after him. Suddenly, she hadn't wanted this anymore. But it was too late. Away from the fire, on the other side of the jetty, the sand and air were cold. And Nick's hands were everywhere, and he was pushing her down, onto her knees. The sand digging into her bare skin. (She had scabs for the first two weeks of the summer, bleeding through her tights.)

No, she had thought. "What about Savvy?" she'd said.

"It doesn't count if we just do this." He started to unzip his pants, but at the sight and smell of him, the vodka was coming up, and he jumped away from her, zipping back up. "Jesus Christ. You need to go home."

The TikTok cut off after she hit Olive, but she was pretty sure now Olive had said something about her dad. After she pushed her away. What was it? As she lay in her bed that night after Nick wordlessly dropped her off, the world spinning, turning, she'd remembered. "Wow. Your dad would be *super proud*," Olive had said angrily. Her dad. Her *daddy*. But he was gone. She could never make him ashamed, and she could never make him proud again.

Ever

E ver sat in the DMV, waiting for Bea to get back from her driving test, too distracted to read the book she'd brought.

"We need to talk to Nick's parents, Bumble," she had said after they got home on Sunday night, as Bea replayed the TikTok again and again, as if it might change each time she watched it. "We need to tell Luke's parents, too."

"Oh god, no, Mom. *Please* don't say anything. Don't *do* anything. Savvy and Olive already hate me. The rest of the girls have basically canceled me."

"*Canceled* you?"

"They've all blocked me on Instagram, on Snapchat. They took me off the Level 6 group chat, Mom. Nobody gets taken off the group chat. Even Mary's still on there."

"But, it wasn't right, for him to take advantage of you when you were clearly drunk," Ever said. She asked Bea to tell her what happened after they disappeared off the screen. "Do you even *remember* what happened?"

"I told you I didn't have sex with him. And he didn't *rape* me. I *wanted* him, Mom. I *wanted* to be with him. You saw the video. Are you blind?"

Whatever she'd seen on the screen didn't matter, though; Ever knew if Bea had been sober, she would never have done this.

"You were drinking. Whatever happened after, he didn't have your clear consent."

"God, Mom, you sound like a PSA. *Consent*," she snorted.

"It's true," Ever had said. "It's your body. Other people don't get to make decisions about what you do with it."

Bea looked at her incredulously. "My *whole life* is based on other people telling me what to do with my body."

This struck Ever like a blow to the chest. What had she been teaching Bea? What sort of twisted lessons had they all unwittingly been teaching these girls?

But instead of letting it go, as Bea had pleaded, Ever felt herself becoming consumed with rage. At Luke. At Nick. At *Olive*. She recalled the explosion at the memorial, the way the gas grill had filled with fumes. It would only take a spark, and she, too, would combust.

She thought of Olive, Bea's best friend out to destroy her. Now that the video was online, it was not going to go away. With every view, with every click, it was spreading. She knew what *viral* meant when it came to the internet, of course, but she'd never thought about *virulence* before. How much like a disease this was: an incurable infection that must simply run its course.

Bea had made Ever promise she wouldn't say anything to Nick or Luke's moms or even to Lindsay about what Olive had done. She just wanted to get through *The Nutcracker* and move on. Rumor had it that Olive was quitting after the show, Nick had already left the studio, and when Savvy got the scholarship, she'd be gone, too.

"How do you know she's going to get the scholarship?" Ever said.

Bea shook her head and said, "Savvy always gets what she wants, Mom. I don't know why I thought it would be different this time."

Ever kept trying to imagine what would bring Olive to the point where she would post that video. She'd seen the altercation, but this act of "revenge" felt off. It seemed like something Savvy would do, not Olive. She suspected that Savvy had somehow orchestrated this, convinced Olive to post the video. It felt like she was the one pulling Olive's strings lately. But even if this were the case, it still wouldn't erase what Bea herself had done that night at the beach. *I wanted him, Mom.* She'd betrayed Savvy. She'd lashed out at Olive. It was all such a tangled mess, and there was no way to fix it. None. If Bea was right, Savvy would walk away the winner here. She'd get the scholarship. And then what?

Bea walked through the DMV doors then, holding her driver's license application. She'd passed. There was a small, sad smile on her face as she walked over to Ever, but no matter how hard she tried, Ever couldn't seem to return it.

Josie

There were only two weeks until *Nutcracker* now, and Savvy wanted to spend every minute she could in the studio. Etienne would do private lessons with her each morning to catch her up to speed with Snow Queen; then she'd go to her regular classes and rehearsals until they moved to the theater for tech and dress rehearsals early next week. They'd be off for Thanksgiving, and the performance would be on the Friday after the holiday.

Most nights that week, Savvy came home from class, disappeared upstairs to soak in an Epsom salt bath. Josie took dinner to her afterwards (healthy protein bowls, steamed vegetables, brown rice), and Savvy ate upstairs, while studying the new choreography on her phone.

Savvy didn't mention Nick, and Josie didn't bring him up. She also didn't bring up what Savvy had done last Monday night after she'd first shown Josie the video of Nick and Bea.

That night, after showing Josie the video, Savvy had wordlessly gone to blow-dry her hair. Alone in the kitchen, Josie had picked up Savvy's phone and played the video again: Bea and Nick making out and Olive, pleading, "Come on. Let's go home." Bea, refusing. She had watched as Bea clumsily writhed against Nick. Nick, that asshole. It was obvious that Bea was drunk; she could barely stand up.

Then the phone had vibrated with a text. From Nick.

Babe

Josie took another swig of wine, felt the fire of it in her throat.

I'm sorry—it was dum

She rolled her eyes and watched Nick dragging Bea by the hand across the sand. Bea was stumbling. Wasted. Josie felt uneasy.

"What are you doing?" Savvy had asked, coming into the kitchen in her bathrobe.

"Just watching the video again," she said. "Nick just texted—"

Savvy grabbed the phone from her hand.

"You aren't answering him, are you?" Josie asked.

"Um, *no*," she said, and clicked and tapped at the phone.

"What are you doing then?"

"I can't upload the whole thing; it's too long. But this should be enough."

"You're *posting* that?" Josie said.

"Well, *I'm* not."

"What do you mean?"

"*I* obviously can't post it, but Olive can."

"Olive?"

"Yeah. I just logged on to her account."

"You posted that from Olive's account?" she asked, stunned. Then, four words she had never said to Savvy. "You shouldn't do that."

"*What?*" Savvy had said, fuming. She had never looked at Josie like this before. Full of venom and fire. "Olive was there that night. She knew about this the whole time and never said anything. He's my boyfriend. And she's supposed to be my best friend. What would you do, *Mom*?" And then she'd stormed upstairs to her room.

Savvy was clearly hurt, lashing out, but still, whenever Josie thought about Savvy so nonchalantly logging on to Olive's TikTok and posting the video of Nick and Bea, she felt prickly. She couldn't help but imagine how different her own life would be if her weaker moments had been captured on film. She wasn't sure why Savvy had felt it was necessary to broadcast it, and hated that she'd thrown Olive under the bus to do so. Yes, Savvy was heart-broken about what Nick did. Of course, she had every right to be furious with him. And with Bea. Josie fully understood the pain of being betrayed, but something about how casually she'd used Olive to upend their worlds was disturbing.

And if all of this was about ruining Bea's chances at the scholarship, it hardly seemed necessary. As far as Josie could tell, Bea was becoming less and less of a threat with each passing day. She was injured, and so Etienne had shifted everyone's roles around. He'd put Phoebe in as Marie, Olive in Spanish, and Savvy as Snow Queen. *Snow Queen.* This role was a dream. In Etienne's version of *The Nutcracker,* the Snow Queen was, in some ways, the star of the show: casting her spell over them all.

Josie oddly felt almost grateful to Bea. Thanks to that stupid video, Savvy and Nick had broken up, which meant that Savvy could stay focused. No distractions now. Nothing standing between her and that scholarship. Savvy wouldn't make the same mistake that Josie had with Johnny: thinking that someone you love at eighteen will love you forever.

Even if it didn't feel that way right now, that video might be the best thing that could have happened to Savvy. Why couldn't she see that?

Lindsay

Olive wouldn't speak to Lindsay. Lindsay texted, called and left messages, Face-timed her. But her efforts went ignored.

"What did you expect? You're breaking up our family," Steve said. "For some random repair guy?"

Lindsay bristled, both at his accusation and his dismissiveness of Victor, the casual classist bullshit she had quietly tolerated for almost thirty years. Olive must have shared her suspicions about Victor with Steve.

"This has nothing to do with anyone else," she said. "This is about *me*."

It felt strange to say this, to call attention to herself in this way. When was the last time anything was about her?

After she'd told him she needed to leave, after she'd packed up her things while he stood dumbly in the bedroom doorway, watching her, she'd suggested they meet in public, where they'd be forced to at least *appear* calm and civil. They'd gotten a table at a new Italian restaurant near the beach. If they weren't here to discuss the implosion of their marriage, it might have been romantic: exposed brick walls, candlelight, Italian music.

"Of course, Olive is mad at *me*," she said, frustrated. "How convenient for you. You always get to be the good guy."

"I *am* the good guy here," he said, his voice rising, as a waitress squeezed behind him with a tray held high over her head. The smell of oregano and garlic was nauseating.

"Can I get you both something to drink?" their server asked. What she wouldn't do for a drink. She motioned to Steve to order.

"Johnnie Walker Blue, neat please," he said.

"Sparkling water. With lemon?"

"Water?" Steve clucked. "Are you pregnant or something?"

"Actually," she said, "I am."

The color drained from Steve's face and seemed to pool in his neck, which blazed red.

"That's not funny," he said.

"Nope. Serious as a heart attack." She reached into the basket the waiter had brought and pulled out a hunk of crusty bread. God, how long had it been since she'd eaten *bread*?

"Jesus Christ," he said, beads of sweat forming on his brow, which he wiped at furiously with his napkin. After a long moment, he said, "What are you going to do?"

"What do you mean?"

"I mean, you aren't possibly thinking about going through with it," he said.

"Actually, I am *going through with it*," she said. She *wanted* this baby. She had never been so certain of anything.

She studied Steve's face, ghostly in the candle's glow. He seemed tired, his eyes turned down in the corners. Serious and sad. He looked *old*. When had that happened? She hadn't seen him either, not for a long time.

"Well, this changes everything," he said, shaking his head, flummoxed.

"Steve, I need to know something," she said. "And please just tell me the truth."

He returned to earth, but stared at her blankly.

"Steve?"

He gave a curt nod.

"Where do you go?" she asked.

"What do you mean?"

"I mean, where are you? Those nights when you get home late. You never text. You just disappear."

He looked down at his plate and took a deep breath.

"Are you seeing somebody? It's okay, if you are," she said, and oddly, she started feeling stupid. "This is crazy, but at first I thought it might be Melissa. And then—the day the hot water heater blew up—I was thinking you were with *Sonia*."

He looked at her, stunned.

"At the movies," he said softly.

"What?"

"I go to the movies. After work."

She was completely confused.

"I know you don't like watching movies in the theater, but I do. I like being able to just forget about everything for a couple of hours. I don't have to think about work, or Olive, or . . . *us*."

The revelation, that Steve was sneaking off to watch movies by himself, was almost more startling than if he'd said he was cheating on her. How had they come to this? To his seeking refuge from their marriage . . . at a multiplex?

"I think we should talk about a divorce," she said gently. There. She'd said it. The D-word was out there like a giant meatball sitting on top of the tangled spaghetti mess of their marriage.

"I'm not cheating," he said. "I would never do that."

Lindsay cocked her head, studying him. He was telling the truth.

Steve reached for a piece of bread and tore at it clumsily. His hands were shaking. The only other time she'd seen him like this was after her father passed. She felt an involuntary tug at one of those frayed heart strings that still belonged to him.

When he looked up at her, his eyes were sad.

"You could stay," he said. *Pluck*.

"Stay?"

"With me. We could do this together." *Twang*. "If this is what you really want? It's not at all what we planned, but if your mind is made up?"

"Steve," she said, willing herself to stick to her guns. To not be pulled in by this, whatever this was he was offering her. She reached out and touched his hand. "You know it's not just me who's unhappy," she said. "You just said—"

Steve studied her face, as if they were playing poker and he was searching for a tell. When she offered him nothing, his eyes filled with tears, but he simply blinked them away and stiffened. Any vulnerability he'd offered up was gone now.

"Well, Olive is staying with me then," he said. "Until she goes to college. She doesn't need to suffer because of your midlife crisis."

Lindsay took a deep breath and exhaled, surprised when she didn't breathe flames in Steve's face. Using their own daughter as a bargaining chip.

"Etienne cast Olive in Spanish lead now," she said. "This means she still has a chance at the scholarship. And if she gets the scholarship, she will be going to Paris in January. If not, she'll be auditioning for trainee positions this winter."

Steve started to protest, to dismiss, to argue, but then a busser appeared with their drinks. Steve just shook his head.

"You're fooling yourself, and giving her false hope," he said. "It's not fair to her. She can't ever be what it is you want her to be."

"Is that what you think? That I'm a bad mom?"

She thought of Victor's words, *You are a great mom*. Which one was right?

"Is that why you don't think I should have this baby? Because I screwed up the first time . . ."

The waiter arrived with their entrees, and the smell of gnocchi smothered in mushroom cream sauce was oppressive. She took a sip of water and closed her eyes. The waiter set down Steve's veal, and it was all too much.

"Enjoy," the waiter said, and walked away.

Steve ate silently as she stared at her plate. Maybe she could bring it back to the hotel, reheat it for lunch tomorrow; she had completely lost her appetite.

Steve stopped eating and looked at her, shoulders slumped.

"Is it even mine?" he asked quietly, and that white-hot anger returned.

"No," she said, slamming the palm of her hand on the table as she stood up, the glasses and silverware rattling. "It's *mine*."

Josie

On Friday night, one week before the performance, Savvy came downstairs after her bath and said she was going to bed early, that she felt like she might be coming down with a little bug. Everybody at the studio was getting sick, she said. Josie made her drink a glass of Emergen-C and take some zinc.

"I really just want to take a shot of Nyquil and crash," Savvy said.

"Okay—there's some in my medicine cabinet. But don't take too much."

Shortly after Savvy disappeared into her room, the sensor lights on the guesthouse lit up, and Josie heard the muffled sound of Etienne's music. Everybody knew he was staying at the guesthouse now, thanks to Melissa.

Savvy had said that Melissa was in Orange County with Jaz this weekend; Jaz was taking a placement class at a new studio there. Some Russian émigré had opened it up recently, and Melissa was convinced that if she played her cards right, Jaz would be dancing with the Mariinsky by the time she was seventeen. It was actually liberating having Melissa gone. She didn't realize how exhausting she was to deal with until she didn't have to anymore. Melissa had gone into overdrive since the *Nutcracker* fiasco. Josie shouldn't have been surprised at all that she'd spilled the beans about the guesthouse, one last-ditch effort to sabotage Savvy. *Whatever.*

When her phone rang, she figured it was Melissa aiming to get some tips for Jaz. Something that might give her an advantage in the placement class. Pretending as if everything was okay between them. She planned to send her straight to voicemail, but saw that it was not Melissa, but Mark. *Oh, good freaking grief. Here we go again.*

"What?" she said.

"I have half a mind to get a restraining order."

"What are you talking about?" Though she knew exactly what he was talking about.

"Erica wasn't going to tell me. But I could tell she was upset about something, and I finally got it out of her. What the hell were you thinking? You can't just go to someone's work like that. What is wrong with you?"

What is wrong with you? Alan had said the same thing when she turned down the Lancôme job he'd gotten her. When she explained she was pregnant, he'd reached into his wallet and thrown five one-hundred-dollar bills at her. "I'm keeping it," she had said, pushing the money back toward him. "Then your career is over," he'd said. And he'd made sure that was the case.

"You know, I've been thinking I should call Johnny," Mark said.

Wait. What did Johnny have to do with any of this?

"*Johnny*?" Mark didn't even know him. They'd met exactly once, at Savvy's eighth grade graduation. "Why?"

"I just think he should be aware of what's going on. The kind of environment Savvy's in right now. You don't seem to be making the best parenting decisions lately."

"Are you kidding? You're the one who decided to put your dick in the hygienist. You're the one who decided to sell our home right out from under us. You're the one who decided to *leave*, Mark. That was *you*."

"You know, Melissa told me about what happened on Halloween. At Maisie's? With your *tenant*."

Wait. When did Melissa see Mark? She'd been pissed about Etienne, but what kind of friend did something like this?

"Well, you can tell Melissa to mind her own business. And you pretty much gave up your right to be jealous when you left me." She hung up the phone and sent him to voicemail when it started to ring again.

Livid, she marched down the stairs into the wine cellar and came back up with the most expensive bottle she could find. So much for things being back on track; just like that, everything had gone completely off the rails. She opened the bottle and poured herself a glass, sat at the island in the kitchen fuming until it was gone and she was feeling a bit tipsy. She poured herself another glass and went to the fridge. She stood there with the door opened for several moments, then reached into the back and grabbed a beer.

The underwater lights made the pool water glow an eerie blue, and that shimmering cobalt dropped off into the blackness of sky. It was unnerving, as if you could simply swim into an abyss.

She shook her head and walked across the cool grass to the guesthouse. Melissa had made sure everyone thought she was sleeping with Etienne; maybe she should really give all those self-righteous bitches something to talk about.

She put the beer under one arm and went to knock with her free hand, but Etienne answered the door before her knuckles met wood.

"Oh, hi!" she said, startled.

"Hello," he said and smiled, his mouth twitching a bit, his head tilted expectantly as he leaned against the doorframe. Had he been expecting her? Did he know this was bound to happen? Had he heard the rumors about himself?

He was shirtless, hair wet from a recent shower, and wearing just a pair of track pants. He smelled like woodsy soap and cigarettes. It was almost more intoxicating than Mark's wine.

He took both the beer and wine from her and set them down on a console table inside the door. Then he reached for her hand, pulling her gently into the guesthouse as if he were beckoning his partner onto the stage.

She tried to think of an excuse for why she'd come. Maybe to tell him that Mark was planning to sell the house. Or how grateful Savvy was for the role of Snow Queen. Really, he wouldn't regret the casting decision. Was *that* why she was really here? Just another transaction? A *quid pro quo*? No—it wasn't that. He'd already given

Savvy the part. And yet—the scholarship still hung in the balance. No. This wasn't about Savvy. This wasn't about an exchange of one thing for another. Of sex for something she wanted. Those days were behind her. Weren't they?

Maybe this was about revenge? About Mark? About *Melissa*? About all the moms who were likely clucking their tongues at her. *No*. This was about her and what *she* wanted. She was in charge here.

But then he was pulling her toward him, against him. He pressed those ropey abs against her, his erection gently nudging her. Her breath hitched as his amazing hands cupped her ass and he carried her to the unmade bed, where he undressed her.

It wasn't until an hour or so later, when her lips were plump, bruised, and her face and inner thighs were raw from his unshaven cheeks, that she opened her eyes. He was flat on his back, the center of the target tattoo pulsing with each breath. She smiled, thinking that Mark probably knew this was going to happen, feared this was going to happen, and was willing to sell the house—displace her and his own stepdaughter—to make sure that it didn't happen. He was no dummy, that Mark.

She had to pee. She climbed off the bed and stepped over their clothes to the bathroom. She flicked on the light and examined her face in the mirror, rubbed a wet thumb under each eye to remove the eyeliner that had smudged there. She needed a Q-tip. She opened one of the vanity drawers. Razors, hair pomade, and condoms—he'd also had a pack next to the bed—but no Q-tips. In the other drawer was some Tiger Balm, an unraveled ACE bandage, and some toothpaste. She flipped open the medicine cabinet and scanned the shelves. Some prescription meds, some over-the-counter painkillers, and a shot glass filled with bobby pins, tangled up in a hairnet. That was odd.

She pulled it out and looked at the door. She plucked a pin from the little nest, and her heart stopped. There, five or six platinum strands, each with about two inches of bright blue at the end.

Act III

Ever

The Santa Anas returned Thanksgiving week, the week of the *Nutcracker* performance. As Christmas carols began to jingle out of every shop, and wreaths went up on the lampposts in downtown Costa de la Luna, the hot winds rolled down from the mountains and whipped through town, stirring everyone into a sort of anxious frenzy. By the time Ever got through a snarl of traffic to The Center for her class on Monday morning, she felt as if there were an electric current running through her, like a live wire.

All weekend, she had been thinking about what Luke and Nick had done to Bea, what Olive had done to Bea, and how it all could be traced back to Savvy. But just as she'd felt completely helpless during the *Black Dresses* debacle, she also had no idea how to stop what was starting to feel like a freefall.

"This is not a competition," Ethan had said, the day that she'd turned on the TV only to see the author of *Black Dresses* chatting it up with Jenna Bush Hager on *The Today Show.*

"Of course, it is," she'd said. "And she won."

"That woman doesn't know you. She probably doesn't even know about your book," he had said. Of course, what he meant was that there was no ill will on the author's part. That this was all just a bit of bad timing for Ever. But she'd snapped at him. "Well, thanks to her, nobody else does, either."

The scholarship, though, was different. This *was* a competition. It was a literal competition with a single prize. And, as always, the stakes were highest for her. Well, for Bea. Bea had the most to lose. None of the girls needed the scholarship like Bea did.

She tried not to think about what Ethan would say if he were here. His assurances that they would make this work. That Bea was a gifted dancer who would find her way. That until three months ago, this scholarship had not even existed. That it had brought out nothing but bad things from all the girls. From all the moms, too. And Bob, of course.

As she briskly walked down the corridor to her classroom, she made a silent wish that Bob would not show up today. It was four days until opening night, and Bea said she still had no idea if Etienne was going to have her or Phoebe dance the lead. The two girls were pitted against each other now, both their futures uncertain. It was cruel, what Etienne was doing to the girls, though she knew this was just the way things were in ballet. After Bea had left the safe bubble of Vivienne's studio, this was exactly the kind of rivalry she'd regularly be facing.

Unfortunately, Bob was already there with the others, sitting in the spot he'd staked as his own. She looked at him, his friendly grin now seeming almost *smug*. Here she'd thought he was just a bumbling dad, but he'd been as conniving and hungry as all the others. He'd angled his way into Etienne's favor, and now his daughter was suddenly at the center of the mess.

"Where are Sid and Clementine?" she asked, ignoring the heavy thud of her heart.

"Sid's sick again," Henry said.

Martha snapped, "You're late."

"Okay," Ever said. "I guess we'd better get started then. Are any of you familiar with 'One Art' by Elizabeth Bishop?" They shook their heads, and so she read it aloud. This poem had meant nothing to her back when she first read it—all that business about the *art of losing*. She'd read it when she was in college: the losses described here were of things she did not yet have: houses, cities, lovers. But now, each line resonated as if she were a Tibetan chiming bowl: hollow and humming.

"Write about something you've lost," she said, but couldn't look Bob in the eye. "Something that is small and seemingly worthless, but that means a lot to you. Make your reader feel its significance."

For twenty minutes, her students hunched over their laptops and notebooks, tapping and scribbling away. But Ever sat still, fingers immobile, thinking of the things she'd lost, that had been taken. She thought of *Black Evenings*—the promise of success, her own idea run away with by another author. Then, Ethan. *God*, Ethan. And now Bea—with so much to lose.

You could drive yourself mad like this, supposing the world was full of thieves. She was so tired of being the victim. So tired of being the martyr, the fool. The casualty at the other end of yet another disaster. She would not allow her children to fall into this same trap. It was too late for her, but it was not too late for Bea.

After class, Bob lingered.

"Hey," he said.

"Hi, Bob."

"I just wanted you to know that no matter what happens, I plan to keep coming. To class, I mean."

No matter what happens. Meaning that if Bea got the scholarship, he wouldn't hold any resentment? Or did he mean this as a threat? If Phoebe was the one to win, did this mean that he'd keep showing up week after week? A living reminder of everything she'd lost?

Stop, Ethan's voice whispered. *Breathe*. No. Bea *deserved* the scholarship. She had earned it, and Ever would not let Savvy, or Phoebe, take it from her.

"I guess there's nothing to do but wait and see," she offered with a shrug. But inside, her body was smoldering.

Josie

For once, she was grateful to Mark. His selling the house gave her an excuse to kick Etienne out that didn't require a conversation about Savvy.

Friday night, after she found Savvy's bobby pins, Josie had hurriedly pulled on her clothes and quietly made her way past Etienne, sprawled on his back and snoring, and out the door. She'd stumbled past the electric blue, shimmering pool, feeling off-balance, the world tilted strangely, almost as though it were trying to shrug her off its surface. Somehow, she'd made her way back to the house, climbed the stairs, and peeked in at Savvy. In slumber, Savvy could be eight instead of eighteen, blankets pulled up to her pointy little chin. Hair in braids and cheeks pink in the gentle moonlight coming through the window. Should she wake her up? Ask her what had happened? Demand to know what she'd been doing in the guesthouse bathroom? But every question hinged on the fact that she, herself, had been in the guesthouse, too. At three a.m., no less.

No. Not now, not when her body was still buzzing from the wine and Etienne's hands and the shock of what she had discovered. Besides, Savvy hadn't been feeling well and had taken Nyquil before bed. Even if Josie could wake her now, Savvy would be groggy; it would be like speaking to a sleepwalker. Now was not the time.

In her own room, she had slipped out of her clothes, which still smelled of him, that earthy scent of cologne and sweat and French cigarettes. She'd balled them up as if they were evidence of a crime and stuffed them in the bottom of the hamper. But even when she curled up under her own covers, she could still smell him. Feel him.

What had she done?

On Saturday morning, she had woken with a pounding headache and a tremendous thirst. The Santa Anas were back. She could feel the frenetic energy in the air. She guzzled at least a quart of water before she began to feel normal again.

Luckily, Savvy was at the studio all day Saturday and Sunday, giving Josie time to think. All weekend, she tried to come up with an explanation for how Savvy's hairpins had wound up in the medicine cabinet. She also devised a reasonable cover story about why she herself had been in Etienne's bathroom: *I was looking for my migraine meds*, she would offer if Savvy asked. *I couldn't find them in the house.* The entire weekend, she'd turned those prickly thoughts around and around, until her brain was scratched raw.

On Sunday night, as Josie waited for Savvy to get home from rehearsals, *she* rehearsed what she might say to her. Practiced asking the question, the questions, that needed to be asked. *When did this happen? Did he hurt you? Why didn't you tell me?*

When Savvy came home from rehearsals, she threw her bag down in the foyer and came into the kitchen, collapsed onto a barstool, and sneezed.

"I really don't feel good," she said. "Everybody's sick."

Josie poured her a glass of orange juice and handed her two vitamin Cs and a zinc pill.

"Thanks," Savvy said.

Josie studied her daughter's face for some recognition, some acknowledgment, some sliver of evidence as to what had happened with Etienne. And *when.*

It must have been recently. She and Nick had just broken up, after all. She was hurt from his betrayal. Angry. Never mind what Beatrice had done. She must have gone to him—in her weakness—and he took advantage.

Savvy swallowed the pills, then pulled the bobby pins from her hair one by one, setting them on the cold marble counter. The plunk of each one felt like a wrong note on a piano.

When her bun was released, Savvy laid her head down across her arms, eyes closed. Josie reached out to stroke her hair, the way she used to when she was a little girl, feeling the same wonderment that something so perfect had come from her. Savvy's hair was silky between her fingers. Josie was glad she'd cut off the indigo-dyed ends, which had felt like blasphemy to her natural, god-given beauty.

She withdrew her fingers as if she'd been burned. Savvy had cut those blue tips off *months* ago. She'd still been with Nick then. It was *before* the video of Beatrice came out. It wasn't long after Etienne had first arrived. And then it hit her; Savvy had cut her hair before her birthday. When she was *seventeen* years old then. A girl. And he was a fucking grown man.

But if he had taken advantage of her, hurt her, why hadn't Savvy said anything? Why hadn't she come to her? They were like sisters, she'd thought. Best friends. Why had she kept this secret? Josie felt her heart lurch. Her little girl.

"Sav," she said. "I found your hairpins in Etienne's bathroom."

Savvy opened her eyes but didn't lift her head from the pillow her arms made.

"Did something . . . happen?" Josie asked, her voice gilded with fear. "Did he . . . hurt you?"

Savvy sat up. "Oh my god," she said. "Are you kidding?"

"You can tell me," Josie said, reaching for her hand. "If he did something to you, I need to know. I'm your *mom*."

Savvy put her head back down. "It's no big deal, Mom," she said.

So something *had* happened?

"He's a grown man, Savvy," Josie said. She had the sudden urge to jump into the pool. As if the cool water could alleviate this sensation of raw nerves.

The pool.

Suddenly, she remembered that night, a couple months ago, the night after *Nutcracker* auditions. The night after he'd given Bea the lead. Had Savvy gone to him, trying to persuade him to change his mind? Had she thought that if she slept with him, he'd give her what she wanted? Is this how she had wound up as Snow Queen instead of Dewdrop? Did she think this was the way to get the scholarship?

No, she thought. This was crazy. But that was exactly what she herself had been trying to do, wasn't it? She was so confused now about her motives. Men muddied things. Desire confused things.

She struggled to remember that night back in September. She'd had wine, the girls had stuffed themselves with pizza, she'd been scrolling on Instagram when she nodded off. It was splashing that had woken her. Olive had been there, too. Hadn't she? She'd sworn she'd seen Olive's pink towel. Though she hadn't had her glasses on, and she'd been drinking.

"I'm going to go talk to him," Josie said, a threat she wasn't sure she had the fortitude to follow through with.

"No, Mom," Savvy said angrily. "Seriously. Nothing happened."

Josie felt heat spreading through her whole body.

"*Nothing happened* meaning he didn't hurt you? Or *nothing happened* meaning you didn't sleep with him?" This came out like a bit of hissing steam.

"With my *teacher?*" Savvy said with disgust. "Just because you think he's hot doesn't mean I do. He's old. And he's disgusting."

Savvy was quiet for a moment before she brushed her hands dismissively. "I always change in there. They've probably been in there since summer." But she wouldn't look Josie in the eye.

Josie pressed her burning hands against the cold marble so that she wouldn't combust. She remembered the way her thighs had burned from his stubble. The way her cheeks and breasts and skin were aflame as she made her way back from the pool house that night. Savvy was lying. Her own daughter was lying to her.

Savvy was still sleeping on Monday morning, so she took two cups of coffee with her to Etienne's door. He needed to go. Now. Luckily, between Mark's threats to sell the house out from under them if Etienne didn't leave, and the rumors she knew were flying around the studio like flies around a dead animal, she had plenty of excuses to send him packing. He had to move out, this much was certain, but confronting him, accusing him, if he'd truly done nothing wrong could be a disaster. There was too much at stake.

Too much to lose. She needed to be strategic about this, use her head.

He stood in a pair of pajama bottoms, rubbing his eyes like a kid, but when he saw her, his pajama bottoms showed he was very much awake. He cocked his head at her expectantly, then leaned toward her and kissed her neck.

Damn it.

"Hey," she said, pulling back, trying not to spill the hot coffee in her hands. "Can we talk real quick?"

"*Bien sûr*," he said, bowing like an usher showing her into a theater.

Inside the guesthouse, he sat down at the edge of the unmade bed, blowing on his coffee before taking a sip. There was nowhere for her to sit.

"Etienne," she said. "You can't stay here."

He frowned.

"Somehow word got out that you're here. It doesn't look good. To the other parents."

He smiled coyly.

"They might think something, um, inappropriate is going on."

"Inappropriate?" he said, forcing her to acknowledge what had happened here, what had happened in those rumpled sheets.

"Exactly. I mean, with everything that's . . . happened . . ." she prompted, then paused, trying not to think about Savvy in this room. She shook her head, as if she could rattle those thoughts loose. "I think, given the line that's been crossed, it might be best if you spent your last week here somewhere else."

He took a sip on his coffee, without taking his eyes off her.

"Also, Mark, my ex-husband? He's jealous. If I don't make you leave, he will take the house from me. Our divorce isn't final yet, and he could take everything. I have to consider Savvy." Her voice caught on Savvy's name, and she waited for his reaction. Some clue, something in his crooked face, that might reveal whatever it was that had happened between him and her daughter. She felt ashamed at the thought that both she and Savvy had gone to this man-child with their need. With their desperate hopes.

But Etienne only set his coffee down and said, "Okay."

"Can you get a room at the motel, where the rest of the crew is staying? With Lotte?"

"Of course," he said, in that oddly deferential way he had.

"I'm really sorry," she offered. "This probably wasn't a good idea to begin with. I wouldn't want anyone to accuse Savvy of having an unfair advantage."

He tilted his head again, like a golden retriever.

"With the scholarship."

Wait. Was he really that stupid? Or was it that Savvy was not a contender? Never had been? Or, maybe, it was a done deal? Nothing that needed to be questioned? Josie's head spun as she tried to figure out what his dismissiveness meant.

"If you could be out by this afternoon, that would be for the best," she said. "And please, don't worry about cleaning the guesthouse. I'll take care of it. Just make sure you don't forget anything. Like in the drawers. The medicine cabinet?"

No reaction. He tipped an imaginary hat at her, and she let herself out.

Back in the house, she called Nancy.

"CLCB."

"Hi, Nancy. It's Josie. Listen, I just wanted to let you know that Etienne's going to need another place to stay for the week. Yeah. There's an issue with the bathroom in the guesthouse."

Lindsay

Olive still would not speak to her. All weekend, she had answered only about half of Lindsay's texts, and then mostly with thumbs-up emojis or one-word answers. Olive was convinced that Lindsay was having an affair, that this was all a simple case of infidelity. Of betrayal. And stupid Steve wasn't doing anything to set her straight. Lindsay missed her. With Thanksgiving around the corner, she was feeling particularly nostalgic. She wanted Olive here with her, though truthfully, she wouldn't really have wanted Olive to see this. The motel room at Seacoast Suites was beyond pathetic, with its dated brown and gold bedding and dinged furniture. Even the "art" was sad: a still life of fruit and flowers that both looked as though they were moments from decomposing. She had been searching her agency's listings for a rental, but until December first, she was stuck with a mini fridge and two-burner stove. At least there was a free continental breakfast, though she stuck to the feeble cantaloupe and pasty oatmeal.

Early Monday evening, Lindsay searched the rental listings again for a place close to work, a place with three bedrooms: one for her, one for Olive, and one for the baby. The *baby*. Dr. Ramachandra had told her that so far, everything looked good with the pregnancy. The latest blood work would reveal its gender and any genetic abnormalities. Oddly, she felt prepared for whatever came her way. The best news of all, though, was that she was off that godawful diet. Of course, she was supposed to eat healthy foods and exercise. But for the next seven months, she wouldn't have to even *look* at a glass of cucumber juice.

Lindsay hadn't told Olive about the baby yet. She'd made Steve swear he would wait to tell her until after *Nutcracker*. He seemed to still be in disbelief that she was serious about leaving him. About going through with any of this. She needed to trust that Steve would keep his word. And she needed to trust that Olive would come around. That her anger would fade, and she'd let Lindsay explain. What Lindsay needed to focus on right now was simply supporting Olive. Unless Etienne did something drastic, she was still slated to perform Spanish, which—in Lindsay's opinion—was the single most vibrant role in *The Nutcracker*. And it was *hers*. Everyone thought they knew what was going to happen with the scholarship, but it wasn't over. Not by a long shot.

She'd run out of bottled water, so she'd locked up her room and gone to grab a few bottles from the vending machine under the stairs. As she made her way back, she heard a raised voice coming from one of the rooms, about four doors down from her own. The door was cracked open, but all she could ascertain was that it was a female voice. Yelling. In *French*.

Her eyes darted to the parking space in front of the door and sure enough, there was the film crew's white van. When she checked in to the motel, she'd known that Lotte and the sound guy were staying here, but it was a big complex. She never would have expected to see the van parked right next to the spot where she had parked her car. But there it was.

She tried to figure out what all the commotion was about, but her French was limited to a few different French dishes and ballet moves, not super helpful unless they were discussing *bourguignon* or *ballonés*.

It didn't take long to realize that no one was responding to the rant, despite pauses in the yelling. Whoever it was must be on the phone. Suddenly, and without warning, the door to Room 103 flew open, and Lotte flew out, phone pressed to her ear.

Lindsay jumped, startled, and nodded stupidly. "Hi!"

Lotte seemed to be trying to place her face. Then recognition set in. She hissed something incomprehensible into her phone and hung up.

"Bonjour," Lotte said. "You are one of *les mamans,* non?"

"Yes! I'm Olive's mom. The redhead?" She quickly added, "Lindsay."

"I remember." Lotte reached into the pocket of her oversized cardigan and pulled out a pack of cigarettes, pinched the cellophane tab, and unfurled it like a ribbon. "You are friends with that woman," Lotte said. Not a question.

Lindsay cocked her head.

"Jo-sie," she said with disgust. "Savannah's mother?"

"Josie Jacobs?" Lindsay asked. "Yes. No. Well, our daughters are friends."

"Well, your friend, she has demanded the *prince* vacate her castle."

Josie had kicked Etienne out? She wondered if Josie thought this might save face, might make up for the fact that she'd been hiding him away in her guesthouse all this time. Lindsay's frustration at the unfairness of it all was rekindled. Who did he think he was, giving the girls hope that they each had a fighting chance, when it seemed his decision had been made a long time ago? Maybe even before he arrived. The more she thought about it, the angrier she got. How could Vivienne allow him to do this? To start a war between the girls. And between the mothers?

Lotte took a lengthy drag on her cigarette and exhaled like the star of a French film. "I am so tired of these secrets."

"Wait, what secret? Him living at the guesthouse? You don't need to worry about that. *Everyone* knows."

Lotte brushed the smoke from in front of her face. "He thinks this film, it will—*comment tu dis*—redeem him," Lotte said. "But he . . . *il est un égoïste, un connard.* I am a filmmaker. My work has won three awards at FIGRA, my last film was nominated for the César Award. I am not here to babysit. *Je ne suis pas là pour tirer ses marrons du feu."*

"I'm sorry; I don't speak French," Lindsay said.

"I am not here to pull his chestnuts out of the fire," she said.

Well, that didn't help.

Lotte's phone rang again, and she huffed before answering and then flicked her cigarette into the bushes and disappeared back into the motel. Lindsay located the butt smoldering in the dry brush and stomped it out. Chestnuts. Cigarette butts.

Lindsay unlocked the door to her motel room and went inside. She sat down on the horrible bedspread and stared at the sad still life. Suddenly, she wanted nothing more than to see Olive.

Liv, she texted, trying again. Maybe if she just kept trying, Olive would come around. **I miss you. Let me pick you up after class? Go get smoothies at the beach?** Olive would drink her smoothie, and they'd look at the stars, the endless sea before them. The future had once felt like that. Limitless and open. She wanted that once more.

But when her phone buzzed with a text, it wasn't from Olive, but Josie. Of all people.

Hey, stranger! Could you give me the name and number for your housekeeper?

Jeez Louise. She ignored the text. She thought about Ever. About how nice it would be to be with her best friend right now.

Hey, Lindsay texted Ever. **Can I come over?**

There was no response for a long time. Then the text dinged. **Sure. Come by tomorrow around noon. We really need to talk.**

Bea

On Tuesday morning, Bea drove herself to her private lesson with Miss V. She knew her mother was watching her back out of the driveway. Bea had been nervous, too, but she had made it to the studio safe and sound, and texted her mom to let her know before she went into CLCB.

It felt so nice to be alone in the quiet studio with only Vivienne's soft voice and gentle hands correcting her. Pulling her back in time to before Etienne arrived, back when the only thing she cared about in the world was the brush of her slippers against the floor, the feeling of her muscles as they warmed and became pliant, amenable to Miss V.'s demands. For once, Lotte and her ever-watchful camera was absent. Not even Nancy was there; she would be at the theater all morning with Etienne, helping the fathers—who came out literally once a year—to load in the new backdrops and updated props from the rental truck. Her dad had been there, too, every year since her first *Nutcracker* when she was a Toy Soldier, to off-load the towering tree and grandfather clock, the sleigh and the throne, and the pounds and pounds of paper snow. Etienne had, apparently, replaced everything though, sets designed to match his new vision. She felt sort of sad for the retired props.

She and Miss V. had been working on the fine details lately, those nuances Miss V. said would one day differentiate her from all the other technically sound dancers, the others with beautiful lines and extensions and turnout. The minutiae—the facial expressions, the tilt of her head, the precise angle of her wrist—that would make her *stand out*.

Today, she spent almost the entire hour addressing her *port de bras*. "Your ankle is healed?" Miss V. had asked when the hour was up.

"Yes," she said. The truth was, it was at about ninety percent now, but she would never admit this. Dress rehearsal was *tomorrow*, and Etienne still hadn't told her whether it would be her or Phoebe dancing the lead.

"This has been a challenging time," Miss V. said.

Bea's heart began to race. She had been sweating, but now the sweat became the cold perspiration of fear rather than effort.

"Come," Miss V. said, and motioned for her to come closer, then put her hands on Bea's shoulders, studied her face.

"I was never a mother," she said, her eyes soft. "Instead, I am a teacher to you girls. It is not the same, I know. But I feel responsible for you. I care for you. I want the best life for you."

Please, she thought. *Please let this be about the scholarship.*

"But I worry about you, Beatrice."

Bea felt like she was going to cry. Why wouldn't she just come out and tell her if someone else would get the scholarship? Is this what she meant? Why did she insist on speaking in riddles, in circles?

Miss V. wrapped her sweater tightly around her slender waist and cleared her throat. "I am not happy. I told Etienne this is enough. It is cruel. He acts as though he is a kitten, and you are all little mice. It is making you girls . . ."

Bea held her breath.

"Hateful. Ugly."

And with a single, disenchanted look from one of the only people whose opinion really mattered, Bea knew: Miss V. had seen the video. Seen the terrible things Bea had done, heard the terrible things she'd said. She'd seen a side to her that even Bea herself hadn't known existed. Miss V. had seen her sloppy and careless and cruel.

But Vivienne was wrong; the bonfire had happened *before* Etienne arrived. What she had done with Nick, the things she'd said about Savvy, to Olive, had nothing to do with Etienne, or the scholarship.

Bea wanted to explain herself. But there was no explaining what she had done. There was no excuse.

When Bea was twelve or so, she had called Danny *stupid* when he didn't get a joke in a movie they were all watching. Her father had reacted in the same way. No anger, just profound disappointment. After pausing the movie and telling her to make things right with Danny, he had told her calmly and quietly, that he had no idea she was capable of such meanness. But she was. Maybe she always had been. And now, it had been revealed to the whole world. She'd let Olive down. She'd let her mom down. She'd let Miss. V. down.

Miss V. took a deep, sad breath. "Beatrice. What you girls do not seem to understand is that it does not matter, in the end. Whether it is Paris or Stuttgart or London or New York City. You will find the company, the director who is best for you. The company *you* will love. The one that will be your home. Hurting each other will not bring anyone success."

Trying not to cry, Bea nodded, pressed her hands together in thanks, and genuflected, an involuntary reflex, curtseying to her ballet mistress. Respect and gratitude, even though it felt like Miss V. had torn her heart from her chest. She felt flayed open. *"Merci,"* she said.

As Bea made her way to the door, Vivienne spoke again.

"I have shared my thoughts with Etienne. But in the end, it is his scholarship." She said this as if she were sucking on a bitter pit. "His *production.*"

After her lesson, she still had several hours before class. Because school was out, Miss V. would have back-to-back private lessons. Etienne would likely be showing up, as well, to work with the soloists.

Normally, she would do homework while stretching in the lobby. But today, she couldn't stay here. Not with Miss V.'s unspoken accusations, her judgment, hanging in the air like so much cigarette smoke. After that incident with Danny, she'd had to sit through the rest of the movie with her family but alone with her shame. She could not endure that today.

She gathered her things and slipped into the greenroom, out of sight of Vivienne and Nancy, who had arrived while they were working.

Her first instinct was to text Olive. Even now, when she needed venting, or advice, or just someone to commiserate with, her impulse was to reach out to Olive. But the connection between them was severed. And it was all her fault.

She was so mortified by what she had done. So embarrassed. But mostly, just sorry. She wouldn't blame Olive if she never spoke to her again. What Bea had done that night was selfish and stupid. She didn't even *like* Nick. And now, she might have thrown away her whole future because of it. Miss V. had said this was Etienne's production, the scholarship his choice to make. But if Vivienne shared what she had done with him, he might decide she was not the kind of girl that the Ballet de Paris would like to see given an opportunity like this.

She packed up her things and pulled her phone out again.

Owen. She could at least talk to Owen.

Hey, she wrote. **Just checking to see if you're coming to class early. I'm here but might go home for a bit. Also, I got my license!**

Several moments passed. Nothing. He was off school for the week; maybe he was sleeping in. Or picking up an extra shift at work. But then ellipses appeared as he drafted his text. Then stopped. Disappeared.

Just as she was about to put her phone in her bag, it trembled in her hand.

I saw the video. Not sure what to think.

Her body felt like it was on fire. Of course, he had seen it. What kind of idiot was she? *Everyone* had likely seen it by now. She started to type and then deleted. Finally, she just said exactly what she felt.

I'm sorry. I'm sorry I did it. And I'm sorry I didn't tell you. I understand if you don't want to. . . To what? To be her friend? To be her boyfriend? Was that even what he was after a single kiss? **I'm just sorry.**

She was shaking as she left the studio, her eyes blurry as she fumbled to find the keys to the Volvo. She got into the car and started the engine. She put the phone in the cup holder, wiped her tears away, and took a deep breath. Focus, she thought. SMOG. Signal (not necessary), Mirror (check), Over the Shoulder (done), Go!

But when she stepped on the gas, she didn't move backwards in reverse, but rather lurched forward, and up over the curb onto the sidewalk. She slammed on the brakes, heart beating loudly in her ears, as the car halted just inches from the studio window. She almost laughed, a maniacal bubble expanding in her chest. *Breathe*, she thought, and quickly shifted the car into Reverse. Hands shaking, whole body quaking, she put her foot on the gas again and started to back out. She felt the curb scrape the undercarriage of the car as she backed over it, and she pressed the gas pedal a little harder.

The honking was close and loud. She slammed on the brakes again. A sharp jerk of her neck. The press of the seat belt as it locked against her chest, making it hard to breathe.

She whipped her head around. She could hear Melissa yelling even through the closed window. The Volvo's rear bumper was inches from the passenger door of Melissa's Mercedes. Bea could see the small *oh* on Jaz's mouth through the passenger-side window.

Shaking, she rolled down the window and cried out, "I'm sorry!"

Lindsay

"Hi," Lindsay said when Ever opened the door on Tuesday. But when she went in for a hug, Ever stiffened and motioned for her to go inside.

"I brought Ralberto's!" Lindsay tried. The biggest perk of all about the pregnancy so far was the freedom to eat Mexican food again. Victor had dropped off a chicken chimichanga her first night at the motel, left it by the door with a sweet note. Today, she'd ordered Ever's favorite veggie burrito and enchiladas for herself. With rice *and* beans.

But it was clear the minute they sat down and Ever waved her hand *no* at her offering, that she wasn't interested in a friendly chat.

Ever took a deep breath and frowned, rubbed her temples. "This has to stop."

Lindsay shook her head. "What's that?"

"What Bea did, at the bonfire, was so horrible. She made a terrible mistake. She's ashamed. But what Olive did? I just . . ."

Lindsay looked at her dumbly; she had no idea what Ever was talking about.

"Oh, did Bea finally tell you what's going on between them?" Lindsay said, "Olive hasn't said a word to me."

"You don't know about the video?"

Lindsay shook her head. *Video?*

Ever shared the video with her. Suddenly, it all made sense. The rift between the girls, Olive's taking Savvy's side. The cruel things Olive said. *Your dad would be super proud of you right now.* This made Lindsay feel like she'd swallowed a cold, hard stone. Where had Olive's anger come from? That meanness? Then it struck her.

This was envy. Because Ethan, unlike Steve, had always been there for Bea, engaged in Bea's life. He'd supported her dreams when Steve had done nothing but diminish Olive's, tried to steer her ship in a different direction. Lindsay's heart hurt for Olive.

"Olive posted this?" Lindsay said.

"She did."

She couldn't believe Olive would ever be so cruel. But then again, she'd turned into someone else since she started hanging out with Savvy. And now, when Olive needed her more than ever—to right that wayward ship, to set her back on course—Lindsay had run away.

"I don't know what to say," Lindsay said. "I'm so sorry. I'll talk to her."

"*No*," Ever said. "I promised Bea I wouldn't talk to you until after *Nutcracker*, but I thought you needed to know. What Olive did. Please wait until you say anything?"

That wouldn't be a problem given that Olive wasn't speaking to her.

"Wait a minute," Lindsay said. "When was the video posted? This summer?"

"No," Ever said. "Last week."

Lindsay's chest heaved with relief. "It wasn't Olive," she said, shaking her head. "We put a parental controls app on her phone in August. You know how I feel about social media. She hasn't had Instagram, or Snapchat, or TikTok since the end of the summer. I took them away."

"Then how . . ." Ever said, mystified.

But Lindsay knew. Olive and Savvy shared everything. Including passwords.

"*Savvy*."

Ever

"We'll figure this out," Lindsay had said. "Together. The first thing I'll do is get Olive logged into her account to take the video down."

Ever nodded. Of course, the damage was done. It was like trying to put toothpaste back into a tube. But at least it was a start.

"Olive is going to be furious. I've been warning her that Savvy was bad news. But I guess sometimes you just have to let kids learn things on their own."

But at whose expense? Ever wondered. Still, she accepted Lindsay's hug, which was softer than it had been two months ago. Pregnant. She could hardly believe that Lindsay was going to start this whole process all over again.

"Would you mind holding off on saying anything to Bea until I've had a chance to talk to Olive?" Lindsay said. "Just in case I'm wrong?"

"Okay," Ever said.

"And please," Lindsay said, handing her the burrito. "Take this. I got it with extra guacamole."

After Lindsay left, Ever took the burrito out onto the back deck and sat on the steps facing the water. She should have known Savvy was behind this. As awful as what had happened between the girls was, as horrible as Bea had been and Olive had been in response, they were still like sisters. They had grown up together. And while Olive was rightfully hurt, Ever should have known that she wasn't capable of being so cruel as to post the video.

Savvy had set out to destroy Bea. She had broadcast her weakest moment, her worst moment, with the intention of humiliating her. And she'd used Olive to do it.

Lindsay had said they would figure this out, but what could be done? Olive might take the video down, but it had already been seen. Other TikTok users had duetted it, preserving it forever, according to Bea. If Vivienne saw the video, there was no way that she would allow Etienne to offer Bea the scholarship. And if Bea didn't get the scholarship, what remained of this fragile castle of sand would crumble. She needed Ethan. She needed his calm, his reassurance, his logic, and his patience and his arms around her.

Ever felt a tidal wave of grief and disappointment and frustration wash over her. Ethan was gone. And she couldn't do this by herself.

When she looked out at the empty ocean, everything she'd been holding in for the last year came rising to the surface.

"*Come back!*" she wailed, just as she had howled that night when he disappeared into the black waves. The keening grief like the roar of the thunderous ocean. She couldn't tell in that moment where her sorrow ended and the sea began. They were the same. Powerful and consuming.

"*Mom,*" Danny said, and she startled.

She turned around, her face flushing with heat, her body an open wound.

"I'm sorry," she said, shaking her head. "I was just . . ."

"It's okay, Mom," he said. "It's okay." He sat down next to her, wrapped his arms around her, and held her until her body finally stopped quaking.

Josie

Josie had thought she'd get Lindsay's housekeeper to clean up Etienne's mess, but Lindsay had ignored her text. She'd probably heard about Etienne living in the guesthouse, too. Jesus. These women.

She didn't have time to clean it up on Tuesday. She spent the whole day running around town getting everything Savvy needed for the show. New false eyelashes and lipstick, extra pairs of tights, and the gel toe pads she preferred. After running errands, she set up shop in the living room with Savvy's Snow Queen costume. Nancy had sent it home with Savvy a week ago, but she'd been so busy she hadn't sat down to see what needed to be done. The costume was at least three or four years old. The cheap tutus, made in China, were always falling apart. She spent hours sewing the loose plastic "crystals" onto the netted skirt, replacing the missing beads on the bodice. Mary was Snow Queen last year, and she had a broader rib cage than Savvy, so she'd had to take it in a couple inches on each side, as well. There were some foundation stains on the bodice that she tackled with a cotton ball and some diluted bleach.

By the time Savvy got home, she'd steamed the wrinkles out of the long tutu, and it hung suspended like a giant, diaphanous snowflake in the living room window.

"Did Melissa tell you about what happened outside the studio today?" Savvy asked as she stripped out of her clothes, tossing everything into the washing machine in the laundry room.

"Melissa? No, what happened?"

"Bea almost backed that piece of shit Volvo into Melissa's Mercedes. She was like inches from Jaz."

"Was anybody hurt?" Josie asked.

"No, she stopped in time. *Unfortunately*, Bea is totally fine, too."

"Sav," she scolded. Josie knew Savvy's heart was broken over Nick, but rather than wallowing, she had clearly moved straight to anger.

Savvy stepped out of the laundry room, wearing only a T-shirt. Some tie-dyed Grateful Dead thing. "I'm just kidding. Jeez. I'm not a freaking monster."

"Whose shirt is that?" she asked.

Savvy started to skip up the stairs. "No idea. Found it in the Lost and Found at ballet."

"How is your cold?" Josie hollered after her.

"Fine, I guess. I took like three shots of Dayquil earlier."

No wonder she was so amped up. But this meant a crash later.

On Wednesday morning, when she checked in on Savvy, she was, as expected, crashed out. Between whatever bug she'd been fighting and the sheer exhaustion of dancing through it, she probably could use as much sleep as she could get. Class wasn't until four; then they would go to the theater for tech and dress rehearsal. It would be a late night.

The costume was done, and she had everything Savvy needed for rehearsal. Normally on the day before Thanksgiving, she'd be prepping for the meal, but Savvy would be with Johnny tomorrow, so no turkey to defrost or pie to make.

Feeling restless, she put on her swimsuit and went out to the pool. The air was dry, charged. The Santa Anas, hot. The news had said there was a significant fire danger, with fires burning a hundred miles or so north of Costa de la Luna.

She climbed into the cool water, allowed it to envelop her. She immediately calmed as her body moved instinctively, propelling her forward. After only a few strokes, there was nothing but water and her skin.

By the time she emerged, she felt refreshed. Her body tired but her brain quiet. It was as if she'd left all those things that had been upsetting her in the cool blue. She wrapped herself in a towel, squeezed the water from her hair, and made her way into the kitchen.

"Oh," Josie said, startled to see Savvy freshly showered and sitting at the kitchen island. She was wearing the same Lost and Found Dead T from last night, and a pair of track pants, but her wet hair was slicked back into a severe bun, and she had full makeup on.

"Morning, sweet pea," she said. "You look like you're feeling better. Let me make you some toast. You want juice?"

She poured juice, and when the toast popped up, she put it on a plate and grabbed the marmalade from the fridge. Savvy used to call it *mama-lade* when she was little.

"Daddy said he'll meet me here after rehearsals tonight," Savvy said.

Johnny had Savvy for Thanksgiving this year, but Josie would have her for Christmas. They alternated each year. This was the first time *Nutcracker* fell smack dab in the middle of his time with her, but so far, Johnny hadn't complained. He'd said he'd take Savvy home after dress rehearsal Wednesday night, and he'd have her back home on Friday morning. He didn't want her out on the roads over the holiday.

"Why doesn't he just grab you from the theater?" Josie asked. The prospect of seeing Johnny in person tonight was not something she welcomed right now. Johnny reminded her of all the ways things had gone wrong in her life. All the mistakes she'd made.

"I want to come home and take a shower before I go to his house. I also don't want to bring all my overnight stuff to the theater."

"Oh, okay," Josie said, and took the crumb-littered plate from her. *Mama-lade.*

Josie felt her eyes burn as Savvy came to her and hugged her. On-stage, she was so powerful, but here, in Josie's arms, she felt breakable. God, what if Etienne *had* hurt her?

Everything she'd shrugged off in the pool started to return, as if blown in with the wind that pushed open the French doors she'd left unlocked. Thoughts of Savvy and Etienne, herself and Etienne, Melissa, the scholarship. Mark and Erica. Mark and her *house*. Despite the rush of hot air that swirled through the kitchen where she sat, she shivered.

Bea

Bea had been too freaked out to drive again after almost hitting Melissa's car, and so she'd gotten a ride to the theater with Rebecca and her mom. Rebecca was eleven, in Level 5 and, miraculously, seemed oblivious to all the gossip. She still looked up to Bea.

Etienne had arranged a half dozen portable barres for class onstage before dress rehearsal. Bea stood by herself at a barre near the back curtains. She thought of her dad's meditation and attempted to conjure the same level of focus. During the adagio combinations, she closed her eyes, went inward, until there was nothing but her body and breath and the music.

She didn't notice Savvy until she opened her eyes and they were all turning to do the combination on the other side. Owen's shirt. What was she doing with Owen's Grateful Dead shirt? Bea searched the barre where Owen and Luke and the younger boys were for some clue, but Owen, lost in his own head, revealed nothing. And when she returned her gaze to Savvy, Savvy looked right through Bea.

She took a deep breath as Etienne walked up and down between the barres, making corrections along the way. He stopped to study Phoebe, fixing her foot—the one that seemed to have a mind of its own. He rotated it, turning it out, and nodded, pleased.

He still had not revealed who would be dancing Marie, and his indecision was maddening. She tried not to think about the awful possibility that she might not even dance tonight.

Lotte was onstage, too. Bea had seen her and Etienne in a heated discussion earlier, but their French had been so rapid, she hadn't been able to follow it at all. Now, Lotte made her way with her

camera behind Etienne, and as he approached Bea, something inside
her fluttered.

"Yes, yes," he said as Bea lifted her leg into *passé,* then *développé à
la seconde.* Lotte trained her camera's eye on her.

When Etienne leaned forward, she expected him to tell her to
lower her hip, to straighten her leg, to turn out her own stubborn
foot. But instead, his words were like a gust of hot wind in her ear.

"*Je t'ai choisi.*" I choose you.

Had she heard him correctly? And did he mean for Marie or something else? Could he possibly mean the scholarship? *Or, my god, both?*

She tipped her chin in response. Just a quick acknowledgment,
instead of the words that just might change everything.

For the rest of class, the butterfly in her stomach fluttered about
restlessly, lodging itself in her throat when, after *révérence,* Etienne
clapped his hands and stood in front of the group.

"In one half hour, please be in costume for Act One. We will run
the show through from beginning to end. Any questions?"

When Phoebe raised her hand, the butterfly almost escaped
through Bea's parted lips.

"Who is . . . will I . . . ?" She could see Phoebe trembling from
across the stage. Her pale shoulders quivering. Her hands. "Who is
Marie?"

He waved his hand dismissively, as if he couldn't be bothered by
such a pesky question. "Beatrice will dance Marie," he said, so casually he could have announced he was having a tuna sandwich for
lunch. Lotte pulled the camera away from her face and caught Bea's
eye. Smiled. Lotte was smiling at her.

But the look on Phoebe's face made Bea feel awful.

"So, I'll be Snow Queen?" Phoebe asked, her voice breaking.

"No," he said. "I have changed my mind."

Savvy would be dancing Snow Queen *and* Dewdrop. Olive would
be dancing Spanish. And Phoebe would have *nothing.*

A sharp cry escaped Phoebe's lips before she raced off stage into
the wings. Bea thought of following her, but was pretty sure she was
the last person Phoebe would want to comfort her.

Etienne sent the girls to the dressing room. Nancy chimed in with some orders about backstage conduct: basically, *shut up, don't eat in your costumes,* and *don't miss your cues.* Then she gathered the parent volunteers. Miss V. was in the control booth, where she would be for the rehearsal's entirety.

Bea grabbed her things and made her way through the wings and downstairs to the dressing room. She had staked claim to the dressing table in the far corner, away from the other girls. It had the worst light and was near the giant trash bin, which was already overflowing with takeout containers, but she figured at least no one would bother her here. And so, she was surprised when Olive sat in the folding chair next to her.

"Hi," Olive said to Bea's startled reflection.

Bea busied herself rummaging through her makeup bag, afraid of what Olive might have to say to her. Had Savvy tasked her with this, whatever this was? Hadn't they done enough? Weren't things even now? Did Savvy have to keep going? She thought of Owen's T-shirt and sucked in her breath before turning to Olive.

"Savvy posted the video off my TikTok account," Olive said. "I had no idea. I swear. And I took it down as soon as I found out."

Bea felt a shock, her body buzzing with it. "What?"

"I was so angry, Bea. You were so different that night. So selfish and hurtful. I'd never seen you act like that before. It scared me."

It was true. She had been selfish, hurtful. *Hateful and ugly*, just like Vivienne said.

She had a poster in her room, a dancer's feet *en pointe*. One foot wore tights and a pristine pointe shoe with neatly tied ribbons. The other foot was bare, ravaged. Hideous. Blisters, and Band-Aids, and blackened nails. The fantasy and the reality. The beauty and the secret ugliness they all hid inside.

Olive was staring at her reflection, imploring her to look at her.

"I was so hurt, Bea. But I would never ever post a video like that. Especially not one of you. Please say you believe me."

Bea turned to Olive. Her auburn hair was already back in a tight bun, a large red rose pinned behind her ear. Olive had been dreaming of being Spanish lead forever. Part of Bea wanted to squeeze her and squeal with delight.

"I should have known Savvy was just using me," Olive continued, voice breaking. "To get back at you. I feel super stupid."

Bea shook her head.

"I'm sorry," Olive continued. "I'm really sorry about what I said about your dad. I didn't mean it. I miss him, too. I do. And I miss you."

Bea didn't try to stop the tears that pooled and fell. She reached out for Olive's hand. "I miss *us,* Livvie."

Olive squeezed her hand and handed her a tissue to sop up the mascara mess under her eye.

"Liv," Bea said. "What can I do, to fix this? To make things better?"

"You can win the scholarship, Bea. I want you to win."

Act IV, Scene I

Josie

With Savvy at rehearsals, she figured now was as good a time as any to go clean out the guesthouse. She'd been avoiding it long enough. Inside, she went straight to the bathroom and threw open the medicine cabinet door. Empty. She pulled open the drawers and scoured the wastebasket, which was overflowing with dirty tissues and empty shampoo bottles and other detritus. He'd left an empty bottle of Ibuprofen, two rusty razors, a can of shaving cream, capless and crusty on the counter, blobs of toothpaste congealed in the sink. But no shot glass filled with bobby pins and her daughter's hair. She wondered for a moment if she'd only imagined it.

She loaded everything he'd left behind into a trash bag and began to clean. To scour the grout and tiles. To wash the baseboards and crown molding. She stripped the bed and climbed up on a chair to clear the cobwebs that had been gathering there. God, men were such pigs. She made her way down each wall with her sponge. He'd been smoking in here, that much was clear. The walls were yellow, and the drapes stank. She stood on a chair and pulled them down; she'd need to get them to the dry cleaners. Outside the window, the sun had set.

When she was finished, and the rooms sparkled and smelled of bleach instead of musky man funk, she took the trash bag outside and closed the door behind her, making sure it was locked, a habit since Mark spent two grand on the exercise bike he kept inside. He'd even installed a security camera on the guesthouse to protect his precious, unused, workout equipment, though stealing the equipment would be no small feat given the six-foot-tall fence and locked gate.

They had the same Wi-Fi doorbell camera on their front door, but she'd forgotten until now that he'd installed one at the guest-house, as well. Mark had tried to explain the whole system to her when he'd first installed it. He was a tech nerd, and loved the idea that it not only captured video of any visitors who arrived but that it also had audio and two-way communication. She had the app on her phone, but she'd never activated notifications for the guesthouse. Why would she? The only people going in and out of there were her and Mark, and Savvy. Until Etienne moved in that fall.

Mark had explained that the camera was triggered by motion.

Triggered by motion. Which meant it recorded anyone who visited the guesthouse. Any of the conversations had outside that door.

Heart racing, she tossed the bag in the dumpster, then walked briskly back to the house. She entered the kitchen in a daze. She grabbed a fishbowl-sized wineglass and filled it with Mark's best cabernet. She took the wine and her phone to the living room and sat down. She opened the security system app and quickly located the guesthouse camera's footage.

Could it really be this easy? There was a timeline, a way to review footage from any specific date. But she couldn't remember exactly what day the auditions had been. She clicked over to her calendar. NUT AUDITIONS. The day that Bea had gotten the part of Marie, and she had seen Savvy by the pool late at night.

She returned to the security app and scrolled back through the timeline of recorded events, stopping when she got to that night, noting there was—indeed—an "event"—meaning some sort of movement had activated the camera.

Fingers trembling, she clicked. But just as Savvy came into view, a call came in.

Melissa. *Goddamn it.* She sent the call to voicemail and returned to the app.

The camera appeared to have been triggered by Savvy's arrival at the guesthouse. The fish-eye view of the entryway revealed Savvy, in shorts and a T-shirt. Her hair in a bun. She watched Savvy lean forward to press the doorbell. Where was Olive?

Savvy's face lit up when, apparently, Etienne answered.

"*Bonsoir,*" his voice said.

"Hi!" Savvy said brightly. Dangling between her fingers was a bikini, and thrown over her other arm was her pink robe, which she tossed onto the bench by the door. "I was wondering if I could use your bathroom to change."

"It is late," he said, his voice all whisky and gravel.

"I know. I'm sorry. My friend's sleeping, and I didn't want to wake her up. But it's like super hot, and I wanted to go swimming."

So she *was* just using the bathroom to change. Just like she had said. But if that were true, why hadn't Savvy admitted that? Certainly, she would remember that Etienne had been there.

When Savvy stepped into the guesthouse, Josie held her breath.

However, Etienne did not follow her. Instead, he walked *outside*, onto the portico, into the camera's view. He sat on the bench, pulled a cigarette from a crumpled pack in his hand, and put it between his lips.

Her phone buzzed with another call. Melissa, again. *Ignore.*

When Savvy came back outside, her hair was down, like gossamer on her bare shoulders. Her belly was exposed, tanned. Her tiny breasts pushed up in the bikini top, the bottoms just shy of scandalous. Etienne looked at her, but not as Josie would have expected—it was a cursory glance, before he said, "Well, good night," and stood to go back inside.

But Savvy didn't move. Instead she blocked his way, hands clasped behind her back, being coy.

Etienne stopped, dropped his arms to his side, and Savvy moved toward him, leading with her breasts. She reached out for his hand. When she placed it on her butt, Josie felt nauseous. *No.* But Etienne retracted his hand as if he'd been scorched, and ran the same hand through his hair, shaking his head.

Still, Savvy persisted. She leaned forward toward Etienne, but he simply took her by the shoulders and steered her away from the doorway. He gazed down at her intently, but when Savvy moved to kiss him, he stepped backwards and gripped the small knobs of her shoulders, gently pushing her away from him. Now, his face was serious.

"No," he said.

Savvy shuddered and then crumpled onto the bench, head in her hands, shoulders trembling.

Etienne stood there for a moment, stupid and helpless, as Savvy sobbed. Then he sat down next to her.

No, Josie thought. *Don't touch her. Please don't touch her.*

Heart pounding, waiting for what would come next, she watched. But Etienne only gave Savvy a paternal side hug, and she wiped her nose on the back of her hand, like a kid.

"Have a good swim," he said. "Hopefully, you will—*cool off.*"

Defeated, Savvy grabbed her robe, stood up, and went to the pool. Josie could hear the faint splash of water offscreen. And Etienne moved to go back inside. But first, he stopped as if he'd forgotten something and looked right into the camera. He lifted his finger and shook it, a scolding *tsk, tsk.*

She shut the app down as if he'd been wagging his finger at her. As if he knew she was watching. Or that *someone* was watching, anyway.

Someone was watching! Holy shit. *Mark* had been watching. This was how he knew about Etienne being in the guesthouse. This was why he'd come here with his jealousy and his threats. How could she be so stupid? He'd been spying on her?

She thought about the times she had stood in this same doorway over the last couple months. When she'd invited Etienne to dinner, when she'd shown up with her muffins and her need, when she came to him with her anger and her desire. Fucking *Mark.*

When her phone rang, she practically dropped her wineglass. Melissa. AGAIN.

"What?" She should have let it go to voicemail.

"Jesus, hello to you, too. I just thought you'd like to know that it looks like Beatrice is getting the scholarship."

Josie felt the last swallow of wine creeping up her throat.

"How do you know that?" she asked.

"Nancy saw some raw footage for the documentary, and the whole thing is about Bea. It's been about her from Day One. Just thought you might want to know, in case you guys were getting your hopes up."

Shaking now, she clicked her phone off and looked up, disoriented. Had she forgotten to turn the lights on? The house was dark. When she glanced toward the French doors to the backyard, there was only the faintest orange glow in the distance. No pool lights. No lights from the neighbors.

The power was out.

Lindsay

Lindsay was in the motel room shower when the lights went out. There were no windows in the bathroom, and she was suddenly swallowed by complete darkness. She turned off the water, then blindly made her way to the towel rack. The floor was slippery, and she was a little dizzy; she felt her foot slip before she caught herself by grabbing the counter. God, just what she needed: to be found naked and knocked out in this sad motel.

A flash of light. Her phone. She'd brought it into the bathroom with her, and now it was buzzing and flashing on the counter. *Olive.*

"Liv?" she said as she tried to wrap a towel around herself with her free hand, though between the darkness and her solitude, it hardly mattered.

"Mom?" she said. "Oh my god. The power went out during Snow. Like, three girls fell. We could hardly find our way back to the dressing room."

"Are you okay?"

"Yeah. And I told Bea what Savvy did. She and I made up."

"You did?" Her heart felt instantly lighter.

"Yeah. Savvy is the worst, Mom . . ." She heard the shuddering sound Olive used to make when she was little right before she began to cry. "And I'm sorry. Can you come get me?"

"Of course, I'll be there. Just wait by the stage door; I'll park in the back lot. The power's out here, too, which means the streetlights might be out. It could take me a while."

★ ★ ★

The theater was in Cascara, the town just south of Costa de la Luna. It was a ten- or fifteen-minute drive on a good day, but it could be a thirty-minute or more trek in tangled traffic.

Outside, everything was eerily quiet. Seacoast Suites was easily two miles from the beach, but she could hear the loud crashing of waves against the sand.

She got into her car, grateful she could at least charge her phone here. It was probably just a rolling blackout; the electric company had done this before during fire season, but normally, it was announced in advance and didn't last long. Blackouts were a novelty, especially on school days: California kids' version of snow days. But this felt different. Ominous, even.

She'd heard on the news that there was a big fire burning north of LA, in Santa Barbara, homes evacuated, UCSB students sent home early for Thanksgiving break. Even so, the fires never seemed to come here. She'd grown up in Costa de la Luna, and not a single home had been lost to a wildfire in her lifetime.

Her Tesla glided down the dark street and onto the coastal highway. It was so strange in this utter darkness. The land and the sea indistinguishable. Everything a molten indigo.

She pulled into the theater's rear lot just as a bunch of other parents were arriving, as well. Car doors slammed, and there was a chaotic buzz, collective chatter and speculation.

Melissa was there, of course, dressed to the nines in a white silk pantsuit and nude heels, as if it were opening night instead of dress rehearsal.

The Littles' mothers were likely already inside, having been assigned to their various charges: Mice and Bon Bons and Toy Soldiers. Lindsay imagined them trying to shepherd the little girls—probably scared and crying—in total darkness. Sure enough, the stage door opened, and one of the Littles' mothers emerged, iPhone flashlight like a beacon, with a trail of costumed mice behind her. Every one of them crying.

Ever's Volvo pulled up, and Lindsay was so glad to see her. When Ever got out of the car, Lindsay embraced her.

"They've shut the power off for the whole town," Ever said.

"On the night before freaking Thanksgiving," Melissa chimed in. "The fires aren't even *close* to us."

Some of the older girls exited through the stage door, still wearing their Snow costumes; in white chiffon and tulle, they could be beautiful ghosts in the weak light of the new moon. The air was warm, but the wind was intense. The girls' long tutus swirled about as if they really were snowflakes. Lotte should be out here to capture this, Lindsay thought; it was oddly beautiful.

The snowflakes quickly scattered in the wind—to their respective parents—but no one dared to leave. Everyone seemed to be waiting for somebody else to take charge.

"Where's Vivienne?" someone asked in the darkness.

"I saw her with the stage manager after the power went out. She was trying to help the younger kids get to the lobby."

"Where's Etienne?"

"He was backstage during Snow."

"Well, I saw him going into the men's dressing room after the Dream Scene."

"Actually, I saw him arguing with Bob. Bob is super upset about Phoebe."

Oh, wow. Did this mean Etienne had given the lead back to Bea? If so, she wondered if Olive had lost her role in Spanish. *No*, she thought. *Please no.* Certainly, Olive would have said something if that were the case.

"Has anybody seen *Bob*?"

"Phoebe would know. Where's Phoebe?"

Then a hushed voice said, "I heard her sobbing in the dressing room. It's not fair what he's done to these girls. Pitting them against each other like this. I mean, for god's sakes, some of them are still just little girls."

"Has anyone seen the film crew? Lotte?"

"Not since the lights went out."

"Listen!" the leader of the Littles said, her usually tentative voice now booming. "Someone needs to find Nancy or Vivienne or *somebody* who can tell us if we should go home."

Another mousy mom chimed in, "If we go home now, does he expect us to come tomorrow? I mean we will, if we need to, of course, but it's Thanksgiving. So maybe not everyone can be here?"

Olive emerged, scanning the dark lot before running to Lindsay. She was in her warm-ups, since she wouldn't have been onstage until Act II. Her hair and makeup were done, however, and there was a bright red silk flower behind her ear. Oh, thank God. He hadn't taken Spanish away from her.

"What's going on in there?" Lindsay asked. With that, Olive leaned into Lindsay, and Lindsay wrapped her arms around her. It felt so good to hold her again, for Olive to need her.

"It's crazy. Pitch black. The Littles are freaking out."

Lindsay turned to the crowd around her and said loudly, "We'll go find Vivienne. Just give us a few minutes. Don't anybody leave just yet." She turned to Ever. "Come with us?"

Ever nodded.

"Liv, do you know where Bea is?" Ever asked as they hurried to the stage door.

"I haven't seen her since the power went out," Olive said.

They made their way through the stage door into the dark corridor that led to the dressing rooms and backstage. For almost fifteen years, Lindsay had been navigating this labyrinthine network of hallways and ramps and stairwells. When Olive was a Little, Lindsay had been charged with making sure she and her friends never missed a cue. She'd led flocks of sheep, clusters of baby mice, and hosts of tiny angels to the stage. As Olive got older, Lindsay had been stationed in the wings to help with quick changes or emergency costume repairs. She'd been there to help girls with their makeup, or hair, or fastening the eye hooks on the back of their bodices. Being with them, the girls and their wishes, their fears and excitement, had been her favorite thing.

It was quiet and dark inside—with only some low, voice-like rumblings coming from somewhere in the building's cavernous underbelly. Olive explained that most people had already exited through the theater and into the lobby. They were probably gathered there now, trying to figure out what to do. That's probably where Nancy was: pairing parents and their children.

"I wonder where Bea is," Ever said uneasily. "She texted when the lights went out, but now texts aren't getting delivered to her. Maybe I should go look in the lobby?"

"Sure," Lindsay said. "And text me if you find Vivienne or Etienne. I can let Melissa know so she can tell everybody out back."

Ever headed down the hallway that would take her to the front of the house. Lindsay knew that she too had long-ago memorized the arterial map of this building.

Lindsay and Olive walked quietly to the stage door, the one that led to the wings.

"You sure you're okay?" Lindsay asked. "I mean, after everything with Savvy?"

"Yeah," Olive said, head hung low. "I don't know why I trusted her. I feel so stupid."

They looked into the darkness together. There was no one backstage. Nobody in the wings, nobody in the bottomless orchestra pit. Nobody at all in the seats.

"What does Daddy have planned for Thanksgiving tomorrow?" Lindsay asked as brightly as she could.

Olive sighed. "He's using the smoker to do the turkey this year. He started already."

"I figured he'd never smoke or grill again after his little catastrophe at Ever's," she said and laughed. "But that should be yummy."

"I like the way you do it, Mom," she said sadly.

Again, Lindsay wondered if all of this was worth it.

"Well, your dad might actually be smart doing it his way; if the power doesn't come back on, he'll probably be the only one with a cooked turkey. I'm thinking I'm going to have to eat out."

"How will this all work now?" Olive asked.

"What do you mean?"

"I mean, where will I live? Daddy thinks you might come home?"

Lindsay felt her heart folding in on itself, like an origami bird.

"I plan to get my own place," she said, and thought of Victor's sad bachelor pad. Would she be living somewhere like that, all alone? "You'll have a room with me, of course. And you'll have a room with Daddy."

"Okay," Olive said softly.

They were standing on the stage, staring out at the seats, into the pitch-black abyss of the auditorium. Suddenly she felt Olive's hand in her own.

"Do you still want to quit ballet?" Lindsay asked softly.

Olive didn't speak, but looked down at her feet, and Lindsay had her answer.

She squeezed Olive's hand in the darkness and summoned the words that needed to be said.

"Sometimes people fall out of love, Liv," Lindsay said. "And that's okay."

"Thanks, Mom," Olive said softly, and squeezed her hand back before letting go and reaching into her dance bag. "Shoot."

"What's the matter?"

"My phone's dead, and I think I left my charger in the dressing room. I'll run down there and then meet you in the lobby?"

"Sure," Lindsay said. "Do you want me to come with you?"

"It's okay. Just go see if you can find Miss V."

Lindsay looked out into the dark house again. Olive told her that onstage, you can't see a single face beyond the front row. So, Olive didn't know that Lindsay cried through every performance; pride so enormous, she felt swollen with it. Olive didn't know she held her breath with every pirouette, every lift. That when the music ended, she was overwhelmed by both relief and tremendous grief: that beautiful moment gone. So fleeting, all of this. Maybe now this really was coming to an end, too.

The sound was deafening. It sounded like an animal. A wailing, a keening. Her first thought was poor Phoebe; was she still weeping in the wings? But no—this wasn't human at all.

It took a few moments, but then it registered. *Sirens.*

Bea

The Party Scene had been a blur. So many dancers onstage, so much activity, until Drosselmeyer arrived in his dark cape and singled her out—little Marie—for the gift of the Nutcracker. Drosselmeyer bewitched the children, made the toys come to life, and Bea felt the scary, dark magic of it. It filled her with wonder and fear. She was onstage for all of Act I: at the party, then as Marie slipped into a dream of giant mice and soldiers fighting, and then as the Nutcracker came to life. She was onstage until the Snow scene, when she fled into the wings.

It was here, between the dark curtains, where she'd found herself when Phoebe's dad came barging backstage. Bob's face was red, his hands curled into fists. Phoebe trailed behind him, head hung low. Bea slipped into the shadows as Bob approached Etienne and started yelling.

"I don't care who you are, or where you're from. This is unacceptable," Bob said.

Etienne was still in his Drosselmeyer costume, though when she was transformed into the adult Marie, he would remove his cape and become the Prince.

Bob was shaking; it was upsetting. She didn't like seeing adults lose their temper. He seemed *volcanic*. And worst of all, *she* was the reason. Or at least part of the reason.

Suddenly, the wings were filled with the Snow corps, three dancers per wing, and the music, that frenzied storm, began. She watched as the snowflakes formed their intricate patterns and Savvy pushed her way to the downstage wing for her entrance. She locked eyes with Bea for a moment, and Bea felt her skin go cold. No, it was just the magic of the performance. The dream of it. Savvy didn't have that kind of power.

As Savvy walked onstage, Bob continued to push Etienne. "Just five minutes. Out here."

"This is not the place," Etienne said. "Or the time for this conversation. We are in the middle of rehearsals. I will speak to you between acts."

"You will speak to me *now*," Bob said, and Phoebe began to cry again.

"It's okay, Daddy. Let's just go home. I don't want to be here anymore."

Onstage, Savvy was transfigured. A white witch. Etienne's choreography turning her into a glistening shard of ice.

Etienne turned away from Bob, and Bea caught her breath as Bob charged forward, turned Etienne around by the shoulder, and swung his fist at Etienne's perfectly square jaw.

That's when the power cut out.

Total darkness, a moment of stunned silence, and then chaos. Girls were screaming, slippered feet scurrying across the dark stage. "*Shit,*" she heard Savvy say. Bodies pushing and running in the wings.

"My ankle," someone said.

"What's happening?" someone else cried.

From backstage, she could hear the mothers trying to restore order.

Terror gripped her in the darkness, and she was enveloped in a moving crush of girls. She had closed her eyes and tried to focus on her breathing.

"Come with me."

She stiffened, shook her head.

"Come on."

Ever

E ver emerged from the dark corridor into the theater lobby, illuminated by a dozen cell phone flashlights. She felt as though
she had resurfaced from the bottom of the ocean, and she let out the
breath she'd been holding.

Nancy was winding through the crowd with her own flashlight
and a clipboard, snapping orders at mothers, and opening the front
doors only when each child was paired with a parent.

Ever made her way through the rumbling crowd to Nancy. "Have
you seen Bea?"

"No," Nancy said. "The Level Sixes all went out the back, I
think."

"I was just there. They're all waiting to find out if they should
stay."

"I'll send Vivienne out to talk to them."

The sirens were louder now.

"What's going on?" Ever asked Nancy. "Out there."

"There's a wildfire," she said. "No info yet, but they cut the
power out to help keep it from spreading. These winds are taking
trees down, power lines."

"Oh, no," she said. "If you see Bea, can you tell her to meet me
at my car out back?"

"Sure," Nancy said, and turned to a distraught mother who'd lost
her twins.

Where would Bea have gone? Why wasn't she with the other
Level 6 girls? Maybe she'd gone to the dressing room? Ever decided
to return to the basement, search the dressing room, and then go

back to the parking lot. There was little to no cell reception down here. That must be why her texts weren't going through.

She walked briskly down the stairwell, then down the ramp to the dressing rooms. Panic crept through her body. As she ran through the bowels of the theater, she recalled the desperate run up and down the beach as the Coast Guard searched for Ethan. She had run until she couldn't anymore, knowing with every passing second that the chance of him being alive was growing slimmer. For an hour, they'd searched, and she'd stood at the edge of the dark world, feeling helpless, and eventually, hopeless. When his surfboard crashed into shore without him, she'd bent over and vomited, then dropped to her knees, the waves lashing her, the sand pulling her under.

For a single, awful moment, she stood in the dark and quiet corridor and felt as if she'd been tumbled by the ocean, unable to discern the sky from the bottom of the sea. Without light, she was disoriented. When she heard the voices, she couldn't tell which direction they were coming from. She stumbled through the dark toward the sound, and found herself standing in front of the girls' dressing room door. The voices were muffled on the other side. She knocked, then turned the knob, pushing the door open slowly. There was just the faintest bit of light inside: someone's cell phone.

It was airless, hot, but a shiver ran up Ever's back. She saw Savannah's reflection in the mirror first. Still wearing her Snow Queen tutu, Savvy stood motionless, her eyes narrowed, and met Ever's eyes in the reflection, her gaze like ice.

And then Etienne emerged from the shadowed depths of the room, holding a bloody tissue to his nose. He caught Ever's eye and lowered his head before pushing past her into the hallway.

Bea

"Please come with me, Bea," Owen said, and took Bea by the hand. Together, they blindly climbed the back stairwell. She was breathless when they reached the roof access door. He pushed it open and held it for her, ushering her outside onto the flat gravel rooftop.

She was still wearing only the nightgown she'd worn for the Dream scene, but the air was warm. More like summer than November.

"Oh my god," she said as he motioned for her to follow him to the far end of the roof, facing the Costa de la Luna foothills several miles away. It looked like a movie. Unreal. The foothills were on fire. The air roared with the sounds of sirens. The winds were intense: hot and violent.

She was speechless, shaking her head.

"Isn't that where Olive's house is? Where your tree is?" he asked.

Her eyes pricked with the thoughts of Olive's house, remembering the hours they'd spent together there, the secrets they'd shared in the branches of their *Toi Toi Toi* tree. She recalled the quiet moments after they'd been talking in the darkness for hours, that magical still point in the middle of the night. What she wouldn't give to go back to a time when the world felt small and safe, to those nights when the girls were nothing but breath, each of them on the edge of their respective dreams.

"I thought you might be able to get reception up here," Owen said. "To call your mom?"

She checked her phone and saw about four hundred texts from her mom. She imagined her freaking out.

I'm fine Mama. I'll meet you in the back parking lot. Give me five minutes. But the text did not deliver; her mom's phone must be off. Or maybe she was in a dead spot somewhere in the building.

"Do we have to go back down there?" she said. "It's crazy. Everyone's losing their minds. Did you see Bob take a swing at Etienne?"

"I know," Owen said. "All of this is insane."

"Did anyone ever find Miss V.?"

"I have no idea," he said. "If I were her, I'd get in my car and drive to Mexico."

She laughed.

Quietly, they stood there surveying the strange scene below.

"What Nick did was awful," he said quietly. "And what Luke did was worse. I'm sorry I freaked out."

Bea shook her head. "No, it was me. It was my fault."

She thought of Savvy, standing at the barre in Owen's shirt. It felt like there was a stone lodged in her throat.

"I saw Savvy wearing your shirt," she ventured.

He sighed. "Oh my god, I left it at the studio the other day. Nancy must have put it in the Lost and Found. Savvy totally knows it's mine, though. Wait, did you think . . ."

She shook her head, embarrassed.

Owen reached for her hand. How many times had he done this in partnering class? They knew this choreography by heart. But when he leaned toward her, and she felt his lips brush hers, it felt like a new dance she'd didn't know yet. In *pas de deux*, trust is everything. You must trust that your partner will keep you safe. Hold you up if you falter, catch you if you begin to fall.

Ever

"Savannah? What's going on in here?" Ever said.

Etienne had wordlessly disappeared down the corridor, and in the dark room, Savvy stood at the dressing table, arms crossed.

"What was Etienne doing in here? I heard arguing."

Ever waited, summoning her patience. Mustering calm.

Savvy uncrossed her arms and leaned against the counter, chin jutted out defiantly. The smell of hair spray and makeup and Etienne's cologne was overwhelming.

"Bob punched him in the nose, and the men's room was out of toilet paper. I was telling him he isn't allowed in here," Savvy said, smirking. "What are *you* doing here?"

"I'm looking for Bea," she said.

At the mention of Bea, Savvy's eyes narrowed, and she glowered at Ever.

"This has all gone too far, Savannah," Ever said, all the anger and frustration she'd been feeling for weeks bubbling to the surface. "What Bea did at the bonfire was wrong. But what Luke did? What *you* did with the video? It's a violation. It's cruel. And for what? You think this is going to help you get the scholarship? That you can somehow destroy the other girls? The ones who have worked just as hard as you have?"

"You *moms*," Savvy said with disgust. "You're worse than we are, you know. You're supposed to be the grown-ups, but when it comes down to it, you're all vicious and jealous and awful."

Ever was stunned. She had never considered herself like those other moms. Not the ones Savvy was talking about, anyway: the ones with their ambition and almost violent need. Not like Savvy's own mom. Her words stung. But Savvy kept on: "You all just see what you want to see. Bea hooked up with Nick to *hurt* me. That's why she did it. She wanted to get back at me, and Nick was the only way to do that. You've seen the video?"

Ever nodded.

"She turned on her best friend, but somehow, she's still the victim. So, she lost her dad. Guess what? So did I. My dad *and* my stepdad. But you don't see me throwing a pity party."

At the mention of Ethan, Ever felt that current of electricity again, alive and dangerous, the energy bigger than she was.

"Olive was right, Ethan would be *so* proud of his sweet girl, wouldn't he?" Savvy hissed.

When Ever reached out to touch her, to press her hand against her mouth, to stop her from saying any more, she expected that Savvy's lips would be cold. Ice. But the moment her palm made contact with Savvy's mouth, pressing her lips against her teeth, willing the vitriol to stay inside her, she felt a startling heat. Savvy's face was burning with it. Feverish.

"Mom?" Bea said behind her, and Ever withdrew her hand as if she'd just put it into an open flame.

Savvy grabbed her bag and pushed past Ever, past Bea and Olive and Owen, who stood behind her in the dressing room doorway.

"Mom, we need to find Lindsay. They're evacuating the foothills."

"What?" Ever asked.

"The wildfire," Olive explained. "It's spreading."

Lindsay

Vivienne appeared, finally, at the backstage door. The industrial flashlight the stage manager was holding shone like a spotlight on her.

"You can all go home now. I will send out an email tomorrow with an update. If the power is restored and there is no fire danger down here in Cascara, we will run through the show at noon on Friday, a break for dinner, and then call time will be at six o'clock. But if we have no power, we have no show."

Melissa's arm shot up, but she didn't wait to be called on before balking, "The show might be canceled?"

"I am sorry, but yes. The theater is not available again until after the holidays," Vivienne said. "All we can do is hope that power is restored. Be prepared either way, and please have a lovely Thanksgiving with your families." She started to go inside, then turned to face them all again. "And *s'il vous plaît*, I know that emotions are running high right now. But *please*, try to behave like adults. Be role models for your children."

Chastised, the parents looked at each other guiltily. There had been whispers that Bob (*Bob!*) had popped Etienne right in the kisser. No one had seen either man since, however.

There was an odd rusty glow to the sky now; they were no longer enclosed in darkness. The sirens were blaring. Someone said there was a brush fire up north.

Bea and Olive emerged from the stage door together with Owen and Ever behind them, and the girls both came running straight for Lindsay.

"The fire," Olive said, breathless.

"It's just a brush fire. Probably in the canyon," Lindsay said. "They'll get it put out."

"No," Olive said, shaking her head. "Owen and Bea went up to the roof and saw the foothills are on fire. Near the house."

"Have you talked to Daddy?" Lindsay asked.

Olive shook her head. "Oh my god," Olive said. "Do you think *Daddy* could have started this? Maybe something happened with the smoker?"

Lindsay shook her head, though it was the first thought that had crossed her mind, as well. That Steve ruined things: never on purpose, but through thoughtlessness. Carelessness. By not paying attention.

"You guys should come to our house," Ever said to them. "It'll be safer at the beach."

"Okay. Thank you," Lindsay said. She figured she could swing by and grab her stuff from the motel on the way. Check out. She didn't want to be there anymore. She wanted to be with Olive. With Ever. Safe.

Josie

The power was out in the house, and when Josie checked the outage map on her phone, it appeared that it was out all across Costa de la Luna and even down in Cascara, where the theater was. She hadn't heard from Savvy, but then again, they were in the middle of dress rehearsal. Certainly, the theater would have a generator. **U have power?** she texted her.

No response. It was seven-thirty—probably just finishing up Act I. But the message had not delivered, and she remembered the dead spots inside the theater.

She stepped outside, and it was as if she were stepping into a black hole. A sinkhole. She felt dizzy. She made her way toward the dark pool, and looked out into the distance, where the foothills glowed an eerie orange. A wildfire. This must be why they shut off the power. When a warm gust of wind blew across the yard, it carried the scent of smoke, and she could hear the faint sound of fire crackling in the distance.

"Mom?"

Savvy was home? She turned, and Savvy had come outside, using her phone as a flashlight, which illuminated her, the white tutu making her look like an ethereal ghost.

"You're home early. Did the power go out at the theater, too?" Josie asked.

"Yeah."

"Oh, no. Will there still be a performance on Friday?" she asked.

Savvy shrugged and started to pull the pins out of her hair, setting them on the glass patio table. And Josie thought again of her in

Etienne's bathroom that night, cringed at what it was she had gone there to do. How lucky she was that Etienne had turned her away. She also thought about what Melissa had told her: the scholarship was a done deal. Beatrice Henderson would walk away the winner. She considered the ways she had compromised herself. The ways she and Savvy both had.

"Sav," she said, feeling the words like shards of ice in her throat. "You *were* in the guesthouse."

"Oh my god. I told you I went in there to change," Savvy said.

"I know you went there when Etienne was home."

"He *told* you?" Savvy said, and in the light of the phone, her face reddened. "Did he tell you what he did to me?"

Josie scowled. "What are you talking about?"

"Did he tell you that he tried to get me to sleep with him? That he promised me the scholarship if I fucked him?"

Josie's eyes burned, and she replayed the video in her mind. That was not what happened.

"And I said *no*," Savvy said bitterly. "So . . . here we are."

Josie shook her head. Why was Savvy lying to her? Fabricating all of this? Etienne didn't do anything to her. She had watched it all play out in HDR on Mark's stupid video.

"Sav, that's not true. I *saw* . . ." Her heart skidded to a stop.

"You *saw*?" Savvy's voice rose to a high pitch. "You were spying on me?"

"No, no, on the video. Mark's security camera . . ."

Savvy gripped the edge of the table, her eyes narrowing.

"He. *Hurt*. Me," she said, banging her palms against the glass with each word. Josie waited for it to shatter. Expected it to shatter. "And I told him tonight, that if Bea gets that scholarship, I'll make sure *everyone* knows what he did to me."

Lindsay

"I could have hurt her," Ever said in disbelief after the girls slipped into Bea's room, where they would sleep tonight. "I *wanted* to hurt her."

Ever told Lindsay she had confronted Savvy in the dressing room, that Etienne had been in there with her. She tried to picture Ever, peaceful Ever, pushed to the edge like this.

"I wasn't myself," Ever said. "I don't know *who* that was."

"It's okay," Lindsay assured her. She, of all people, understood exactly what it felt like to lose oneself.

"No, it isn't," Ever said. "She's a child."

"Actually, she is not a child anymore. Not technically."

The alert sounded on all their phones as Ever was making up the couch for Lindsay: **Mandatory Evacuation for the following areas: The Foothills, Chesapeake Canyon, Northridge Estates.** It felt unreal that this was happening in Costa de la Luna. Somehow, they'd been immune to this. But now, the foothills and canyons were burning.

Lindsay had finally gotten in touch with Steve. The house was okay so far; he'd been outside hosing down the stucco, the roof, the backyard for hours when she and Olive were trying to reach him. He'd been pissed when she asked about the smoker, if there was any chance it was his fault. But at least it wasn't his turkey that had started the fire, thank God.

"I got all the art and photos," he said. "The safe, your jewelry box."

He'd gathered their most valuable things and loaded up his car before heading to his brother's house. Lindsay insisted she didn't need anything, but Olive had pleaded with him to gather a whole list of items: her baby blanket, her laptop, the Tiffany bracelet she got for her sixteenth birthday. She asked him to find her favorite worn pair of Vans, her favorite sweatshirt.

"But first please get my ballet scrapbook. It's under my bed. Promise you won't leave without it. And all the DVDs from my shows?" She was sobbing, and Lindsay felt gutted.

Even here, at the water's edge, they could smell the smoke. Several miles east, the fire was creeping through the canyons, edging toward the neighborhoods, fueled by those wicked winds. Within hours, it had spread from a small brush fire to thousands of acres.

Ever lit candles, and even the contained flames made Lindsay uneasy. The girls had returned to the living room and were chatty, restless.

"Why don't you guys go take showers," Ever said. "I put candles in the bathroom."

They slipped down the hall, and Lindsay was scratching Cobain behind his ears when her phone dinged again. This time, it was a text from Victor.

You okay? I saw your neighborhood is evacuating

We're fine. At Ever's house by the beach. Your family okay?

Yes. Thx. My son is home for Thanksgiving break, but he's with my wife at my in-laws' in San Diego.

Oh good. I'll call you tomorrow. Exhausted.

"When is Danny supposed to be back?" she asked Ever. Ever said he and his best friend, Dylan, had gone to a concert up in LA.

"I told him to stay there until they open the highway. They can camp in the van."

Lindsay couldn't imagine letting Olive sleep in some parking lot overnight. But maybe it was different with boys. She had no experience with boys. Oh my god, what if this baby was a *boy*?

The house was dark, but cozy and warm. When Ever sat next to her on the couch, it felt familiar and right. Despite the chaos going on outside, it was as if order had been restored. The tilted world turned upright.

Ever looked at Lindsay, her eyes wet in the candlelight. She glanced toward the hallway, where the girls had disappeared.

"I think I need to sell the house, Linds," she said.

"Oh, Ever," she said. "*No.*"

"My book deal isn't happening. So even if Bea gets the scholarship, I'm not sure I can keep the house. And if she doesn't, I don't think I'll have a choice. Not unless she quits ballet. And I can't do that to her. I just can't."

Lindsay glanced around at the living room, the lovely home that Ever and Ethan had spent two decades building. There was more love in this little room than there was in her entire monstrous house. The idea of Ever having to choose between Bea's ballet and their home was unimaginable.

"What if I moved in?" Lindsay said. "Just for a while? I can pay rent. I can also help with groceries. With household expenses? I'm up early and at my office all day; you'll hardly know I'm here. And maybe with a little less on your plate, you'll be able to start writing again."

Ever leaned into Lindsay. "I love you, Linds. You're a good friend."

The alert sounded again. **Mandatory Evacuation: The Foothills, Chesapeake Canyon, Northridge Estates. Voluntary Evacuation: Briar Canyon Estates.**

"Wait. That's Josie's neighborhood," Lindsay said. "But that's all the way on the other side of town."

"It must be a second fire?" Ever said.

"Shit."

Josie

"You can't do that," Josie said to Savvy. "Accuse him. Etienne did not hurt you."

Savvy looked bemused, her face as pale as her tutu.

"*Sav,*" Josie said, gripping her arm. But Savannah stood motionless. Her skin was hot, feverish. "*Savannah.* You cannot do that. He's an asshole, but he's not—he's not—he's not what you're saying. That's . . . extortion."

Savvy was silent, but her shoulders rose and fell with each contained breath. Josie had seen her do this after a performance, heart pounding, breathless, but—to the untrained eye—she appeared remarkably still.

"Listen, honey," Josie implored. "It doesn't matter what you say or do. Bea is getting the scholarship. Nancy saw the documentary. It's already over."

"What?" Savvy asked, her chin quivering.

"I'm sorry, baby," Josie said, and her heart hurt. She wanted to hold Savvy. To comfort her. Let her know that none of it mattered. She'd audition elsewhere. New York. Boston. London. She was so talented. She would find a home somewhere. They would love her.

"Men like Etienne," Josie started, trying to capture exactly what sort of wisdom she could impart, to articulate something she had experienced a thousand times but still had no words for. "You can't count on them." Was this stupid truth all she had to offer her daughter? The advice that men would always fail her? Father, bosses, lovers, boyfriends, husbands?

Josie shook her head sadly, and she searched Savvy's face. And

there, behind her rage, she saw the little girl who'd thrown herself
to the floor the night her father moved out. It had torn Josie apart,
watching her holding onto Johnny's ankles with her small hands,
pleading with him to stay. The way he had reached down and pried
her fingers from him before scooping her up, only for her to cling
to him with her legs and fingers. It was agony, that desperate need.

"Men, will always disappoint you," she said firmly. The truth. "It
doesn't matter what we do . . ."

"We?" Savvy said, scowling.

Josie's face felt hot. "Yes, I mean . . ."

"You slept with Etienne," Savvy said calmly, cold. Not a question.

Josie's body stiffened. Should she deny what had happened? Pretend she hadn't gone to him, hoping for what? The same exact thing
Savvy was hoping for now. How was this any better than what Savvy
was doing?

"I'm sorry," Josie said, reaching for her, but Savvy pulled her hand
away. "I was just so angry with Mark, and I'd had a little too much
wine."

"Mark?"

My god. Savvy didn't know about Mark. About the house.

"Oh, Sav. He's selling our house. He's the bad guy here. Not
Etienne."

"I cannot believe you slept with him," Savvy said. "You really
didn't think I could get the scholarship unless you fucked him?"

"Sav, come on. That's not fair . . ."

Savvy's phone dinged. Josie's phone dinged. A voluntary evacuation for their neighborhood. The fire had looked so far away; was it
possible it was coming toward them now?

Savvy's phone lit up again. Her expression softened as she read
the text.

"Daddy's going to be here in ten minutes," she said, and moved
to her dance bag. She fumbled around inside, pulling out the sewing
kit where she kept her ribbons, the dental floss she used to sew them

to her pointe shoes, matches for singeing the ribbon's edges. Then she walked across the yard toward the guesthouse. Josie could hardly see her in the darkness. The distant orange glow of the fires beyond made her a strange silhouette.

Josie smelled the smoke before she saw it, curling around Savvy, who held a cigarette in her hand. When had she started smoking? Was this Lotte's influence?

"They were right," Savvy said. "All of them." Her voice was so cold, her words icy.

"Who?" Josie asked, confused.

"The *moms*," Savvy said, and dragged on the cigarette, exhaling a plume of smoke into the dark sky.

"Right about what?"

"About what you *are*."

Josie thought about Melissa, spewing her hate on Halloween. Calling her a whore. Her daughter thought this, too?

"Well, fuck them," Savvy said.

Josie felt nauseous.

"And fuck *you*, Mark," she said angrily, staring into the eye of the camera.

"Sav. Honey. You're sick; you shouldn't be *smoking*."

But when Josie went to Savvy, and touched her arm gently, Savvy yanked her arm away. "Actually, fuck you, too," she said. "You and Etienne."

The words felt like a slap; her whole body stung with it.

"I'm going to Daddy's," she said, and with that, she flicked the burning cigarette into the canyon.

"Sav," Josie said, and rushed to the canyon's edge, heart racing. It was pitch black, but she knew that the canyon was filled with brittle brush: manzanita, juniper, eucalyptus. She looked around, frantic, watched the single spark as it caught. "Sav, go get the fire extinguisher. It's in the kitchen."

Savvy ignored her and marched back across the lawn. She picked up her phone. "He's waiting out front," she said.

"Please, Sav," she said. "We have to put this out." But she didn't know if she meant the fire or what was suddenly ablaze between them.

Savvy calmly tossed the pack of matches on the table and grabbed her dance bag, which she slung over her shoulder.

"Actually, I think I should stay with Daddy for a while."

It felt like Savvy had stabbed her in the heart. She looked away from the canyon at her daughter, who was just a shadow now.

"Also?" Savvy said, her voice breaking. "Don't bother coming to the show on Friday."

And then she turned and disappeared through the sliding glass doors.

Josie let out a cry of horror as she looked down into the canyon, at the little fires jumping from bush to bush, plant to plant, at the fire climbing steadily toward the yard.

She ran into the guesthouse, found the now-empty wastebasket in the bathroom, and came back out with it. She dipped it into the cool pool water and poured it into the canyon. But it did nothing to extinguish the flames; instead, it seemed to enrage them even more.

She looked back at the guesthouse, and her knees weakened. The blue light on the security camera winked.

And suddenly, she was overwhelmed. She paced back and forth along the pool's edge. What was she supposed to do now? Everything she had done for the last eighteen years had been for Savvy. She'd hurt Savvy, and now she'd lost her. Savvy *hated* her.

But she couldn't let Savvy set her life on fire; she couldn't allow her to burn her own future to the ground. She was eighteen. An adult. Old enough to go to jail for this. This was *arson*.

Josie was trembling as she went to the grill, where she had set her phone. She picked it up, hands shaking so badly she could hardly keep it steady. She opened the security app but couldn't locate the footage that would show Savvy standing by the guesthouse, the flick of the match, the spark, her rage-filled face. The security camera had a battery backup, but with the power out, the Wi-Fi was out. It hadn't uploaded to the cloud. She let out a relieved sigh.

As she studied the sky, glowing red now, she remembered Ethan's memorial, the lanterns that floated to the heavens. How beautiful it was. How sad. She remembered thinking that all she'd ever wanted was to have the kind of love that Ethan and Ever had. How unfair it all was.

She'd lost Johnny. She'd lost Mark. But none of that hurt like this. *Savvy.*

She thought about Ethan's memorial again, about the explosion.

Her body quaking now, she went to the grill, blew out the pilot, and turned the gas on high. She closed the lid and waited, the air growing smokier and smokier as the fires scattered across the canyon. Then she went to the table and picked up Savvy's matches.

This way, she thought, when they came to investigate, it would look like an accident. Just a tragic mistake. She'd turned the grill on to make dinner, she imagined explaining to the fire marshal. It was so hot; she hadn't wanted to cook inside. But then the voluntary evacuation alert came, and she panicked. She must have forgotten to turn it off.

As the flames crept toward the hedges by the guesthouse, she walked slowly across the yard, listening to the crackle of the burning brush. And then she lit the match and lifted the lid.

The explosion wasn't as big or as loud as it had been at the Henderson's, but it was enough to rattle the ground beneath her feet. In the patio window's reflection, she watched as the flames leapt from the grill. She listened to the fire licking and ticking and spreading. It wouldn't be long before everything was consumed.

Act IV, Scene II

Bea

On Thanksgiving morning, Bea woke to snow falling outside her window. She rubbed her eyes and sat up in bed. Olive was asleep next to her, snoring softy, her red hair fanned out across her pillow. For a moment, Bea was transported. A long-ago family trip to the mountains. Olive had come along; it was the first time either one of them had ever seen snow. She, Olive, and Danny spent the whole day trudging up the steep hill behind the rented cabin, flying down on orange sleds her dad bought at a nearby gas station, Cobain chasing behind them. They stayed outside until the sun went down; until their shins and ankles were numb with the sting of snow, and their cheeks were raw. In the cabin that night, her dad had built a fire, and they played Scrabble and ate homemade pizza. It was one of the happiest days of Bea's life. She and Olive had fallen asleep together in front of the fire, while her dad strummed his guitar, waking to find another twelve inches of snow had fallen that night.

Olive rolled over, mumbling in her sleep.

It was ten o'clock in the morning, but outside, the sky was the color of sunset: hazy and orange and still. Was she dreaming? She went to the window and looked out toward the water, watching as the snowflakes twirled and danced in the sky. Then she realized it wasn't snow; of course it wasn't. It was ash. And it was blanketing everything.

She heard helicopters, the whirring of their blades against the ash-filled sky. They were likely lifting water from the ocean to drop on the fires, dousing the scorched earth, trying to quash the flames

that—as of midnight, when they all went to bed—had already devoured three thousand acres.

She lay back down, closed her eyes, recalled other Thanksgivings.
The smell of pumpkin pie, her dad up early to surf and then bake
the pies before her mom got the turkey in the oven. She and Danny
would sit in the kitchen while he rolled out the pie crust and blasted
The Roots or Digable Planets. Their mom could sleep through anything. He used to make them mini pumpkin pies, with the scraps
of dough and filling, for breakfast. She remembered the taste of the
pumpkin, the smell of nutmeg and cinnamon, and the buttery crust,
and she missed him. She wished she could sit in her pajamas at the
kitchen table and eat little pumpkin pies with her dad. To drink the
"coffee" he made her: hot milk with a splash of espresso and tons
of sticky-sweet honey. She needed him. She needed him to tell her
how to move on. How to handle what was gearing up to be a huge
disappointment. The world was on fire; there might not even be a
production.

She quietly got out of bed and made her way to the kitchen. She
could hear her mom and Lindsay chatting in the kitchen. Another
voice, too. The power was still out, so there would be no pie. No
turkey. Then why did it smell like this?

In the kitchen, a man she vaguely recognized was setting a box
down on the counter.

"Morning, Bumble," Ever said.

"Hey Bea, this is my friend, Victor," Lindsay said.

Olive had told her last night as they were about to fall asleep
after hours of catching up, their words and apologies cartwheeling
between them, that Josie and Savvy had started a rumor about her
mom cheating with some guy from Freezey's, but that Lindsay swore
he wasn't the reason she was leaving her dad. Could this be him?

He reached into the box and pulled out a foil-wrapped turkey,
followed by takeout containers of mashed potatoes and sweet potatoes and stuffing. Two pies: apple and pumpkin.

"Also, here's a tofurkey roll," he said. "In case anyone doesn't eat meat. They said the power will be coming back on sometime around noon. You can just pop it in the oven. I brought some ice to keep it cold until then, if you have a cooler."

"This is so kind of you. Where did you get all this?" Bea's mom asked.

"They're handing out meals at Vons," he said. "I've got a car full to bring over to the emergency shelter. Call me if you need anything else. There's a bottle of white and a bottle of red in there, too."

"Can you join us for dinner later?" her mom said to him. "Please. This is so lovely and thoughtful."

"No, no," he said, shaking his head. "That's okay. I'll be pretty busy getting these distributed. Please, just enjoy your meal." With that, he gave Lindsay's shoulder a quick squeeze and slipped out the front door.

Later that afternoon, the power did come back on, and they ate dinner around the table; Danny had called and said the highway was still closed, that he and Dylan would grab Burger King and keep them posted. After dinner, they cleared the table, and everyone checked their phones: their only connection to the outside world right now.

"Have you heard anything from Vivienne yet? About the show?" she asked her mom.

Dress rehearsal had been such a disaster; even if they were able to perform, she had no idea how they would manage to pull it all together by tomorrow night. They hadn't even rehearsed the second act; they'd need to get into the theater early tomorrow to run the show at least once without an audience. She tried not to think of what would happen if the show was canceled. Would there be a documentary still? A scholarship?

"I haven't heard anything yet. I was just checking the news. They say the fire's only ten percent contained. But at least it's not near the theater. I guess we'll just wait and see?"

Bea's phone buzzed in her hand, and she jumped. "It's Owen," she said, and excused herself, walking down the hall toward her room.

"Hey, Happy Thanksgiving," he said. There was a lot of background noise: chatter and laughter. "Sorry, my whole family is here from New York. I have like four hundred cousins."

"That's okay. I can hear you." Bea went into her room and reflexively began to stretch, gently rolling her ankle, making the alphabet with her foot.

"So, my mom finally heard from Nancy," he said. "She's sending an email out in a bit."

"Finally!" she said, though her heart raced at the thought of a cancellation. "Will there be a show?"

"Well, at this point, nobody knows," he said.

"What do you mean?"

On the other end of the line, there was a crash, and then his voice was muffled.

"Sorry. One of my cousins just dropped a pie. There's glass everywhere. And eight hundred bare feet."

"So . . . what did Nancy say?"

"Savvy's house totally burned down."

"Are you serious?"

"Yeah. And nobody knows where her mom is."

Josie

Josie had had nowhere to go when the fire started. She was an evacuee. A refugee. From her home, from her life. Her hands had been trembling so hard, she could barely start the car.

She hadn't expected there to be a room at the extended stay, but she'd pulled up into the Seacoast Suites parking lot anyway and sat in the car for fifteen minutes, trying to figure out what to do next. Where to go from here.

Finally, she had gone into the dark motel lobby, and a harried-looking girl behind the desk had rifled through the paper receipts to determine if there were any empty rooms.

"Oh! I just had a guest check out early. She'd reserved it through the end of the month. It's a suite, with a kitchenette?"

"I'll take it," she said.

"Okay. It should be ready in about thirty minutes. I'll text you when it's ready. The restaurant is closed, but the bar is open. Cash only, though."

"*Great*," Josie said.

She was walking toward the restaurant when her phone rang. *Johnny*. She could barely breathe.

"Hey," she said, as casually as she could, hoping he couldn't hear the pounding of her heart.

"*Jo*," he said, his voice distant and sad.

"What's going on?" she asked, trying to steady her breath.

"Jo," he said, his voice breaking. "Savvy told me everything."

She felt like she might collapse. She moved to a grassy area by the parking lot and sat down under a tree. She hung her head between her knees and pressed the phone to her ear.

She closed her eyes, but when she squeezed them shut, all she could see were the flames, licking the edge of the property, creeping like fingers across the grass toward the guesthouse.

"I know this summer has been hard for you. And I'm sorry for what Mark did. It was shitty. And you didn't deserve it."

Wait. Where was he going with this?

"Sav says he's selling the house? She also says you've been drinking. A lot," he said, and paused. "That she came home from rehearsals tonight and you were drunk. She also says you slept with that man? Her teacher? She doesn't really feel . . . safe at home."

The knife that Savvy had thrust in her chest twisted.

"She's asked to stay with me, which, of course, is totally fine. Until you can get things under control again."

Why was Savvy doing this to her? Her eyes welled, and she shook her head.

"Jo, I'm really worried about you."

"I have to go, Johnny."

God, she needed a drink.

She stood up, brushed the grass from her jeans, and headed to the restaurant.

It was nautically themed, tacky. She looked around for someplace to sit. The dining room was full of fellow evacuees. She located a booth in the far corner and sat down. When the waitress explained that the kitchen was closed due to the power outage, she said, "That's fine. Can I just get your house cab? Wait," she said. "Can I get a Lemon Drop, please?"

She pulled out her phone, checked the cloud for the security footage. Still not there. Then she realized, if the guesthouse burned down, the security camera and its hard drive would be destroyed, too. There would be nothing to implicate Savvy.

She considered texting Savvy, but then sighed and opened Instagram instead. She found Savvy's ballet account, located the first posted photo, and began to scroll. Eyes burning—as if the room

were filled with smoke—she watched Savvy grow up. Baby ballerina in a tutu. Six years old, working so hard, tongue protruding
a little from her lips as she concentrated in class. Twelve years old,
trying on her first pair of pointe shoes, delight and pride in her pale
blue eyes. Video after video of her onstage. Competitions and performances, just goofing around in the studio. The most recent photo
was of her being fitted for her Snow Queen costume. She searched
the photo for some clue. Some explanation for how her daughter
could turn on her like this. Just ice her out.

"*Bonjour*," he said, and Josie jumped.

As Etienne sat down across from her, she clicked her phone off and
shoved it into her purse. She felt like an elastic band that had snapped.
She would have run, but her legs would not have carried her.

Etienne scowled, studying her from across the sticky Formica
table.

"What happened to *you*?" she asked. Even in the dim candlelight,
she could see his eye was black and blue, swollen. The whites rivered
with red.

"Phoebe's *papa* happened to me. *Connard.*"

"*Bob?*" she said in disbelief.

When the waitress delivered her cocktail, he asked for a cognac.

"The fire, it is close to you?" he asked as she took her first sip.
Confused for a moment, she thought about the fire burning in her
throat as the liquor made its way down.

"Yes," she said. The fire, the fire was in their backyard. Consuming everything. So, she recited the speech she had been rehearsing
since she left. "There was a voluntary evacuation. Savvy's with her
father. And I'm . . . I'm here."

"I cannot find Lotte," he said, looking around as if she might
simply materialize in this shitty restaurant.

"Hmm," she said, and took another drink.

"She's angry at me," he said.

"Is she your girlfriend?" Josie asked.

He snorted. "No. A girlfriend would not be so . . . *têtue* . . . stubborn?"

"What do you mean? Stubborn about what?"

"This film, it was supposed to be a *documentaire* about *me*. You know, I have a reputation," he said. "My company is not happy. *Avec moi.*"

"A reputation for what?" she asked. *Sleeping with dancers?* she wondered. *With their mothers?*

"I do things my own way," he said. "But this film, it was supposed to be different. It was not supposed to be what she has made it."

Josie took a deep breath and another pull on her drink; the lemon was sour.

"What has she *made* it?" she asked.

He pulled his own phone out of his pocket and studied the screen for a moment, before clicking and passing it to her.

She looked around the sad restaurant, then clicked Play and watched as the footage began.

A dark screen, and then the lights began to appear. Lanterns, dozens of red lanterns filling the sky. The camera took them all in, a breathless wonder and hush.

"Why don't you tell us when you knew?" the voiceover said. *Lotte.*

There was a pause, and then the camera panned from the fire in the sky above the beach, to the silhouette of a girl alone on the sand. The water was illuminated by so many paper lanterns.

There was another voice. A little raspy, uncertain. *"Knew?"*

"Yes. That this was serious. Your daughter's dancing."

The girl on the screen began to dance. She was completely alone. The camera zoomed in on her face, and her eyes were closed. Oblivious to the world around her. *Beatrice.*

"You lost your father. Recently?"

"Yes."

"La vie est un flambeau toujours prêt à s'éteindre," the voiceover said, as Bea danced. "Life is a torch, always ready to go out. And that is why we must make art; to keep the flame burning."

So, this *had* been the plan. All along. From the moment that Etienne arrived. Just like Nancy had said. This had never been a documentary about *him*. It had always been about Bea. Poor, fatherless

Bea. Lotte knew that people didn't want to hear about someone who had lived a charmed life, who was blessed with gifts. They wanted to see the struggle. And Bea was that scrappy underdog. Josie felt as if she might collapse.

The video stopped, the screen dark. This was some sort of draft, it seemed. Rough footage, clips crudely pieced together.

The next image was of a tree's twisted limbs, a hundred pairs of pointe shoes strung from their branches. What was this?

It was Bea's voice now—that tinkling bell. "We called this our *Toi Toi Toi* Tree . . . every time we retired a pair of pointe shoes, we strung them up here and made a wish."

And then a male voice . . . who was that? Nick? No. *Owen.*

"Did they come true? Your wishes?"

Oh Jesus. Josie shoved the phone back at him.

"So now what?" she said.

"Your daughter. *Elle veut me détruire.* She wants to destroy me. But I am innocent. You know this. She said that if I do not give her the scholarship, that she will accuse me. But Lotte, she will not allow me to do this. She said I must give the scholarship to Beatrice. Or she will use the film against me. She will twist things. She said I will never work again. She knows about us."

"How does she know about *us*?" she asked, livid.

"I had to explain why you evicted me."

"Well, what the hell do you want from *me*?" she asked, laughing. Because really, in the end, every relationship she'd ever had was like this. Every exchange an actual *exchange*. Tit for tat. Quid pro quo.

"I want you to stop your daughter," he said, sounding like a petulant child.

If she somehow convinced Savvy not to go forward with this, what would he have to offer? Not the scholarship. It was all so laughable. Lotte's film was about Beatrice. The ending predetermined. Lotte would be there tomorrow night to film Beatrice performing the lead role and then receiving the scholarship. It was *over.*

"Please. You are her *maman.* She will listen to you."

She felt the sting of his words, like little flames. And she thought about the way she had pleaded with Savvy, and the way Savvy had looked right through her as if she were a ghost.

Josie thought about the fire again. The way a single flicker could make everything go up in flames. She thought of her own career. Her marriages. How combustible everything was.

"It seems to me," she said, "you're screwed either way. One way, you just lose your comeback. But the other way? You lose everything."

She left him at the dark restaurant and checked into the suite, where she fell asleep the moment her head hit the unforgiving pillow. Despite the rigid mattress and cheap sheets, she didn't wake at all during the night, and not even the next morning. She might have slept through all of Thanksgiving Day if there hadn't been a knock on her door at eleven that morning.

"Who is it?" she grumbled, and stumbled out of bed.

"Costa de la Luna PD," the man said. "We're looking for Josephine Jacobs?"

Première

Bea

A performance is like a sandcastle. Something you spend hours and hours crafting, building, something gorgeous and whole made of nothing more than a zillion grains of sand: the tiny movements of ankle, wrist, and neck. But no matter how carefully, how meticulously you work, its destiny is to last only a few hours before it is carried away again.

When the curtain rose, she tried to hold onto *this* moment. To bask in the lights and the music, to be mindful of each inhalation and exhalation.

It's no mistake that *aspiration* means "to breathe"—to aspire, to want to be glorious, beautiful, flawless—that wild untamed hope—that desire for achievement. It is the same as drawing breath. *Wanting*, *aspiring*, is what makes us human.

Tonight, she *wanted*. In the Party Scene, she wanted the Nutcracker, that beautiful wooden soldier doll that Drosselmeyer brought just for her. She wanted to dance when he gave it to her, to hold it in her arms. When her brother, Fritz, was careless and broke it, she wanted only for it to be repaired again. Then, as she fell asleep, she dreamed of other things. Battles and rats and dolls coming to life. A magical tree that grew until it towered above her.

When the snow came, when the storm of girls swirled about her, swallowing her, and Savvy came onstage, she was mesmerized. Captivated, literally held captive, by her spell. She felt her body becoming less childlike, more womanly. Her desire for the Nutcracker becoming a desire for something scarier. She wanted a prince. She wanted a man's hands holding her up, lifting her, carrying her above the snow to someplace new.

As the curtain fell, she bent over in the wings, trying to catch her breath.

She aspired and aspired and aspired.

Ever

She had never seen Bea dance like this. Ever sat spellbound as her daughter grew from a little girl into a woman before her eyes. It was as if she were watching the last ten years spool out, like a ribbon unfurling so quickly she could barely comprehend what was happening until it was over. Until she was suddenly and mysteriously grown.

An old lady in a grocery store stopped her once to coo over Danny and Bea when they were both babies. "The days are long, but the years are short," she said. It had struck her as clichéd and sentimental at the time; but now, it seemed wise.

She held her breath through most of the first act, and felt almost light-headed when the lights came on, when the audience around her materialized again. The crumpling of programs and squeezes of her shoulder by those around her who knew: she had been sitting here for years, waiting for this moment.

She wanted nothing more than to reach for Ethan's hand, to hold it tightly. Let the energy of what she was feeling flow into him. She wanted him to be with her, to put his arm around her as they watched their daughter make something so beautiful, she could hardly breathe.

"She's amazing, Ever," Lindsay said. "It makes my heart ache to watch her dance."

"Me too," Ever said. "Thank you."

"Now, I'm going to get snacks," Lindsay said. "I am freaking ravenous. I have been thinking about Pringles since the Party Scene."

The second act was much shorter than the first, but Ever tried to

absorb everything. Owen's playful Chinese. Olive's stunning Spanish. Bea and Etienne's magical *grand pas*. And before she knew it, the
curtain fell, and rose again, the cast assembling for their bows.

The Littles made her heart ache, too: for all the years their mothers had ahead of them. For all that delicious possibility. For their
small hands and clumsy feet and round tummies. What she wouldn't
give to go back, just for a day, and brush Bea's hair into a bun, to
hold bobby pins between her teeth.

When Savvy came onstage to bow, the crowd roared. It felt violent, the way the world responded to Savvy. Like the audience was
hungry for her. Bea was not this kind of dancer. Savvy breathed fire
in her dancing, while Bea quietly stole their breath away.

Etienne, as the Prince, ushered Bea onto the stage, presenting her
in the way that male dancers do, and Ever flew to her feet, applaud-
ing. She didn't care what anyone thought of her. Soon, the entire audience was standing, cheering. Vivienne came out of the wings and
handed Savvy and Bea flowers, kissing them both on each cheek.

Etienne gestured for Bea to step forward again, and she curtsied
deeply to the crowd.

Eventually, Vivienne motioned for the audience to quiet, and the
stage manager hurried across the stage to hand her a microphone.
Ever held her breath.

Josie

The world is on fire. This is what she thought as she gripped the wheel and accelerated, the inferno blazing behind her, the world alight on both sides. As fire consumed the canyons, pressing in on the town, enclosing them, she focused only on the road to the theater.

She looked at the clock on the dash. The performance would be ending soon; because of the fires, the main roads were blocked, and she had been forced to detour. To take the circuitous route. Miles in the wrong direction before spilling her onto the right path again. If that wasn't an apt metaphor, what was?

She raced along the freeway now, focusing not on the journey but on the destination. The world behind her was on fire, the house she left behind just a pile of blackened bones, but one must always think of where one is going, not where one has been.

She pulled into the back parking lot and reached to the passenger's seat for the fiery bouquet of flowers: crimson peonies and orange roses. Savvy's favorites.

Outside, she studied the night sky, the ash as it swirled and fell gently around her. The air smelled of smoke, and the sky was a hazy bronze. It was beautiful, really. Like a stage cast in orange and red color gels. Like a luminous dream.

At first, when the officer came to the motel door, she thought he knew what Savvy had done. That somehow, they'd gotten the security camera footage, that Savvy had been recorded flicking her cigarette into the dry canyon. And that someone, *Mark*, had given her up. Josie had almost collapsed at his feet, before he even spoke, imagining them taking Savvy away.

"What happened?" she'd asked, her voice cracking.

He'd quickly clarified he was there to notify her that her home and guesthouse (*thank god*) had been casualties of the fire. He and his colleagues had been visiting all the shelters and motels to locate residents whose homes had been impacted.

"Though, I suspect you already knew that?" he asked.

She froze. The insinuation, the accusation, was clear.

"I left as soon as they announced the voluntary evacuation. I could see the fire in the canyon, and I didn't want to risk it," she said.

He studied her.

"I was about to cook myself dinner. A burger on the grill," she added. "Oh my god, did I leave the grill on?"

She thought about the explosion. The flames.

"Ma'am, we're actually going to need you to answer a few questions. We spoke to your husband earlier."

"Ex-husband."

"Ex-husband," he said. "He mentioned that you made a threat to his girlfriend recently? Something about burning the house down?"

Erica. *Mark.*

"Oh Jesus," she said. "I wasn't serious."

And yet.

"You can't possibly think I had anything to do with this," she said. "What kind of idiot sets their own house on fire?"

"Well, ma'am," he said, "technically, the house belongs to your husband."

"Ex," she said, head pounding now.

"Anyway. We'd like to have you make a statement, on the record. The fire marshal will be heading over to investigate tomorrow. Given that your house was the only one on the block affected. It shouldn't take too long."

Her heart had started to race. She wondered what kind of evidence they might find. What might have survived that could implicate Savvy.

"Sure," she had said.

He'd asked her nearly a dozen questions about who was in the house that night, what she was doing at certain times, and at what point she left the house.

"And there was no one else in the house with you?" he asked.

"No. I was alone."

He'd looked at her, given a curt nod. "Ma'am, I'm real sorry for your loss but glad you made it out. We'll be in touch as soon as we have more information from the fire marshal. I suggest you stay put here until the investigation's complete. Okay?"

She'd nodded. Unable to speak.

She'd gotten call after call from Nancy, checking to make sure she was okay. Of course, they wouldn't go on with the performance if one of the students had lost their home. "No," she had insisted. "Please. It's okay. We're okay. And Savvy will want to dance."

Now, flowers in hand, she entered the theater through the stage door, mustering a smile for a mom who stood guard with her clipboard and a walkie-talkie.

"Oh, Josie!" the woman said, her face equal parts surprise and masked horror. "You're here! Everyone's been so worried about you."

She knew this was bullshit. That this mom, and every other mom, was secretly thrilling at the possibility of disaster.

But she was no Juliet, no Odette. She was the Firebird, ascending.

"You missed the performance," the woman said, pouting sympathetically. "Savvy was beautiful. As always."

At this, her heart stirred. Savvy had told her not to come to the performance. But she had not banned her from coming afterwards.

"They're about to announce the scholarship," the mom said. "You should hurry in and grab a seat."

Ever

"Thank you all for coming to our performance," Vivienne said. She was dressed in elegant, camel-colored slacks and a cashmere turtleneck. Heels. Onstage, she glowed.

Applause. Ever felt numb with anticipation.

"But before we go, it is my great pleasure to introduce Etienne Bernay. I invited him to my school, because he is a brilliant dancer. He graciously agreed to direct the performance, and to capture this process in a documentary about our conservatory, filmed by the FIGRA Award-winning filmmaker, Lotte Paquet. As you know, he will also bring one student back to the Ballet de Paris with him, where he will sponsor a scholarship to the Académie for the spring session."

Ever took a deep breath and smiled at Danny next to her.

Onstage, Vivienne paused as she waited for the crowd to quiet down. "Mr. Bernay will now present the recipient of the scholarship."

Etienne, shiner covered with makeup, accepted the microphone and spoke softly into it. "*Merci.* Thank you so much for coming tonight. There are so many gifted dancers here, and it has been my pleasure working with them all."

A small swell of applause.

"This has been a most difficult decision," he said, turning to the girls, most of whom looked at him expectantly. Bea stared at her feet. Ever's heart lurched; she felt unmoored.

"I am pleased to present the first Bernay Scholarship," he said, turning toward Savvy and Bea behind him. "To Savannah Jacobs, our Snow Queen."

To . . . Savannah.

Not Bea.

Saltwater filled Ever's eyes, her lungs. She was drowning.

Anemic applause filled the room, and a couple of hands reached out and gripped Ever—though now in commiseration, or consolation, or something. She looked up at the stage and watched her daughter maintain her composure. Bea nodded and smiled at Savvy, clapping her hands together. And Savvy glittered in the bright lights.

"Thank you all, and please, have a safe drive home tonight," Vivienne added. "I pray you all remain safe from the fires."

The curtains closed. Ever let out a shuddering breath. She'd known what to expect, but disappointment still coursed through her.

Danny put his arm over Ever's shoulder.

"Fuck Ballet de Paris," he whispered.

She leaned into him, shaking her head. It was over.

Lindsay

The houselights came on, and the crowd lingered, though the excited din that had preceded the show turned into a disgruntled grumbling.

Ever and Lindsay sat in the front row, waiting for the girls to change. Lindsay grabbed Ever's hand, and Ever smiled at her.

"Well, then," Ever said. "I guess this is it."

When Josie approached them, Lindsay's jaw clenched.

"Josie," Ever said, looking disoriented. "You're okay. Everyone has been so worried."

Josie smiled, though somewhat sadly, Lindsay thought.

"I'm fine," Josie said.

Lindsay forced herself to say what was expected. "Well, congratulations. You must be so happy for Savvy."

"She works very hard," Josie responded distractedly.

"I'm so sorry about your house," Ever said. "Do you and Savvy have a place to stay?"

"Savvy's at her dad's," she said. "I've got a room at the Seacoast Suites."

Lindsay thought about the pitiful room she'd left, tried to imagine Josie Jacobs camped out at a place like that.

"Do you need anything at all?" Ever asked.

"I was actually wondering if you could do me a favor," Josie said.

Ever and Lindsay looked at each other first and then back at Josie, who was visibly trembling now. It was unsettling. Granted, she'd just suffered an enormous loss. Her house! But her daughter had just won the coveted prize, and Lindsay just couldn't make all the pieces fit.

"Can you make sure Savvy gets these?" Josie asked, and held out the bouquet of flowers.

What?

"Don't you want to give them to her yourself?" Ever asked.

"I can't stay," she said vaguely. "Thank you. And, Ever? I just wanted to say that I'm sorry."

Josie walked briskly toward the exit, leaving them behind and baffled.

"That was weird," Lindsay said.

"Very weird," Ever agreed.

Bea

Backstage, Bea stared at her reflection in the dressing room mirror, and slowly began to peel the false eyelashes from her burning eyes, then ran a makeup wipe across her forehead and cheeks. Her own face emerged from behind the stage makeup, Marie slipping away, the magic waning.

Behind her, the younger girls swarmed around Savvy, who held court in the center of the dressing room. In the mirror's reflection, she could see Savvy hugging Lizzy, then Jaz. "Oh my god, Sav! Paris!" Jaz squealed.

Olive came to the dressing table and sat down next to her, and Bea studied her glowing face.

"You were incredible, Livvie," she said. "I've never seen you dance like that before."

"Thanks," Olive said as she carefully removed the rose from behind her ear. She fiddled with it before setting it down. "I'm sorry, Bea. That should have been you." She nodded toward Savvy.

Bea took a deep breath, and two hot tears ran down her cheeks.

"'Tis just a flesh wound," she said, and wiped at them with her makeup wipe.

"At least she'll be gone soon," Olive offered. "A whole continent away."

"True," Bea said. She could hardly imagine what it would be like at the studio without Savvy there. "So, what are you doing now? Do you and your mom want to go get pizza with us? Is your dad here?"

"No, he didn't come," Olive said.

Bea grimaced. She couldn't imagine her father skipping a performance.

"It's okay. I told him not to," Olive said. "I think I was able to dance like that because he *wasn't* there. Does that make sense?"

Bea nodded.

Savvy posed for photos with some of the baby mice, as the moms clucked and cooed.

"So Owen's coming with us for pizza, too," Bea said. "I hope that's cool?"

"That is *very* cool, Bea," she said. "He's liked you forever."

Someone knocked on the doorframe, and everyone turned. The boys were notorious for "accidentally" coming in while the girls were changing. But it was only Lotte.

Savvy emerged from the thicket of fawning girls and mothers, approaching Lotte, beaming.

Bea's eyes filled again, and she studied the eyelashes on the counter, like a dark pair of butterfly wings, next to Olive's crushed rose.

But Lotte walked briskly, dismissively, past Savvy, toward Bea.

"May I speak with you a moment?"

Ever

The curtain eventually lifted, and the stage crew set to sweeping up the lingering bits of snow and scattered bobby pins and sequins.

Lotte appeared onstage, scanning the nearly empty theater, ubiquitous camera at her side. When she spotted them, she waved.

Lindsay huffed. "Oh, for the love of God. I hope she doesn't want to interview us."

Lotte climbed down the steps from the apron and came to them, but when she sat down in the empty seat next to Ever, she put her camera away in her bag.

"Bonjour," she said, smiling.

"Hi," Ever said. It took everything she had to make small talk. "The show was so lovely. I hope you recorded it?"

"Mais oui, of course," Lotte said.

"I'm sure the parents would love to have a link to the performance video," Lindsay said. "Especially for the girls who are graduating."

"Of course," she said.

Lindsay asked, "Any idea when the documentary will come out?"

"Ah, my project," she said, and sighed. "This is all," she said, motioning toward the stage, "how do you say, a little *wrench*?"

Ever cocked her head.

"It is not the ending I expected," Lotte said.

"That's funny, because it's exactly the ending the rest of us did," Lindsay said with a laugh. "Anyway, I'm going backstage to find Olive. I can bring these to Savvy if you want," she said, and took the flowers from Ever. "We'll meet you in the lobby and then head out for pizza?"

Ever sat back down in one of the seats, and Lotte sat next to her.

"I am sorry," Lotte said. "The scholarship should have gone to your daughter. She is magnificent."

God, everyone was sorry. First Josie. Now Lotte.

"Well, thank you. She'll be okay. We'll figure out a way for her to audition in January. We can always send videos. If she can't travel." She and Lindsay really needed to sit down and talk about listing the house. It was the only option she had now.

"Actually, that is what I wanted to speak to you about," she said. "Of course, I had hoped that she would be given the scholarship, to study at the Académie in Paris. But since that is not to be, I took a . . . liberty?"

Ever cocked her head.

"Last night, I shared some of the footage I have of Beatrice dancing with a colleague in New York. He is a dear friend of the director at NYRB. Vivienne told me that NYRB is where Beatrice has been spending her summers?"

"Yes," Ever said. "She's done their intensive for the last four years."

Lotte nodded. "My proposal was that if the company's school were to admit her, on scholarship, we would follow this step in her journey as part of the film."

Ever's ears felt as though she were under water, Lotte's words far away.

"And I just received a call from NYRB's director himself. He was able to review the video, and he thinks it is a wonderful idea."

"You mean she's been offered a scholarship to NYRB's school?" Ever asked, with each word the weight lifting from her shoulders.

"Full tuition and a stipend to assist with room and board. If Beatrice agrees to continue with the documentary, I will see that we make up the difference," Lotte said.

"New York Repertory Ballet," Ever said dumbly.

"*Oui.*"

Finale

Bea

Normally, Vivienne gave everyone the week after *Nutcracker* off. But Lotte wanted to film Bea working with Miss V. one last time before she returned home to France for the holidays. Lotte would not see Bea again until they both arrived in New York in January.

Bea dropped Danny off at school on Monday morning and then drove to the studio alone. She took deep breaths as she navigated rush-hour traffic, still a little gun-shy after the near miss with Melissa's car, but feeling more confident with every venture out. She and Owen had even talked about taking a road trip together to Big Sur when she came home for Easter in a few months. She thought about driving up the winding coast with Owen, and felt a stir of excitement.

The CLCB parking lot was empty except for Lotte's van and Miss V.'s car. Etienne and the sound guy had already flown back to Paris, and Nancy was on a plane to Hawaii—her usual break after *Nutcracker*. She would return suntanned and refreshed in a week.

"*Bonjour,*" Bea said as she entered the cold studio.

Miss V. was sitting on her little wooden stool, studying her laptop. She looked up and smiled at Bea, though her eyes looked tired. *The Nutcracker* was exhausting. Lotte beamed from behind the camera.

Lotte had said she wanted to film Bea doing a warm-up at the barre. The show was over; time to get back to work. This was the real life of a dancer. Hundreds of hours at the barre before, and after, each performance.

"Pretend I am not here," Lotte said, smiling.

And Bea did, losing herself in the familiar music, in Miss V's gentle corrections and encouragement. The quiet *whoosh, whoosh* of her slippered feet against the floor. She felt her body warming up, her muscles becoming pliant and loose.

"Come to center," Miss V. said to Bea after *grand battements*. And then to Lotte, "Would you excuse us for a moment?"

"Of course," Lotte said, reached for her tote bag, and then stepped outside. Bea could hear her lighting her cigarette, smell the heady scent of the smoke wafting through the open back door.

Bea stood awkwardly in the center of the room. She never knew what to do with her hands when Miss V. was speaking to her. Those warm limbs felt suddenly awkward, her body taking up too much space. She hadn't spoken to Miss V. alone since that awful discussion about the video.

"How are you, my dear?" Miss V. asked.

"My ankle is all better," she said.

"That is good," she said. "But I did not mean your ankle."

Bea nodded. "I'm grateful. To Lotte, for helping me get the scholarship at NYRB."

"Yes," she said. "It is a good opportunity for you, though it is not Paris as you hoped."

Bea's face felt hot.

"This is a difficult life you have chosen," she said. "I will not pretend that it is not."

Bea nodded.

"You are at mercy to the whimsy of your directors. To the rivalry of your colleagues. It can feel unfair at times."

Bea looked down, mouth twitching. She thought of Savvy, somehow managing to steal the scholarship out from under her. Bea had been so close, but Savvy had still won. Still, Bea tried to muster up some compassion for her. Savvy couldn't be having an easy time right now, despite getting the scholarship. Her house had burned down, for one thing, and her mom had been arrested right after the *Nutcracker* performance. Luckily, no one had been harmed—Savvy had been safe at her dad's that night—but Josie would likely be charged this week. So yes, Savvy was going to Paris. But what a mess she was leaving behind. Bea, honestly, wouldn't have traded places with her if she could.

"Have you heard of the bonfire ballerinas?" Miss V. asked.

Bonfire ballerinas. She had learned about them in the mandatory Ballet History class she took at her summer intensive. Everyone else had groaned about the class, but Bea had loved it. Miss V. was talking about the last dancers of the Romantic period. Poor girls, sold to the ballet by their families: for purchase by the wealthy opera patrons. They were the starving girls, the rats of the ballet world. *Gutter sylphs,* they were called, seeking flight from their stations in life through dance. And dressed in dreamy tulle, ethers of fabric, they really were transcendent. But the gaslights that illuminated the stage were uncaged flames, and if the girls got too close—like diaphanous moths—they would ignite. The irony was, it could all have been prevented; the fabric could have been fireproofed, *cartonerised.* But this made the dresses heavy, clumsy, and the girls chose beauty over safety. Their livelihoods depended on it.

So many incendiary girls.

"Then you have heard of Emma Livry?"

She had read about Emma Livry, a dancer whose claim to fame was her role as a butterfly whose wings got too close to a flame: life imitating art when she fluffed her skirts and promptly combusted.

"I have," Bea said.

"Savannah Jacobs will fluff her skirt too close to a flame one day," Miss V. said. "Not today maybe, but one day."

Bea looked at Miss V. in disbelief, but Miss V. only smiled at her warmly, apologetically even.

"I will miss working with you, Beatrice. It has been one of my greatest joys, watching you become the artist you were meant to be."

Bea's eyes filled with tears, and she started to speak, to thank her, but then Miss V. clapped her hands, startling Bea. "Okay, please go to center for adagio." Back to work.

Bea nodded quietly and hurried to the center, where she stood patiently in the stillness before the music began.

Lindsay

On Christmas Eve at the Hendersons', they all gathered in the living room to exchange gifts. Ever and Lindsay sat together on the velvet couch. Danny sprawled on the floor by the tree. Olive and Bea sat on the floor by the fireplace, pillows propping them up.

Normally, the packages for Olive would have held silky ballet skirts and leotards, hand-knit warm-ups, and extra pairs of tights. However, Olive had—as promised—quit ballet after *The Nutcracker*. Lindsay knew it was coming, but it had still felt like a shock to her system. But Olive was eighteen now. An adult. And it was time for her to start making her own decisions. So instead of ballet gear, Lindsay had purchased all the things Olive might need in New York: beautiful sweaters and scarves, a puffy down coat, and fur-lined boots.

Lindsay had often envisioned Olive going to New York, though she'd pictured her dancing there. Instead, Olive was hoping to study screenwriting, of all things. Lotte, in addition to helping Bea out, had put in a good word for Olive at NYU, where she had a friend in the film department. Olive had gotten the application in under the wire, but she would have to wait another couple months to find out.

"We don't even know if I'll get in yet," Olive said, but even as she did, she held the soft butter-colored sweater to her cheeks. "But thank you, Mama. For always believing in me."

Lindsay pressed her hand to her aching chest.

"Now you," Olive said, and handed Lindsay a small package from under the living tree they had all decorated together.

Inside the box was the tiniest pair of ballet slippers she had ever seen. Lindsay held the pink satin shoes in her palm. Imagined the baby's tiny feet inside them.

"Oh my goodness," Ever said. "Look at how little they are!"

"You will put her in ballet, right?" Olive asked. "When she's old enough?"

"Maybe," Lindsay said, and she thought about starting again. Watching a little girl stuffed into a pair of pink tights and a small black leotard. She imagined the Littles' teacher, Eloise, taking her by the hand and leading her to the barre. Demonstrating how to put her heels together in first position. "Or, I was thinking softball? Maybe swim?" Lindsay said, tears filling her eyes. She was such a blubbery mess these days. It didn't take much.

"How about ice skating?" Bea said.

"I totally vote for hockey!" Danny said.

The baby kicked, and Lindsay gasped. "I'm thinking *krav maga*, actually."

Olive gave Bea a NYC sweatshirt, and Bea gave Olive a novelty New York license plate with her name on it. New York—a whole continent away. She was pretty sure an umbilical cord couldn't stretch that far, though it was never meant to. But at least, if this worked out, the girls would have each other.

"Danny," Lindsay said. "Can you grab that gift over there by your surfboard?" Ever had found an almost-new longboard for Danny on Craigslist, wrapped a big red ribbon around it. "Yeah. That one for your mom."

Danny got up and found the present and handed it to Ever, who looked at Lindsay as if to say, *You shouldn't have.*

Inside, wrapped in tissue, was the ceramic plaque Lindsay had commissioned Ever's dad to make. Hand-painted numbers, reading: 501.

"Are these address numbers?" Ever asked.

Lindsay nodded.

"But we're five-o-five," Ever said, frowning apologetically, as if the error was Ever's own.

"I know." Lindsay smiled.

Ever looked at her quizzically.

"Five-o-one is that house for sale down the street," Danny said.

Recognition finally set in, and Ever reached for her hand. "You bought the house? We're going to be neighbors?"

"We are!" She'd put in an offer, and the desperate owners had agreed when she said she'd waive the inspection. Victor had offered to help her with the necessary repairs. Closing was right after the new year. *The beginning of a new life*, she thought. Two new lives.

Victor arrived at eleven-thirty to take her with him to midnight Mass. The kids had disappeared into the bedrooms by then, after hanging their stockings on Ever's mantle. Olive had insisted on leaving cookies and milk out for Santa, as well. These relics of childhood tugged at Lindsay's heart. Tomorrow would be strange, with Olive off to spend the day with her dad. She and Victor volunteering at the homeless shelter. But for now, at least, things felt somewhat normal.

Inside St. Mary's, Lindsay spied Vivienne in a pew near the back, as always.

"Merry Christmas," Lindsay whispered, touching Vivienne's shoulder gently.

"And to you and Olive, as well," Vivienne said. "And please, let her know that she is welcome to come back any time to take class. They miss it, you know, the ones who leave. But it will always be her home."

"Thank you," Lindsay said. "I will let her know."

Candles flickered in the alcoves, and when the choir began to sing, she felt a strange new sense of peace. It was as if she were simply a tightly wound ribbon, slowly unfurling. She looked at Victor, and he smiled at her, squeezed her hand.

After mass, back at Ever's house, she said goodbye to Victor and quietly let herself in. She expected everyone would be sleeping, but Ever was at the big oak table in her pajamas, laptop open, cup of tea steaming next to her. The plate where the kids had left the cookies was empty save for one coconut macaroon.

"How's it going?" Lindsay asked as she grabbed the macaroon and sat down at the table next to her, kicking off her heels. "Working on the new book?"

"Yes," Ever said, looking up from the screen.

"So can you tell me about it yet?" she asked. "Just a hint?"

"I think it actually might be kind of a . . . thriller?" Ever said, her bright eyes dancing.

Ever

One night not long after *The Nutcracker* performance, the first lines had come to her, a warm whisper in her ear.

It was late August when Mathéo Thibaut arrived in Calypso Cay, and another hot summer without rain had left the earth parched. Fire season. The quiet canyons surrounding the tiny coastal town were a dangerous place. Everything was dry and brittle. Ready to ignite. The tick of a match, that hushed brush of the tip against the grit of the striker. This was all it would take to start a fire. A single spark, the hiss of a tiny flame, could be the beginning of disaster.

The rumor was like this. No one knew exactly where it started, who first uttered it. But it spread. The ti-ti-ti of his name, the crackle and hiss. Igniting, then leaping from house to house, from neighborhood to neighborhood. Just that little flicker fueled by so much breath. Within minutes, the whole town was aflame with his name.

Mathéo, Mathéo, Mathéo.

Mathéo Thibaut was coming to Calypso Cay Conservatory of Ballet.

She wrote this story—this odd amalgam of experience and imagination, certainty and speculation, fact and fiction—faster than any of her other novels. It was as if she were a glass that had been slowly and quietly filling up and now was spilling over: love, grief, ambition, rage. It was a thriller, yes. But it was also a love letter. To Ethan. To her children. To motherhood. To *ballet*. She wrote the first draft in the month between *The Nutcracker* and New Year's. Even if no one wanted to publish it, it was the book she needed to write. She'd sent it off to Leona with few expectations, but then Leona had called to tell her she loved it.

Now, at the restaurant in Union Square, Leona ordered champagne. Expensive champagne. With a cork and an intricate cage of thin gold wire to protect it.

"This seems premature." Ever laughed when Leona toasted her. "It's just a first draft."

"Well, Edward will definitely make an offer on it as-is. But if he can't give us what we want, I've put feelers out and have at least four editors chomping at the bit for it. I think I could even get an auction going. Once you've had a chance to revise."

Ever knew better than to get her hopes up, though this felt like trying to hold down a helium balloon intent on rising.

"Hoping we'll get Edward's offer early next week. You'll be back home then?"

"Yeah. I'm just going to get Bea settled in first before I head back. Can't leave my students that long."

She thought of her class at The Center with a bit of heartache. Doris had emailed her to let her know that Sid had passed away (relayed all in CAPS, of course). Clementine was devastated. As soon as she got home, she planned to visit her. She wanted to assure her she'd be okay. Eventually.

Bob had also texted, said he'd gotten an idea for a new book and was writing furiously away. "It's a thriller," he said. "About a female arsonist. A housewife. A mom. Of course, I really just started." Ever's heart sank, and she tried not to think about what this might mean for her book, then snuffed that thought out before it could burn.

Leona squeezed Ever's hand. "We'll have an offer soon. A good one. I promise you."

She hadn't told Bea or Danny yet. She knew better after *Black Evenings* to say anything before it was real. But it *felt* real. If it didn't happen, of course, she'd need to figure something out. Lindsay refused to let her put the house on the market, though, insisting there were other options. She told Ever she could leverage her equity in the house, use it to buy another property,

which she could rent out for some passive income. Think of
how it would free up her time for writing! Maybe they could
invest in a property together. Melissa had done it, why couldn't
they?

"Where is Beatrice today?" Leona asked.

"She's having lunch with some of the girls at NYRB. Her roommate from the summer is showing her around. We're meeting at the
Met in a bit."

"Well, make sure she still has my number. In case she needs anything at all, now that she'll be living here."

Ever went straight from lunch with Leona to the museum, where
she found Bea waiting for her on the front steps. It was cold, and Bea
was bundled up, a baby-blue scarf wrapped around her, making her
easy to spot in the crowd.

Bea used the museum's map on the app on her phone to navigate
through the immense building, and when they finally found what
they were looking for, Bea lit up.

"Oh! Take a picture?" Bea said, and positioned herself next to the
bronze statue.

Degas' *Little Dancer, Aged Fourteen* stood proudly in fourth position. Hands locked behind her back.

"She was a ballet student in Paris," Bea said. "People actually
hated the statue at first. They thought it was vulgar, because she
was poor. They called the dancers *rats*. The wealthy patrons of the
opera, the men, took advantage of them." Bea continued talking,
excited, as she circled the *Little Dancer*. "The original was made of
wax. But it was too fragile. Easily damaged. That's why he cast her
in bronze."

As Ever studied Bea on her phone's camera, she wished she could
do the same. She wanted to gild this girl-woman at this very moment of her life. Preserve her. Here. At the still point. At the beginning of everything.

"I wish he were here," Bea said, after Ever had taken the photo.
"Daddy."

"Me too, Bumble," she said, and went to her. Together they studied the statue.

"But we're going to be okay?" Bea said, turning to her. A question.

Ever framed her sweet face with her hands, looked into her eyes. "Yes, we are."

Curtain Call

Josie

Josie sat down on the soft leather couch, with her laptop open and a fresh cup of coffee at her side. She curled her legs under her, suddenly aware of the clunky ankle bracelet, a constant reminder. Irritated, she stretched her legs out. Though, of course, it could have been so much worse.

She'd confessed when it became clear that the cops weren't buying what she was selling. *Making a burger on the grill.* She and Savvy were vegetarians now, not a single piece of meat in the Sub-Zero freezer which, apparently, was fireproof. Lord. And after the confession, Johnny had encouraged her to take the plea bargain—admitting to "reckless burning" rather than second-degree arson. *Tomato tomahto,* she'd thought then, but in the end, it was the difference between house arrest or sleeping in a concrete cell.

Bob had left an hour ago, and the girls were at school. He'd been so generous, letting her stay with him during this whole mess. It was his pleasure, he said, and he sure appreciated the help with his daughters. He had wanted to start dedicating more time to his writing and had rented an office space downtown, where he went every day to work on his novel.

He said he couldn't imagine who could possibly be more helpful with Phoebe than a seasoned ballet mom. She'd set to work right away, sewing pointe shoe ribbons and making healthy snacks. With Savvy and Bea gone now, she promised Bob that Phoebe would be the next star at CLCB. She'd been cast as the White Swan for the spring show, with Jaz as Black Swan.

Bob had offered her his guest room in exchange for getting the girls off to school each day, and delivering Phoebe to the studio every afternoon. He'd put her on his payroll as a nanny so her probation officer would allow her to shuttle the girls to wherever they needed to go. Though Josie knew better than to stick around at CLCB after drop-off; she'd gone in with Phoebe for the *Swan Lake* auditions, and you'd have thought she was an axe murderer, the way all those miserable mothers gawked at her. Even Nancy suggested next time she should just drop Phoebe off at the door.

When Bob had reached out to her, she'd been shocked. She figured that she'd be shunned by the other parents, maybe even banished from Costa de la Luna entirely. She'd briefly considered moving to her mom's in Orange County, but Johnny told her she wasn't allowed to leave town.

But Bob had been such a good listener. So attentive. He wanted to know exactly what happened, what had been going through her mind that night. Why she had snapped. He'd invited her over and just let her spill for hours, chin in hand as he listened.

Bob's girls had gone to their aunt's house that night. And so, they sat alone at the table after eating the dinner he'd made, though she declined when he offered her wine. Not allowed, not even a sip. And so, over tea, she'd explained. She'd been so distraught about Mark selling the house out from under her and Savvy. That everyone had been so mad about Etienne staying in her guesthouse, assuming the worst of her. She'd been devastated that it looked like a sure thing that Beatrice would get the scholarship, when Savvy had worked so, so hard. She wept when she confessed that she felt like a pariah at the studio, all those mothers hell-bent on making a monster of her.

Of course, she kept a few key details to herself.

She simply hadn't been herself that night, she said, and he had nodded sympathetically. Who was he to judge? He'd attacked Etienne, after all.

"You'd do anything for her," he said, his eyes warm with understanding.

"I *would*," she said. Bob got it.

Now, she looked at the clock on her laptop, quickly calculating what time it was in Paris—6:45 p.m. Almost time for curtain. She tried to imagine what Savvy was doing backstage at the opera house. She dreamed her costume, the crimson satin and tulle. She'd been cast as the Firebird in the Académie's end-of-year production. The lead. Etienne had brought them a star; they were so pleased with Savvy, they'd reinstated his contract. Savvy had saved his tight little ass.

What she wouldn't give to be sitting, watching Savvy's European debut from the front row. But, sacrifices had to be made. *Had* been made. So she picked up her phone and quickly shot off a text: **Merde, Sav. Love you.** Savvy quickly responded with a ♥.

Then she sat back and waited for the performance to begin.

Glossary of Ballet Terms Used in *The Still Point*

À la seconde—"to second position"—to the side.

Adage/Adagio—"at ease or leisure"—1. A series of slow and graceful movements. 2. The beginning of a classical pas de deux.

Allegro—"at a brisk tempo"—1. Petit allegro consists of small, quick jumps. 2. Grand allegro consists of large, traveling jumps.

Arabesque—a position in which the dancer is supported on one leg, with the other leg extended behind the body. Both legs are turned out and straight.

Ballet master—a professional employed by a ballet company or school to instruct and rehearse dancers for performances.

Balloné—a bouncing movement repeated on one leg (supporting) while the other leg (working) extends from a cou-de-pied in plié to a straightened leg, then returns to cou-de-pied.

Barre—1. A stationary handrail used for warm-up exercises. 2. Ballet warm-up exercises done at the barre.

Battement—"beating"—a movement in which the leg is extended to the front, side, or back.

Coda—the conclusion of a pas de deux.

Combination—a choreographed series of movements either at the barre or in the center.

Corps de ballet—the members of the lowest rank of a ballet company, who dance together as a group.

Curtain Call—the return of a performer to the stage after the final bows.

Développé—a movement in which one leg is first bent, foot raised to the knee of the supporting leg, then straightened and extended.

En dedans—movement in an "inward" direction.

En pointe—when a dancer, wearing specially designed shoes (pointe shoes) dances on the tips of their toes.

Entrée—the opening piece of a grand pas de deux.

Extensions—the dancer's ability to lift and hold their leg to the front, side, or back.

Facility—a dancer's body's natural ability or potential based on body proportions, shape of head, length of neck, natural turnout, shape of feet, etc . . .

Fifth position—a ballet position in which both feet are turned outward, with one in front of the other so that the heel of the front foot touches the toe of the back foot (and vice-versa).

Finale—the closing scene of a performance.

Fondu, fondue—"to melt"—the slow bending of the supporting leg.

Fouetté—a ballet turn which incorporates the whipping movement of the working leg while executing a pirouette.

Fourth position—a ballet position in which both feet are turned outward with one in front of the other, with a small distance between the front and back foot.

Line(s)—the aesthetic of a dancer's body, the pleasing image created by the dancer's form as they move.

Marking—an energy-saving approach when learning new choreography. The dancer goes through the motions without performing full-out, focusing on learning the movements.

Merde—an expression of "good luck" to a dancer before a performance. It purportedly originated in nineteenth-century Paris, when, during performances, the streets were filled with horse-drawn carriages (and manure). Saying "merde" (which means "shit" in French) was meant to ensure a packed house.

Partnering—the dancing performed by two dancers (usually one male, one female), focusing on congruous movements between the two.

Pas de deux—a dance for a pair of dancers.

Passé—"passed"—a movement in which one foot of one leg passes the knee of the other leg.

Penché—"leaning"—a movement in which a dancer bends forward over one leg, while the other leg is held in arabesque, at between 90 and 180 degrees.

Plié—a movement in which a dancer bends the knees and straightens them again. This can be done from first, second, fourth, or fifth position.

Port de bras—"carriage of the arms"—in ballet, a dancer's arm movements in general, but also specific exercises aimed at improving the quality of the upper body's movements.

Première—a debut performance.

Principal dancer—a dancer at the highest rank within a professional ballet company.

Promenade—"a walk"—usually seen in a pas de deux, with the female dancer supported on one leg, the other in arabesque or attitude, as the male dancer supports a slow turn.

Raked stage—a stage which slopes upward, away from the audience (raised at the upstage end).

Relevé—to rise from a flat foot onto the toes.

Révérence—a series of movements executed as a gesture of reverence and respect for the teacher, pianist (or orchestra), or audience.

Rond de jambe—"round of the leg"—a circular movement of the leg.

Saut de Basque—a turning jump in which the dancer rotates in the air with one foot of one leg drawn to the knee of the other leg.

Saut de chat—"a cat's jump"—a jump in which the legs are in a split position.

Solo—a performance executed by a single dancer.

Summer Intensive—rigorous ballet training offered to young dancers (usually 8-18) over the summer months when school is out.

Tendu—"tight or stretched"—a movement in which the dancer's leg extends to the front, side, or back with the toe pointed.

Toi Toi Toi—an expression of good luck prior to a performance. The German expression originates from the superstition of spitting over one's shoulder three times to ward off evil spirits.

Turnout—the rotation at a dancer's hips, causing the feet (and knees) to turn outward.

Variation—a solo dance.

Bea's Playlist

"Can I Kick It?"—A Tribe Called Quest

"Me Myself and I"—De La Soul

"Last Chance for a Slow Dance"—Fugazi

"Heart-Shaped Box"—Nirvana

"Le Bien, La Mal"—Guru feat. MC Solaar

"'Round Midnight"—John Coltrane

"Cantaloop (Flip Fantasia)"—Us3

"Song of Home"—Van Morrison

"Ripple"—Grateful Dead

The Nutcracker Suite—Tchaikovsky

THE STILL POINT

Tammy Greenwood

ABOUT THIS GUIDE

The suggested questions are included to enhance
your group's reading of Tammy Greenwood's *The Still Point*.

Discussion Questions

1. This is a novel about ballet moms, which might seem like a very specific sub-culture. However, do you find that there are aspects of raising a dancer that are similar to other parenting situations?

2. *The Still Point* follows three mothers and three daughters during a short period of time during which the daughters are competing for a scholarship. However, each character has her own issues she is contending with. How do you think that the scholarship competition affects each of these journeys?

3. Ever is a newly widowed mother whose financial struggles are compounded when she learns that her husband's life insurance policy has been nullified. This amplifies the need Bea has for the scholarship. Do you feel more sympathy for Ever because of this? Ever says near the end that she never considered herself like the other mothers. Is she right? Or is her ambition the same?

4. Lindsay's relationship with her husband is crumbling. She blames his inattentiveness and disinterest for this dissolution. But does she bear some of the burden for the marriage's demise? Do you think she and Victor might find themselves in the same position years down the road? How do Steve and Victor differ?

5. Josie is a woman who has used men to get what she needs for her entire life. She can sometimes come off as a villain in this story. Do you sympathize with her at all? If so, why?

6. Beatrice and Savvy's competitiveness began long before Etienne's arrival at CLCB. And Bea's behavior at the bonfire is indicative of a longstanding animosity toward Savvy. Do you feel like Beatrice gets what she deserves when Savvy steals her

best friend? Or, is Savvy doing, as Bea suggests, what she always does—just "being her awful self"?

7. Etienne has an agenda with his stint at CLCB. He hopes to repair his reputation via Lotte's film. But Lotte has other plans. Discuss how Lotte's own ambition plays into the story.

8. We also watch Ever's artistic ambition play out in her chapters. Describe the parallels between the *Black Evenings* fiasco and Bea's competition for the scholarship.

9. There is a literal fire in this novel. Discuss the use of fire imagery throughout the story.

10. Is this a story about second chances? If so, what does that look like for each character?

11. What do you make of the Curtain Call scene? Josie has made an enormous sacrifice for her daughter. And Savvy, as always, gets what she wants. But is there trouble on the horizon for them both?

12. At one point, Bea says that beauty isn't meant to last. That beauty, by nature, is ephemeral. Is this true in this story? In your own life?

Don't miss the previous novel by the
award-winning Tammy Greenwood:

SUCH A PRETTY GIRL

**Perfect for fans of Taylor Jenkins Reid, Jodi Picoult, and Emma
Cline, this vividly lyrical, evocative novel from the award-winning
author transports readers to the gritty atmosphere of 1970s New
York City as the precarious lines between girl and woman, art and
obscenity, fetish and fame flicker and ignite for a young girl on
the brink of stardom and a mother on the verge of collapse.**

"A gorgeously written, emotionally resonant novel about mothers and
daughters." —Jillian Cantor, USA Today bestselling author

In 1970s New York, her innocence is seductive.
Four decades later, it's a crime . . .

Living peacefully in Vermont, Ryan Flannigan is shocked when a text
from her oldest friend alerts her to a devastating news item. A controver-
sial photo of her as a preteen has been found in the possession of a wealthy
investor recently revealed as a pedophile and a sex trafficker—with an in-
scription to him from Ryan's mother on the back.

Memories crowd in, providing their own distinctive pictures of her
mother, Fiona, an aspiring actress, and their move to the West Village in
1976. Amid the city's gritty kaleidoscope of wealth and poverty, high art,
and sleazy strip clubs, Ryan is discovered and thrust into the spotlight as a
promising young actress with a woman's face and a child's body. Suddenly,
the safety and comfort Ryan longs for is replaced by auditions, paparazzi,
and the hungry eyes of men of all ages.

Forced to reexamine her childhood, Ryan begins to untangle her young
fears and her mother's ambitions, and the role each played in the fraught
blackout summer of 1977. Even with her movie career long behind her,
Ryan and Fiona are suddenly the object of uncomfortable speculation—
and Fiona demands Ryan's support. To put the past to rest, Ryan will need
to face the painful truth of their relationship, and the night when everything changed.

"Magnetic . . . This knotty story leaves readers reflecting
on the limits of family obligations." —*Publishers Weekly*

Available wherever books are sold.

Visit our website at
KensingtonBooks.com
to sign up for our newsletters, read
more from your favorite authors, see
books by series, view reading group
guides, and more!

Become a Part of Our
Between the Chapters Book Club
Community and Join the Conversation

Submit your book review for a chance to win exclusive
Between the Chapters swag you can't get anywhere else!
https://www.kensingtonbooks.com/pages/review/